THE HEADHUNTERS

By the same author

WOBBLE TO DEATH
THE DETECTIVE WORE SILK DRAWERS
ABRACADAVER
MAD HATTER'S HOLIDAY
INVITATION TO A DYNAMITE PARTY
A CASE OF SPIRITS
SWING, SWING TOGETHER
WAXWORK
THE FALSE INSPECTOR DEW
KEYSTONE
ROUGH CIDER
BERTIE AND THE TINMAN
ON THE EDGE
BERTIE AND THE SEVEN BODIES
BERTIE AND THE CRIME OF PASSION
THE LAST DETECTIVE
DIAMOND SOLITAIRE
THE SUMMONS
BLOODHOUNDS
UPON A DARK NIGHT
THE VAULT
THE REAPER
DIAMOND DUST
THE HOUSE SITTER
THE CIRCLE
THE SECRET HANGMAN

Short stories

BUTCHERS AND OTHER STORIES OF CRIME
THE CRIME OF MISS OYSTER BROWN AND OTHER STORIES
DO NOT EXCEED THE STATED DOSE
THE SEDGEMOOR STRANGLER AND OTHER STORIES OF CRIME

THE HEADHUNTERS

Peter Lovesey

Published by
Soho Press, Inc.
853 Broadway
New York, NY 10003

Library of Congress Cataloging-in-Publication Data
Lovesey, Peter.
The headhunters / Peter Lovesey.
p. cm.
ISBN 978-1-56947-490-7
I. Title.
PR6062.086H43 2008
823'.914—dc22
2007037815

10 9 8 7 6 5 4 3 2 1

THE HEADHUNTERS

'I COULD CHEERFULLY MURDER my boss,' Gemma said.

'Is he a slave-driver, then?'

'Oh, no.'

'A groper?'

'No. He's nice.'

The logic was lost on Jo, but her friend had a wild imagination—which was why she was fun to be with. 'You want to kill him and he's nice?'

'Not nice.' Gemma stretched her small, neat mouth into a large, forced smile. 'Na-eeeeece.'

'I get you,' Jo said. 'I've met people like that. Drive you mad.'

'Imagine working with one.'

Starbucks on North Street, Chichester, was frantic as usual. It was always a haven for mothers with fractious children but on Saturdays entire families with shopping and strollers rearranged the seating and turned the narrow walkway into an obstacle course. Mercifully, the staff turned up the music to drown the sound of infants. But the coffee tasted right and the eats were fresh so where else would you go? While Jo got in line Gemma used her one-time hockey skills to shimmy to the far end and bag two of the much-sought-after purple armchairs, almost knocking over the elderly couple who had just got up from them.

'So?' Jo asked when they were seated with their cappuccinos.

'What?'

'How would you do it? What lurid little fantasies have been whirring in that head of yours?'

'Kill my boss, you mean?' Gemma was shouting to be heard above a Robbie Williams track. 'With something extremely slow-acting. I'd definitely want to clock that stupid smile being wiped off his face when he sees what's coming to him. I could force-feed him marshmallows.'

Jo took a moment to think and laughed.

'Or drown him in golden syrup,' Gemma said, her weird mental process churning away now.

Jo joined in the game. 'Sit him in a jacuzzi until he passes out. They say it's dangerous to overdo it.'

'You've got the idea. A non-stop massage by a team of gorgeous Polynesian girls until he's rubbed to nothing.'

'I can't top that. You've obviously given this some thought.'

'It keeps me going.'

'What exactly is your job? You've never told me.'

'I'm his PA. In the office next door, guarding the inner sanctum. Anyone wants to see old sweetie-pie, they have to get past me, the battleaxe. I take the phone calls, open the mail, tell the staff he's in a meeting when he isn't. Anything unpopular, I break it to everyone else. The result is I have no friends at work. They see me coming and they think extra duties at best.'

'What's the work?'

'Printing. Everything from parish magazines to pizza vouchers. It's massive and hi-tech. Well, the machinery is, not the staff. We're small and plodding. The old printing skills have been replaced by laser technology. A halfwit could do it. And a halfwit is running it.'

'Your nice Mr Cartwright?'

'You want the measure of the man? This is something that happened this week. Some political agent ordered some election literature, the stuff that gets pushed through your door. We printed his leaflet and there was a typo in the headline. It read, "'My Erection in Your Hands Again.'"

Jo almost choked on her blueberry muffin. 'Gemma, that's priceless!'

'Our client didn't think so. His people delivered two hundred before someone noticed.'

'Love it.'

'Yes, but who took the rap? Muggins, as always. Our charming Mr Cartwright never picks up his phone. "Tell him I'm out, my dear," he said when I tried to transfer the rabid caller. "And remind him politely that he must have been sent the proof to check and passed it. But as a gesture of good faith we'll reprint the entire batch." So it all comes down to me. And that isn't the end of it. I have to find the wretched printer who cocked up and tell him he's in deep shit and had better stay late and redo the job and deliver it himself.'

'I'm getting the picture now. Your Mr C is a delegator.'

'Some sort of reptile, for sure.'

'I don't think you heard me.'

As likely as not she did. Her brain had its own anarchic way of working. She was already planning a better fate for Mr Cartwright. 'I wonder if he's allergic to anything. You can kill someone with a single peanut.'

'That wouldn't be slow, would it?'

'You're right. No pleasure looking at that. Forget the peanut. Here's a neat one. We tell him he's been selected for one of those reality programmes on TV and it's going to be rigged so that he wins a million. All he has to do is a filmed sky-dive, and then, of course, when he tries to open the parachute . . . '

'That isn't a slow death either.'

'But it's on film, sweetie. I can watch it again a million times and in slo-mo if I wish.'

This whole conversation was off the wall and not meant to be treated as real, but you'd be a party pooper to say so. Instead, Jo prolonged it by injecting some logic. 'All these ideas have a fatal flaw. You're going to be left with a dead body and they'll do a post mortem and trace it back to you.'

'The Polynesian girls?'

'If we're not in fantasy land, Gemma, the Polynesian girls won't massage everything away. At some point he's going to expire and they won't want to massage a corpse.'

The mouth turned down at the edges. 'You're saying I'm stuck with Denis bloody Cartwright, aren't you?'

'Unless you want a life sentence, yes.'

'He isn't worth that.' Gemma's eyes gleamed as yet another idea came to her. 'How about getting *him* a life sentence?'

'What—stitch him up?'

'Worth thinking about. It would get him off my back, wouldn't it? It's the sort of lingering fate I was talking about. I could visit him in prison and gloat.'

'How would you do it—stitch him up, I mean? You'd need a body.'

'Trust you to throw a spanner in the works.'

'And if he's as charming as you say, the jury might give him the benefit of the doubt.'

Gemma sighed. 'Dead right. He'd charm their socks off.'

'THE WOMAN sounds mental,' Rick said when Jo told him. Rick was her latest bloke. He ticked most of the boxes: confident, clever and gorgeous to look at, with sun-bleached hair and blowtorch blue eyes, but there's always a drawback. The drawback was Sally, a so-called 'older woman' Rick had met when he did a survey on the big house she bought in Bosham. He insisted on seeing this Sally every Sunday for a roast lunch—and Jo didn't like to think what happened after lunch. She wasn't thrilled with the arrangement, but she had the feeling it wouldn't be wise to interfere—yet.

'She wasn't totally serious. We were being silly, dreaming up ways to kill this freeloading boss of hers, but it was obvious she's thought about it quite a lot, so there's a little bit of intent behind the joking.'

'Waste of space, is he, this Mr Cartwright?'

'A complete nerd, according to Gemma. I haven't seen him, but I've met his sort before. They ooze charm and get what they want without ever doing a hand's turn.'

'He can't be clueless if he's managing a print business.'

'It gets managed no thanks to him, Gemma says.'

'Is he married?'

'I've no idea.'

'The thing is,' Rick said, 'scarcely anyone is alone in the world. You rub Cartwright out and then you find there's a wife and six kids, or a little old mother. If he's as charming as we're led to believe he's going to leave behind a bunch of friends desperate to find out what happened to their dear old buddy.'

'Good thing she isn't serious,' Jo said.

'How did you meet this Gemma?'

'In yoga. She and I are the ones who couldn't lie on our backs without laughing. We had a giggle about it in the break and decided to leave at the same time. I haven't known her long. Don't know much about her.'

'Except she'd like to murder her scumbag boss.'

'Her na-eeeeece scumbag boss.'

'I've always thought the right way to go about it is to make them disappear,' Rick said. 'Without a corpse the police are buggered.'

'Easier said than done.'

'There are plenty of ways.'

'Such as?'

'Lost at sea is one.'

'What—push him overboard?'

'Preferably with a ton weight attached. The sea idea isn't perfect, though. I'll give you that.' He raised his finger. 'Here's a better method. I remember reading about a woman who was kidnapped back in the sixties. It went on for weeks. She was the wife of some rich guy in the newspaper industry. In the end, after several attempts to set up a ransom arrangement, they arrested two brothers, but the poor woman was never found. These kidnappers had a farm, you see, and the police reckoned she must have been fed to the animals. Pigs are supposed to eat everything—skin, bones, the lot.'

'Ugh!' Just like a man, making the whole thing grotesque. At least Gemma's zany ideas had been redeemed by humour. 'I'm going to change the subject. Where shall we go this evening? Fancy Portsmouth for a change?'

'Is that, like, a joke?' he said. They'd gone clubbing in Portsmouth's Gun Wharf for the past two Saturdays.

'Name someplace else, then.'

AFTER FOUR frames, she was getting nowhere in the bowling. She should have guessed Rick would be good at it. He'd already scored two strikes and was way ahead on the screen. She didn't mind really. It wouldn't be long before he offered hands-on advice how to pick the right ball and improve her action: the game within a game that girls play to win.

From infancy Jo had been burdened with high expectations. As the only child of a domineering mother, she'd been pushed to excel, whether in music, producing a sound on the violin like triplets being born; dance, in the fifth row back, extreme left, where they could grab her from the wings when she tripped; or skating, with an apparent mission to bring down everyone else on the ice. At school she'd been average, so her mother had arranged for private tuition to bring out her hidden talents. All it had brought was a mental breakdown, a gap year with a meaning all its own. Instead of university she'd gone to an undemanding, stress-free job at a garden centre. She'd left home (the best thing she ever did) and got to enjoy her work and feel like a human being again.

While Rick was waiting for the ball to return, she spotted a familiar figure just two lanes away: Gemma, looking the total athlete in stretch jeans and stripy top that revealed a flash of scarlet bra straps. The way she released the ball and immediately flapped her hand in disappointment showed she was used to winning at this game.

'Your go,' Rick said. He'd cleared the pins again.

'See that girl with the ponytail? She's the one I was telling you about, wants to murder her boss. Shall I tell her we're here?'

'We're in the middle of a game.'

'If she looks this way I'll wave. You'll like her. She's fun.'

'Okay, but let's get on with it.'

She took her turn, not thinking about the aim, and struck down all ten—her first time ever.

'Hey—how did you manage that?' Rick asked.

Next time up, her next ball slipped to the side and disappeared down the back without a score. She heard her name being called.

Gemma was waving.

'Meet you after for a bevvy,' Jo called back.

Suggestions like that, made with the best of intentions, sometimes have unplanned results. Not long after, they were in Chicago Rock knocking back spritzers and eyeing up the possibility of grabbing a table as soon as some other people left.

'Jake will give them one of his looks and they'll get up and leave, no problem,' Gemma said. She pointed a thumb at her bowling companion, who'd had to dip his head when he came through the door. Dressed entirely in black, Jake could have stepped out of an old Hammer horror movie. There was no question that his eyes were scary. With his pale face and twisted mouth he would have seen off Dr Phibes, no problem.

Rick was getting on fine with Gemma—a touch too fine, Jo thought—praising her bowling skills and saying she must have played the game before. There was no 'How did you manage that?' Strange. He hadn't seen much of her play unless he'd been taking stock of her before Jo had pointed her out.

Jo tried talking to big Jake and found he was no conversationalist. Besides, he was working his influence on the people at the window table. His stare was making them increasingly ready to leave.

'So do you like dancing?' Rick asked Gemma.

'Why—are you guys going somewhere later?' she said.

'Nothing planned. I was just thinking you move so well you have to be a dancer.'

'Bit of a Sherlock Holmes, isn't he?' Jo couldn't stop herself saying. 'We'll get you a pipe and deerstalker, my love.' It sounded more sarcastic than she meant. She didn't want Gemma thinking she was jealous.

'We could all go clubbing,' Rick said.

'Me and Jake haven't talked about what we'd do,' Gemma said. 'D'you want to go clubbing, Jake?'

Clubbing seals would be more to Jake's taste, Jo thought.

Without looking away from the people by the window he said, 'Whatever you want.'

'Jongleurs?' Rick said.

Jo couldn't believe her ears. This was the same guy who'd bellyached about another evening in Portsmouth. Now he was pushing to go there. True, there wasn't much in Chichester, but Jongleurs was scarcely a novel experience.

'Cool,' Gemma said. 'Shall we drink up and get on the road?'

'Hold on, I'm sure those people are about to leave,' Jo said. 'It's early, anyway. Let's sit down for a bit now we've got a chance.'

The other party moved out with some backward glances at Jake. He was too large and scary to take on. His knee rubbed against Jo's under the table and it wasn't because he was getting frisky, just that a leg the size of his had nowhere to go. She was opposite him and would have got the full force of the stare except that he was focusing somewhere over her head. I do believe the poor guy is shy, she thought, getting all maternal.

'Are you from round here?' she asked him.

He shook his head, still without eye contact.

'Jake's a Cornish lad,' Gemma said for him. 'Would you believe there's a place called Bugle down there?'

'Get away.' Rick held an invisible bugle to his mouth and sounded a fanfare.

Jo tried again. 'So what brought you to Chichester, Jake?'

'Motorbike.'

'You're a biker?'

Another shake of the head.

'He was riding pillock,' Gemma said for him.

'Pillion,' Jake said.

'All right. Have it your way.'

'I like it Gemma's way,' Rick said with a laugh. 'Riding pillock.'

Jake gave him a look and he went quiet.

'What I meant,' Jo said to Jake, doing her best to take the mockery out of this, 'was what are you doing here?'

'Having a drink.' It was becoming clear that if you wanted information you had to phrase your question precisely.

'Are you in work?'

'Yup.'

'You're keeping her in suspense, Jake,' Gemma said. 'She's asking about your job. He's in nature conservancy, looking after the wildlife. He knows all there is to know about birds and before you say anything, Rick, we're talking ducks and moorhens, right?'

'Did my lips move?' Rick asked.

'So what do *you* do when you're not ten-pin bowling?' Gemma, too, seemed to have decided Jake needed a break from the ribbing.

'Me? I'm a chartered surveyor. I can tell you when your house needs money spending on it.'

'All the time.'

'How did you guess? And you work at the printer's out at Fishbourne.'

She flushed scarlet. 'Who told you? Jo, I suppose.'

Jo gave a shrug and a smile.

Someone had to compensate for Jake's non-existent social skills, and Rick was doing his damnedest. 'Hey, I heard all about this creepy boss you want to do away with. Mr Cartwright, Yeah? Between us we ought to be able to help you out. I was saying to Jo, it's not enough to top him. You've got to think the whole thing through. Make him disappear as well. That's the biggest challenge. I was telling her about the case of a woman—'

'Rick, don't,' Jo cut in. 'We don't want to hear it.'

'We only ever hear about murders that get discovered,' Rick said. 'Those are the failures. There are plenty that go undetected. Hundreds, if not thousands. Think about all the people who go missing and are never seen again.'

Gemma's eyes widened. 'Do you think some murderers get away with it?'

'You're joking. All the time.'

'The perfect murder?'

'I wouldn't call it that. Getting rid of a body is no big deal. All it wants is some planning. In my job, for instance, I visit building sites, roadworks, motorways. When the foundations go down, they have to be approved. I get to know when a piece of ground is ready to be laid over with a few tons of cement. Come to that, I've surveyed old cemeteries that are getting turned into car parks and supermarkets. Who's going to know?'

'You've still got to get on the site and bury the body. I wouldn't care for that,' Gemma said.

'Better than keeping it in your front room.'

She laughed. 'Well, yes, but there must be easier ways.'

'I'm sure there are. Take Jo's job.'

'What?' Jo said. She'd been listening to this and wishing Rick would shut up. 'This is nothing to do with me. He's not *my* boss.'

'She works in a garden centre,' he told Gemma as if she didn't know already. 'All she has to do is stick him in a raised flowerbed in one of the glasshouses and cover him with compost. You can get stuff to rot anything down. He'll be pushing up next summer's bedding plants and no one will be any the wiser.'

'That's ridiculous,' Jo said.

'She'd find it difficult on her own,' Gemma said.

'You'd help her, wouldn't you?' Rick said. 'It's your boss we're knocking off.'

Gemma exchanged a look with Jo that said, some men never know where to draw the line. 'I meant it wouldn't be easy moving his mortal remains.'

'What are those little carts for that they have in garden centres?'

Gemma burst out laughing again.

Jo had heard more than enough. 'If you think I'd risk my job to carry out your crazy scheme, you're nuts.'

'Lighten up, babe,' Rick said. 'I was only using you as an example. Who knows? You might need our services if your boss turns nasty. We'd better think up a team name.'

'The Cretins?' Jo said.

'I was thinking the Headhunters.'

Gemma said, 'Neat.'

Rick gave her a smile and continued stirring. 'Between us, we've got it made. Take Jake, for instance. I expect he goes out in a boat looking at his waterfowl. I guarantee he knows places where you could shove a body overboard and it would stay there. What do you reckon, Jake?'

Jake appeared to ponder the matter for a while. Finally, he said, 'I don't dance.'

A real conversation-stopper.

Rick frowned. 'Get with it, mate. We're dumping a body.'

'No problem, Jake,' Gemma said. 'Jongleurs is a comedy club as well. You can sit and have a laugh. And if we do some dancing no one's going to notice you. It's too crowded.'

'Don't know about that,' Rick said. 'He *would* stand out in a crowd.'

Gemma giggled again. It seemed unkind.

Jo said, 'We don't have to go dancing. We could see a film.'

'Bor-ing,' Rick sang out.

'You haven't even checked what's on.'

'*March of the Penguins*,' Jake said at once, belying the impression that he was slow.

'That's a documentary, isn't it?' Rick said. 'Came out yonks ago.'

'I didn't see it,' Jo said. 'It's supposed to be a classic.'

'What else is on?' Rick said. 'There must be something better than a line of bloody penguins walking across the screen.'

'It's good,' Jake said.

'What—the penguin film?' Rick said. 'How do you know, mate? Have you seen it?'

Jake nodded.

'You wouldn't want to see it again, then.'

'Would.'

'Oops, I'm forgetting. Hands up anyone who wants to look at the penguins with the bird man of Chichester.'

Jo hesitated. She'd become increasingly irritated by Rick's attempts at humour. She said, 'If you and Gemma would rather see something else, maybe we can all meet up after.'

A pivotal moment. Rick looked shocked, Gemma disbelieving. To Jo it seemed obvious that she wasn't making a play for Gemma's Neanderthal boyfriend, and at this minute she didn't care what Rick thought. Besides, Gemma hadn't declared yet. She had the chance of seeing the penguins if she chose.

Rick recovered enough to say, 'Fair enough, but count me out. Don't know about you, Gemma, but I'd like to find out what else is on.'

'Suits me,' Gemma said.

So it was that Jo found herself seated next to Jake in a dark, almost empty cinema. He watched the film intently. Jo, too, was absorbed in the drama of the penguins' long treks across the ice. It was only towards the end that her attention strayed as she tried to think of her strategy for when the lights came on. She couldn't get up and walk away. The others had gone to see the latest Russell Crowe on Screen 3 and she'd noticed the running time was at least an hour longer than the penguins.

'Amazing,' she said after the credits had rolled. 'What an existence.'

'Migration,' Jake said.

'I know, but under those conditions.'

'They get on with it.'

'Yes, I suppose it's a mistake to think of them in human terms, but I can't help sympathising with them. How about you?'

'I'd like—' Jake said, and stopped.

'Yes?' She almost completed it for him by saying, 'A drink?'

'—to turn off the commentary.'

She had to think for a moment. 'But it needs explaining to people, doesn't it, or we wouldn't appreciate the distances they march and the reasons?'

'I can watch the pictures.'

'True, but . . . '

'Don't need the voiceover.'

'I suppose it would grate a bit if you've seen the film before.'

'Five times.'

'*Five?*' She laughed and Jake gave a faint smile. Next time you'd better take earplugs. Do you fancy a bite to eat? After all that ice and snow I'd like to get something warm inside me. The others won't be out for some time.'

He thought about that and gave a nod.

They went to Frankie & Benny's, where the music was from the fifties. A Johnny Mathis CD was playing.

'How did you and Gemma meet?' Jo asked.

'Print job,' he said, as if that explained all. She wasn't going to get the romantic version, for sure.

'I think that boss takes advantage of her,' she said. 'He leaves all the decisions to her and if there's any credit going, he takes that for himself. I wonder if she'll leave.'

He didn't seem to have an opinion.

After they'd ordered, she tried another tack. 'Do you live in Chichester, Jake?'

'Selsey.'

This, at least, was a place she could talk about. 'I like Selsey, the seafront, anyway. I sometimes go there for an early morning walk. Doesn't matter if the tide's in or out. Always interesting.'

'Seolesig.' His eyes focused directly on hers for the first time and weren't so off-putting. Dark and deep-set they might be, but now they wanted to communicate, as if to make up for his halting conversation.

'What was that you said?'

'Anglo-Saxon. Seolesig.'

He'd surprised her. 'Does it have a meaning?'

'Seal Island.'

'But it isn't an island, is it? Oh—did it used to be? Of course, you can see when you drive out there. The road is raised up in parts, like a causeway.'

'Big question,' he said.

'What is?'

'Managing the landscape.'

'Whether to shore up the sea defences or let nature take its course?'

He nodded. 'Pagham Harbour. East Head. Habitats.'

'All this comes into your work?'

'One time—' he began to say.

She waited.

He drew another breath. Long sentences were definitely an ordeal. '—at Sidlesham—'

She encouraged him with a nod.

'—there was a ferry.'

'I didn't know that,' she said. 'Tell me again. Seal Island. Seole—'

'—sig.'

'Seolesig. There you go. I've learnt something. I suppose it was a favourite place for seals in the old days.'

He made a simultaneous movement with his mouth and

shoulders that conveyed that he didn't know for certain, but she could be right.

There was more to Jake than she'd first appreciated. He was hard work, but when you persevered he had depth to him, unlike golden boy Rick. 'Next time I go for one of my walks I'll think of it in a different light. Don't suppose I'll spot a seal, though.'

'Might.'

'I never have up to now.'

'I see them.'

She gave an uneasy laugh and said, 'Really?

'Common seals. Grey seals, too.'

'Where?'

'Where I work. Pagham.' A place just along the coast from Selsey. He paused, making a huge effort to say more. 'On the mudflats at low tide.'

After that, she had to believe in the seals. She'd lived locally for some years and never seen or heard of one before.

The food came. Jake had chosen a cheese and tomato pizza. She had fish and chips. It was predictable but embarrassing that the waitress assumed they were a couple and tried to talk them into buying the house wine, with some remarks about putting them in the mood. Jo handled it smoothly and said they were meeting friends later and just wanted water at this stage.

'Was that all right, speaking for us both?' she asked when the waitress had left them.

Jake nodded. 'Water is good.'

'We could have ordered coffee.'

He shook his head.

The food provided a break from conversation, and gave Jo a chance to reflect on how this evening had turned out. First impressions can be misleading. Jake's looks were against him and his problem communicating hadn't allowed him to appear as anything but oafish, even sinister. In company he was fated to be the victim of the quips Rick excelled at. But like this, one-to-one, if you persevered he had thoughtful things to say. She couldn't imagine him starting a conversation, not with someone who was virtually a stranger, but he'd made efforts to respond. Was he short of confidence? There wasn't any speech impediment she could detect. Maybe he'd been given a hard time at school by people like Rick. Being so tall and—well—grim-faced, he'd no doubt been picked on by other kids, particularly when they sensed he wasn't the threat his size suggested.

She wanted a chance to know him better. And if Rick disapproved, tough. She hadn't liked what she'd seen of him tonight.

The situation with Gemma was more complex. She valued her as a friend. You can't take over your best mate's boyfriend the first evening you meet him. But was Jake her regular bloke? Gemma had never mentioned him before. She seemed to treat him without much affection. She'd blithely gone off with Rick.

Hard to tell.

'I go for my walks at the weekend, really early, before many people are about,' she said. 'Doesn't matter what the weather is doing. I always enjoy it.'

'Nice,' he said without looking up from his plate.

'Won't be there tomorrow, more's the pity. I sometimes have to work Sundays.'

'Me, too.'

A short time later they returned to the multiplex and waited in the foyer for the others to come out. When they did, Rick's face suggested the Russell Crowe film was a turkey. His mood had taken a plunge. He'd changed his mind about Jongleurs. He complained of a raging headache and said he needed to get home right away. They called a taxi. Jo did the decent thing and joined him in the cab.

He closed his eyes most of the way.

'I'd ask you in for a coffee,' he said when they reached the block where his flat was, 'but I'm damn sure I'm running a temperature and I don't want to pass some bug on to you. The driver will take you home.'

'Make sure you take something for it.'

Before getting out, he said, 'Messed up your evening, didn't I?'

'No,' she said. 'I had a good time.'

He took out his credit card, but she said she'd got change and would take care of the fare. He thanked her and turned away.

It was difficult to be certain, but he hadn't carried total conviction as a headache victim. Jo had her own theory and wondered if Gemma would confirm it the next time they met in Starbucks.

two

A WEEK LATER, JUST after seven on Sunday morning, Jo got in her Fiat Panda and took the winding road to the coast. The shoreline at Selsey had always appealed to her as a place to walk: stimulating, never the same. And now its possibilities had increased.

The night had been mild for late September, but when she arrived in the car park at the end of the High Street, an offshore wind was whipping foam off the crests of some sizeable waves. A few people, as always, were sitting in their cars watching from behind glass, as if it was television. Jo had definitely come to walk, but before getting out she checked her face in the mirror. She'd decided not to wear the woolly hat she sometimes pulled on for blustery days. Instead she'd fastened her hair at the top with two red clips and let the rest hang loose.

She stood for a moment to savour the smell of beached sea-weed and feel the spray against her cheeks. The last high tide had spread pebbles and bits of driftwood across the concrete path above the sea wall. She picked her way through for a few paces and then took the steps down and crunched into the shingle. A real beach this, she thought, where you could hear the rattle of stones shifted by the waves and see the stacks of lobster pots. Free of day trippers, too. Most favoured the broad, clinically clean sands of West Wittering, a few miles up the coast.

The breakwaters at this end were almost submerged and easy to step over. She continued down to where the stones got smaller and blended with tiny shells. Strips of sand were exposed in places. In another hour there would be a clear stretch to walk on.

When she'd rounded the narrow section below the high sea defences at Bill Point, the southernmost tip of Sussex, she returned to the path for a bit and was treated to the long view of the East Beach stretching for a couple of miles to Pagham Harbour, the conservation area where Jake worked. Much closer stood the grey lifeboat house and slipway at the end of a pier long enough for launchings, even at low tide. Around it was moored the last of Selsey's ancient fishing fleet, much favoured by photographers, about twenty small, brightly coloured craft moored to orange buoys. Beyond, a good six miles off, looking as if it was just a continuation of the walk, was the tentlike roof of Butlins at Bognor.

As always there were people walking their dogs, although fewer than usual this morning.

You could spot anyone coming from a long distance. A man of Jake's height would be more obvious than most. She passed one tall guy a good bit younger, in a fleece top and tracksuit trousers. A jogger, maybe, though he was walking. He had iPod earphones.

Not that she expected to see Jake. Nothing had been arranged. But a chance meeting wasn't out of the question. She told herself she wasn't even sure if she wanted it to happen today. He might think it was a set-up. How cringe-making would that be? Far better at some time in the future.

Only a short way on she was reconsidering. A chance meeting might not be so hard to handle. The way she pictured it, they would exchange a few friendly words and then move on. Unless. Unless what? Well, unless he suggested they stop and sit on one of the benches facing the sea.

Get real, she told herself. He's Gemma's boyfriend and she's your friend from yoga. You can't behave like that.

Absorbed in these thoughts, she strolled for another ten minutes or more, past the lifeboat station and the upended dinghies opposite the place where the fish was sold.

It was increasingly obvious that Jake was nowhere on the front.

This end of the beach was divided by stout wooden breakwaters, and the tidal movement had produced a strange effect. On the side facing her the stones were heaped almost to the top, but on the reverse the wood was exposed, producing a drop of at least ten feet.

At one point she paused to watch a youngish man in army fatigues throwing a ball for a large frisky poodle. They'd been hidden below the breakwater until she got level with them. The dog was running fearlessly into the waves, emerging with the ball and insisting on a repeat performance.

What now, then? She had the choice of continuing the walk on the path above the beach or venturing down in one of these sections between the breakwaters and coming to a forced stop. This, in the end, was her choice. She picked a stretch inhabited only by herring gulls bold enough to stand their ground as she approached, the wind ruffling their feathers. She stood for a while watching the breakers until the same wind that was producing the spectacular choppy sea started to chill her, threatening a headache. She wished she'd put comfort before image and worn the woolly hat after all. Time to turn back, she decided. She was struggling up the bank of stones when her attention was caught by a pale object in the shadow of the breakwater.

All kinds of rubbish is cast up on a beach, particularly when the sea is rough. At first sight this had the smooth curved surface of a large fish, a beached dolphin perhaps.

Jo went closer and lifted away some seaweed. This was no dolphin, nor any other marine species.

She had found a human body.

'No way! All I ever find is lolly-sticks and fag-ends. What did you do?' Gemma asked when they met the next Saturday in Starbucks.

'Went up the beach and knocked at the door of the first house I came to. They called the police.'

'So whose body was it?'

'Some woman. She was nude except for her pants.'

'Drowned?'

'They thought she probably fell overboard and got washed up.'

'In her Alan Whickers? That doesn't sound likely.'

'I don't know. If she was sunbathing on the deck of some yacht, a freak wave could have swept her overboard.'

Gemma raised her eyebrows in mocking disbelief. 'You reckon?'

'It's only a suggestion. There has to be an inquest, doesn't there? They look at reports of people lost at sea.'

'What age would she have been?'

'Late thirties, the cop said. I didn't go too close when I took them down to see. I just pointed to where she was. They took my details and said I could leave. They're going to put something in the paper in case anyone knows about her. A reporter phoned me later.'

'Didn't you get a look at the face?'

'No, thank God. She was turned away from me.'

'Are they certain she'd been in the water? She might have snuffed it on the beach.'

'Some seaweed was twisted round her. It's more likely she came in on the tide. They say the sea gives up its dead, don't they?'

Gemma was remembering something. 'When I was having my winter break in Tenerife last year there was a body washed up on the beach and the locals said he was an asylum seeker. These poor bloody Africans put to sea in boats that are unsafe and hundreds of them never make it. Was your woman black?'

'Extremely white, by the time I saw her. I don't think she was an asylum seeker.'

'Escaping from the Isle of Wight,' Gemma said, that fertile imagination at work again.

'Oh, yeah?'

'You're smiling, but there are prisons on the Island.'

'Her pants didn't look prison issue to me.'

'Honey, these days they don't wear kit with little arrows over it.'

'Naff off, will you?'

They were perched on tall stools by the front window watching the people walk by. The pedestrianised North Street in Chichester, stiff with shoppers, was a far cry from Selsey beach last Sunday morning. 'The way you tell it,' Gemma said, 'you don't seem to have panicked. If it had been me, I'd have run a three minute mile, screaming all the way.'

'Strangely enough, I didn't feel anything at the time,' Jo said. 'I mean, I didn't trip over her, or anything. If I had, I might have screamed. I noticed something large and pale under the seaweed and walked over to where she was and that was it.'

'I've never seen a dead body.'

'That was my first. There isn't much to it.' She gave Gemma a faint smile. 'If you're going to murder your boss like you said the other day you'll have to face up to it.'

'Won't be so scary if I'm expecting it. What I wouldn't like is finding one I didn't know was there, like you did. They're always doing that in films.'

'The people who make films are out to shock you, aren't they? The quick burst of music and the sudden close-up? Real life isn't like that.'

'Real death.'

'All right. Real death. It's not the big deal we're all led to believe. Don't worry, Gem. When the time comes, you'll be fine, just fine.'

'I'm going to need someone like you to keep the heeby-jeebies at bay.'

'I'm not sure I want to be party to a murder.'

'A brilliant undiscovered murder.'

'If you insist.' She smiled and sipped her coffee. 'You know, if they served this in smaller mugs, everyone would drink it quicker and the place wouldn't get so crowded.'

'It's their marketing strategy. You bet they've worked it out. There are good commercial reasons for large mugs, but don't ask me what they are.'

A tall, good-looking guy in a suit paused outside the shop and appeared ready to come in, then changed his mind and walked on.

'Did we do that?' Jo asked.

'We were the reason he stopped in the first place,' Gemma said. 'He'll be back.'

'You wish.' They weren't teenagers. They were in their thirties. Jo had been thinking for some time it would be no bad thing if they started behaving like grown-ups.

But Gemma wasn't of the same mind. 'Did you see the size of his feet?'

'No. Should I have? Why?'

Gemma shook with laughter. 'If you don't know by now, I'm not going to tell you.'

'Oh, that.' Jo sniffed. 'It's a myth.'

Gemma spooned some of the froth from her coffee and licked it. 'Mind if I ask something personal?'

'Ask away. If it's off limits I'll tell you.'

'You and your squeeze. Have you known him long?'

'Rick, you mean? Not very. Why?'

'Doesn't matter.'

They watched more people cross their vision. In her mind Jo was running through the reasons for Gemma's question. Could it be the solution to the dilemma she'd been facing all week?

'You want to know if I'm serious about him? As it happens, I'm not. He's just someone I've been out with a couple of times. We don't have much in common, as you probably noticed last weekend. Was he coming on to you in the cinema?'

'A bit.'

'What a prick.'

'Don't get me wrong,' Gemma said, and she was actually blushing. 'It wouldn't have bothered me normally.'

'How embarrassing. It crossed my mind when he mentioned the headache. His excuse to cover up what had been going on, was it?'

'To be fair it was only a problem because I thought you and he were, like . . . you know. I let him know he was out of order.'

'What did you do—mark the back of his hand with your fingernails? I would have.'

'I just told him to leave off.'

'Bastard.'

A customer looking for a place to sit caught the full force of Jo's annoyance and slopped coffee over his tray.

Gemma said, 'Oops.'

Jo ignored the guy. 'Him, not you. I'm not saying just because I've been out with him a couple of times he's got to be totally loyal to me, but you are my friend and it was the first time he'd met you. That entitles you to some respect.' She gave a sharp, angry sigh. 'That's Rick and me finished. I wasn't that keen on him anyway.'

Gemma said after a pause, 'Are you sure about that?'

'You heard me, Gem. He's just a bad memory now.'

'Then you wouldn't curse me and my progeny for a thousand years if I went out with him?'

Jo, tiptoeing as lightly as Gemma, said, 'But what about Jake? Isn't he your boyfriend?'

'Jake?' Gemma squeaked at the suggestion. 'God, no. Don't run away with that idea. He's only a customer—at the printer's, where I work. We're doing some Christmas cards for the wildlife thing he's part of, and he said he'd seen me at the bowling. When he asked me to play some ends with him I thought it was naughty talk, but it wasn't. The guy's got the sense of humour of a wombat. I felt sorry for him, so I went as an act of charity. He hasn't a clue how to chat up a girl.'

'He got a result with you.'

'Get away.' She laughed. 'A game of ten-pin. Call that a result? Not where I was brought up, ducky. If you want the truth I was trying to think of ways of unloading him on someone else when we met last week and you were the unlucky one who copped him.'

'So you won't be seeing him again?'

'The son of Frankenstein? You're joking. I've done my bit for customer relations.' She clapped her hand to her mouth. 'You don't actually fancy him, do you? Omigawd, Gemma puts her foot in it again.'

'I didn't say I fancy him,' Jo said—which was true. She hadn't said anything about him. She hoped she looked indifferent. 'He was okay with me. I've nothing against him.'

'Me neither,' Gemma said, 'but you wouldn't want to wake up in the morning and find that face next to you on the pillow. Know what I mean?'

'His looks don't bother me.'

Gemma gave her a nudge. 'I think you do fancy him on the quiet. A bit of *Rocky Horror*, eh?'

'I wouldn't call him that.'

'Nor would I—to his face. Well, you have a clear run as far as I'm concerned.'

'Oh, thanks,' Jo said, and tried to make it sound ironic.

'Got any plans for tonight?'

'Nothing definite.'

'Not for publication?'

'Yet to be decided.'

'He hangs out at the bowling place most Saturdays, I heard. Play your cards right and you could even get to see the penguins again.'

Jo screwed up her paper napkin and threw it at Gemma.

'I was going to give you the latest goss on Mr Cartwright,' Gemma said. 'Don't know if I will now.'

'Goss on the boss? Go on. It had better be good.'

'Well, he's started chatting up this woman in accounts called Fiona. She's a good twenty years younger, about twenty-four. This isn't like him. Whatever I've said about him in the past, he's not a skirt-chaser.'

'Given the incentive, they all are,' Jo said. 'Pretty, is she?'

'I suppose. Well, yes. A redhead.'

'Say no more. Is he married?'

'Divorced. He lives alone.'

'Then I don't see what the problem is.'

'Fiona is the problem. The thing is, she's a single mum. There's a four-year-old son. She needs the work and she's afraid if she gives him the big E she'll lose her job.'

'Are you sure she isn't out to pull him?'

'Jeez. You want to work with him.'

'Some women are turned on by power.'

'Running a print business in Fishbourne? It's not exactly Microsoft International.'

'Have you talked to her?'

Gemma nodded. 'She's the homespun type, a bit short of confidence. Doesn't know how to handle it.'

Jo giggled a bit. 'Handle what? What exactly has he been up to?'

'Get a grip, girl. You're positively slavering. No, it isn't physical. Not yet, anyway. But the early signs are there. Yesterday he was in the stock room showing her the papers we use, telling her about quality and sizes.' With a glare at Jo, who was grinning again, she said, 'Sizes of *paper*. Today he was with her for over an hour explaining how the big colour printer works. She's in accounts, Jo. She doesn't need to know that stuff.'

'And she spoke to you about it?'

'In the loo at the end of the day. She knows I'm his PA. We haven't talked much before this, but she said she's getting embarrassed about all this interest and some of the other women are noticing. Basically she was asking if I think he's got the hots for her.'

'Obviously he has. Is that what you said?'

'Come off it. I was trying to reassure the poor wee lass. I said I've never known him get heavy with a female employee, which is true.'

'There's always a first time. Was she asking for support?'

'Not directly. No, I wouldn't say so. I guess she wanted me to know it wasn't welcomed—in case I was jealous, or something. Which I most definitely am not.'

'But you'd like him to cool it?'

'For everyone's sake, yes.'

'Does he know she's got a kid?'

'He ought to. He interviewed her when she joined. He could easily look at the file.'

'I expect he's conveniently put all that out of his mind. Randy old men are like that.'

Gemma rolled her eyes. 'Tell me about it.'

'But you just said he hasn't tried it on with you.'

'Please! I was speaking generally. This is about Fiona, not me. She's got to find a way of giving him the elbow without putting her job at risk.'

'You want my advice?' Jo said. 'Don't get involved or you'll end up getting grief from both of them. She's a grown-up. She can deal with this herself.'

SHE DIDN'T, after all, go bowling. There was a phone message from her dad to say Mummy was in Southampton Hospital with concussion after falling off Penrose, her white gelding.

'Wasn't she wearing a riding helmet?' Jo asked him when they met outside the ward.

Daddy was a silent man with a large moustache that was his defence barrier. 'You know Mummy,' he said, as if that explained all. Really it did. This was the third time she'd fallen and ended up in the hospital.

'Couldn't she get a safer horse?'

'I'm not sure it was the horse's fault.'

'He's so tall. It's a long way to fall.'

'You could be right, but I don't see your mother on a pony.'

'She ought to think about giving up riding.'

'Try telling her.'

Telling her wouldn't aid the recovery. Margaret Stevens was a stubborn woman. The mother-daughter relationship had foundered years ago when Jo went through teenage rebellion and Mummy went through her room looking for unsuitable reading and cannabis. Harmless things all her friends were trying at the time, like coloured hair and ripped jeans, became issues. If her mother had treated her with a modicum of understanding some of this might have made sense, but it was handled in a vindictive way. Mummy's own self-indulgence, the gin and cigarettes and all the expense on the riding, was not for comment. Jo had a suspicion there were other dissipations, and it had suited her mother to turn the spotlight elsewhere. The trust between them had never recovered.

She was in a side ward in Accident & Emergency and as pale as the pillow but still in good voice. 'You look like death, darling. What's wrong? '

'You're what's wrong, Mummy, giving us a shock like this. How did it happen?'

'Don't ask me. It's a blur. They're keeping me in overnight. What a bore. You two had better go out for a meal. Your father won't cook for himself. If I remember, there's a good Italian restaurant opposite the hospital.'

Typical of her mother, directing operations.

'Don't suppose I'll get much,' she ranted on. 'They have a system of ordering here and I missed the chance to see what's on offer. I'll get the leftovers, I expect, cold stew and semolina.'

'You must be feeling better if you can think about food.'

'I wouldn't mind a drink right now.'

Jo reached for the jug of water on the cabinet.

'I mean a tipple, not that stuff.'

'You're here to get your head right, Mummy.'

'Fiddlesticks. What have you been up to? Ages since we saw you. It's a funny old world when it takes something like this to get you calling on your parents. Are you still working in the glasshouse?'

'Garden centre, Mummy. Yes, I am.'

'What do you do—water the plants?'

'I've told you before. Lots of things.'

'It's not good for you, working under glass. It's no protection from those rays. You can get skin cancer. Tell her, Willy.'

'I'm not telling her anything,' her father said.

Mummy was unfazed. 'She should get a different job. With the education we gave her, she ought to be doing something better than watering pansies.'

Daddy rolled his eyes and was silent.

'Come on, dear,' Mummy insisted. 'What have you been up to? Is there a man in your life? I wish there was, someone you could start a family with, legally of course. No such luck, I suppose?'

Jo was beginning to think she would leave. She hadn't come here for an inquisition into her private life. 'How is the horse?'

'Which horse?'

'Penrose. Did he fall as well?'

'I've no idea. I told you it's a blur and you're trying to change the subject.'

Her father said, 'The stable lad who phoned said you went under a tree and got knocked off by a low branch.'

'That doesn't add up,' Mummy said. 'I'm too experienced for that.'

'It happened before.'

'Willy, I was a novice then. I don't make basic errors these days.'

'Something unseated you.'

'I expect the horse reared. You can't do much when that happens. A dog must have frightened him. People should keep them on leads. And muzzled. Josephine, you didn't answer my question. What sort of company are you keeping?'

'Mummy, I'm thirty-six years old. I don't have to account to you for the friends I have.'

'Be like that. I wouldn't mind betting you won't be so reticent when you want us to fork out for a big white wedding in the cathedral.'

'Ha!'

'What does that mean?'

'It means don't worry. It won't happen.'

'I'm not worried. We took out insurance shortly after you were born.'

'You what?'

'Tell her it's true, Willy. She can have a white Rolls Royce and a champagne reception for a hundred guests.'

He confirmed it with a shrug.

Instead of feeling grateful for such foresight, Jo thought it mercenary. She decided if she ever did get hitched she'd go to a register office and tell her parents later. The last thing she wanted was a monster shindig managed by her mother.

'You're getting overwrought,' she said. 'I'm going to leave. Get some rest while you've got the chance.'

Driving home, Jo had to admit she was the one who was overwrought. They still had the capacity to make her feel eleven years old. Maybe she should have gone for the Italian with Daddy. Stupid old man, he was no use at fending for himself. Never had been. Even if he'd offered, Mummy wouldn't have wanted him in her kitchen.

One night of cheese sandwiches wouldn't hurt him, she told herself, but she still felt bad about it.

THERE WAS a message on the answerphone. 'Jo, this is only me.' (It was Gemma's voice) 'Disappointed? I bet you are. I don't know if you've seen the local rag, but you're in it, babe. Front page news. "Woman's Grim Discovery at Selsey. Miss Josephine

Stevens, twenty-nine." That's pushing it a bit, isn't it? I thought we agreed we were roughly the same age and I won't see thirty-five again. The rest of it seems reliable, though. I thought you might want to get a copy. I'll keep mine in case you can't. See you Saturday, I hope. 'Bye.'

Nine thirty, just gone. She wasn't going out again. If she wanted to see the paper she could pick one up in the morning. She wasn't too excited about making the front page. Finding a body on a beach wasn't much of an achievement, not like swimming the channel or rescuing someone from a blazing building. Any fool could stumble over a body.

She regretted being economical with her age to the reporter. Gemma was right. Twenty-nine was pushing it. Why did newspapers always want to know your age, as if it mattered? The people at work were going to have a ball. Twenty-nine and counting, they would say.

As she cooked herself a late supper of a mushroom omelette, she had a mental picture of her father alone at home with his cheese sandwich. She was still thinking what a mean cow she was when the smoke alarm went off. The omelette was burning. All in all, this hadn't been one of her better days.

three

A REGULAR AT THE garden centre was Miss Peabody, a white-haired, straight-backed woman always in the same pink hat like a huge scoop of strawberry ice cream on top of her head. She was in each day shortly after opening time, but emphatically a visitor rather than a customer. None of the staff could recall her buying anything. Her routine was to wander the aisles noticing plants that were ailing. 'I know about plants,' she would say to whichever of the staff she could buttonhole, 'and you've got pansy wilt. Come and see.' She was usually right, but on a busy morning when a consignment of bulbs had to be checked and bagged up, pansy wilt wasn't a high priority. Adrian, the manager, advised the staff to treat the old lady with courtesy and find a reason to move away. He said he couldn't ask her to leave. She lived just down the road in Singleton and regarded the garden centre as an extension of her own small garden.

This Monday morning, she'd crept up behind Jo.

'Did you know you've got black spot?'

Jo dropped the trowel she was using. 'For crying out loud! You gave me a start, Miss Peabody.'

'Black spot, my dear, on your heart's desire. Do you want me to show you?'

'If it's there, Miss Peabody, we'll deal with it.'

'You shouldn't have let the fallen leaves lie there. It's a fungus and they're spreading it.'

'The roses aren't really my responsibility, but I'll pass it on. Oops, I've just remembered I should have made a phone call. Excuse me.'

Jo started walking fast, too fast for Miss Peabody. Any direction would do.

She hadn't gone far when something else brought her to a stop like a cartoon cat. A man in a black leather coat striding up the next aisle. Was it wishful thinking that he was unusually tall? He was in sight for a moment, then hidden behind the camellia display. Automatically her hand went to her hair and checked it. She wasn't certain this was Jake, but she'd be an idiot not to find out.

At the end of the row she slowed to a dignified walk. Karen, one of the sales staff, was with the man. From the back he looked right. He was tall enough. Please God, she thought. And Karen was clearly having difficulty understanding him.

As if by telepathy, he turned, blinked, frowned, and gave that lopsided smile that made him look as if he'd come from a session at the dentist's.

Heart pounding, she stepped closer. 'This gentleman is a friend of mine, Karen. May I help?'

'Please do.' For Karen it was as good as the U.S. cavalry arriving. 'We've established that he wants some plant labels. I was about to show him the range, but if you'd like to . . . ' She was round that display stand and out of sight before finishing the sentence.

'This is a surprise, Jake.'

The big man shrugged, but it was a friendly shrug. If nothing else, he remembered her.

'You didn't know I work here? No, you wouldn't.' She was floundering for the right words, wanting to show how pleased she was without overwhelming him. 'It's labels you want, then. Is that to do with the nature reserve? I thought everything grew wild.'

'Shingle plants,' he said.

'Single?'

'Shingle.'

'Oh.' It meant nothing.

'Sea campion.'

She was all at sea herself.

He struggled to get something else out. 'Vi—.' At the second and third attempts he didn't get past the V. He grimaced and the words came in a rush. 'Viper's bugloss.'

How unfortunate after so much effort that she'd never heard of it. 'I don't think we stock anything like that.'

He flapped his hand. 'Labels.'

'Of course. Labels. Karen said. For some special plants?'
Much nodding.

'Ah. So people can tell what they are and respect them?'

He nodded again and she breathed a sigh of relief. The point
was made and they could move on.

'I get the idea. You'll be wanting something easy to read and
quite robust.' She sorted through the selection of plant labels
while thinking how she might turn the chance meeting into
something more. 'These might be just the thing, don't you think?
They're on tall metal spikes, so you're not tying anything to the
plant.'

'They'll do.'

'But you may like to see some others.'

'How much?'

He wanted to get out fast and it could only be because of shyness. The opportunity was slipping. 'But they are a bit expensive,'
she told him. 'How many do you need?'

'Hundred and fifty.'

'That's a big order. I'll see if we can get a reduction. Look, the
manager will have to okay it. He's expected in ten minutes or so.
Would you mind waiting? I can get you a coffee.'

He took a step backwards. For a privileged customer he was
giving a fair impression of a trapped animal.

The garden centre had its own café, used mostly by the staff
and known unofficially as the Down Tools. She sat opposite him
at a white wrought iron table, hardly believing her luck. 'I was in
Selsey recently.'

'I saw.'

She was confused again. 'Really? I didn't see you.' Then it
dawned on her. 'Oh, you read about me in the paper? Horrid.
That experience has put me right off the place.'

A look of rejection came into his eyes, as if she was blaming
him for what happened.

'I don't mean that,' she added at once. 'What a wimp. I've got
to get over it, haven't I? Actually, I like the beach a lot. I'm sure
it has some of those plants you were mentioning.'

The brown eyes still looked as if there was no hope left in the world.

She wasn't giving up. 'In fact I was thinking—before I found what I did—it was a pity you weren't there to point out some of the features. You must know the beach well, being local. It even crossed my mind that you might have been out that morning, but of course you weren't.'

He was silent.

This was awfully hard work, but Jo persisted. 'Are you sometimes down there for a walk?'

'Depends.'

'Oh?'

'Some weekends . . . ' His voice trailed off.

She widened her eyes and smiled in encouragement.

He cranked himself up again. ' . . . I have to work.'

'Like me. We do most of our business at the weekends, but I can usually switch with someone if I need time off.' She took a breath. She was about to push harder at the door than she ever had with a man. 'Jake, I enjoyed being with you that time at the film. I'd really like to know you better.'

Too hard.

He uttered a loud, 'Ho,' and looked away, towards the exit.

She fingered her hair, coiling some and then releasing it, wishing she hadn't spoken, but what else could she have tried?

It seemed that the 'Ho' wasn't a putdown, because he turned his eyes back to her and said, 'For real?'

'Yes.'

'Me?'

'That's what I meant.'

He raked a hand down his face and the fingers made pale lines in the flesh. The guy was under terrific stress. The dire possibility crossed Jo's mind that he might be gay and hadn't come out yet. Finally he managed four pitiable words. 'Not much company, me.'

'Jake, that's for others to judge, isn't it?'

A long pause followed. 'Where, then?'

'How about a walk on the beach?'

He tugged at his shirt collar as if it was too tight.

'I was thinking Selsey, in spite of what I said. I don't want one bad experience to spoil it for me, so I ought to go back as soon as possible. Having you for company will make it so much easier.'

After more work on the collar he gave a nod.

She turned a mental cartwheel. 'Cool. And I'll try not to stumble over a body this time.'

He gave the novocaine smile.

By the same painstaking process they worked out that they would both be off work on Friday. She went to look for Adrian, and negotiated a reduction on the plant labels. Jake paid for them, muttered his thanks, and was gone.

THERE WAS excitement of a different sort after lunch. Over the public address she was called to Adrian's office. Unusual: it was his custom to seek people out on the shop floor, see what they were up to. Mystified, she checked her appearance before obeying the summons.

A young man in an off-the-peg suit that didn't hang well was standing just inside Adrian's door. Also, seated on the opposite side, a woman better dressed, in a navy two-piece. They didn't look as if they'd come to buy flowers. 'This is Miss Stevens,' Adrian told them without addressing Jo at all.

The woman spoke. 'Perhaps you'll leave us for a while, then.'

Adrian quit his office like a greyhound from the trap.

Jo understood why when the woman said, 'We're police officers. DCI Mallin, Chichester CID,' and showed a warrant card. The rapid way she spoke made the DCI sound like a forename. The card showed she was a detective chief inspector.

The guy in the cheap suit—plainclothes in an extra sense—was evidently playing the nice cop. He introduced himself as Gary Pearce, Detective Constable, placed a chair for Jo and said as if she had done the police a great favour, 'You found the body on Selsey beach and reported it, right? Would you mind telling us about it.'

'I already told—'

'No you didn't,' DCI Mallin cut in. 'Not to us. Sit down, please.' She was a small woman with a substantial presence.

Jo was glad of the chair. This sudden face-to-face with the law had thrown her. Her legs had gone wobbly. She'd been trying to move on from that gruesome business. 'There isn't much to say. I drove to Selsey and went for an early morning walk along the front.'

'Any special reason?' DCI Mallin asked.

'Exercise, I suppose.'

'Why Selsey?'

She wasn't going to tell them about Jake. He had no conceivable connection with what had happened. 'I like it there, that's all.'

'Many people about, were there?'

'A few. Some in cars, some walking dogs. Not many. It was early and quite breezy down there.'

'See anyone you knew?'

'I don't live there.'

'We know that, Josephine,' DCI Mallin said in a withering tone that made Jo even more uncomfortable. 'If you simply answer the questions, you'll help yourself as well as us.'

'It's Jo. My name. No one calls me Josephine.' But my mother does, she thought. No wonder the name humiliates me.

'Jo it is, then. I have the same trouble,' the chief inspector said as if she realised she'd been a touch too severe. 'I was named Henrietta and that's a mouthful I don't care for. People close to me call me Hen. Not him, though.' She tilted her head at DC Pearce but she didn't smile and neither did he. 'My question, Jo, is did you see anyone you know on Selsey beach?'

'No.'

'That's all right, then. Carry on with your statement.'

She hadn't thought it was anything so formal as a statement. She was just telling what happened that Sunday morning when she found the dead woman. 'I don't know how much you want to hear.'

'Start from when you first got there,' DC Pearce suggested, seating himself quite close to her on the edge of Adrian's desk.

She found it easier speaking to the young constable. She cast her thoughts back. If they wanted the entire story, they could have it. 'I parked the car at the bottom of the High Street and walked all the way along the front, past the lifeboat station and the fishermen's huts. I'd been on the path for some time, at least twenty minutes, and I wanted to get closer to the waves before I turned round, so I picked a section of the beach at random. After I'd been at the water's edge a few minutes I turned and climbed up, and that was when I saw her against a breakwater. Well, at that point I didn't know it was a person. I saw her pale skin under some seaweed and wondered what it was and went to investigate and had the biggest shock of my life.'

'Against a breakwater, you said?'

'Yes, they're really massive, about ten feet tall on the side where she was. She was right up against the wood, partly hidden behind one of those posts that support it all.'

'Was anyone else about?' DC Pearce asked.

'No one I noticed. I would have asked for help, wouldn't I? I had to go up to the top and call at the nearest house that backs onto the beach. The people phoned nine-nine-nine and I waited for the police to come.'

'Hold on a bit,' DCI Mallin said. 'Before you went up to the house, didn't you try to resuscitate her?'

'She was well dead.'

'How do you know that? Did you feel for a pulse?'

'I didn't touch her. I could see.'

'See she wasn't breathing, you mean?'

'It was obvious,' Jo said, more annoyed than defensive. 'Her skin was deathly white. There was seaweed clinging to her. Flies.'

'Have you ever done a life-saving course? People apparently dead can be saved with mouth-to-mouth or chest compressions. Drowning cases offer the best hope of recovery. But I won't labour the point. We've established that you did nothing. Carry on.'

Jo's so-called statement had long since ground to a halt. 'I don't know where I was.'

'Waiting for the police,' DC Pearce prompted her.

'Where?' Hen Mallin asked.

'What?'

'Where did you wait? On the beach?'

'Of course.' To keep up her confidence she reminded herself that this hard-nosed chief inspector was Hen to her friends. She'd also noticed that the chief inspector's fingers were nicotine-stained. Even the police experienced stress.

'Did you notice anything of interest?'

'What do you mean?'

'Stuff lying around.'

'What sort of stuff?'

'We're asking you, Jo,' Hen Mallin said. 'It isn't our job to put words in your mouth. Apart from the dead woman, was there anything you noticed along that bit of beach?'

'I don't know what you're talking about.'

Hen Mallin spelt it out as if to an Alzheimer's patient. 'You were there, Jo. We weren't. The place has been covered by the tide many times since that morning. Things get moved, washed out to sea, covered over. The site isn't of much use to a crime scene investigation team now, but while you were there it was fresh.'

At the words *crime scene*, Jo's insides clenched. 'Are you saying there was a crime?'

'Didn't you notice?'

'Notice what?'

'The marks on the flesh.'

'I expect there would be some. It's a stony beach.'

'Bruising to the neck consistent with finger pressure.'

A pulse throbbed in her temple and she thought she would faint. 'No—how dreadful!'

'We're treating it as a violent death and possibly murder.'

Gooseflesh was forming on her arms.

'She drowned, as you must have guessed,' DC Pearce said in a tone meant to make it less of a shock, 'and the marks suggest she was held under the water.'

'Horrible.'

'Yes.'

'I had no idea. And this happened at sea?'

'Not in the way you mean,' Hen Mallin said.

'I don't follow you.'

'You're assuming she was attacked on a ship. We don't think so. Human skin immersed in water for any length of time gets bleached and wrinkled. It used to be called washerwoman's hand, but these days we don't use the term. This woman's skin was in good condition, wet from the waves, and no more. We think the attack happened close to the beach.'

'I can't believe this.'

'It seems she was in the water with her killer and held under until she stopped breathing. Now do you see why your recall of the scene is so important?'

She released a large, shaky breath. And nodded.

Hen Mallin pressed on with her questions. 'You found the body at the base of the breakwater, right?'

'Yes.'

'As you pointed out, they stand ten or twelve feet high, those breakwaters. On the one side, that is. On the other, the stones are stacked almost to the top, so you don't see much timber at all. It's the action of the tide, dragging the stones from under one breakwater and heaping them against the next one.'

Jo waited for her to get to the point.

'And the sea was quite rough. Had been for some hours. Do you follow me? If the body had been washed up, it wouldn't have got where you found it.'

It was as if they were questioning her account. 'That's where it was.'

'So it looks as if the tide went out and the body was left there, more or less where she drowned. That would explain why it was on that side of the breakwater.'

'I suppose.'

'You didn't find any clothes nearby?'

'No. Why?' She knew the question was stupid as soon as it left her mouth, but all this had come as a shock.

'She's not going to be on a public beach in no more than her knickers.'

'There weren't any clothes that I could see.'

'You must have wondered where they were, surely, finding a poor dead woman almost naked.'

'I don't know what I thought. I was very upset when I discovered what it was I'd found.'

'You didn't look around, then?' Hen Mallin's brown eyes regarded her with disbelief, if not disapproval.

Jo felt annoyed by the question. 'I'm not an expert like you. I thought she'd been washed up by the tide. I'm only the person who happened to find her.' She almost added that they were making her feel like a suspect, but she stopped herself in time. 'Was she . . . ?'

'Raped? Apparently not. The signs weren't there, but who can say what was in the mind of the killer? Something that starts out as sex play can turn ugly if the woman doesn't welcome it.'

These words, 'raped,' 'killer,' 'sex play,' and 'ugly' struck Jo with near-physical force. 'Do you think they knew each other, then? They went to the beach together for a swim?'

'That's our present assumption.'

'And he held her under and she drowned?'

'He, or she. We consider every option.'

'Why?'

'Why was she attacked?' Hen Mallin turned up her palms. 'No one can say yet. The killer could have planned it, expecting she'd be taken for some unfortunate woman who fell overboard. You understand why I'm asking if you remember anything from the scene?'

'Who was she?'

'We don't know yet. She could be local. Equally she could have come from miles away. Or been brought there by her killer.'

'Poor woman.'

'Yes. Whoever she was, her luck ran out that weekend. Cast your mind back, Jo. Who did you see along the front?'

'Nobody I knew.'

'That isn't what I'm asking. I don't expect names. I want your recollection of everyone you noticed.'

'That's hard.'

'Think for a bit. Take your time.'

She frowned. The finding of the body had pushed everything before that moment into a hazy, unimportant background. For much of the walk she'd been absorbed in her own thoughts, hoping against the odds to meet Jake. She'd been on the lookout for tall men, that was one sure thing.

'There was a young guy who passed me early on. He was tall, over six feet, and wearing a fleece and tracksuit trousers. Grey, I think. And he had an iPod. Well, I saw the earphones.'

'You say he passed you. Do you mean overtook you?'

'No, he was coming towards me.'

'From the direction of the body?'

'Yes, but I don't think—'

'Hair colour?'

'God, this is difficult. Darkish brown and short.'

'Age?'

'Younger than me. Mid-twenties probably.'

'Was he in a hurry?'

'He was walking quite fast when I saw him. He could have been a jogger.'

'Did you speak?'

She shook her head. 'There wasn't even eye contact.'

'But you'd remember him if you saw him again?'

'I might. I can't say for sure.' She felt responsible, drawing attention to this guy who probably had nothing to do with the body. 'He wasn't the only man I saw along the beach. There was another, in combat clothes, down at the water's edge throwing a ball for his dog.'

'What—near the body?'

'No. I told you nobody was there. This was further back, closer to those wooden buildings where the fish are sold.'

'Go on,' DC Pearce said. 'We're with you.'

'I watched the dog running into the waves to collect the ball. It was a large black poodle.'

Maybe a pit bull would have impressed them more. The two detectives lost all interest in the dog owner. They didn't even ask the colour of his hair. 'When you saw the first man, the guy in the tracksuit,' Hen Mallin said, 'it was early on in the walk, you said?'

'I think so.'

'Not far from where you left the car?'

'Probably.'

'You wouldn't have noticed if he got into a car himself?'

'I told you. He passed me. I didn't look back.'

'Fair enough.' Hen looked at her colleague. They'd run through their repertoire. 'There's nothing else you remember from that afternoon?'

'I've told you all I know.'

They left soon after. Although something was said about thanks and cooperation, Jo felt it was only lip service. She'd had a mauling. She needed another coffee before she could face work again.

THAT EVENING one of those small cars that look as if it they've been sawn off at the back was parked in the spot she always used outside her flat, so she had to go looking for another place. Typical. The only space she could find was way up the next street. Serious damage to property (namely, one yellow Smartcar) was on her mind as she finished humping two bags of shopping the two hundred yards to her door.

Before she got there someone stepped out of the offending car and stood waiting for her.

Gemma.

'Can I help with those?'

'You'd better, seeing that you nicked my parking place.'

'Sorry.' Gem sounded worried, more worried than ill-judged parking warranted.

'Problems?'

'Mind if I come in? I've had a godawful week and it's still only Monday.'

Supper would have to wait. Inside, Jo opened the bottle of merlot she'd bought for herself and carried two drinks to the sofa. The two friends sat facing the switched-off television.

'It's my butthead boss again,' Gemma said. 'You remember I was telling you about Fiona from accounts? Well, it seems I read the signs all wrong. She's giving him the come-on now. In the last couple of days she's appeared at work all done up like the next *Big Brother* contestant in really unsuitable clothes, low-cut tops and skirts a teenager would think twice about wearing.'

Jo was still feeling frayed from her session with the police and it wasn't easy to take Gemma's problems seriously, but she made the effort. 'I thought she was the homespun type. That's what you told me.'

'And how wrong I was. That line she gave me about being embarrassed by all his interest was a load of horse hooey. She was sounding me out, making sure I wasn't going to make a play for him myself.'

'And what does he make of it?'

'Laps it up, naturally. He's starting to give her jobs that mean reporting back to him directly. Every time she comes in he sends me out on some errand.'

'Do you think they're at it in the office?'

'Parallel parking? I wouldn't put it past them. There's some fooling around for sure, but that isn't here nor there. What really upsets me, Jo, is that I think he's grooming her for my job.'

'Really?' For all her efforts, Jo wasn't sounding as outraged as the story demanded.

Fortunately Gemma didn't seem to notice. 'Yesterday she was told to take a spess—that's a specification—from a client. That's what I do. I should have done that.'

Jo rallied a bit. 'Bloody cheek. Did you tell him he's out of order?'

'No. I'm a coward basically.'

'You've got to stand up for yourself or she'll trample all over you. If it happens again, you march into that office of his and tell him you won't stand for it.'

Gemma shook her head. 'I know what'll happen if I do. My office experience up against her pulling power? No contest.'

'The place can't run without you.'

'I wish that was true. I was talking to Rick and he said no one is indispensable.'

'You've discussed it with Rick?'

'We had a drink last night.'

'And he wasn't much comfort by the sound of it.'

'He said the writing is on the wall. I'd better see what's on offer at the job centre.'

'Oh great!' Jo's fighting spirit surfaced. 'Listen, Gem. Rick is way off message here. You've done nothing wrong. You're practically running that firm on your own. If you want out, okay, but if you want to keep the job you've got to hit back.'

'What can I do? Call in the Headhunters?'

'Let's think. Like you say, she's played the sex card, and that's got him all fired up. We give him the cold shower treatment.'

'How?'

'You say he's giving her the chance to meet clients. What if she makes a mistake that costs the firm a lot of money?'

'I'm sure she will, given time, but I can't afford to wait for it to happen.'

'Exactly. You help it along. I don't know how your office works, but if, say, an order comes in for three hundred booklets it won't look good for the fair Fiona if her paperwork says thirty thousand.'

'I add some zeros? She'd notice. She's trained in accounts.'

'It's a matter of when it's done. You intercept the order after it's left her and before it goes to the printer. You can find a way of doing that, can't you?'

'I guess I can . . . but it's sneaky.'

'Gem, I don't get you. Don't you think *she's* being sneaky, doing you out of your job?'

Gemma looked as if the sun had come out. 'Back of the net. Yes, I could use her computer and alter the figures at source and reprint the order. It would be simple to do.'

'Remember, for this to work it has to be several zeros, not just one.'

'A major boo-boo?' Gemma's eyes shone again.

'Precisely. And the beauty is, she won't know for certain that she didn't make the mistake herself. We've all done that, pressed one key too hard and made a row of letters.' Jo was surprising herself with her relish for this underhand plot.

'Do you think I'll get away with it?' Gemma said. 'I'll be the obvious suspect.'

'If she points the finger at you, she's admitting she's made an enemy of you by targeting your job. She won't want to do that.'

'What about Mr Cartwright? He's going to think it was me.'

'Let him. He won't be able to prove a thing. And he can't be certain it wasn't Fiona who screwed up. The main thing is he won't dare put any more of your work her way.'

'I'm going to do it,' Gemma raised a clenched fist. 'I feel heaps better now.'

Jo, too, was much recovered.

'I knew I could depend on you,' Gemma said. 'You know what?'

'Tell me.'

'When I top the bastard, you're definitely on the team.'

four

'THIS IS GETTING TO ME,' Hen Mallin said to Stella Gregson, who was managing the mobile incident room on the front at Selsey. They were sitting on the steps in front of the open door so that Hen could smoke one of her evil-smelling cigarillos. 'I never fancied a caravan holiday.'

Stella had worked with Hen ever since their days at Bognor police station and knew when the boss was in danger of erupting. Ten days into the investigation they still hadn't identified the victim. 'Things could be worse. Makes a nice change from the nick. Fresh sea air.'

'You think so? I'm an Essex girl, raised on petrol fumes.'

'A tough case brings out the best in you.'

'It isn't a case at all yet.'

'I can't think what else we can try, guv. The posters are everywhere. We had the front page in all the local papers. Television news.'

'And what have we got for it? Sweet FA.'

'There can't be anyone left in Selsey who hasn't heard.'

'Have we scared them off, parking this Port-a-Loo at the scene, or what? Even the attention-seekers are shunning us. We might as well shut up shop and shift back to the nick. At least you get a burger and chips there.'

'You get freshly caught fish here. I took home two beautiful fillets of plaice last night.'

'Great—if you've got the energy to cook at the end of the day.'

'My fellow does the cooking.'

'Be like that.' Hen lived alone in a Bognor terrace. Her police career had always come first, and, unlike Stella, she'd never thought of sharing her home with a cop. She'd been raised in a

working class family in Dagenham, but the raising had stopped at
five foot one, and when she'd confided to her sister and two older
brothers that she wanted to join the police they'd teased her without mercy. For the next year she was PC Shortarse and had to put
up with ee-ah siren sounds whenever she appeared. She'd refused
to be downed and answered a recruitment ad as soon as she was
old enough. For the interview she'd added extra inches with plat-
form shoes and her hair on top in a bun. Even the interviewer had
poked fun, telling her the ballet school was up the street, but
she'd toughed it out and said she had her own version of the
Nutcracker called the ballbuster. And here she was, twelve years
on, running a murder squad.

Stella switched the talk back to the investigation. 'I've been
asking myself why it's so quiet. It's a small community, just a village really. Suppose word got round that talking to us is not
encouraged?'

'A conspiracy of silence? I don't think so, Stell. You don't see
that in their faces. Nobody cares enough. If we could put a name
to the victim, we'd get a response, believe me.'

'There are still no reports of missing women.'

'I'm wondering about house-to-house.'

Now it was Stella's turn to get uptight. 'Do you want my honest opinion, guv?'

'Save your breath,' Hen said. 'I know where you're coming
from. It wouldn't be cost-effective. If we knew what happened to
the victim's clothes, we might get somewhere.'

'Taken by the sea?'

'I doubt it. You've seen the tideline all the way along. Enough
rubbish to fill a quarry. Things get washed up here, not swept out.'

'And everything along the beach has been sifted by the search
squad.'

'I'm not complaining at the effort,' Hen said. 'I want to know
why, that's all. Either some local ne'er-do-well found her kit and
nicked it and is scared to own up, or the killer saw the sense in
disposing of it. I would, and so would you.'

Uncomfortably close to home. Stella hesitated before asking,
'So are we talking about someone with police experience?'

'Not these days. Any couch potato with a telly gets the basics about forensics most nights of the week.'

The dialogue was interrupted briefly by some screaming gulls fighting over a fish head. Burgers still got Hen's vote.

Stella threw in another suggestion. 'What about the woman who found her?'

'Jo Stevens?'

'What's she like?'

'Ordinary. Profoundly shaken up by the experience. Lives in Chi and has the occasional walk down here at weekends. I got the impression she was keeping something back. It could be down to nerves, but she was pretty tight-lipped when I asked.'

'Could that be because she picked up the victim's clothes?'

Hen turned to look at her. 'That's a thought.'

'Is she short of a few bob?'

'Shouldn't be. She's in work. Mind, we don't even know if the clothes were worth taking. No, on second thoughts she'd have found nicking them difficult. She was still at the scene when the patrol car answered the shout. The things must have walked before she got here.'

'What's she holding back, then?'

'Don't know. It's just the vibe I was getting from her.'

'Would you like me to have a go at her?'

Hen shook her head. 'I don't want her retreating into her shell.'

Stella wasn't known for bullying tactics, but she let the remark pass. 'Could she be a suspect?'

Hen flicked ash on the pebbles. 'What, drowned the woman and raised the alarm herself? It wouldn't be unknown in the annals of crime. I dare say there's a syndrome with a special name for it. In the absence of any other suspects, Stella, I'm keeping an open mind on Miss Jo Stevens.'

'And the men she saw along the beach, the jogger and the dog-owner?'

'Still trying to trace them. Like I said, Selsey people aren't the best at coming forward. This box on wheels looks too much like a prison vehicle. Speaking of which, I'm still interested in local villains.'

'We checked the sex offenders' register on the first day and drew a blank, as you know.'

'This may not be about sex.'

'Nothing showed up in the post mortem.'

'My point exactly. It's easy to get carried away with the idea that because she was undressed it was for one thing only.'

'What else is there?'

'Skinny dipping, for starters. This was a warm September night. At this end of summer, the sea temperature is as high as it gets.'

'I haven't heard of nude bathing down here.'

'These things go on, Stell.'

'In Selsey?'

'All along the coast. There's an entire beach in Brighton that is set aside for the birthday suit brigade. I once walked by out of curiosity. Didn't exactly inflame me. And then there's art.'

'There's what?'

'Photography in the main, celebrating the naked form, usually female. Page three girls. Not just the *Sun*. Lads' mags. Even posh Sunday colour magazines pay big bucks for that kind of stuff. Beaches are favoured locations. Not that your average girl-fancier wastes much time looking at the background.'

'And they call it art!'

'I hope I haven't got a Philistine on my team. This is com-mercial art. Cash for the models, fees for the photographers, and sales for the newsagents.'

'Do you think our victim was a model, then?'

'Actually, no. At thirty plus, she was a bit old for that. Unless it was amateur photography. The local camera club.'

'A Women's Institute calendar. What was that film?' Stella asked, playing to Hen's improving mood.

'It had a thousand imitations. The world's moved on.'

'But has this place?'

'Going by Bognor, where I live, probably not. But I haven't heard Selsey is planning anything quite so risqué. Someone would have told us, wouldn't they?'

'Are they telling us anything?'

'You can't get up to frolics like that without half the village knowing about it.'

'We don't know half the village.'

'Which is why house-to-house has its attractions,' Hen said. 'You walked into that.'

Behind them, a phone went. One of the computer operators inside the van would take it.

'What we need is someone out here under an awning,' Hen said. 'Know what I mean? A canvas thing with coloured stripes. We're on a beach, for God's sake. Let's meet the public as they walk by.'

She was called to the phone.

Stella waited, hoping whoever it was would put the awning out of the boss's mind. Outside was no place to be when the wind got up.

'Breakthrough,' Hen said, stepping out again, elated. 'A witness has surfaced. Says he was on the beach on the day she was found. He was exercising his dog. This is the guy with the poodle.'

TWENTY PAST two and Jake was late. They were supposed to meet on the path opposite the lifeboat station, and it wasn't the best of choices. The sharp east wind coming off the sea was getting through Jo's padded jacket and chilling her. Unusually for her, she was shivering. She wasn't sure how much longer she could stand here.

She should have asked for his mobile number. She assumed he carried a phone. He'd need one in his line of work, just to keep in touch with colleagues. She wasn't sure what nature conservancy entailed, except that labelling shingle plants was part of it. A man out on the reserve would need to stay in contact.

The arrangement had been clear, she thought. Friday at two. If something had gone wrong he could have called the garden centre and left a message for her. She'd just checked and she had no voicemail. He wouldn't have reached her at home because he didn't know her number, or even where she lived. This early in a friendship you don't exchange addresses.

Plenty of things might have delayed him, and she kept playing them through her mind. She didn't wish to face the other possibility: that he'd stood her up. It was hard to know how any man's mind worked, and Jake's shyness was an extra barrier. So for the moment she preferred to think something had gone wrong at home, a burst pipe or a gas leak. He'd get the problem fixed as soon as possible and come hurrying to meet her.

If she was wrong and a domestic emergency wasn't the reason, she supposed he could have made a mistake about the time. Or even the day. Forgetfulness would be preferable to rejection.

Clutching at her arms, trying to rub warmth into them, she looked again along the path in each direction. Few scenes are so bleak as the seaside on a grey autumn day. To the east, where the wind was coming from, she could see the black trailer the police had parked opposite the place where she'd found the body. It just depressed her more.

He'd said he lived in Selsey but she had no idea which part. No one else was in sight. The only life in view was the gulls gliding on the stiff wind, and they were pretty inactive, not needing to move their wings. This was looking like a lost cause.

I hate this place, she thought. Once it was all right, but now it's linked with that poor woman's death and the hard time I was given by those detectives. If I'm honest with myself I'm only here for the chance to spend time with Jake. I don't really have to put myself through this.

She looked at her watch again. Maybe the poor guy was ill, too far gone to make contact. That would be dreadful, but was it realistic? People his age didn't get ill very often, not ill enough to be stuck indoors. If she stayed here much longer she'd be the one who was ill. Soon she'd have to admit he wasn't going to appear and hadn't bothered to let her know.

Ten more minutes, then.

Those minutes passed and he didn't come.

ON SATURDAY in Starbucks Gemma was even more hyper than usual. 'You're a crafty minx, putting those wicked ideas in my head. I've done the dirty now. There's no going back. The ordure hits the air conditioning next week, about Tuesday morning, I reckon.'

'You went through with it?'

'Calm down. You look like the bird that went for a worm and pecked through the electric cable. This was your suggestion, remember. Yesterday she left about three-thirty and so did he.'

'Together?'

'Take a wild guess. So it gave me the chance to get into her computer. To be honest, I was in two minds even then, but I didn't know the half of it. You wouldn't believe the amount of stuff he's syphoned off to her in the last week. I went mental when I saw it all on screen. These aren't jumble sale posters, Jo, they're major projects, colour magazines, and Christmas catalogues for some of our top clients. Work I've always handled.'

'So what did you do?'

'Just like you said, I bumped up one of the orders from five thou to five hundred thou.'

'Good. Which one?'

'A council booklet about waste disposal.'

Jo raised a clenched fist. 'I like it. She'll be waste herself when this gets found out.'

Gemma rolled her eyes upwards. 'I'm not so comfortable with it now.'

'Why?'

'Basically, I'm a coward. I'm hoping the printer queries it with Mr Cartwright.'

'That's no use,' Jo said. 'The business has to suffer, or she'll walk all over you and so will he. You want half a million useless booklets stacked up for everyone to see.'

Gemma whistled. 'Half a million? Is that how much it comes to?'

'Five hundred thou, you said.'

'I'm wetting my pants over this.'

'Believe me, if it doesn't hurt him where it matters, in his pocket, your Mr Cartwright is going to forgive and forget and Fiona will be sitting at your desk before the end of the year. Be strong, Gem.'

Gemma's way of being strong was to bite her lip and flap her hand in front of her face, and Jo felt her own confidence falter, in spite of all she'd said. She'd set this up and people's careers were at risk. Someone was going to suffer, whatever the justification for the thing.

Jo changed the subject. 'How are you and Rick getting on? Have you been out with him again?'

'A couple of times,' Gemma said. 'The lad is shaping up. We've got the same taste in films, which is good. But we haven't had sex yet, if that's what you're asking.'

'D'you mind? I wouldn't be so nosy.'

'Did you sleep with him when you two were going out?'

Jo smiled. 'I see. It's all right to ask me. As a matter of fact, I didn't. Things got a bit physical, if you get me, but I wasn't ready for the main course.'

'I bet he was.'

'Possibly, but it takes two.'

'He behaved like a gent, then? Adjusted his dress and wished you a polite good evening?'

'Something like that.'

'I don't plan on telling him about my war with Fiona,' Gemma said. 'That's between you and me, right?'

'Fine.'

'I know I can trust you not to blurt it out. Can't count on Rick keeping it to himself. Know what I mean?'

'Understood.'

'I've nothing against him. He's fun to be with, but I've got to keep this schtum. I mean, it doesn't reflect very well on me. I don't mind you knowing because it was all your idea.'

'As you keep reminding me.'

'That's me accounted for, then,' Gemma said. 'How about you and old motormouth? Are you two an item yet?'

'Hardly.' Jo felt the colour rise. 'Where did you get that idea?'

'Come on, babe, it's obvious you fancy him something wicked. Look at you now, a poinsettia in full bloom.'

'You're so wrong.'

'Don't mind me. Just because I call him names it doesn't mean a thing. I'm always slagging off blokes. It's a sport. You've got to make the first move, you know. He's chronically shy. If you wait for him to ask, you'll still be waiting when you get your bus pass. Fix a time and place and tell him to be there.'

Jo didn't enlighten her about Selsey. 'He isn't interested.'

'Bet he is. Want me to find out?'

'No,' Jo said sharply. 'Absolutely not.'

'Look at the state you're in. Simmer down, babe. You've got it bad, haven't you? All right, do it your way. I won't interfere.'

'You've got this all wrong.'

'I'm sure. Be funny, wouldn't it, if we swapped blokes?'

'Oh, hilarious,' Jo said.

BACK AT home the light was winking on the answerphone. She pressed it before taking off her coat. The voice was not Jake's. It was female. And familiar.

'Miss Stevens? Hen Mallin—DCI Mallin. We spoke the other day. Give me a call directly you get back, would you?' She gave the number.

What did they want now? Jo hung up her coat and looked at the mail. Junk, all of it. Nothing with a local postmark.

She went back to the phone.

'Thank you for calling in, my dear,' Hen Mallin said, all sweetness and light now. 'I've got a favour to ask. When you told us about finding the body at Selsey you mentioned seeing a couple of men.'

'Did I?'

'The one in the tracksuit and the one with the dog. What I'd like is for you to see if you can recognise the jogger.'

'How do you mean?'

'Pick him out from a line-up. An identification parade.'

Jo gasped and her mouth went dry. 'I don't think so. I didn't see him well enough for that.'

'When you get a proper look at him again, you might find it refreshes your memory. No pressure. It's all done through one-way glass and you get a cup of tea if you want.'

'But the people I saw just happened to be out for a walk that morning like me. They weren't acting suspiciously or anything.'

'Understood. They're probably innocent, but we do need to eliminate them from our enquiry, and only you can help. I'll send a car. It will take a couple of hours to set this up. We'll pick you up about four-thirty.'

How could she refuse? She wished she'd left that beach without reporting what she'd found. You just don't know what it will lead to when you help the police.

SHE WAS still trying to think of a get-out when the police car drew up outside the flat. She hated the idea of fingering someone who might be innocent.

They'd sent a chatty policewoman to fetch her. She was worse than some taxidrivers, on about the government and public sector pay rates and the price of housing and the problems of immigration. When Jo stepped out of the car in the police station yard she scattered umpteen shreds of paper tissue on the ground. She hadn't noticed herself doing it.

Hen Mallin greeted her like an old friend and took her upstairs. 'I won't be at your side, I'm afraid,' she said, as if that would disappoint. 'The rules require that you're taken in by an identification officer who isn't on the investigation.'

'I've given this a lot of thought—' Jo started to say.

'Not a good idea,' Hen said. 'Relax. You'll know at once if you recognise the guy. The eyes have it, as they say—much better than trying to remember.'

'I don't want to do it.'

'No one ever does. Look at it this way. It's better than a visit to the mortuary. We're not asking you to identify the corpse.'

There seemed to be no option. Hen introduced her to Sergeant Malcolm, a young man looking more anxious than Jo was. 'My first time,' he said.

'Mine, too.'

'There's a gentleman in there already. He's a solicitor. It's important this is done properly or he'll be down on me like the proverbial ton of bricks. The parade is also being videoed. When we go in you'll be shown nine men, including the suspect.'

'Suspect?' Jo said. 'Have you arrested someone?'

'That's the whole point of this.'

'Then I don't want to do it. Definitely.'

'You can't back out now,' Sergeant Malcolm said in alarm. 'All these people have given up their time. The solicitor came in specially. It isn't scary at all, not for you. They can't see you.'

'What if I don't recognise any of them?'

'Not your problem. You'll help me, won't you, miss?'

'If I must.'

'Each of them has a number. When you identify anyone, you just say the number. But please take a really good look at each of them. Walk along the line twice, at least, and take as much time as you want. Ready?' He opened a door.

It was almost dark in there. She was aware of a man in a suit standing at the opposite end, and someone with a camera. Then some lights came on and the area to her right was revealed through glass.

Her stomach lurched. She was facing a row of nine men, and the third one in was Jake.

five

HER EYES MISTED OVER. She blinked several times. She wasn't mistaken.

'You're supposed to walk the line, miss,' Sergeant Malcolm said.

Confused emotions bombarded her. Jake looked dreadful, as if he hadn't slept for two days. He seemed to be dressed to make him an object of ridicule, in a skimpy grey fleece zipped to his throat and black tracksuit trousers that didn't even reach to his socks. She wanted to speak to him, but they were divided by soundproof one-way glass.

'Take a good look at each one.'

Her impulse was to tell the sergeant they'd made a dreadful mistake and Jake shouldn't be there. He was a good man, not a murderer. He cared about the living world and the ecology. No way would he take another person's life.

Better judgement ruled. She stayed silent and tried to make a cool assessment. Innocent men were brought in off the streets to make up the number on these parades. The police dressed them to match a witness's description. Now that she took a wider view this entire line-up had ill-fitting tops and tracksuit trousers like Jake's and she remembered giving DCI Mallin a description of the man she'd passed that day at Selsey. Well, one thing was certain: that guy wasn't Jake. Only through coincidence had Jake been brought in. Probably he'd come into town for the afternoon and some policeman had picked him at random and asked him to take part.

Convincing?

Not really, she thought. I can see the strain in his face. He's their suspect and the rest are there because they faintly resemble him. Tall, dark men, not one of them anything like the man she remembered seeing.

'Make a start, miss.'

Her anger mixed with fear as she forced herself to glance at the first man. A white card with the number one was on the floor in front of him. She'd never seen him before. He looked faintly bored. So did number two.

She took a deep breath and moved on. It was painful looking at Jake. His eyes were red-lidded and dark all round. Stress lines at the side of his mouth made him seem twice his age.

She stepped past him, trying to appear unaffected. All the others seemed untroubled, indifferent to this whole procedure. No one was stressed and exhausted like Jake.

'Take your time. No need to hurry.'

Her thoughts still in turmoil, she started walking back.

'You're not facing them, miss. You're supposed to look at them all at least twice.'

She didn't trust herself to speak. Her throat ached. To satisfy the rules she paused in front of each man and gave another glance. Except for Jake. She couldn't bear to look into his face again, so she fixed her eyes at the level of his chest. When she reached the end of the line she faced Sergeant Malcolm and shook her head. It was the truth. She hadn't seen any of them at Selsey.

'For the record, would you mind saying if you recognised one of these men?'

The way he put the question sounded like a trap. If they could choose their words, then so could she. And still speak the truth. 'I saw two men at the beach and they aren't here.'

'Are you quite sure, miss?'

She nodded.

He glanced at the solicitor, who shrugged and spread his hands. 'Would you like to walk the line one more time?'

She shook her head.

DS Malcolm held open the door and she came out. He offered tea. She needed something to calm her jangled nerves. On the way down to the canteen he said, 'It's not too late to say if you spotted one of them. You can tell me now and I'll inform the solicitor.'

To emphasise the truth of what she was saying, she stopped on the stairs, looked straight at him and spaced her words. 'They were not the men I saw at the beach.'

'I thought you reacted to one of them.'

This time she couldn't be as truthful. She turned away and moved on again. 'It was the situation. I wasn't comfortable being so close and having them stare straight through me.'

In the canteen, her spirits plunged. A small familiar figure was waiting at a table with a teapot and cups. Hen Mallin stood to greet them, eyes wide in anticipation.

Sergeant Malcolm shook his head.

The start of a smile turned into a puzzled frown. 'You'd better get back, then. You've got work to do.'

The sergeant nodded to Jo and left her with Hen Mallin.

'Milk and sugar?'

'Black, without, please.'

'Help yourself.'

She poured it and slopped some in the saucer.

'So you weren't able to help?' Hen said with a sharp note of accusation.

'I did what I was asked.'

'A waste of everyone's time.'

That stung her. 'I can't think why, if it proves you've got the wrong man.'

'It doesn't prove anything,' Hen pointed out, 'except that you didn't see the killer. Apparently.'

'All I saw at Selsey were people acting normally. God knows why you asked me here. It's not as if I witnessed the murder.'

'You placed two men near enough to the scene to be of interest to us. If you'd picked out the suspect we'd be a damned sight closer to charging him. We'll have to release him now. There's a limit to how long we can hold a man and we've just about reached it.'

'Don't you have any other witnesses?'

Hen watched her, level-eyed. 'There is one actually.'

Jo suppressed the spasm of panic she felt. 'Did they see the woman killed?'

'Christ, no. If we'd got that lucky we wouldn't need you. Just some guy who was out walking that afternoon like you and gave us a description.'

'And did he identify the man?'

'In a parade, you mean? No need.'

'Why not?'

'He's local, like the suspect. He gave us the name of the bastard.'

BACK IN her flat, she tried to calm herself enough to get a sense of what had been going on. She was in no doubt as to whom their suspect was. She'd never seen anyone so shattered, looking just as you would after hours of questioning. The only conceivable reason for putting Jake through this ordeal was that the other witness must have seen him on the front at Selsey that fatal morning.

Jo couldn't think how she had missed him.

Was one sighting enough for them to pull him in as a suspected killer?

They'd need more. What else had they got on Jake? Whatever it was, it could only be circumstantial. Maybe he was linked in some way to the victim. Had they managed to identify the dead woman? She hadn't asked, and they weren't telling.

Out of all this wretched business there was one consolation. She now understood why Jake had failed to meet her at Selsey yesterday. Not because he'd forgotten, or lost interest. It could only be because they'd arrested him.

Whatever the police suspected, she was sure Jake was innocent and he would get her backing. Poor guy, he needed oceans of support after this. Unfortunately there was a difficulty. She didn't have his address or phone number. And it was too late in the day to phone his work and leave a message.

She spent the next hour trying to think of ways of contacting him. The police had said they couldn't hold him any longer, so he'd be home by now. How frustrating was that?

JUST BEFORE seven, her phone rang. She picked it up and gave her name. At first no one answered. She waited in dread that it was only a cold call, someone in India trying to sell her cheap electricity.

Then a man's voice said, 'Sorry about yesterday.' And she knew instantly who it was.

'Jake. How are you?'

'In a spot of trouble.'

'I know. I know all about it.'

'You do?'

'I was there today for that stupid identification parade.'

'You?' There was a pause, then a despairing, 'Oh, Christ.'

'They made me do it because it was me who discovered the body on the beach. I was supposed to see if I recognised one of the men I'd seen. Jake, it freaked me out when I saw you in the line-up. God knows what the police think they're doing. Anyway, you're home, are you?'

'Mm.' He sounded preoccupied, still absorbing what she'd told him.

'How did you get my number?' she asked.

'Number?'

'The phone. I'm ex-directory.' How it was done didn't matter squat, but talking about it was giving her time to get her own jumbled thoughts in order and decide what to say next.

'Gemma,' he said.

'Of course. Good old Gem. She's in the book. She put you onto me. I really appreciate this call, Jake.'

'Can we meet?'

'Meet?' Her pulse quickened. 'I'd love to.'

'To talk.'

'I understand. All right. When? Tomorrow?'

'Tonight.'

'Are you sure? You looked out on your feet.'

'A pub would do.'

'What's the one near the beach in Selsey? The Lifeboat Inn.'

'I can come to Chichester.'

'I won't hear of it after all you've been through,' she told him. 'Selsey. Definitely Selsey.' She looked at her watch. 'Eight-thirty in the Lifeboat?'

* * *

He was already at a corner table with a pint in front of him when she arrived. The sight of him here, a free man again, was a huge reassurance. The dark rings were still around his eyes, but some of the strain had gone from his face. She said she'd have a tonic.

'How long did they hold you at the police station?' she asked when he put the drink in front of her.

'Since yesterday morning.'

'Oh my God. Is that legal?'

He nodded.

'But you haven't done anything.'

'It's a murder case.'

'They told me you were seen by someone at the beach the day I found the body,' she said. 'Surely that isn't enough for them to arrest you. Were you really there? I didn't spot you.'

'Thought I might get lucky,' he said.

'What do you mean?'

'You said . . . ' The words stopped coming.

'Go on.'

' . . . you walk there sometimes.'

Her heart felt like Big Ben striking. 'You were there because of me?'

He shrugged. 'Anyway, it's not a bad place to walk. Normally.'

If his remark was meant in humour, it escaped her. She was seized by the need to let him know she'd shared his idea. 'That's why I went, in hope of meeting you. How could we have missed each other? Jake, I'm sorry. If I'd known you were about, I wouldn't have gone back to the car. Do you know who it was who spotted you?'

'Some local guy.'

'And what was he doing there?'

'Walking his poodle dog.'

'Him! In combat clothes. I saw him. I told the police about him, but they didn't show any interest.'

'He knows who I am.'

'It doesn't mean he's in the clear. He could be shifting the interest away from himself. I was really shocked when I saw you in that line-up. Did they rough you up? You looked awful.'

His mouth twitched into a half-smile. 'So what's new?'

'I don't suppose you slept at all. They should have found out in the first two minutes that you had nothing to do with it.'

He sighed and stared into his drink. The broad shoulders sagged. 'There's something you don't know.'

Her skin prickled. Were the new shoots of joy about to be trampled? She was so certain he was a decent man, unfairly accused.

He said, 'I've got form.'

'What?'

'A record. Been in prison.'

She shook her head in disbelief. 'Tell me.'

'When I was nineteen . . . ' He primed himself with a sip of beer. 'When I was nineteen, in Cornwall, there was a main road built near where I lived, a bypass.'

She nodded, but so much was going on in her own shocked brain that she was hearing his voice as a distant sound.

He passed a hand over his head and held it against the back of his neck. He was making a terrific effort to speak more than his usual few words. Gaps came between sentences, but he persevered and Jo heard him out. 'I was against it. Habitats were under threat. Trees, ecosystems . . . I joined the protesters. We set up camp, lived rough, in the trees. Said the developers would have to kill us if they felled the trees. That didn't stop them. . . . They sent in the police, then the army. Ordered us down through loudhailers. We refused, but they had the equipment.' He paused for longer at this point. The words had been flowing more than anything he'd communicated before. 'It was no contest. I'm lashed to a branch in a sixty-foot beech. Three squaddies come for me. I try to hold them off, but one gets a grip on my foot. I stick my free boot against his shoulder and brace my leg. He falls off. He's on ropes, but he hits a branch and breaks his spine. Paralysed.'

Jo had a vivid picture in her head. She whispered, 'What a nightmare.'

'Lots of people saw. It was filmed. They got me down soon after. Threw me into a van with the others. Charged me. Grievous bodily harm. When it came to court . . . ' He paused to summon up more words. 'In court the judge said the injury warranted a long custodial sentence.'

'Jake, how horrible.'

'On top of that, I was acting unlawfully by resisting arrest. But he said there was doubt about the intent. I got two years.'

'That's awful.'

'Not so awful as spending the rest of your life in a wheelchair.'

'I suppose. But you didn't mean that to happen.'

'If I hadn't put up a fight he'd be okay.'

'You were young and idealistic. Committed to the cause.'

'Impetuous.'

'You must have gone through a terrible time in prison.'

'Rather not talk about that.' He sat back in the chair. 'You serve your time, but your record is always there. Something violent happens. . . . They pick you up and find you did time for GBH and they're not going to pat you on the head and send you away.'

She reached across the table and put her hand over his. 'I had no idea about any of this. You didn't say.'

The skewed smile appeared. 'Not much of a chat-up line, is it?'

'Makes no difference. I still want to be friends.'

Gently, but firmly, he withdrew his hand from hers. 'Better not.'

She felt the chill of rejection. 'I don't see why. They've freed you now. You're entitled to meet anyone you choose.'

'They see us together, they'll think we cooked something up. Likely they'll pull you in for questioning.'

'So what? I can put them right.'

He shook his head. 'It's uncool linking up with an ex-con.'

'We're together right now, aren't we?'

'I asked to see you just so you'd know about me.' He paused and then emphasised each word. 'And we draw a line and no one is hurt.'

'Jake, I'll be far more hurt if I can't even speak to you.'

'They're sure I did it,' he said. 'They only let me go because they don't have the evidence yet.'

'But that's ridiculous. This woman was murdered, strangled by the sound of it. Your so-called crime was pushing a soldier out of a tree. That wasn't murder, that was accidental.'

'An act of aggression.'

'I don't accept that.'

'The words of the judge who sent me down.'

'Nuts to that judge. I don't believe you're a violent man.'

'That's good to know,' he said nodding, 'but it doesn't change anything. It's out of our hands.'

'The police have their own agenda?'

'Exactly.'

'And you think they'll arrest us both if you're seen with me? That's crazy, Jake.'

'Crazy things happen to me. I don't want you drawn into it.'

She bit her lip, on the verge of tears. She could tell he meant every word and truly cared about her. From his perspective, separation made sense. From her own selfish point of view what he was suggesting would be an outrage, a denial of freedom. 'I'd rather take the risk and stay friends. Let's at least exchange mobile numbers so we stay in contact.'

He looked startled, then acquiescent, then pleased. 'Okay, but don't put the number . . . don't put it in the memory. The first thing they do is go through your directory.'

'And I'm not ruling out a walk on the beach,' she said, writing hers down and handing it to him. This was a moment to be strong. Poor guy. He needed to know she was in his corner. 'Now let's talk about something really serious. Tell me what music you like.'

THE FIRST BARS OF Colonel Bogey sounded in Jo's bag. She took out her mobile and pressed the green key.

'Sweetie, how are you placed?'

Too bad. The caller wasn't Jake. Five days had gone by and she'd heard no more from him. It was Gemma.

'You mean right now?'

'I mean can you come over?'

'Where to?'

'The print works. Fishbourne. You know it, don't you?'

'Is that wise? I might meet someone.'

'It's okay. The boss isn't in.'

'What's the problem, then?'

'Bit of a mystery. Tell you when you get here—if I haven't spontaneously combusted by then.'

Even allowing for Gemma's dramatising, this sounded like an emergency. The last week had been stressful enough, but you back your friends when help is asked for. Wondering what she was getting into this time, Jo told Adrian the boss she was feeling woozy, got into the Panda, and drove the couple of miles to Fishbourne.

Kleentext Print Solutions was housed near the railway station in a boxlike 1950s utility building with a cluster of wooden annexes where the real work was done. Jo parked beside a silver delivery van and used the main entrance, under a sign saying ADMINISTRATION. Inside, she was confronted by a six-foot wall of cartons that screened off the reception desk. She squeezed past.

'I hope you're from the council.'

The receptionist's voice was confrontational.

Jo gave her name and explained why she was there.

'So you're not.'

'Not what?'

'From the council. They should have sent someone to collect that lot,' the receptionist said, eyeing the cartons. 'They've been there two days, blocking my light. How can I do this job when I can't see people coming? It's really inconvenient.'

'Nothing to do with me,' Jo said, privately suspecting the opposite.

Gemma was waiting on the top floor when the lift opened, arms wide in welcome. 'You're a true amigo. Where would I be without you?' She gave Jo a hug. 'Come and see the office. It's all right. I'm entirely alone.'

Her workplace was carpeted and comfortable, with veneer panelled walls and framed scenes of Chichester with picture lights over them. Her desk was on one side and a large leather sofa on the other. Copies of *Country Life*, *Trout and Salmon*, and *Today's Golfer* were displayed on a low glass-topped table. The aroma of coffee came from somewhere.

'Cosy.'

'Have a seat.' Gemma waved her to the sofa. 'Did you notice all those boxes downstairs?'

Jo smiled. 'Is that what half a million brochures look like?'

'Until we pulp them, yes. Hillie on reception throws a wingding every time I walk by.'

'How did your boss take it?'

'This is the kick in the pants. The ratbag hasn't seen them. It's Thursday and he hasn't shown his face all week. The last I saw of him was Friday when he sloped off early with Fiona. He hasn't phoned or anything.'

'How about Fiona?'

'She's off work too.'

Jo raised an eyebrow.

Gemma nodded. 'You're onto it. She's reeled him in, hasn't she? What's your reading of it? A week in Paris?'

'It does look suspicious,' said Jo.

'Suspicious? I've heard of dirty weekends, but a whole week is gross. And not so much as a postcard to say sorry.'

'Mean.'

'Mean? You can do better than that.'

'All right,' Jo said. 'What a prick!'

Gemma added seamlessly, ' . . . as Fiona remarked in the honeymoon suite at the Paris Ritz. She's way ahead of us. It knocks our little scheme on the head, doesn't it? He's not going to sack the creature for incompetence if he's just spent the week playing mothers and fathers with her—not unless she's rubbish at that as well.'

'Smart lady.'

'All those bloody council brochures, Jo. What am I going to do with them?'

Sometimes it takes an outsider to think of a solution. Jo sensed she was expected to supply one. 'Does everyone know they were ordered by Fiona?'

'Not really.'

'Spread the message, then. Fiona ordered these by mistake. Shout it from the rooftops. It's ammunition for later. Then get them pulped, like you said. They've lost their impact now.'

'What a waste.'

'Spoils of war. The reckoning comes later.'

'He can't invoice the council for the true cost.'

'I should hope not,' Jo said. 'I don't want it going on my council tax.'

'You'd think he'd have been in touch,' Gemma said, and it was apparent how deep this had gone with her. 'Muggins is running the show here.'

'Bosses can do stuff like that, take off when they want. He knows he can depend on you to hold the fort.'

'Yes, and when he comes back I'll be shown the fort door. It's so bloody unfair. I feel like stamping my little foot.'

'You can do better than that,' Jo said.

And Gemma responded to the challenge. 'Nail him to the wall and play darts with him. Put him in the lion enclosure wearing a zebra suit. Dose him with laxative and stand him on guard at Buckingham Palace.' She sighed. 'Help me, Jo. What can I really do?'

'What we need,' Jo said with a show of sisterly defiance, 'is a master plan.'

Gemma held up her hand for a high five. 'Put it there, hon. I knew I could rely on you.'

Jo slapped her palm against Gemma's without the faintest notion what to suggest.

Fortunately Gemma had it worked out for herself. 'This may sound sneaky. Well, it is sneaky, but this is war, right? I'm not supposed to know Fiona is off with Mr Cartwright. On the face of it, as the temporary team captain, I ought to be getting worried about her. Not a word has come in. She could have had a heart attack and be lying dead in her house. There's a four-year-old kid. She's obviously farmed him out to the father, or some friend, but I'm not to know that, am I? The poor wee bairn could be in that house in total squalor trying to feed raw potatoes to his dead mother.'

Jo was amused and showed it. 'This is good, Gem.'

'So I already phoned a couple of times and left messages on the answerphone asking Fiona to get in touch urgently.'

'That's good, too.'

'The decent, caring thing is to go round to the house and speak to the neighbours. Chances are they don't know anything. I doubt if she told the people next door she's shacking up with the boss for a week. All this fuss is because we're worried about the kid. You see where I'm coming from?'

'It's being responsible.'

'*Exactement*. I knew you'd have the answer.' She'd supplied it herself, but for some reason she wanted Jo to take the credit. 'The next step is to try and break in, but that's a matter for the police.'

At the mention of police, Jo's heart rate stepped up. She didn't want another meeting with Hen Mallin. She tried not to show it.

Gemma was still in full flow. 'They force an entry and listen to the answerphone and look at the letters and find she hasn't been there all week. After that, it's in the lap of the fuzz. They may take no further action.'

'Unlikely.'

'That's what I think. They'll want to know when she was last seen. They'll probably come here and talk to the workforce. Someone may have seen her getting into Mr Cartwright's car on Friday afternoon.'

'Right, and you'll be in denial, appalled at the idea.'

'Do you think it'll make the papers?' Gemma's hyperactive imagination was ahead of Jo's.

'The absent mother? Could do. In any case, the affair will be all round the office, and none of your doing. All you did was act responsibly.'

Gemma's big eyes locked with Jo's. 'Tell me, wise one. Can it go wrong?'

'I can't see how. It may not unfold exactly as we think, but whatever happens they'll walk into a hotbed of scandal when they get back. He'll find it impossible to promote her.'

'Or sack me?'

'Or sack you.'

'So will you come with me?'

Jo played the question over.

'Where?'

'To Fiona's house, of course. Doing this alone will spook me out.'

A volley of no's exploded in Jo's head. She'd had her brush with the police and it hadn't turned out nicely. 'Couldn't you take someone from work? It would look so much better if you did.'

'Why?'

'When you go to the police station they'll be sure to ask who we are. If I say I'm your friend it won't sound half so official as if I'm another Kleentext employee.'

'Does that matter?'

'It does to the police. They could think you're wasting their time.'

Gemma heaved a huge sigh. 'Ain't that the truth and no mistake. But sweetie, I don't know who else to ask. Like I said to you the other day, I'm not the flavour of the month here.'

Jo had some sympathy, but nothing would induce her to cross swords with DCI Mallin again.

Now Gemma gave a self-pitying sniff and her eyelashes moistened. 'Please?'

A compromise was wanted here. 'Tell you what,' Jo said. 'Why don't I come with you for company, but stay out of sight so it will look as if you're acting all alone for the good of the firm?'

'Cool.'

Jo seemed to have got it right.

'Babe,' Gemma said. 'I'm going to pay you the supreme compliment. You're better than a line of coke.'

FIONA LIVED in Emsworth, a coastal resort, small, red-brick, and with an unfortunate history. Once noted for the excellence of the local oysters, said to excel those of Whitstable and Colchester, the town supplied some for a civic banquet in Winchester in 1902. Within days a number of the guests became ill with typhoid and died, among them the Dean of Winchester Cathedral. You don't kill a dean without repercussions. In the enquiry it was alleged and later admitted that all of Emsworth's sewage was pumped into the harbour beside the oysterbeds. Mischief makers suggested that the oysters owed their unrivalled size and flavour to their food source. The Worshipful Company of Fishmongers imposed a national ban. Cause and effect was never established beyond doubt, but Emsworth oysters became notorious and the industry collapsed overnight. These days the town was better known for its large colony of swans. Fiona had a terraced house facing across the Mill Pond, a less than adequate name for a ten-acre sheet of water that took a half hour to walk round. Here a hundred or more swans were ever-present, along with mallard ducks, coots, and gulls. Jo drove the Panda up the narrow road between the water's edge and the houses.

'Here we go, then,' Gemma said.

'Here *you* go,' Jo said. 'I'm sitting here. Remember?'

She stopped some way short of the house and watched Gemma step up to the front door and try the bell. No one came, but of course it would have surprised them both if Fiona had appeared. Gemma tried a couple more times and bent down and peered through the letterbox. Then she turned towards the car and flapped her hand to let Jo know she was getting no response.

'Idiot,' Jo said between gritted teeth. If anyone was watching they'd know for sure that the two of them were in this together. She looked the other way at a group of swans.

Gemma stepped around the dividing hedge and tried next door. An upstairs window opened and a shaven-headed man in a white vest leaned out.

In the car, Jo pulled down the sun visor.

The man seemed to be a caring neighbour and a typical male as well, all brass and swagger. He came downstairs and out to the front and tried Fiona's doorbell himself. He stepped onto the small front lawn and looked through the living room window. A short consultation followed. The man went back inside his own house and returned with a mobile. The plan was racing ahead. This was clearly phase two: Call the police.

Jo slid so far down in her seat that her head was below the steering wheel.

Presently the passenger door opened and Gemma looked in. 'Trying out a new position?' She was on a high again. The neighbour's show of cooperation had pumped up her adrenalin. 'Take it from me, it wouldn't be comfortable in the driver's seat. I'd say it was damn near impossible.'

'I'm trying to stay out of sight.'

'And succeeding. For a moment I thought you'd gone AWOL. He's a hunk to die for, that neighbour. Did you check those pecs? He's called Francisco and he works nights as a bouncer in Portsmouth. What a waste. Hasn't seen anything of her or the child for a week and said we should definitely report it. He saved me the trouble of calling the police.'

'You don't have to relay all this to me,' Jo said. 'You can tell me later. I'm supposed to be invisible, okay?'

'Lighten up, poppet. He's back in his house putting on a shirt. Funny, he didn't mind me seeing his tattoos, but he gets dressed for the rozzers.'

'They're definitely coming, are they?'

'Relax. They won't be here for ten minutes.'

Jo wasn't waiting for that. 'Look, Gem, I think this might work better if I get out and take a walk along the path. I'll come back after they've gone.'

'Be like that.'

'We agreed I keep a low profile.'

'Sure thing, kiddo.'

'You don't sound nervous any more.'

'It's turned out rather well. Francisco could be the find of the week. The last time I set eyes on a hunk of manhood like that, he was tossing a caber. Well, I think it was a caber.' She rolled her eyes and laughed.

'Hold on a mo. You're forgetting what this is all about. You're supposed to be worried about Fiona and the little boy, right?'

Jo got out of the car and started a brisk walk along the bank, intent on putting distance between herself and Gemma. She'd lost all confidence. No way would that daft creature play her part convincingly with the police. Still, she reminded herself, that was down to Gemma. This was her show. The overriding need at this stage was not to be a part of it.

Annoyingly a flotilla of swans and ducks swam beside her, keeping up. She had missed a trick here. Anyone patrolling the Mill Pond had a duty to toss in pieces of bread or, preferably, seed. She was ignoring them and they weren't giving up.

Ahead was the sailing club. Soon she would disappear from view behind the clubhouse, safe from waterfowl and nosy parkers. She risked a glance back. The find of the week had put on a red shirt and was striking a pose in the middle of the road, arms folded, legs astride, like the genie of the lamp. Gemma was sitting on his garden wall swinging her legs, anything but anxious about Fiona and her son.

People, Jo thought. The ones who are most fun are the least reliable.

The walk brought her past the club to the southern extreme of the Mill Pond where the road became the top of a harbour wall. She would head back on the side opposite the house, where she could safely watch any developments while seeming to admire the scenery.

She now had a view of the sea, the marshy inlet between the islands of Thorney and Hayling. Here, through the narrow Emsworth Channel, waves of invaders had come in times past. It wasn't beyond imagination to picture a Viking ship approaching on the high tide.

The sea wall curved and she faced inland, with the town as a backdrop. To her right were mud flats with boats beached by the low tide. Across the Mill Pond she didn't yet have a sight of Fiona's house. She quickened her pace and crossed the little bridge to the quay where another sailing club, the Emsworth Slipper, occupied the former mill. The road turned past a tea room and a malt house and emerged as Bridgefoot Path. Across the water she could see everything.

A police car had arrived and stopped just ahead of her Panda. It wasn't flashing its emergency light. This was evidently just a routine enquiry. Two men in uniform were in conversation with Gemma and the hunk of manhood, Francisco. Presently one returned to the patrol car and took something bulky from the boot. It proved to be an enforcer, the miniature battering ram used to gain entry. They swung it only once. The door sprang open and the police went inside.

On her side of the water, Jo found a bench and sat down to watch. From this distance no one could connect her with what was going on. Gemma was still outside, chatting with her new friend Francisco. Jo expected the police would soon emerge and confirm that Fiona and her son were not inside, an anticlimax everyone ought to welcome.

Activities on this side of the Mill Pond went on regardless of what was happening across the water. Two teenage boys were fishing near the malt house. To Jo's right, a mother and toddler were throwing bread to the swans and finding that the gulls swooped in and took most of it.

The police emerged from Fiona's door. One was using his personal radio. The other said something to Gemma. There was no apparent excitement about what they'd found inside. Some time was spent making the door secure again and then they got in their car and drove off.

Jo got up and resumed her walk towards the little bridge at the top end. In under ten minutes she was across and back to where she'd left her car. Francisco had gone back inside his house and Gemma was waving to her, incapable of keeping a low profile.

'Hi, poppet. Mission accomplished. No rotting bodies inside, I'm glad to report. They're going to check with her ex and see if the boy is with him. They listened to the answerphone and picked up my messages, so our master plan worked beautifully.'

'Let's be off, then.'

'No hurry. If we stick around I'm thinking Francisco might offer us a cuppa. The phone inside his house started ringing, so he left me here.'

'Gemma, I'm not supposed to be here.'

'Doesn't matter any more, does it? The fuzz have gone. He's not just muscle. He's got personality in buckets. I don't know what aftershave he uses, but it's turned me into a tart.'

'Look, I only agreed to do this if you kept me out of it.'

Gemma folded her arms. 'What is it with you, Jo? Are you on their most wanted list?'

'I found the dead woman on Selsey beach. Remember? They made me feel like a suspect. It was horrible.'

'Chill. I keep telling you, they've done their job and gone. Francisco won't blab when I tell him you're my best friend.'

Jo let out a sharp, angry breath. 'You don't get it, do you? The whole point is that you're not supposed to have brought a friend. Listen, I'm out of here. It's up to you if you want a lift.' She turned and walked towards the car. This was no empty gesture. When she started the motor she would be off.

Behind her, Gemma shouted, 'I fancy the guy. Since when has that been a crime? I'm not a fucking nun, you know.'

And that's an oxymoron if ever I heard one, Jo thought. She didn't turn her head. She unlocked, got inside and then realised there was a hitch. The car was facing south and the way home was north. A three-point turn in that narrow road was an invitation to reverse into the Mill Pond. Instead of making a speedy getaway she would have to pass Gemma and find a turning point at the end where the sailing club was.

So be it, she thought. She switched on and moved off.

Gemma was in the middle of the road, waving her arms like ground crew showing a jumbo where to taxi. No way could the car get past without running her over.

Jo braked.

Gemma came to the side and jerked open the door. 'All right, I've reconsidered. Give me a lift and I'll take my vows. Promise.'

Jo gave a rasping sigh. At this minute the humour didn't appeal.

Gemma got in and they drove on. But they hadn't gone thirty yards when she said, 'Bloody hell. Stop the car.'

'For Christ's sake.' Jo glanced in the mirror, fully expecting to see Francisco outside his house again. He was not. 'What's up now?'

'In the water.' Something was definitely amiss. There was urgency, if not panic, in the voice.

Jo braked and turned her head to see. Not a duck was swimming there. The only thing worthy of comment was what she took to be a clump of seaweed close to the surface, its reddish-brown tentacles shifting gently with the water's slight movement.

'I've got to check.' Gemma flung open the door and ran to the edge.

'Check what?' Jo switched off the engine and joined her.

From the bank she saw what had shocked Gemma. They weren't looking at seaweed. The tentacles were fronds of reddish hair. Just visible at a lower level in the murky water was the rest of the corpse, face-down and dressed in a black top and jeans.

seven

'Is that Fiona?' Jo asked, thinking as she spoke that it was not the brightest question considering that the body was face-down. But when your legs are shaking and your last meal wants to make a comeback, you're not best placed to offer an intelligent remark.

'She's got red hair,' Gemma said.

'I can see that.'

'I mean Fiona's a redhead.'

'That does narrow it down.'

'This is where she lives and she hasn't been seen for nearly a week.'

'Not much doubt, then. Dreadful.'

'Gets me right here—in the gizzard.'

Jo happened to know that a gizzard isn't part of the human anatomy, but she let it pass. In her unique fashion Gemma was paying respect. She let a few seconds go by before raising the next obvious question. 'What happened, do you think?'

'Accident?'

'Must have been.' She was quick in her response, too quick to carry conviction. Faced with a shock like this the normal impulse is to look for the least upsetting explanation.

Gemma said in support, 'It's a risk she took, living so close to the water.'

'I guess.'

Neither of them spoke while they continued to gaze down at the figure submerged in front of them. Both must have sensed that there was more to this than Fiona's choice of where to live.

When Gemma broke the silence she was clearly making a

bigger effort to convince herself. 'I feel sure it was an accident.' Nodding as if someone else had spoken and she agreed, she put her imagination to work again. 'She could have had a few too many, stepped outside for some fresh air and fallen in. Or she may have come home in the dark and missed her footing. Hit her head and knocked herself out. So easy to see how it could happen.'

Jo said nothing.

'I feel such a cow,' Gemma added. 'All the mean things I've been saying about her. Jo, what are we going to do?'

This was the moment to make one thing clear. 'Not so much of the "we."'

'What?'

'I'm staying out of this.'

Gemma turned to look at her. 'How do you mean?'

'I found one body already. That's enough to be going on with.'

'But if I report it, what are they going to think?' Gemma said in a panicky voice. 'Suppose they get the idea someone pushed her in? I've got a clear motive. She's known to me. She was a threat to my job.'

'That's a fact.'

As if she'd won the point, Gemma said, 'But you haven't even met her. You can call the police and they'll accept it for what it is, a chance discovery.'

Jo wasn't swallowing that. 'What—and tell them I was here all the time when they checked the house? Tell them I left my work and drove you here? Does that sound like a chance discovery? To the police it's going to smell like a set-up. I'm sorry, but I'm not doing it, Gem. After going through Saturday's line-up, I've done more than my share of public duty.'

'Line-up?'

'The ID parade.'

Gemma frowned. 'You didn't say anything about an ID parade.'

'Didn't I? I was trying to forget, standing in front of strange blokes and being expected to pick one of them out.'

'What for?'

'The murder of the woman at Selsey. I'm supposed to be a

witness. They think I could have seen the killer when I was walking along the beach.'

'And did you? Did you spot him?'

'Of course not. Look, this isn't helping us now. We've found a body. I don't want to report it and neither do you.'

Their presence on the bank and facing the water was starting to attract the swans. Some were swimming across from the opposite side expecting to be fed.

'We can't leave her here,' Gemma said. 'How would you like that if it was you?'

'I wouldn't know anything about it. I'd be dead.' Jo took a deep breath and made an effort to sound calm. 'I think we should get back in the car and drive off. Someone else is going to find her soon. People are always walking round this place. I'm surprised she wasn't found already.'

'You don't know how long she's been in the water.'

'Agreed.'

'It could have happened this afternoon.'

'Even more reason why we don't want anything to do with it.'

Then Gemma came up with her most stupid suggestion yet. 'I could tell Francisco and ask him to call the police and leave us out of it.'

'That's dumb. You don't even know him that well.'

'He's really helpful.'

'Have you thought why? He could have done it.'

'Francisco?' Gemma pulled an appalled expression.

'He's the neighbour. He was on the spot. We don't know if he had a relationship with her, or if he wanted one and was given the elbow.'

'You're making this up.'

Rich, coming from the queen of make-believe.

'I'm trying to make you see sense. It's stupid asking Francisco or anyone else to report what we found. It throws suspicion on us. He'll think we're hiding something. He could get the idea we killed her.'

'I don't buy this, Jo. I don't buy it at all.'

'But you don't want to get involved, right?'

'Only because it would look so bad for me.'

'Me, too.'

The first swans arrived and glided between the body and the bank, ignoring the grim presence of death, intent only on getting fed. Others were converging fast.

Jo said, 'Do you want out, or are we staying here in full view of all the curtain-twitchers?'

Without more being said, they turned from the scene and walked briskly back to the car. Jo started up and drove the short distance to the turning point at the sailing club. They were soon back on the A259 heading for Chichester.

Conscience was a third passenger sitting between them.

'What about your boss?' Jo said, trying to shake off the guilt. 'Where does he fit into this?'

'Mr Cartwright?'

'He was last seen going off with Fiona on Friday and he hasn't been at work since. Don't you think he might have something to do with it?'

Gemma took a sharp breath. 'Wow! You're way ahead of me.'

For once, Jo was, and it gave satisfaction. 'He's the one with questions to answer, isn't he?'

The accident theory slipped out of the reckoning and Gemma was only too ready to speculate. 'Maybe she overplayed her hand with him and demanded too much, like . . . like a share of the firm's profits. He wasn't having it and got rid of her.'

'Is he the violent type?'

'I've never thought of him like that.'

'I know. You said he was nice, but there's obviously a selfish side to him. Even the so-called nice ones have a snapping point.'

'Dead right. All his schmoozing never impressed me. I've often wondered what would happen if push came to shove.'

'Ho-hum.'

'It's an expression.'

'I know. Fiona got the push.'

'Don't! I'm starting to believe this. Where is he now?'

'Gone abroad, I should think.' For a change it was Jo who embroidered the theory. 'He'd want to put some distance between himself and the crime. He knows she'll be found in the Mill Pond and he'll hope it's seen as an accident, something like we assumed when we saw her. He'll have kidded himself nobody knows about the affair with her.'

'He's wrong about that.'

'Yes, but we're not saying anything yet.' She was surprising herself by finding extra strength while Gemma's confidence ebbed. 'Let's see how this pans out. Soon enough you'll have the fuzz crawling all over your office. When they start asking questions that's the time to let them know what you noticed. Not before. Don't volunteer anything.'

'You're bloody good in a crisis.'

'Trying to be sensible, that's all. Do you want me to drop you at the print works?'

'I need a drink to steady me.'

'All right. Let's find a quiet pub.'

They called at the Cricketers on the Chichester Road and had the public bar all to themselves. Gemma ordered a gin and tonic. Jo was content with a lemonade and lime. She wanted to think straight.

'Are you still seeing Rick?'

'On and off. Well, yes, actually,' Gemma said.

'It wouldn't be such a good idea to tell him—or anyone else—about this afternoon. Let's have a pact, shall we? What we saw in the Mill Pond is strictly between ourselves.'

'It didn't happen,' Gemma said. 'Erased, deleted, wiped.' She took a gulp of her gin and tonic as if to speed the process. 'Have you been out with Jake yet?'

'I had a drink with him Saturday night.'

'I don't get it—you and him. You're poles apart.'

'Attraction of opposites.'

'If you say so.' Gemma rotated the lemon and ice in her drink. 'Not like Rick and me. We're two of a kind, really. Funny.'

'What is?'

'Remember when the four of us were talking in Chicago Rock about my boss, dreaming up ways to get rid of him? The

Headhunters. Wasn't it Rick who suggested the best way was to get him a life sentence?'

'No,' Jo said. 'It was you.'

'Me?'

'Rick was going on about gruesome methods of making people disappear altogether.'

'Oh, yes.'

'The idea of stitching up Mr Cartwright was yours. You thought of it in Starbucks. There were just the two of us. I distinctly remember you saying it.'

Gemma's eyes widened. 'With a memory like that, you should be on *Mastermind*. And now you've said it, I can remember something else. It was you who said we'd need a body to get a conviction.'

Jo cast her thoughts back. 'True. And now we've got one.'

'Weird.'

'Bit of a coincidence, certainly.'

'I'd say it's creepy. The stitch-up could really happen if Mr Cartwright gets pulled in for murdering Fiona. He could be banged up for life.' Her mouth curved upward. 'I'll be leading the cheers.'

'Hold on,' Jo said. 'You're racing ahead again. We don't have any reason to think she was murdered. I thought we decided it was an accident.'

'We talked in the car about him pushing her in.'

'We were both feeling guilty for not going to the police. It was a relief to throw suspicion on someone else.'

Gemma frowned. 'You've changed your mind already?'

'We should take a more balanced view now.'

'Accident?'

'Unless someone proves us wrong.'

'They'll do a post mortem, won't they?'

'Sure to.'

Gemma gave a wicked smile. 'And you're going to look pretty damn silly when they find the mark where the poisoned arrow went in. Did I tell you my boss took a cruise up the Amazon last year and met one of those tribes who use curare for hunting?'

'You didn't, and I don't believe a word of it.'

'He's also a Russian spy.'

Jo laughed. 'Working at the printers' in Fishbourne? I don't think so.'

'All will be revealed.'

'I can't wait. That drink must be doing you good. You're sounding more like the Gemma I know.'

'Permanently pissed?'

'Nicely relaxed.'

'I did panic a bit, seeing the body. First time for me. You're more experienced.'

'By a few days only. I don't intend to make a habit of it.'

'Do they know who she was—the dead woman on the beach?'

'If they do, they haven't told me.'

'What if there's a link with Fiona?'

'It would be surprising.' Time to draw the line, she thought. 'Gemma, this isn't getting us anywhere. We ought to stop speculating and get back to normality.'

'Coffee in Starbucks on Saturday?'

'Good suggestion.'

They drank up and returned to the car.

Jo DIDN'T have much confidence in Gemma. She'd soon be chirping like a sparrow to Rick about the body in the Mill Pond. She might even tell all to the police if they arrived at the print works. There were people constitutionally incapable of keeping anything to themselves and Gemma was a prime example. The best hope was that this death would be treated by the police as an accident and dealt with by those constables in uniform who searched the house. Not CID. Please God, not Hen Mallin.

After dropping Gemma in town she drove home, trying to put the best spin on what had happened, but getting increasingly anxious. She took a lasagne from the freezer and popped it in the microwave before listening to her messages. Her mother home from hospital and asking her to visit. Someone from a call centre wanted to know if she was satisfied with her electricity bill. The bank needed her to call in about some query on her account.

The overdraft, no doubt. It didn't seem to matter so much any more.

Nothing from Jake. She'd hoped to hear from him. A whole weekend was coming up and they hadn't fixed to meet. She didn't like doing all the chasing.

Nothing, either, praise be, from DCI Mallin about the dead woman at Selsey. Was it too much to hope she'd found other people to question?

She transferred the lasagne to the cooker to crisp up the top. Then she pressed one of the preset numbers on the phone.

'Mummy?'

The voice that answered was steeped in self-pity. 'Is that you, Josephine? Good of you to call at last. I'm home now.'

'That's why I'm phoning. I got your message.'

'The standard of care in that hospital was nil. They push you out as soon as they can.'

'I thought you couldn't wait to leave.'

'That isn't the point. I'm not fit to cope and your father's a dead loss, as you know. Shall I see you this weekend?'

'Mummy, it's the worst possible time. They want me in at work and I've got all the chores to catch up on. I've had one hell of a week. Can we leave it that if I do find a space I'll let you know?'

The disapproval would not have disgraced Lady Bracknell. 'Find a space? Is that how you think of me? If you've got more important things to do don't trouble yourself.'

'It's not like that.'

'I'll survive, no doubt. The migraine attacks will calm down eventually, they told me. Meanwhile I can't do a thing. Can't sleep, can't relax. Watching television is out of the question. What were you doing at Selsey, anyway?'

'You heard about that?'

'It was on the front page of the paper. I couldn't miss it. They got your age wrong, of course. If they'd come to me I could have put them right. I see that they're still trying to identify the dead woman. You'd think they'd know by now.'

'When did you hear that?'

'This evening on the local news, that nice Sally person. I always think she'd make someone a wonderful daughter.'

'So you've seen *some* TV?'

There was a pause for rapid thought. 'I expect your father mentioned it. He watches far too much. Do you want to speak to him? He's in the kitchen trying to boil an egg for me. It's sure to be like concrete.'

'Don't disturb him, then. Just give him my love. I'll call as soon as I can.' She usually finished with, 'Take care,' but the sentiment might not be appreciated this time.

Strange that the woman at Selsey remained a mystery. You'd think someone would have reported her missing by now, more than two weeks on. Presumably Hen Mallin and her team were studying all reports of missing women. In a way, Jo wanted to know who the victim was, yet at the same time she dreaded finding out. A name and a life and family ties would make her more real, and give the whole experience more potential for lasting trauma.

Lasting trauma? More like Mummy every day, she thought.

She poured herself a glass of red wine and ate her supper listening to local radio. News bulletins came every half hour, but there was nothing about the Selsey woman or the body in the Emsworth Mill Pond. Maybe Fiona was still in the water, condemned to another night. She recalled what DCI Mallin had said about the appearance of a body after a lengthy immersion and then she couldn't finish the lasagne.

About eight she took the plunge and called Jake's number.

'Yes?'

She warmed to his voice, even though it sounded strained. 'It's me—Jo.'

'Hi.'

'We said we'd stay in touch. I was wondering if you've got plans for the weekend.'

'Oh?'

'Don't sound so surprised, Jake. We spoke in the pub about this. Have the police been onto you again?'

'No.'

'That's all right, then. You sound kind of guarded. I'm a bit frazzled, too, and I'd really like to see you.' The difficulty dealing with anyone as reticent as Jake was that you were forced into making all the suggestions and so seeming manipulative. 'Are you free Saturday? I'd enjoy some more time with you.'

'Where?'

'I'm still wanting to get up my courage and take a walk along the front at Selsey. We were all set to meet on the day you were picked up by the police.'

'Selsey?' He spoke the name as if it was Death Valley.

'Restoring my confidence. Remember?'

'Yes.'

It wasn't clear whether he was confirming the memory or agreeing to meet, but Jo was sure what she had in mind. 'Shall we say the car park at the end of the High Street?'

'I suppose.'

'At two?'

'All right.'

She was disappointed he wasn't more animated. Last time they'd spoken she'd thought he was getting confident with her. He sounded uncomfortable now. That experience of being arrested was preying on his mind. Understandable, considering his time in prison.

ON LOCAL radio at ten-thirty the same evening it was announced that a woman's body had been found in the Mill Pond at Emsworth. She had not yet been formally identified, but she was believed to have been a local resident who had been missing for about a week.

The phone rang shortly after.

'Did you hear?' Gemma gasped in end-of-the-world mode. 'It was on Southern Counties Radio. They found Fiona, just when I was starting to convince myself we imagined it. She's dead, Jo. It really happened. I'm clawing at the walls here, I feel so guilty.' No problem over poor communication from this caller.

Gemma seemed to expect a show of panic. Instead, Jo said, 'We should be pleased they found her, Gem. Personally, I wouldn't have got much sleep tonight thinking she was still in that water.'

'Yes, but I'm a prize bitch for trying to get her in trouble at work. That dumb trick with the council leaflets makes me squirm.'

'That dumb trick wasn't your idea. Anyway, she didn't find out about it. She wasn't there all week.'

'Even so, it's bound to come out, isn't it?'

'There's no reason why it should if you do what I said and get them pulped. If anyone wonders what you're doing it's going to look like an act of kindness. She made a blunder and you're quietly covering up out of consideration for her memory.'

'That's good. No, it's bloody brilliant. I didn't think of it that way.'

'Stay cool, Gem.'

Out on the beach where it shelved steeply Hen Mallin treated herself to an intake of ozone mixed with nicotine whilst listening to the small pebbles being raked by the tide. She had a flat scallop shell in her hand and was using it as an ashtray, over-fastidious, but smokers have learned to cover their tracks. She kept a tiny spray of Ralph Lauren's Romance for when she needed to suppress the fumes. Behind her, the mobile incident room was being tidied prior to removal. She'd decided this abomination was serving no useful purpose here on the beach. The fingertip searches, the appeals for witnesses, had been tried with limited success. Some of the staff had been so under-employed that she'd seen them down at the water's edge playing ducks and drakes. Little was in the computer system except the statements by the woman who had found the body and the two local men known to have been on the beach at the time: Ferdy Hamilton, the dog-walker, and Jake Kernow, the ex-con. Hamilton was the nearest they'd got to finding an informant. He'd named Jake as a suspicious character he'd seen along the beach on the morning the body was found. Jake was the big, laconic fellow who had been tracked down, interviewed, and put through the ID parade, but with a negative result. That didn't mean he was in the clear. Jo Stevens had failed to pick him out, that was all. He remained the only suspect. With his prison record and his shifty responses under questioning he had to be a serious contender. But there wasn't enough to charge him, and no one else had come knocking at the door of the mobile incident room with names.

She heard the shingle being crunched behind her as one of the team approached.

'Saying goodbye to it, guv?' Stella said.

'Damn good thing, too,' Hen said. 'Let it go back to being a beach instead of a crime scene.'

'Don't you think people will remember?'

'Not for long. The tides come and go. The whole thing changes. By next summer there'll be children bathing from here.'

'And we'll have put the case to bed?'

'Don't count on it. This one could stay unsolved.'

'I hope not. It's an ugly crime.'

'Too bloody true.' Hen had been locked for too long in her own morbid thoughts. Sharing them was a relief. 'I was watching the waves and thinking about the physical and mental demands of holding someone under the water until they stop breathing. Apparently death by drowning can take all of five minutes. Longer, even. Can you imagine holding someone under for that long?'

Stella gave a shudder. 'Slow murder. Horrible.'

'Different from pulling a trigger or knifing them. Plenty of time to think about what you're doing. You'd have to be pitiless.'

'Imagine being the victim, held for that long.'

'Yes, you'd fight for your life, but it wouldn't be easy. All your efforts are constricted by the water. You might inflict some scratches or bruises, but if your killer has a good grip, it must be bloody hard to break free.'

'I'd give it a go.'

'Anyone would. You're also trying to hold your breath until you have to let go and give way to the inrush of water into your lungs. You're panicking and getting weaker all the time. To be honest, Stell, this is the first case of homicide by drowning I've had to deal with, and it gives me the creeps just thinking about it.

They're mercifully rare. Pathologists don't like them, either. Drowning is difficult to prove at post mortem.'

'You'd think it would be obvious.'

'For one thing—and this is what I learned from the guy who did the autopsy—a fresh water drowning produces a reaction quite different from sea water. The blood volume increases rapidly when fresh water pours into the lungs and there's a strong chance of it causing a heart attack. It can be quick, very quick, if there's a cardiac arrest, as there often is, from the shock. Then they die from submersion, rather than drowning. But almost the opposite happens in the sea. Water is sucked from the plasma into the lungs, so the heart isn't under the same strain. Your chance of survival is higher in the sea.'

'Plenty of people do drown.'

'I'm not disputing that. You're more likely to have an accident at sea than you are in the bath at home or the local pool. I'm simply saying that if you're immersed in salt water you may last longer. When someone holds you down the result is the same; it takes more time, that's all.'

'I suppose if they first got you drunk, or drugged, it would be quicker.'

'True.'

'Do we know the time of death?'

'You're joking, of course. Does a pathologist ever give you a time of death? They can only make informed guesses. The body was found between eight and nine in the morning, so it's likely she was killed the evening before, or during the night, or in the early hours of daylight.'

'The reason I asked is that if she was given alcohol or drugs it could have been at some kind of beach party the night before. It was a warm September night, wasn't it?'

'Warm enough for a barbie, yes.'

'But no signs of one? Was any alcohol found in the body?'

'A small amount. The signs are that she hadn't had much.'

'Except that she'd stripped almost naked. I'd need a few drinks before I did that on a public beach. Even on a dark night.'

'I'd have to be out of my head,' Hen said.

'Moon bathing, guv. You must have tried it some time.'

Hen returned the cigar to her lips and visited old times. 'Once in my youth—and in a decent one-piece costume. I'm an Essex girl. The only beach I knew was Southend. I wouldn't recommend romping in the nude there.'

'Do you think he undressed her?'

'The heavy seduction scene? I can't picture it happening. It's much more likely the stripping was voluntary on her part. If, say, we forget the moon bathing and think about an early morning photo call, our lady there to have her picture taken, a boob shot, she might have agreed to strip down to her pants.'

'Back to the calendar idea?' Stella asked.

'Or some sort of glamour picture. We agreed she wasn't young enough to be working as a model, but any woman in her thirties is vulnerable to some guy with a camera suggesting she'd look gorgeous flashing her tits.'

'I still favour the midnight bathing. They go skinny dipping and—just like you—she's too shy to do it in the buff so she keeps her pants on.'

'Either way, there's a nasty element of deception. She's conned into stripping off by someone she trusts. She'd be crazy to do it for a stranger.'

'Is it possible he removed the clothes after the drowning?'

'Why would he do that? To make identification more difficult, I suppose.' Hen weighed the possibility for a moment. 'It's not out of the question, but I can't see it. Struggling with wet clothes wouldn't be easy or quick. Any killer's impulse is to quit the scene as soon as possible. And why would she enter the water fully clothed?'

'Dragged in?'

Hen pulled a sceptical face.

'I guess you're right,' Stella said. 'It's pretty unlikely.'

'It's all unlikely until we find out who she was and why she was there.'

'I came down to say that we're about ready to move off.'

'Let's go, then.' She stubbed out the cigar and felt for her scent spray. 'Things can only get better.'

eight

WHEN THE CALL CAME, early Saturday morning, Stella Gregson was at the window of the relocated incident room in Chichester Police Station looking out at the car roofs and thinking East Beach had its attractions. A sudden movement from behind her was reflected in the glass. DC Gary Pearce was waving frantically. He couldn't shout because he was on the phone.

Stella picked up another receiver and was instantly all attention. An educated voice was saying, ' . . . got back from St Petersburg last night and she wasn't here and there was no message, so I called a few people and no one could tell me anything. We don't live in each other's pockets, but I was surprised and a little concerned. I decided to sleep on it and this morning I phoned my local police station and gave a description. They put me through to someone else and I've been transferred several times and now I'm being asked to go through it all again with you.'

Offering a silent prayer that they'd finally nailed it, Stella took over. 'Thank you, sir. This is Stella Gregson, Detective Inspector, Chichester CID.'

'Did you say Chichester?'

'Yes.'

'I can't think why I've been put through to you.'

'Forgive me, I just came in on the call,' she said. 'Thank you for getting in touch. I didn't catch your name.'

'Austen Sentinel. It's about my wife Meredith. She's missing.'

'And you're from?'

'London, that is to say, Islington.'

'You were saying you've been abroad?'

'A British Council trip to Russia for a conference. I'm a geologist at Imperial College and I'm speaking from London. Look, we're wasting each other's time if you're in Chichester.'

'Not necessarily. Would your wife have visited Selsey lately?'

'Selsey, on the south coast? Not to my knowledge. Why?'

'Would you describe her?'

'For the umpteenth time this morning? Five foot six, thirty-seven years of age, hair coloured blonde, slimly built. She's from Kentucky, so she speaks with an American accent.'

She won't be speaking to us, Stella thought.

'But I've no idea what clothes she's wearing.'

And that's not a problem, Stella thought, but kept it to herself. 'Do you have a computer, sir?'

'What's that got to do with Merry?'

'It will speed things up.'

'I'm sitting in front of one.'

'Could you send us a jpeg of your wife?'

'I'm with you now. Yes, there are several on the machine.'

'Have you got a pen and paper there? I'll give you an email address. Then if you send it right away we'll know if we're talking about the same person.'

'Do you know where she is, then? Is she all right?'

'Be patient with me, sir. We can't confirm anything until we've seen the photo. Hold the line for a bit. I'll need your contact details.'

GEMMA DIDN'T appear in Starbucks at the usual time so Jo carried her coffee to one of the side tables, sat in an upright chair, and waited. The chatter from other tables, the music—the pure, warm sound of Ella in her prime—even the caffeine, did nothing to relax her. She was increasingly troubled.

'Hi, babe.'

She jerked and slopped some coffee.

'Easy,' he said, seating himself across from her. 'Anyone would think I was the law.'

Rick.

She asked what he was doing there.

'It's Saturday and I'm off work and this is a coffee shop and I happen to know you. Is that enough?' he said. 'No? Well, I'll come clean. I was sent to find you.'

'By Gemma?'

'She called this morning and updated me on the Emsworth episode.'

Just as predicted, Jo thought bitterly. Big-mouth Gemma ignoring the pact of secrecy at the first opportunity.

'So here I am, ready to pass on a message,' Rick said, and stopped, insisting on a response.

'Well?'

'She can't meet you because she was called to the print works. The police are there wanting to talk about Fiona.'

Typical Rick: playing on her nerves. Jo tried to appear unmoved.

In case she'd missed the point, Rick added, 'There isn't any doubt now. It was definitely Fiona's body you saw in the Mill Pond yesterday.' He watched her with expressionless eyes for a moment, then reverted to the role of friend. 'Listen, I'll get a coffee and join you.'

Obviously he knew everything. She felt like throttling Gemma. What was it she'd said with such sincerity about the incident being erased, deleted, wiped? And that was after she'd been warned not to tell Rick.

But Rick was spilt milk now. Real trouble was looming and she had no influence over it. She didn't think of herself as a controlling person, but she felt helpless and alarmed about what Gemma might be saying to the police.

She tried telling herself the two of them had committed no great crime. She wasn't even certain that failure to report a body in a millpond *was* a crime. It was more of a civic duty. Okay, they'd shirked their responsibility. Had anyone suffered as a result? Fiona had been long dead when they'd spotted her. They weren't the first to turn their backs on a scene of sudden death. Surely the guilt she and Gemma shared was moral, not criminal?

Rick returned, Americano in hand, and sat opposite, enjoying himself, eyes like wasps over a cream tea. This morning he was another species from the wimp she'd shared the taxi with the last time she'd seen him, at the end of that evening at the cinema.

Being in on the secret of their discovery in Emsworth had acted like something pumped into a main vein.

'Lighten up, little lady,' he said, at his most patronising. 'I'm not going to shop you. I'm a friend, remember?'

She stared through him.

'Besides, the police won't be interested in you and Gem doing a runner. They've got more important stuff to find out, like how the body got in there in the first place. I think the boss man— what's his name? Cartwright—has to be the main suspect. He's done a runner himself by the sound of things. What a lamebrain. It's no way to cover up a crime.'

'We don't know it was a crime,' Jo said. 'It could have been an accident.'

'Get real, Jo. Cartwright killed her. They'll find out why. Maybe she was pregnant and he didn't want his wife to find out.'

'There isn't a wife as far as I know.'

'Who told you that, Gemma? I wouldn't bank on anything she says. When the imagination was being given out, Gem got a triple helping. Don't get me wrong. She's great company, but I take anything she says with a pinch of salt.'

'What did she tell you about Fiona?'

'That she was making a play for Cartwright and putting Gem's job under threat.'

'She said the same to me and I believe her. Fiona has a child. Did you know that?'

'Poor little brat, yes.'

'That's why we went to her house, for the sake of the little boy, in case she'd had an accident, or worse, and he was with her. We called the police and they made a search.'

'I know all this.'

'They weren't inside. The boy must be staying with the father.'

'You don't have to convince me, of all people,' Rick said as if he could walk on water. 'I don't think you guys murdered her.' He followed that with a sly smile. 'You were planning to bump off her boss. Take it from me, I wouldn't be sitting here with you drinking coffee if Cartwright's body had been found.'

'Don't joke about it.'

'You're so wound up this morning.'

'I've reason to be.'

'Why?'

She felt so isolated that telling Rick—even Rick—might be a crumb of comfort. 'You heard about the dead woman I found on Selsey beach? The police gave me a really hard time over that, like I was holding back information.'

'That woman was murdered, wasn't she? You don't want to take it personally because they fired some questions at you. They've got their job to do.'

'I know, but if it gets back to them that I found another body, they'll give me the third degree. I'm worried sick what Gemma might be saying to them.'

'If they come knocking at your door, you just have to tell the truth. Stuff happens, as the man said about the war.'

She nodded. She wasn't going to tell Rick about the print order she and Gemma had sabotaged to try and get Fiona into trouble. He might have had heard about that already, but he hadn't mentioned anything yet, so maybe Gemma had *for once* had the sense to keep something to herself. 'I'm hoping they treat Fiona's death as an accident.'

'Dream on.' He couldn't resist another twist of the knife.

'You don't think they will?'

'What you have to hope is that she had no marks. The woman on the beach was marked, wasn't she?'

'So they told me. Bruises on the neck that showed she was held under the water. But the two cases aren't similar. The woman I found was nude except for her knickers. Fiona was fully dressed.'

'They both ended up in water. That's one thing they had in common. And they were both discovered by you. That's the other.'

'Pure chance.'

'Sure.' He gave that evil grin again.

'I didn't even know Fiona,' Jo said, goaded by him. 'And nobody knows who the other woman is. They're appealing for help.'

'They should show her face on TV. Someone would know her. The face wasn't damaged, was it?'

'I don't think so, but I didn't look. I saw the back of her head, and that was more than I wanted to see.'

He leaned forward on his elbows, his face a foot away from hers. 'So you can't be certain if you knew her?'

'Come on, Rick. There's no reason I should have known her. It was a chance discovery.'

'Be strange, wouldn't it, if that corpse was someone you knew?'

'Highly unlikely.'

He pointed to her mug. 'Care for a top-up?'

'No. When are you seeing Gem again?'

'Tonight, supposedly, if she's still in the mood to go clubbing.' He drew back from the table, trying to appear less confrontational. 'How about you? I heard you were getting friendly with the big, silent guy.'

'Jake? I had a drink with him the other evening.'

He smiled. 'A drink and two words. Or did he manage three?'

'He's okay. Not everyone has your gift of gab, Rick.'

'Ouch.'

'Life hasn't been easy for Jake.'

'So we make allowances, is that it?'

'No, but you don't have to pick on him at every opportunity. When we meet again as a foursome, as I hope we will, it would be good if we could all be more relaxed with each other.'

He tilted his head and ran his fingers down the stubble on his cheek. '"Life hasn't been easy." The big guy's got to you, hasn't he? I missed a trick here. Should have told you how my wicked stepmother threw out my teddy bear and made me join the boy scouts. I might have got my leg over.'

'A knee in your groin.'

'Charming.'

'And your ouch would have been heard in Australia.'

'I'm outta here. I only came to pass on the message.'

HEN COMPARED the jpeg of Mrs Sentinel with the photo they had of the woman in the mortuary. 'No question,' she announced to everyone in the incident room. 'It's our mystery woman. Nice work, everyone. Let's treat ourselves to a lunchtime drink.'

'Don't know about that, boss,' Stella said. 'The husband, Dr Sentinel, is on his way. Should be here in another hour.'

'The rest of you can get a drink, then. Stella and I will be offering condolences.' She lowered her voice for Stella alone. 'We celebrate later. You gave him the bad news?'

'I said there was a resemblance.'

'So now he knows we have a dead woman here. Does he also know she was murdered?'

Stella took this as criticism. 'There was no point in being mysterious about it. The rest of Britain knows it's a murder.'

'He didn't?'

'He's been abroad, hasn't he? Someone was going to tell him.'

'Was he shocked?'

'Disbelieving.'

'Kept his cool, then. What's he like?'

'Toffee-nosed, if I'm any judge, but I suppose he would sound like that to one of the plod, with all his education,' Stella said. 'He seemed to think it was a bit off, his wife being killed down here.'

'He'd have preferred the stockbroker belt?'

The remark was meant to ease the stiffness between them. Stella took it for what it was, smiled and shrugged. 'Quite possibly.'

'Does he have any explanation?'

'For her death? No. They haven't spoken on the phone since he flew to St Petersburg three weeks ago. He's often away at conferences, he said, and he doesn't call her, phoning from hotels being such a rip-off.'

'Were those his exact words?'

'I was giving the sense of them. He said "exorbitant."'

'He must have a mobile.'

'"The price of using one from Russia is iniquitous." His words.'

Hen shaped her lips into a silent whistle. 'Has the romance gone out of this marriage, by any chance?'

'His wife wasn't wearing a ring.'

'I wouldn't read too much into that, Stell. A lot of wives don't.'

'You're giving him the benefit of the doubt, are you, guv?'

'Well, he cared enough to make enquiries. And he's wasting no time in coming here.'

'To make a good impression, maybe?'

'He doesn't seem to be succeeding with you. What's wrong with the guy?'

'You know what voices are like on the phone. You can tell a lot.'

'Are you suggesting he might have a guilty conscience? I can't think why, when he has a cast-iron alibi.'

'It's not unknown for a spouse to hire a hitman.'

This earned a chuckle from Hen. 'So we have a theory already, and we haven't even met the poor sod. Give him a chance, Stell.'

'The main thing is, we know who our victim is.'

'Yes,' Hen said, 'I knew our luck would change when we got out of that lousy caravan.'

JAKE WAS waiting at the entrance to the beach car park when Jo drove in. Good thing he was so tall, because she wouldn't have known him otherwise. He was in a navy blue jacket with the hood over his head like a boxer ready to enter the arena. Maybe he thought of this outing as a contest. She hoped not. More likely he wanted to be inconspicuous. Difficult when you're six foot six.

'We made it this time,' she said.

'You made it last time.' His response came fast and free, a promising start.

The rain had given way to a spell of sunshine and there was a sharp breeze. The sea looked choppy, if not quite so wild as when Jo was here last time. She locked the car and they started along the path. Not many people were out.

On the drive down, she'd decided to tell him the whole sorry story about Fiona. Gemma had blabbed to Rick, so why shouldn't Jake be told? He wouldn't use the information to score points as Rick did at every opportunity. He'd be a sympathetic listener and wise counsel.

She missed nothing in the telling: the plot to undermine Fiona, the search of the house by the police, the finding of the body, and the news that Gemma was being questioned. Jake heard her in silence, occasionally using his foot to steer away pebbles the tide had deposited on the path.

'I haven't heard anything directly from Gemma,' she finished up, 'so I don't know what the police got out of her. She could still be with them at the print works, I suppose. I don't like to phone her in case they're with her.'

'She'll call you,' Jake said.

'That's what I'm hoping. I've brought my mobile. Do you think they're holding her?'

He shook his head. 'What for?'

'I mean if there was some suggestion that Fiona was pushed in.'

'Is there?'

'I don't know. How else did she get in the water?'

He shrugged. He didn't seem to have thought of this.

She said, 'I'm wondering if she's ashamed to call me because she dropped me in it. There could be a police car waiting outside my house.'

'If there is . . . ' He opened his hands in a gesture of emptiness.

'I shouldn't panic?'

'They've got nothing on you.'

'That's true.'

'They'll be wanting to talk to someone else.'

'Mr Cartwright, Gemma's boss? That's for sure. He's got a tale to tell. Yes, he's got to be a crucial witness.'

'Have you met him?'

There was a change in Jake, and it was positive. He wasn't just responding to prompts from her. He was making points and asking questions.

She shook her head. 'We've only got Gemma's word for what he's like, and I'm not sure she's a good judge of character. She pictured him as a freeloader who got others to do all the dirty jobs while he kept his hands clean and worked on his image.'

'Doesn't sound like a killer.'

'I agree—but where is he?'

'Keeping out of the way.'

'There is another possibility,' she said. 'He could be dead as well, lying in the Mill Pond. I bet they're searching it as we speak. All that joking about thinking up ways to kill him was fun at the time, but it may have taken an ugly turn now.'

'I don't think so.'

'You think he's hiding somewhere?'

'It's more likely.'

'Especially if he killed Fiona.' She almost wished it were true and all the uncertainty were over.

'Why would he?'

'His motive, you mean? Fiona was overplaying her hand, according to Gemma, wanting a place on the board at the printer's, or just demanding money. She was on the make, by all accounts.'

'That's only one version,' he pointed out.

'Well, yes, Gemma's, like I said. Can we believe her?'

He didn't answer.

Jo said, 'All this speculation isn't helping, is it?'

He smiled.

She said, 'I know. I'm my own worst enemy. Not good for my nerves.'

They'd passed the southernmost point of Selsey Bill and now the East Beach came into view. First there was a large step down. Jake jumped into the shingle, turned, and held out his hand to help her down. A thoughtful gesture. She gripped the hand gratefully and made the jump. Her first physical contact with him. It was short-lived. He relaxed the grip and thrust both hands in his pockets.

'You see the lifeboat station?'

She wasn't certain if he was being serious. You could hardly miss it. The raised steel gangway projecting over the waves to the boathouse and slipway was about the only feature of the long stretch ahead. 'Yes, I see it.'

'Sixty years ago a prep school stood a short way back from there.'

'What—on the beach?'

'Above high water . . . then.'

'Erosion got it?'

He nodded. 'They built a lifeboat house in the twenties, close to the beach. They had to keep adding to the gangway. In thirty years it was eight hundred feet out to sea.'

'Oh, my.' She felt as she made the response that she sounded a touch too impressed. She wanted so much to encourage this dialogue he'd started.

'Shingle and sand over clay,' he said. 'Easily eroded.'

'But a whole building like a school going. That's scary.'

'It didn't get washed away.'

'I understand. It was no longer habitable, so it was pulled down.'

'Soon after that, in the mid-fifties, the sea wall was built. Until then, this coast was disappearing faster than anywhere in Britain.'

'I know erosion is a hot topic with the locals, but I didn't realise it had been happening on that scale.'

He stretched out his arm and made a sweeping movement in the direction of the sea. 'Somewhere out there is a deer park.'

She laughed, 'Oh, yes?'

But he was serious. 'In the time of Henry VIII, it was hunting country. Fishermen still call that stretch of sea "the park."'

'Hard to imagine.'

'And still further out is a cathedral, they say.'

'Under the sea?'

Jake didn't waste words on make-believe. 'There was this Bishop of York called Wilfrid.' He drew a long breath, priming himself for the story. He related it slowly and with pauses, and the impact was stronger than a more fluent speaker could have managed. 'Wilfrid was banished from the north for opposing the king, so he came south. Arrived in Sussex at a bad time, after three years of drought. Crops failing, desperate times, so he taught the people to fish. And the rain came, and he could do no wrong. He preached and built a monastery and a cathedral. When I say "built," I mean he was the overseer. The locals did the heavy work. That was in the seventh century.'

He'd got through. She felt like hugging him. 'An entire cathedral?'

'Wilfrid knew about building. He'd already built them at Ripon and York. It was Benedictine.' In his hood, staring out at the water, Jake could have been taken for one of the monks.

'How did a building of that size get destroyed?'

'Three centuries later, the Church ordered a new one to be built in Chichester.'

'There's gratitude. Enough to turn the locals right off Christianity.'

'Maybe their cathedral was already under threat from the sea.'

'You shouldn't be finding excuses for the Church,' she said, tongue in cheek. 'Selsey people built that cathedral and they deserved to keep it.'

'They did, in a sense.'

'How do you mean?

'In bits. You can still find chunks of marble and Caen stone in local buildings.'

'They looted it?'

'Reclaimed,' he said, looking out to sea.

Dr Austen Sentinel looked slightly older than his picture on the internet but still didn't fit their stereotype of an academic. He was lightly tanned, casually dressed in linen jacket, T-shirt, jeans, and Reeboks. On another day in a different situation, he could have passed for a sportsman.

Little was said during the drive to the mortuary. Until formal identification had taken place there was no justification for asking questions about the marriage, so Hen confined herself to summarising the few known facts about the finding of the woman on the beach. Sentinel contributed nothing except single-word responses. His thoughts seemed to be on the ordeal to come.

When the sheet was drawn back to display the dead woman's face there was a moment of uncertainty because he stared, frowned, and shook his head.

'Isn't that your wife?' Hen said.

He released a long breath, vibrating his lips. 'I'm at a loss to understand how this happened.'

'But she is—'

'Merry, yes.' Death has a way of making everything sound tasteless.

'You're confirming that this is your wife, Meredith Sentinel?'

'I just said. Can we leave now?'

Hen closed the car door on the widowed man and used her phone to call the incident room.

'That's a relief,' Stella said after she was told. 'Are you bringing him in now? Because we'll need to break the news as soon as possible. Don't ask me how, but the hounds have picked up the scent. They know you took someone to the mortuary, at any rate. I've taken two calls in the last ten minutes.'

Hen was philosophical about the leak. She doubted if it originated with the police. Obviously she'd been spotted entering the mortuary with Dr Sentinel. The public were quick to pass tips to the press. So, for that matter, were mortuary attendants. 'No problem, Stell. You can say we'll be issuing a statement within the hour.'

She walked round to her side of the car and got in. 'You have my sympathy, sir.'

Dr Sentinel said, 'I'm finding this difficult to take in. You'll have to make allowances.'

'Of course, but we need to talk at the police station.'

'I can't help you. I can't get my head round this.'

'You know a lot more about her than we do.'

He sighed. 'She drowned in the sea, you said?'

'Someone murdered her, sir, and it's our job to find out who, and why.'

'You'll be making this public, I expect?'

'Very soon. That's part of the process.'

THEY STROLLED on, past the lifeboat station and the fishing boats. The world was a happier place now. In Jake's company, the worries of the last twenty-four hours were not so threatening. Jo would have liked to tuck her hand inside his arm. It was a pity the moment didn't seem right. An opportunity might come, but it wasn't yet. She cared too much to risk giving him the wrong impression. Like some chaste woman out of a Victorian novel, she thought.

'How are you feeling?' he asked. An unexpected question. Mostly he avoided anything personal.

'Fine. Just fine.'

'About walking here, I mean.'

She grasped what he was saying. They were almost level with the section of beach where she'd found the corpse and she hadn't given it a thought. The mobile incident room was no longer parked there. Briefly she wondered how Jake knew which section it was, and then decided anyone with an interest in the matter would have no difficulty finding out. Everyone local would have seen that big police trailer and it was obvious that the bit of beach was just below there.

'I think I'm over that,' she said. 'Being with you makes it all right.'

As if embarrassed, he stepped a little to the right, putting distance between them.

This process of getting to know him was a learning curve. She tried to sound more objective, more fact-based. 'You're from Cornwall and yet you know this place as if you were raised here.'

'My job.'

'Local history?'

'Erosion and such. Or conservancy, I should say.'

'It's a lot more than that, what you've told me about this strip of coast. So unexpected. I mean on the face of things it's just a long stretch of shingle, pretty unromantic. Then you tell me it looks out onto a hidden deer park and a cathedral.'

'Folklore says you can hear the bells at low tide.'

She turned to look at him. He *wasn't* all factual statements. 'Now you're laying it on.'

He shrugged and looked down towards the water's edge, and she had a sense that he was enjoying this. 'Good place for fossils, too.'

'Do you collect them?'

'I have a few at home. And just about here . . . ' He stopped and measured a slice of the seafront with his hands ' . . . the skeleton of a woolly mammoth was found.'

'On the beach?'

'At low tide, after a storm raked off the shingle and sand and laid bare the clay.'

'A mammoth?'

'A fisherman found it and marked the place. The bones were recovered by a team from Brighton University.'

'When was this?'

'Twenty years ago. A young specimen that would have stood about nine feet tall.'

'Big enough.'

'Elephant-size, at any rate. The biggest mammoths grew to fourteen feet.'

She gazed at the foreshore, trying to imagine the scene. 'What an experience, excavating something like that. Those university people must have been over the moon to get such an opportunity.'

'You never know what will show up here. Mostly relics of the last ice age. Bones from rhinoceros, straight-tusked elephant.'

'Where is the mammoth now?'

'London. Natural History Museum.'

'The Selsey Mammoth. Has anything else been found, other than bones, I mean?'

'We get the metal detectorists here looking for Roman gold.'

'And finding any?'

'They were finding it before detectors were invented. A hoard of three hundred coins on the West Beach. A solid gold bar. A pair of armlets.'

'Have you found anything?'

'Only fossils. But you have to wait for the right conditions when the clay beds are exposed.'

'Low tide?'

'Spring tides are best. If you like, I could take you when the chance comes.'

'I'd enjoy that.'

Her phone rang.

'Sorry. This could be Gemma.' She put it to her ear.

It was, and she sounded in good heart. 'Jo darling, is this a good time?'

'Sure.' Considerately, Jake had turned away and stepped down the beach towards the sea. She wouldn't have minded if he'd stayed.

'Sorry to miss Starbucks,' Gemma was saying, requiring a shift in thought of half a million years. 'Rick told you about my problem.'

'How did it go?'

'Well, after much thought, they didn't bang me up in jail.'

'I should think not.'

'It wasn't so hairy as I expected at first. Would you believe they called me at seven-thirty in the morning on a Saturday, when I'm trying to get a proper lie-in? What they wanted was to be let into the office and shown where Fiona worked. They asked me all about her, and the boss.'

'Did they know she had something going with him?'

'They did when I'd finished with them. They spent a long time in his office and took his computer away. Asked me loads of questions about his attitude to women and where he takes his holidays and if he drinks and stuff like that. He's the prime suspect, for sure.'

'Are they treating it as a crime, then?'

'You bet they are. These were CID, not plain old cops in uniform.'

'Who was in charge? A woman detective called Mallin?'

'No. Have you got friends in the police?'

'Far from it. She's the tough cookie who interviewed me about the dead woman I found at Selsey.'

'She'd be West Sussex, then. Emsworth is Hampshire. Another county. Different set of cops. Didn't fancy either of mine, if you want to know.'

Something to be thankful for, Jo thought. 'I don't see why the CID have to be involved. It could have been an accident, or suicide.'

'Get with it, Jo. We've been through that already.'

'But the police haven't. They should be keeping an open mind.'

She gave a hoot. 'You think?'

'Was she injured, then—besides being drowned, I mean?'

'They didn't say. I was in no doubt they were serious.'

'Was anything said about why you called at Fiona's house?'

'I did the right thing, apparently. They praised me up. I'm a star, a copybook executive who cares for the staff she manages. An absolute credit to Kleentext Print Solutions.'

'Gemma, be honest. Did they really say all that?'

'Not word for word, but that was the gist of it.'

'And you didn't let on that we saw the body in the water?'

'What do you take me for, dumbellina? No way. That's a closed book. We agreed.'

Jo was tempted to say it wasn't a closed book to Rick, but why waste her breath?

'Are you sure you kept me out of it?'

'No chance. I said I was with this dangerous woman called Jo who drives a Panda and works at the garden centre and shits a brick every time I mention the word "police."'

'You said *what*?'

Gemma's laugh rattled the phone. 'Give me a break, sweetie. I wouldn't rat on my best mate.'

'Piss off, Gem.'

'As a matter of fact, they showed a lot of interest in Francisco.'

'The neighbour? I told you he could have done it.'

'They seemed to think I was his chick. I should be so lucky.'

'You were at his side when that police car arrived.'

'They're sure to question him. I hope they treat him well.'

'I hope they get the truth out of him,' Jo said. 'It wouldn't surprise me at all if he's the killer.'

'He's a bunny rabbit.'

'I'm not convinced of that. He was overplaying the part when I was watching.'

'What part?'

'The helpful neighbour.'

'He's a Latino. You've got to make allowances. You didn't get up close like me. I could tell he was legit.'

'We're obviously not going to agree about Francisco. I thought it was Rick you fancy. He told me he's going out with you tonight.'

'Yes, he's got lucky. But if Francisco makes a move, Rick is history. Don't tell him, will you?'

Jo ended the call and walked down the steep bank of shingle to where Jake was standing, still with the hood up. 'Can we get a coffee somewhere?'

He shook his head. 'I don't think we should. People know me here. It's only a small place.'

He was being protective, not wanting to draw her into the suspicion he felt was still attached to him. Concern like this was a new experience for Jo. 'Somewhere else, then?'

They returned to the car and she drove back to Chichester without telling him she was heading for her flat. In his present state of mind he might think it was entrapment. All she said was she knew of a place where they could get coffee. It was a calculated risk that could backfire, but she was going to have to make the first move. Any other guy invited back would think he'd hit the jackpot, but Jake was the exception.

nine

THE VISIT TO THE mortuary hadn't put Austen Sentinel off food. He went through a round of egg and cress sandwiches and two cups of black coffee while Hen was agreeing to the text of the press release. When she joined him in a side room he looked and sounded much recovered.

'You're about to break the news, then?' he asked. 'Those jackals will soon be after me, no doubt. I've watched grieving spouses forced to appear on television. Is that being suggested yet?'

The subtext, Hen suspected, was that the poor bereaved guy wanted his five minutes of fame.

'Not unless it becomes necessary.'

Disappointment spread over his face like a maiden's blush. 'I thought it was standard procedure.'

'It could still happen.'

'I'll do anything to help catch the monster who murdered my wife. I'm willing to face it today.'

'Thanks, but that would be too soon. We've got all the publicity we need at this stage.'

'What if they call me at home and ask for a statement?'

'You say "no comment" and refer them to our press office. You've got enough to cope with. You'll be wanting to contact her family and friends, I expect. Are her parents alive?'

He clapped his hand to his forehead. 'God, the old couple. They'll be devastated by this. I ought to speak to them before they hear it from someone else. They live in Kentucky. What time is it now?' He looked at his watch. 'They'll be up and about.'

'Do you have a mobile?'

His hand went to his pocket, but not inside. 'Oh, hell. I doubt if there's enough credit for a call to America. It needs topping-up.'

'So you'd like to use one of ours?' Making a mental note that he was a tightwad as well as a self-admirer, she took him into the CAD room and found him a seat.

She sought out Stella in the incident room. 'Check the St Petersburg flight arrangements both ways with the British Council and compare them with the airline passenger lists. Let's be sure he was on the flights he said he was. And see what you can find out about this conference and his part in it. I've no doubt he was there, but I want to know where he stayed and for how long and if he attended all the sessions.'

'Do you think he's flaky?'

'As a bowl of All-Bran. But I don't know if he's a killer as well.'

Dr Sentinel had finished speaking to his parents-in-law when Hen returned to him. 'One of the most difficult calls I've ever had to make,' he said. 'You can't imagine.'

'Actually I can,' she said. 'I had to break the news to you.'

'So you did.'

'And it wasn't my first time. Every copper has to do it.'

'I suppose.'

'Feel ready to answer some questions? Not here. We'll use an interview room.'

He frowned. 'Shouldn't you be going after the monster who did this?'

'I am. You offered to help. I'm asking for information.'

'Is there anything we haven't already covered?'

'Quite a bit.'

In Interview Room 2, with DC Gary Pearce at her side, Hen explained that it would streamline the process if they videoed what was said. Sentinel commented that in modern Britain you never knew when you were being secretly videoed anyway, and he had no objection. He didn't require a solicitor. Why should he?

For the record, Hen spoke the preliminaries, and then told him, 'I want as much as you can give me about your wife. Her personality, likes, dislikes, interests, friendships. It's our job, with your help, to work out what she was doing in Selsey.'

'That's a closed book to me,' he said. 'Let's try, but I don't hold out much hope that I can be of use to you. Personality-wise, Merry was charming in the way American women are, or most of them. She charmed me, anyway. We first met in the late nineteen eighties when she was an undergraduate at Brighton and I was a visiting lecturer attached to the geology department. I led a course in palaeontology for a couple of terms there.'

'And she was on it?'

'No, it wasn't that old cliché.'

'What do you mean?'

'Tutor seduces student. She wasn't even my student.'

'So what was she reading?'

'Zoology. Got a first, in spite of me. Merry could have excelled in any of the sciences, including my own. She had that sort of brain.'

'"In spite" of you?'

'She could so easily have been sidetracked. Academically, I was bad news for her. You see, I was on attachment from Brunel, twenty-five years of age, full of myself, not bad-looking. She was eighteen, a fresher.'

Not a million miles from that old cliché, Hen mused.

'The ratio of women students to men at Brighton was outrageous compared to what I was used to. I was the proverbial kid in the sweetshop. For me it was ideal, but not for Merry. I came along at a critical stage in her studies and took far too much of her time. It's a measure of her ability that she still got the best degree going.'

Something in his favour. He had a conscience.

'When did you marry?'

'Nineteen-ninety-two, after she graduated. The wedding was in Louisville, where they have the Kentucky Derby. Her father owns a string of racehorses. It was a society do. And they do their best to convince you America has no class system. You wouldn't believe the hats. Like that scene in *My Fair Lady*.'

'But you chose to live in England?'

'My career. I was hoping to get the chair at Imperial. I'm still waiting. I worked damned hard establishing myself, writing books and so forth. Merry was a huge support.'

'Did she continue her studies?'

'She took her doctorate at University College, but she wasn't cut out for lecturing, so she didn't stay in education.'

'What did she do?'

'Various things. She worked mornings at the Natural History Museum in South Ken, classifying bones and fossils. Yes, I know it sounds like the ultimate dead end, but the work had a link with her zoology, you see. And once a week she was doing what she really believed in, helping living species as a volunteer for the World Wildlife Fund.'

'Doing what?'

'Stuffing things into envelopes mainly.'

Hen had pictured her bottle-feeding baby pandas. 'And she found that fulfilling?'

'She valued the animal kingdom above mankind.'

Was that what irked him?

'The whole ecology, in fact,' he added.

'Flora as well as fauna?' A new thought came to Hen. 'She wasn't, by any chance, a campaigner for trees?'

'Not unless they were homes to one-toed sloths.'

'She must have made some friends in these jobs she did.'

'I expect so.'

A vague answer. 'You didn't meet any of them?'

'She didn't bring them home, no.'

'You're private people?'

'We gave the occasional dinner party for colleagues of mine.'

It seemed equality hadn't penetrated the Sentinel household.

'Did she ever mention names?'

'Of her friends? If she did, I wouldn't recall them. I have more than enough going on at Imperial to occupy my attention.'

Hen felt some sympathy for Meredith Sentinel. Marriage to this self-serving man must have been a pain. 'Enemies, then?'

'None that I heard of. She was difficult to dislike. I can see where you're going with that question, but I can't help, I'm afraid.'

'You mentioned the work she did at the Natural History Museum. Did she go on field trips?'

'What's that got to do with it?'

'Parts of the coast down here are well known for deposits of fossils.'

'I'm aware of that. They aren't short of specimens at the museum. She hasn't been here since her student days.'

'She was here last month when she was murdered.'

'And you're suggesting she came fossil-hunting? I don't think so.'

'So why did she come to Selsey as a student?'

'That was the woolly mammoth.'

'The *what*?'

'Twenty years ago some large bones were exposed in the clay after an unusually low tide and they turned out to be the complete skeleton of a young mammoth. My lucky day. This happened during my lecturing stint at Brighton—what is it?—thirty miles up the coast, and I was the obvious person with the skills and knowledge to supervise the excavation.'

'You were in charge?'

'The man on the spot. Palaeontologists don't grow on trees.'

'Neither do mammoths, I guess.'

'Not in nineteen-eighty-seven, anyway,' he said, causing Hen some puzzlement. She didn't interrupt. 'The dig had to be done swiftly because of the tidal conditions. And this was towards the end of September, before the university session began. I'd come up early to prepare and I recruited all the help I could, local volunteers and students from anywhere and everywhere, including Merry.'

'So that was the start of your romance?'

He was quick to scotch that notion. 'No, she was just a fresher, then. The mammoth dig was before I started going out with her. I took note of her, of course. You tend to spot the pretty ones on an excavation and they were in bikinis, if I recall correctly.'

Hen trusted his memory on that. 'How long did this dig go on for?'

'Three or four days only, at extreme low tide. Very demanding conditions. It's a pity, because a lot can be learned from the clay the bones are embedded in. You can isolate fossil plant-seeds that provide insights into the conditions at the time the mammal met its end.'

'This was an important find, I imagine?'

'Sensational, yes. The press came, and radio and television. Nowadays it wouldn't be the story it was. Global warming has led to wonderfully preserved mammoths being hacked out of the permafrost. In Russia they have so many you can buy them on the black market.'

One little query answered. Mammoths didn't grow on trees in 1987, but twenty years later was another story.

'To your knowledge, Dr Sentinel, that was the last time your wife visited Selsey?'

'I can't think of any other reason she would have come. We don't take our holidays here.'

'There are other local sites where ancient remains have been excavated.'

'Boxgrove,' Gary Pearce put in.

'Didn't I make myself clear?' Sentinel said. 'She doesn't— didn't—go on digs. The mammoth was a one-off.'

'And you can't think why she would have come to Selsey this September, or who might have come with her?'

'If I knew the answer to that, I'd have told you already.'

'Did she own a car?'

'A Volvo Estate. It's still in the street outside our home.'

'So either she took the train or she was driven here.' Hen let a few seconds pass. 'There's something I'm bound to ask and it's vital that you give me a frank answer. Was your marriage in any difficulty?'

The colour rose in his face. 'Certainly not. Hasn't everything I've said up to now demonstrated the strength of our affection for each other?'

'You've no reason to suppose she might have met someone else?'

'That suggestion is in appalling bad taste in the circumstances.'

'Sorry to give offence, but I had to ask,' Hen said. 'She acted out of character, according to you. Whilst you were away, she came to a place you knew nothing about and was found half naked on a beach.'

'Obviously she was abducted and brought here by her attacker.'

'Why? A public beach isn't the ideal place to conceal a murder.'

'He must know the area. You're looking for someone with local knowledge.'

It was a reasonable comment, but was he deflecting suspicion?

He continued, showing remarkable detachment, 'Sadly, bodies are washed up on beaches from time to time and most of them are victims of drowning. He must have assumed you would think she went swimming and got into difficulties. He didn't expect to leave those marks on her neck. That's my reading of it.'

On this, Hen agreed with him.

Jo LIVED on the north side of Chichester in a 1930s semi converted into two flats. She had the upper one. Doreen, a widow in her seventies, lived downstairs and did all the gardening, one of those hardy Englishwomen who knew about plants and was never happier than when out there watering, weeding, and pruning. They shared the front door.

She noticed Jake getting tense as the car left the main road into town and headed along suburban streets.

'You don't mind?' She was doing her utmost to sound relaxed. 'I thought my place would be less public than one of the coffee shops in town.'

He said nothing. At least he didn't protest.

Fortunately Doreen wasn't working in the front. She would have insisted on being introduced and asking questions, well meant, but liable to alarm anyone as wary as Jake.

Jo parked on the drive and switched off. Jake remained in his seat with the belt fastened.

'I know,' she said. 'You're wondering if this is wise.'

He gave a nod.

'There's no hidden agenda. It's coffee and biscuits and a chance to talk.'

After a pause for thought he said, 'Suits me,' and got out.

First base, she thought, and then gave herself a silent reprimand.

Upstairs in the living room Jake said, 'Nice place.'

'Not to everyone's taste,' she said. 'The colours are on the strong side, but I like the orange to red range. Shall I take your coat?'

A small courtesy, but the reaction was symbolic of trust when he unzipped the jacket and handed it to her.

'Have a seat and I'll get the kettle on.'

Had she prepared for this by some trick of the subconscious? She'd left an unopened packet of chocolate biscuits beside the kettle. She found a plate for them.

'I seem to remember you like yours black without?' she called from the kitchen. 'Put some music on if you like.'

The Lazy Sunday brand of coffee would have to do for Saturday. Humming to herself, she spooned some into the cafetière and poured on the water. Then she noticed there was a message on the answerphone. Gemma? Unlikely. Gem would have called her mobile. I know who that is, she thought with resignation. Her mother always used the land line.

Jake had chosen her CD of the *Goldberg Variations*. Glenn Gould, another guy with a personality problem.

'Do you play?' she asked as she came in with the tray.

'Badly.'

'Better than me. I lasted one week on the violin. My parents were keen for me to learn and that turned me right off. I have a pushy mother, though I have to admit she pushes herself hardest of all. She's mastered all kinds of skills, from marquetry to martial arts.'

'I won't pick a fight,' he said.

'Yes, she'd see how tall you are and take you as a challenge. Are your parents anything like that?'

'Tall?'

'No. Cringe-making.'

'Died when I was too young to know them,' he said.

'Oh.' Another gaffe.

'I was a Barnardo's boy. Have you heard of it?'

'I've seen the charity shops. That must have been a tough time. Were you in a children's home?'

He shook his head. 'They closed all the homes some time ago.'

'So?'

'I was fostered, three times.'

'That's a lot of changes. Weren't the parents suitable?'

'I wasn't. A right little tearaway.'

She smiled. 'Hard to imagine.'

'Oh, yeah? I took advantage. Didn't settle down until I went to school. Other kids put me in my place, let me know I was different.'

'Kids are cruel.'

'I have the hide of a rhino.' He managed a rare smile while working himself up to say something else. 'Your mother might knock me over, but she wouldn't hurt me.'

He did have a sense of humour. 'She still knows how to needle me,' Jo said. 'There's a message on the answerphone and I'm certain it's going to be from her. I don't visit enough for her liking, but when I do she makes me feel guilty.'

'Do you want to listen?'

'Right now I'd rather listen to Glenn Gould. And to you. Can I be personal and ask how you and Gemma got together?' She'd heard it from Gemma already, but his version would be more reliable.

'I don't think we did,' he said with the beginning of a smile. 'Needed some printing done for my job. Found her firm in the Yellow Pages.'

'So you visited Kleentext. Who did you meet?'

'A tough lady on reception.'

'That would be Hillie. I met her, too. She keeps throwing wingdings, to quote Gem. I think I've got the general idea, but I'm not always sure what her expressions mean.'

'It's a party, isn't it?'

'A wingding? More like some kind of outburst, I think. Yes, from what I saw of Hillie she isn't the sort to throw a party. Did you get to meet the mysterious Mr Cartwright?'

'Saw him. He walked through the office. Didn't speak.'

'What does he look like?'

'Dark hair, slicked back. Suit and bow tie. Glasses. Average height.'

'Bow tie? You know the saying? Dicky bow, no dick below.' The moment she spoke, Jo wished she hadn't. It was girl talk, strictly, strictly girl talk, of the sort she'd have a giggle over with Gemma.

'Haven't heard that one,' he said, straight-faced. Then smiled and said, 'Like fur coat and no knickers.'

'Much the same, yes.' He'd spared her blushes and she was grateful for that. 'And was Fiona about?'

'I couldn't tell you. Gemma took over.'

'I know what you mean. Meeting Gem for the first time is an experience. We were in the same yoga group and for some reason she homed in on me and we were asked to leave for being disruptive. Embarrassing really, but yoga classes are two-a-penny and Gemma's a one-off. And I've interrupted what you were telling me.'

'It's all right,' he said. 'You know the rest.'

'She chatted you up?'

'Told me I should get a life. Offered to take me bowling. That's where you came in.'

'At Chichester Gate. Wasn't that a strange evening? Rick being difficult and I'm not sure why. Maybe he was miffed about spending the evening with other people. It's not as if he and I were close. We'd been out together a couple of times and he kept on about this older woman called Sally he's known for ages who lives in a big house and cooks a roast for him on Sundays, so I was very much the second choice of date, or so I felt. He was totally open about her. I wonder if he's told Gemma.'

'Are they going out now?'

'Rick and Gem? She's dead keen. He can lay on the charm when he wants. She cleared it with me. We'll stay friends. Have one of the biscuits.'

'Thanks.'

'They're total opposites,' she said, 'so they ought to complement each other, like the two hemispheres of the brain. I never remember which is the intuitive, creative side, but that's Gemma.'

'The left.'

'And Rick is the analytical one. Put them together and you get something formidable. Gemma talks about murdering her boss—which is pretty outrageous—and Rick thinks of ways to go about it. Her ideas are off the wall, but he thinks it through like a chess player. Creepy. He's harmless, I'm sure, but I felt uncomfortable that evening we discussed it.'

'The power of suggestion.'

'Yes, and when I actually discovered a body not long after, it was very weird indeed. Then, on top of that, Fiona dies.'

The phone rang.

She said, 'Sod it.'

'Could be important,' Jake said.

She picked it up and of course the voice was her mother's. 'Didn't you get my message? Does that machine of yours work?'

She carried it through to the kitchen. 'I only just came in. Is everything all right?'

'Where were you, then?'

'Out for a walk. Does it matter where I was? If you want to reach me, Mummy, I carry the mobile almost everywhere. I wrote down the number for you. It's tucked in with your credit cards.'

'You haven't been listening to the radio, then?'

'No. Is something going on?'

'You'd better switch it on. Or look at the television. They've identified that poor woman you found on the beach. You'd like to know who she was, wouldn't you?'

'I suppose, yes. Did they say how she got there?'

'It's still a mystery, apparently, but now they know who she is they'll soon sort it out.'

'How did they find out?'

'From the husband. Why don't I get off the line and let you hear it for yourself?'

One of Mummy's better suggestions. 'All right. Take care.'

She stepped back into the living room. 'I don't know if you heard. That was my mother. It seems we ought to be listening to local radio. They've named the woman I found at Selsey.'

'Who was she?'

'Don't know yet.' She crossed the room and switched off Glenn Gould. 'Do you mind?' She tuned in to Southern Counties Radio. They were playing Westlife. 'Damn. Some other station must have it.'

'Stay with it. They keep giving the news,' Jake said.

'I suppose. More coffee?' She topped up his cup. 'Mummy said the husband came forward. It's been at least two weeks and more like three. I wonder why he left it so late?'

The question couldn't be answered yet. Jake gave a shrug and looked at his watch. Radio bulletins generally come on the hour and half hour.

Jo remained standing, more tense than she expected, gripping her arms to stop them from shaking. She couldn't explain why she was reacting like this. Hearing the name of the murder victim on the radio wasn't going to resolve anything. In a subversive way the woman was about to become more real. The sight of the almost naked body draped with seaweed and curled against the breakwater was still vivid in her memory, often returning, but it was just that, a shocking image. Now it was as if the poor woman was about to acquire a personality and make a stronger claim on the imagination.

The music ended, and the news jingle followed. Then: 'Southern Counties Radio at five o'clock. The stricken tanker in the Solent has been brought under control and is being towed towards Portsmouth. Coastguards report that the spillage of oil is less than was first feared and is being managed with booms. The woman found dead on the beach at Selsey two weeks ago and believed to have been murdered has been named as Mrs Meredith Sentinel of Islington. She was identified by her husband, Dr Austen Sentinel, a university lecturer, who has just returned from an overseas trip. Police are now trying to establish her movements prior to her death.'

Jo picked up the remote and switched off. Just as she'd feared, the dead woman seemed more real, more tragic, now that she had an identity. 'A lecturer's wife. I wonder what brought her to Selsey.'

Jake didn't say anything. He'd taken out his mobile and was texting someone. If anyone else had behaved like that it would have been rude.

'I mean she must have had a reason,' Jo said. 'It's a long hike from London.'

He didn't look up from the display.

'If she came by car they would have found it, surely,' Jo said, as much to herself as Jake, the thoughts tumbling from her in pity for a real woman, no longer just a corpse. 'They didn't even find her clothes. Well, I guess they'll have more to go on now they know who she was. The husband must be devastated, poor man. Fancy coming home from abroad and finding your wife was murdered.'

Jake stood up. The colour had drained from his face, leaving an unhealthy sallow that picked out the dark hollows and crevices as if a spotlight was on him. 'I must get home.'

'Is something wrong?' she said. 'Are you ill?'

He shook his head. Back to minimal communication.

'I've got painkillers if you want.'

'No.'

She collected his coat. She wondered if she'd touched on some painful memory when she commented on the news of the dead woman. A man with a stricken past was a minefield.

They went downstairs to the car and were soon south of the city on the Selsey Road.

'It's been a good afternoon, anyway,' she said to break the silence.

He said nothing.

One thing she'd learned was that you didn't force Jake to communicate. Trying to hold back her tears, she gave all her attention to the series of sharp bends. The light was fading fast.

'I don't know exactly where you live,' she had to say when they were approaching Selsey.

'Keep going.'

They had driven some way up the High Street before he said, 'Next left.'

She made the turn and he immediately said, 'Put me down here.'

'Now?'

'Here. Don't hang about.'

Up ahead, under a lamp-post, a police car was parked. He got out and started walking towards it.

ten

ALL THE WAY BACK to Chichester Jo was trying to make sense of Jake's behaviour. She drove as if on autopilot and when she got out she had no memory of being in control of the car.

Her neighbour Doreen was in the hall, smiling and blocking the way, poised for a chat. Jo muttered something about being in a hurry, brushed past, and dashed up the stairs.

For a long time she sat in her living room staring at the wall. She wasn't able to be rational. Her emotions had taken charge. Until now she hadn't appreciated the impact this man had made on her. She was locked into his destiny. She cared enormously what happened to him. If he was in trouble, then so was she. Whatever had happened, she couldn't believe the fault was his.

Eventually she composed herself enough to think back to the news item that had triggered the change in his mood. This, she was sure, had affected him more than anything she'd said herself. Affected him? Poleaxed described it better. His features had crumpled into an image of pain. Was it just the knowledge that the murder victim had been identified, or did the woman's name mean something to him? He'd texted someone as if to confirm the news.

Whilst driving him back to Selsey in that almost unbearable silence, Jo had convinced herself that he'd recognised the name. He knew who the woman was and was grieving for the loss of a friend. Not an intimate friend—she was someone's wife, for God's sake—but someone he'd known from way back.

The police car in his street had come as more of a shock for her than Jake. When he'd insisted Jo didn't drive up to the house she was reminded that he didn't want her involved in whatever had to be faced. This was his overriding concern, the reason he'd been so reluctant to be seen with her in Selsey, why he'd worn the hood and why he wouldn't even sit in a café and drink coffee. He was being protective. The moment he saw that police car he'd got out and walked towards it, dignified, resigned, and alone.

It was as if he'd expected the police to be there. His moment of shock had come earlier. By the time they'd driven to Selsey he was in control, calm, and resigned. He knew what to expect because he'd texted the police to tell them he was coming in.

She remembered his words that evening in the Lifeboat Inn after he'd been released from custody: 'They're sure I did it. They only let me go because they don't have the evidence yet.'

A moaning sound, primal in its despair, came from the back of her throat.

She wanted desperately to know what was happening, but phoning Jake was not an option. He'd made a point of giving nothing away to the police about their friendship. To call him now would be a betrayal of all his efforts. She had to wait.

Her eyes moistened. Tears would not be long in coming. She felt for the box of tissues on the table beside her and her hand came to rest on something smooth and square—the Glenn Gould CD case. Jake had been the last to handle it. Instead of a tissue she pressed the cool perspex against her cheek. The disc, his choice, was still in the player. She reached for the remote and pressed PLAY. The music was a solace.

Jake was a suspect because of his time in prison. In his own harsh phrase he was an ex-con. 'Crazy things happen to me,' he'd said. 'I don't want you drawn into it.'

They would question him again. Presumably they'd found out about his connection with the dead woman, his friend. Or maybe, Jo reasoned—looking for a more acceptable explanation—the woman hadn't been a particular friend, but just one of the many birdwatchers who visited the nature reserve at Pagham and were shown where some rare species could be observed. Something as innocent as that. Under questioning he would explain the coincidence and they'd have to release him.

In her heart she knew that couldn't be so. Jake would fold. He wasn't capable of explaining anything under the workover he'd get. They'd harass and bully him until he broke down. They'd find some spurious evidence and stitch him up.

She used the Kleenex this time.

Stop being a wimp, she told herself. All this speculation was negative and wouldn't help Jake or herself. The sensible thing was to get more information. Knowledge was strength, and if anyone needed some strength right now, she did. The dead woman's name was distinctive and so was her husband's. He was a university lecturer. Lecturer in what, and where?

She collected her laptop, switched on, put the name 'Sentinel' into a search engine and waited to see if anything came up.

Over a hundred hits appeared straight away. This was hot news:

Selsey Murder Victim Named

Police investigating the murder by drowning of a woman in Selsey have today named the victim as Mrs Meredith Sentinel, 38. She was the wife of Dr Austen Sentinel, a geology lecturer at Imperial College, London, who has recently returned from a conference in St Petersburg. He was not aware of his wife's disappearance. Upon finding she had not used their Islington house for several days he informed the police. From his description they linked her to the murder victim and confirmed the identity with photographs. This morning he formally identified the body as that of his wife.

Mrs Sentinel was American by birth and came to this country to pursue an academic career. She met and married Austen Sentinel in 1990, when she was an undergraduate and he a visiting lecturer at the University of Sussex. She later obtained a D.Sc in Zoology and was employed part time at the Natural History Museum, South Kensington. Her parents still live in Louisville, Kentucky, and are reported to be devastated.

As yet the police have been unable to account for the circumstances of Mrs Sentinel's death. Her almost nude body was found on the beach at Selsey, West Sussex, on September 30. The post mortem revealed that she was held under water until she drowned. Despite an extensive search of the beach and adjacent gardens her clothes have still not been found. She had not indicated to her husband that she intended to visit Selsey while he was abroad.

DCI Henrietta Mallin of Chichester CID is leading the enquiry and has appealed for help from the public. 'We have interviewed a number of individuals who were on the beach on the day the body was found, but we still know very little about Mrs Sentinel's last hours. Anyone with information should contact Sussex Police using the emergency number.

Another website had a photo of the couple wearing evening clothes and holding glasses of wine. Meredith Sentinel was blonde and her hair was pinned up except for some wayward strands suggesting that the party had passed the point when perfect grooming mattered. The look in her blue eyes helped to create the impression. A gorgeous, sexy woman, Jo thought. The birdwatcher theory was unravelling already. She couldn't imagine this charmer sitting in a freezing hide waiting for a Brent goose to fly in.

Austen Sentinel, too, was a looker, quite a hunk for an academic: broad-shouldered, tall, and tanned. The hair was dark, a mass of tight curls. The confident brown eyes left little doubt that his plans for later matched his wife's. His hand curled over her bare shoulder.

On another website Jo was startled to see her own name. Little else was accurate. Described as a resident of Selsey (wrong), she was supposed to have stumbled over the body (she didn't stumble over anything) whilst exercising her dogs (what dogs?) on Medmerry Beach (East Beach). A salutary reminder not to believe everything on the internet.

Austen Sentinel's name cropped up on numerous websites unrelated to the murder. He'd written books and articles and was much quoted in scientific literature. Apparently he was a serial attender of conferences in foreign countries. Was this significant? How did the beautiful wife amuse herself while he was away? Selsey, for all its charms, wasn't the obvious place a lively lady might choose to visit.

The phone went. She let the answerphone play to find out who was on the line. The voice was Gemma's.

'Have you heard, poppet? They've discovered who your mystery woman was.'

Trust Gem to want to chew it over. But she wasn't the only one. Jo badly needed shaking out of her embattled state of mind, and no one was a better shaker than Gemma. She switched off Glenn Gould and picked up the phone. 'Hi. Just heard your voice. Yes, I caught the news on local radio.'

'A university wife in nothing but her kecks,' Gemma said. 'Am I completely out of touch, or is this the end of civilisation as we know it?'

'I know. I'd already convinced myself she must be some poor homeless woman with a stack of problems.'

'My thought exactly,' Gemma said. 'Mind, she was probably an alky. They're well known for irrigating the tonsils, aren't they, university types?'

'Some of them,' Jo said. 'There's a picture on the internet of these two holding wineglasses.'

'Completely stonkered.'

'I don't know about that. No, I think that's unfair. Everyone's been snapped with a glass in their hand at some stage.'

'If it's the same picture I just saw on South Today, "stonkered" is being charitable.'

'She'd had something to drink before she died,' Jo said. 'There were traces in her blood, but not a huge amount, the paper said.'

'She was probably gaga. The stress gets to these lecturers' wives, trying to keep up with intellectuals. In the end they don't know if it's pancake Tuesday or half-past breakfast time. It's not all it's cracked up to be, you know, university life.'

'I didn't know you went to uni.'

'Chichester Tech—as was. They're all universities now, aren't they? Doesn't matter if it's Oxbridge or Chi. The same things go on. You know the saying, don't you? If you want to get laid, go to college, but if you want an education use the library.'

'Oh, Gem!'

'True. They arrive as freshers thinking it's all about lectures and essays and quickly find out their pointy-head tutors are expecting a shag. Some of them are dim enough to come across. And a few get spliced. It never lasts. A couple of words out of turn at high table, the confidence goes, and they're ready to jump off a cliff.'

'It wasn't suicide, Gem. Someone drowned her.'

'Okay, she was such a misery-guts she drove him to it.'

'Oh? What are you suggesting now? The husband killed her? I thought he was in St Petersburg.'

'His story. Who's going to check?'

'I'm sure the police will if they have any suspicions. He must have given a lecture there.'

'It might have been scheduled but there's no telling he actually gave it. Or—how about this?—he gave his spiel on the first day and caught a plane home the same night and did the deed.' Gemma on cracking form, weaving an entire whodunnit out of nothing.

'Why would he bring her all the way down to Selsey?'

'You don't piss on your own doorstep.'

'We're talking about an intelligent guy, Gem. There are cleverer ways of killing your wife than drowning her and leaving the body on the beach.'

'Ah, but he meant it to be taken for suicide or an accident. He didn't bargain for the marks on the neck.'

'You really think he did it?'

'The spouse is always the main suspect.'

'They don't seem to have charged him.'

'Like you say, they'll check the alibi first. See if he really was in St Petersburg.'

'A moment ago you said they wouldn't check.'

She chuckled. 'I could have been wrong there. Actually I don't have a lot of confidence in the rozzers. Plenty of crimes go undetected and it's only thanks to informers that any get cleared up at all.'

'There's some truth in that.'

'They take the easy option every time. The next thing is they'll put Dr Sentinel on TV appealing to the public for help. That's the giveaway. You see it so often. Men think they can bluff it out. Can they, hell?'

'You don't think they suspect anyone else?'

'Like you, for instance, just because you found the body? No, babe, don't waste any sleep over that.'

Jo wasn't thinking about herself. 'Someone local, maybe?'

'I doubt it. Selsey's got its share of weirdos, I'm sure, same as every other place, but this looks like a domestic. If it was a sex crime, you could be right, but this wasn't, was it? I know she was practically starkers, but there was no sign of ground rations that I heard of.'

'Ground what?'

'Naughties. Brace up, ducky.'

'It would be all over the papers if there was.'

'The lines are open again. Have you asked yourself why she wasn't wearing clothes?'

'They went for a midnight swim?' Jo said. 'People do. It's supposed to be liberating.'

'You're firing on all cylinders now. Think about it. She'd have to know her killer pretty well to skinny dip with him. Which is precisely why I don't think it was some yobbo she'd met over a couple of drinks the same night. It's got to be the husband or a lover.'

'I think you're right.' Jo hoped the police were working along the same lines. She was feeling better for talking to Gemma. 'But in the picture I saw he appeared to be quite fond of her.'

'That's the one he gave the fuzz, I expect. He's not daft.'

'He doesn't look like a killer.'

'They don't all have slitty eyes and bad teeth. The Boston Strangler was a dish. Tony Curtis played him in the film.'

'Gemma, you're the bloody limit, did you know that? Speaking of murder suspects, have they found your boss yet?'

'No chance. If you ask me, he's living it up on the Costa del Crime.'

'And are you still running the business?'

'Trying to. I did what you said and pulped all those council pamphlets. Even Hillie on reception has gone quiet now. The next thing will be Fiona's funeral, I suppose. Some of us will have to show our faces there.'

'Has it been arranged?'

'I don't think they've released the body yet. I say . . . ' Gemma took a gasp that could be heard down the phone. 'I just had a thought. What if Dr Sentinel murdered Fiona as well as his wife?'

'I don't see how,' Jo said. Gemma's capacity for invention knew no bounds.

'He was in the area.'

'He was in St Petersburg.'

'We dealt with that. He came back. First he drowned his wife and then Fiona.'

'Why?'

'That's for the Old Bill to find out. Far be it from me to speculate but if I was in charge I'd look for a connection, like was Fiona ever a student of his?'

'Unlikely,' Jo said. 'She was trained in accountancy, you told me. He's a geologist.'

'Yes, and he gets his rocks off by drowning women.'

'Oh, come on!'

'It's worth investigating. I may have a word in that inspector's ear if she comes by again.'

'Do that,' Jo said, deciding to humour her.

'I'd better go and put on some face. I'm meeting the gorgeous Rick tonight.'

'It's still on, then?'

'Bubbling nicely. We had a slight falling-out over this woman he sees on Sundays, but we're over it now.'

'Sally.'

'I call her his dinner lady, which irks him a bit, because she's posh and very rich. Lives in a mansion overlooking the harbour at Bosham. It's got a studio, a games room, and an indoor pool. I wondered why he was wasting his time with me until I found out Sally's fifty-three.'

'As old as that? I didn't know.'

'A mother-figure, you see. Some men have a lifelong need for them.'

'He won't get much mothering from you.'

'Christ, no. And how's yours?'

'Mine? You mean Jake? I still like him, yes.'

'Cool. Why don't we all meet for a drink tonight, mend some fences?'

'I don't know about that.'

'Just for an hour. We don't have to spend the whole evening together. Rick and me are going clubbing, anyway, and that's not Jake's style. You two could go bowling after. He likes that. But it's not for me to organise your evening. Let's say we'll be in the Slug & Lettuce between seven and eight and we'll look out for you guys.'

'I don't think so.'

'Go on. Give it a whirl. Jake won't mind. I'll call him if you like.'

'No. Don't.' To fend off that possibility, Jo said, 'If we can get there, we will, but don't wait around.' The right moment, she thought, to end the call. 'Thanks for phoning, Gem. I don't believe half of what you say, but you always cheer me up.'

After putting down the phone, she shook her head and smiled at the riot of fantasy she'd just heard. A lecturer not only drowns his alcoholic—or insane, or depressed—wife while skinny dipping, but is confirmed as a serial killer by drowning Fiona as well. All of this while he's attending a conference in St Petersburg.

INSIDE THE terraced house Jake rented in Selsey, Hen Mallin picked a lump of stone off the top of a bookcase. 'Tell me about this, Jake.' She'd learned at the first interview that she'd get more out of the man when he relaxed a bit. The rocks on display weren't things of beauty, so they had to hold some other appeal for their owner. 'Looks to me like an oyster.'

He emitted a long, tense breath. Even in his own setting he was stumped for words.

Jake may have preferred to move on. Hen didn't. 'It's not shell any more. It's rock, so this is a fossil, yes?'

A definite nod this time.

She exchanged a glance with Stella, then pressed Jake harder.

'You're going to have to help me here. I suppose it has a Latin name?'

'Gryphaea.'

'Cop that, Stell. And it's special, obviously. Very old?'

'Hundred and fifty.'

'Thou?'

A shake of the head.

'Million? Hundred and fifty million? That's prehistoric.' She tossed it across the room to Stella, who made a one-handed catch. 'Have you handled anything as ancient as that, Stell, not counting that sandwich in the police canteen today? And it looks just like a modern oyster to me.'

'Me, too,' Stella said. 'Except this is a Gry—?'

'—phaea,' Jake said and volunteered something else. 'Extinct.'

Now that he'd broken cover, he had to be pursued. 'Ah,' Hen said, 'but it takes an expert to tell the difference. How can you tell it isn't a common or garden oyster, a mere ten thousand years old?'

'Thicker,' he was moved to say. He retrieved the fossil from Stella and returned it to the bookcase. 'The valve is thicker. In folklore . . . ' His voice trailed off, as if he suddenly realised he'd been manoevured into uttering more than a couple of words.

'Go on, Jake. We're listening.'

'In folklore these are devil's toenails.'

'So this innocent-looking oyster gets a bad name. I guess devil's toenails are easier to remember than Gry— whatever.' She eyed the rest of the exhibits, thinking there wouldn't be much mileage in them. They were uninspiring. She wouldn't have minded insects in amber or sharks' teeth. These were plain old rocks, even if they had Latin names like the extinct oyster.

He was shaping to say something else.

'Go on,' she encouraged him. 'I'm all ears.'

'Good for arthritis.'

'Are they, by all that's wonderful? But how do you take them? Not swallowed, surely?'

'Grind them to powder.'

'When my joints start giving me gyp, I'll know where to come. You're an authority, obviously.'

'Amateur.'

'Shall we talk about the reason you texted me?' she said, deciding that the confidence-giving had run its course. 'You say you know the dead woman, Meredith Sentinel.'

'Met her, yes.'

'Well, *there's* a thing. You're pulled in for questioning for being close to the scene and having a record and now it turns out the victim is known to you.'

'Coincidence,' Jake said, reddening.

'Really? Let's look into that. Where did you meet?'

'Natural History Museum.'

'London? You visited there?'

'A few times.'

'I get the connection, I think. Mrs Sentinel had a part-time job in the fossil department. Not such a thumping great coincidence, then. Showing her some of your specimens, were you?'

He shook his head. 'Looking at theirs.'

'Did you meet Mrs Sentinel outside the museum?'

The question startled him. 'No.'

'But you knew her by name?'

'She introduced herself.'

'Bully for you. Pretty woman, wasn't she, Jake?'

He didn't answer that.

'I thought we might agree on that,' Hen said. 'Most guys like a good-looking blonde. She must have made an impression, for you to remember her. How did you find out she was the dead woman on the beach? Saw her picture on TV?'

'Radio.'

'I follow you . . . I think. You recognised the name and decided to tell all before we kicked your front door in. Wise move, Jake.'

He lifted his shoulders a fraction.

'Where were you when you heard this news?'

'With a friend.'

'I said where, not who with.'

'Chichester.'

'How long was it before you texted?'

'Immediately.'

'Aside from the discussions you and Meredith had about fossils, did you get to know the lady at all? Was she friendly?'

The inevitable nod.

Hen was annoyed with herself. She needed to phrase her questions better to get a response. 'What did you learn about her life outside the museum?'

'She cared.'

'Cared about you?'

'The rainforests.'

'Conservation? She shared your opinions, then?' She saved herself from another nod by saying, 'You don't need to answer that. I'm thinking aloud. I'm interested in where you talked about such matters. Must have been difficult in the fossil gallery, or whatever it's known as.'

'Over coffee in the restaurant.'

'Ah—it got as friendly as that? I'm getting the picture now. And what did she have to say about personal matters?'

He frowned.

'Like life at home?' Hen prompted him.

'Not much.'

'But there was something?'

'Her husband wasn't in—' The statement stopped there.

'Are you saying you went to the house, Jake?'

'No.' He backtracked. 'Wasn't in agreement.'

'With what?'

'Climate change. He said it was cyclical.'

'Right,' she said, the disappointment obvious in her tone. She didn't want to get into a debate on global warming. 'Did she at any point talk about coming to Selsey?'

'No.'

'You didn't invite her down to see your fossils or go looking for them on the beach?'

Another shake of the head.

'We don't know why she was here and neither does her husband. Fossil-hunting seems as likely a reason as any. Do you have any suggestions? No? I wasn't expecting any, but I had to ask.'

His small living room was pretty basic, emulsioned in the universal off-white called magnolia, with a patch of blue carpet over brown-stained boards. Three-piece suite, vintage 1970, portable TV, bookcase stacked mainly with maps and magazines, coffee table with a bunch of Fair Trade bananas still in their wrapper. A Vernon Ward on the wall of wildfowl flying over water. Not a family photo in sight.

'How long have you been living here?'

'Four, five years.'

'Get on with the neighbours, do you?'

'No problems.'

'Do you get out much?'

'Got an outside job.'

'Yes, but do you have a social life? Know what I mean?'

He lowered his eyes as if his large feet held the answer. Finally he said, 'I'm okay.'

IN THE car, Stella said, 'Am I missing something here, guv?'

'What's the problem?'

'You don't think we should pull him in?'

'Why, do you?'

'He's our only suspect apart from the jogger we haven't traced. And this links him to the victim.'

'It was a voluntary statement.'

'I know that, guv. If he's our man, he's made a smart move. We would soon have made the link. I happen to think he's a whole lot brighter than we take him for. He can't string six words together at a time, but when he does say anything, it's measured.'

'I don't underrate him,' Hen said. 'He's holding down a responsible job. The problem is that the custody clock starts ticking and what do we get out of him? We've been over his movements in the hours leading up to the murder. He isn't fireproof, but any connection is circumstantial.'

'This link to the victim has some clout, surely?'

'Not enough to make a charge stand up. Next time I don't want him to walk away.'

'So you rate him as the killer?'

Hen tossed it back. 'Do you?'

'I was trained to look for motive, means, and opportunity. He had the means to hold her under. He's a big, strong guy. He had the opportunity. She came to Selsey knowing he lived here. He takes her down to the beach on a fossil hunt. But what would have been his motive?'

'The visit turned sour,' Hen said. 'He's an ex-con trying to hide his past. Maybe she got wind of it and he panicked and attacked her. Or she told him his fossils are a heap of rubbish.'

'She was supposed to be a charmer,' Stella said. 'I can't see her treating him like that.'

'All right. Here's another angle. She was the first woman who'd agreed to go out with him in five or six years.'

'She was married, guv.'

'Yes, and we've both seen what the husband is like. Would you stay loyal to a self-regarding berk like Austen Sentinel? You'd find it a strain.'

'To say the least.'

'Let's say Meredith was tempted to play away. She had interests in common with Jake and he was the opposite of her old man, the strong, silent type. But it turned out he wasn't up for it. He was thinking fossils while she was thinking sex.'

'Or the reverse.'

Hen frowned, thought about it and gave a nod. 'I guess. Either way, there's a fatal moment of discovery. He's big and strong and violent in a crisis. All the frustrations of the past erupt in him. He grabs her and holds her under till she can't struggle any more.'

'I can believe that,' Stella said.

'I've only got one problem with it,' Hen said.

'What's that?'

'How come you and I just went to and his house and felt so safe with him?'

eleven

ON THEIR RETURN TO Chichester police station, Hen and
Stella were met inside the entrance by DC Gary Pearce looking
like the wildebeeste who couldn't work out why the rest of the
herd had bolted.

'Something up, sunshine?' Hen asked.

'Don't know, guv. The ACC was asking for you.'

'The main man? What time is it? He'll have left by now.'

'I don't think so. It sounded urgent,' Gary said.

'Got to be. I hope you told him I was out seeing a witness.'

'I said you'd left the building, anyway.'

'Oh, thanks a bunch.'

'Not long after, he came downstairs.'

'Got up from his chair to come looking for me? That's a first.'

'He asked me to call you.'

'What stopped you?'

'I tried. I kept trying.' He shot her an apprehensive glance. 'Is
it possible your phone was switched off?'

'When was this?'

'Twenty minutes ago.'

'Ten past six. It could have been. We were dealing with an incident, weren't we, Stell? Did he say what the flap is about?'

'No, but he wants to see you the minute you return.'

'I'd better give him the pleasure, then.'

Stella waited until Hen was out of earshot and then told Gary,
'The incident was a shortage of cigarillos. We had to find a pub
that sold them. You did good, Gary.'

* * *

JUST WHEN she was resigned to not hearing anything, Jo's mobile sounded and it was Jake. 'Me again.' His voice was strong. 'I thought I'd better call.'

'You sound okay,' she said.

'I am. It's all right.'

'It's great to hear from you,' she said. 'I was spooked when I saw the police car. Are you at home?'

'Actually, no. On the bus to Chichester. There was a message from Gemma about meeting in the Slug and Lettuce.'

That Gemma! Bloody nerve. 'Was there indeed?'

'You're going to be there, aren't you?' Now the anxious note returned to his voice. 'Gemma said you would.'

'Em, of course. You bet I am.'

'We don't have to . . . '

'Spend the whole evening with them? No. That's for sure.'

'See you soon, then?'

'Quick as I can make it.'

WHEN HEN came back from the ACC's office, something had changed. She seemed smaller, less jaunty, more thoughtful. 'Going outside for a smoke,' she said. 'No one is to leave. Mother Hen will address you shortly.'

There were some puzzled looks. 'Trouble?' one of the newest detectives said.

'We'll know soon enough,' Stella said.

Gary said, 'Do you reckon she'll be quick? I was hoping to go off duty. Pompey have an evening match.'

'I wouldn't bank on it.'

But in five minutes the boss was back and some nicotine-assisted bounce was back as well. 'Listen up, people. Things have moved on. Eighteen days after Meredith Sentinel's body was found, another woman drowned. Why the hell didn't we find out? You may well ask. Two reasons. First, it looked like an accident. Second, it wasn't on our patch. It was at Emsworth, over the county border. The woman was floating face down in the water in the Mill Pond, that big stretch where all the swans are. Why am I telling you this? Because the post mortem report is out and the pathologist noticed some pressure marks on the back of her neck and shoulders suggesting she was held under.'

Someone whistled.

'Just like ours,' Stella said.

'Fainter than ours,' Hen said. 'The marks, I mean. The victim was wearing clothes, but you can still see bruising. Up to now the post mortem report hasn't been made public. The incident hasn't had much publicity, a paragraph on an inside page of the local paper. Our case, as you know, has had plenty of attention. Hampshire Police knew all about it and got in touch this afternoon. The assumption is that the two drownings are connected, that we have a double killing. Clearly it calls for cooperation across the county border. Seeing that our investigation is already under way, Hampshire have agreed to me being SIO in both cases. We'll have two or three of their detectives on the team, but basically it's our show. A double murder—unless it's Sod's Law that two similar drownings happened within twenty miles of each other.'

'Sod's Law?' Gary Pearce queried softly.

'Something that can go wrong will go wrong,' the sergeant behind him said.

Hen had heard and said, 'AKA Murphy's law. Isn't that right, Sergeant Murphy?'

'Yes, guv,' Paddy Murphy said, 'but this should help us.'

'Right. Good news and bad news,' Hen said. 'We've doubled our chance of learning something about the killer. But the bad news is that the pressure to make an arrest will more than double. The media will go bananas.'

'A serial killer,' Murphy said.

No one doubted this was how the press would portray the news, but Hen was a stickler for accuracy. 'For my money, Paddy, a killer doesn't rate as "serial" until he has at least three to his name. And before you tell me he could have killed in the past and no one spotted the signs, I've got a little job for you.'

DS Murphy gave a twisted grin, resigned to what was coming.

'Check the drownings of all adult women in the past five years in Sussex, Hampshire, and adjacent counties. Accidental as well as homicidal. Get hold of the PM reports if you can. Anything remotely similar to these two cases, speak to the coroner.'

'Do we change our focus now, guv?' Stella asked.

'In what way?'

'I've spent a lot of time trying to establish if Dr Sentinel was in St Petersburg for the full three weeks he claimed. He's unlikely to have killed this second woman as well.'

'Let's make no assumptions. How far have you got with the check?'

'He definitely flew out on the day arranged and back three weeks later. The time between is less certain. He gave his lecture the first weekend. His hotel was paid for by the organisers. The hotel can't or won't tell me if his room was in use for the whole of his stay.'

'Why not? The chambermaid must have noticed.'

'I think they're being cagey for their own reasons. If he was absent for some days they may not be entitled to claim full board from the conference people.'

'God help us. It's the same the world over—people on the make. Did you get the impression he wasn't there?'

'Something dodgy was going on. I'm not sure what.'

'Keep at it, Stell. We need to know. Coming back to your question, we don't change focus. Everyone in the frame remains there.'

Gary Pearce asked, 'Do we know the identity of the Emsworth victim?'

'Good question, and we do. She's Fiona Halliday, aged twenty-four, and she couldn't be more local. The house she rented faces onto the Mill Pond. She was found fifty yards from her front door. Everyone assumed it was an accident until the pathologist reported the marks.'

'Who found her?'

'Some old dear who feeds the swans. We can eliminate her as a suspect. Aged nearer to ninety than eighty, I'm told. The interesting thing about Fiona Halliday is that she went missing from work a week before she was found, and so did her boss, named Cartwright. I should explain that Fiona was divorced and had a four-year-old son.'

'Poor kid.'

'Yes. When the mother didn't call in, some of the staff where she worked were worried that she'd collapsed or died and the boy was with her in the house. They're a good bunch of people by the sound of things. They reported it and a patrol car was sent. The officers forced the door and took a look around. No sign of the child. It's since been discovered that he was with the father by arrangement. His turn to have the boy for a week.'

'Has Cartwright shown up yet?'

'Not yet. Another mystery.'

'Another victim, maybe?' Stella said.

'Or another suspect,' Gary said.

'What do we know about him?' Stella asked.

'Only what I've learned from the Emsworth police. He's manager of the printing firm in Fishbourne where Fiona worked in accounts. The staff there had the impression he fancied Fiona. Last seen leaving the building with her mid-afternoon on the Friday. She was found six days later.'

'We have to find this guy—and fast,' Stella said. 'Is he married?'

'Divorced. Lives alone in Apuldram.'

'Does he have form?'

'Nothing known. But you're right, and we're putting out a description. We'll need a warrant to search his house. That's another job for you, Stell.'

'Now, guv—at the weekend?'

'You weren't thinking of putting your feet up?'

'It's finding a magistrate to issue a warrant. Not easy on a Saturday night.'

'Nonsense. They'll be propping up the bar at the golf club. Droves of them. You need to be in Cartwright's house tomorrow morning.'

'I'll get onto it.'

Hen knew she would. She could depend on Stella.

'And we visit the print works and question the people there.

That can't be done till Monday, I guess. Right now I'm off to Emsworth to look at the scene and inside Fiona's house. Gary.'

'Guv?' He looked as if the whistle had blown for a penalty against Pompey.

'You can come with me.'

THE SLUG & Lettuce, in South Street, gets crowded on a Saturday night. The noise level is pretty high. But there was no problem hearing Gemma from the far side. 'Over here, amigo.'

Jo went over. Rick and Gemma were sitting close together on the banquette opposite Jake, upright on a chair as if he was asking the bank manager for an overdraft. Something about Rick and Gem had changed. They gave the strong impression they had just shared a secret.

'Check that outfit,' Gemma said. 'Doesn't she look fabulous, Jake?'

A quick change after the phonecall, shimmery silver top over white leather skirt and ankle boots. Yes, it was dressy, but Jo could have done without the fanfare from Gemma.

Jake gave his customary nod.

'Well, I know you're a man of few words,' Gemma said to him, 'but you could show your appreciation by drumming on the table. She didn't dress like that to please me or Rick.'

Jo said, 'Gem, I'm sure you mean well, but do us all a favour and put the stopper in it. Who wants another drink? Don't get up, anyone. My round.' A tip she'd got from her canny father: always get your round in early. Then you can leave when you want with a clear conscience.

When Jo came back with the drinks Gemma was holding forth about some weird website she'd discovered. 'It's a bit like those African water holes where they have a camera rigged up permanently and anything coming to drink gets on the screen. If you're patient and you get lucky you might see a lion. Well, this is outside a nightclub in Bristol, and you get to clock all the glam and glitz as people arrive. Of course you also get the bouncers turning away the troublemakers and the drunks coming out and the druggies dealing and the fights. Nonstop action.'

'Who'd want to look at that?' Rick said.

'Maybe,' Jake started to say, and everyone waited, ' . . . a lion.' Bemused looks all round.

'Nice one. Hey, I go for that,' Rick said, and earned Jo's approval. He'd remembered her appeal to be civil to Jake. 'A lion with a computer.'

'Surreal,' Gemma said. 'Comical, though, I must admit. I hope there isn't a camera outside Jongleurs. I couldn't get my hair right tonight. I wouldn't want it on the world wide web.'

'It looks fine to me,' Jo said.

'Liar. It's like a cornfield a flock of sheep have been through. I can't get anything right at the moment.'

'Maybe you're working too hard.'

'Tell me about it!'

'Any news of your boss coming back?'

'Old Cartwright? He won't be back.'

'You sound very definite.'

'I am. He's history now.'

'Wrong,' Rick said. 'He could be tomorrow's news.'

'I hope not,' Gemma said. 'That's the last thing I want to hear. Ah!' She started to giggle. 'I get you. Tomorrow's news. Wicked.' She shook with laughter.

This was some kind of private joke between Gemma and Rick. Jake looked as mystified as Jo was.

'Are you going to let us in on this?' Jo said.

'No chance,' Rick said, so quickly that he almost cut her off.

'Why not?' Gemma said. 'They were here when we first talked about it.'

'They don't need to know.'

'Be like that. I think it was genius. Deserves to be appreciated.'

Rick didn't want appreciation. He gave Gemma a look that could have drilled through concrete. 'Let's change the subject. Did you hear about the woman you found on the beach, Jo? She was American, married to some university lecturer.'

'Yes, I heard on the radio.'

'They're London people. God knows what she was doing half-naked in Selsey.'

'Being murdered,' Gemma said.

'Apart from that.'

'Obviously she had a lover.'

'How do you work that out?'

'Get with it, Rick. The husband was away at some conference, wasn't he? We all know what conferences are for—tax-deductible sex. She thought she'd get a bit for herself.'

'Who with—one of the locals?' Jo said.

As always, Gemma had a whole storyline worked out. 'I doubt if he was a Selsey guy. Some old flame of hers who lived in one of the grander places inland, like Arundel or Petworth. They meet up—the first time in years—and have a couple of drinks and at her suggestion he drives her down to the coast to look at the sea by moonlight, all Mills and Boon, she thinks, but he's humouring her for old time's sake. What she doesn't realise is that she's lost all the sex appeal she had and he's lost the desire. When they get to the beach she starts coming onto him, flinging off her clothes. Jo, you and I know what blokes are like about their libido. They go in the sea for a midnight dip and she makes a grab for his popsicle. He panics, gets in a strop and pushes her under, simple as that.'

Looks were exchanged around the table. Gemma's 'simple as that' hadn't convinced everyone.

'Even if it happened like you say, she'd fight for her life, struggle like hell,' Rick said. 'You don't drown straight away.'

'And we know she must have fought because it said in the paper there were marks on her neck and shoulders where he held her down. All the time he's thinking how am I going to deal with this if I let go? He's attacked her, tried to murder her. If he stops now he's going to get done for attempted murder and God knows what. Better to let her drown. Then at least he has a fighting chance of getting away scot free. And he has. He pulled it off.'

'So far,' Jake said.

'You think they'll find him? They don't have any clues. It happened in the water, so the traces are minimal.'

'Now you're talking sense,' Rick said to Gemma. 'The fuzz have two ways of catching criminals. One is through informers. The other is DNA, and there ain't none.'

Jake wasn't so sure. 'Someone will have seen them together.'

'What, earlier, you mean?' Rick was still on his best behaviour. He had the grace to give it a moment's consideration. 'Maybe. And you think they'll come forward?'

'When her picture gets in the papers.'

'And on TV,' Jo said, to support Jake. 'I'm confident they'll catch up with him.'

'Personally,' Rick said, 'I hope not.'

'Why?' Jo said in disbelief. 'He's a killer.'

'One of us, in other words.'

'Rick, that's bullshit.' He'd just lost all the credit he'd been earning. 'Just because we had a light-hearted fantasy trip the other day about Gem's appalling boss you can't lump us in with a real-life murderer.'

'Can't I?' Rick said with a triumphant smile, as if she'd sprung the trap. 'Face it, we all had ancestors who killed to survive. It's in the genes, yours and mine and everyone else's, kiddo.'

'You're talking about cavemen?'

'Survivors. The ones who came out winners. Quit talking about killers as if they're another species. You may not care to admit it, but you'd take another person's life if you were driven to it.' He was in earnest now. This wasn't idle chat.

'I wouldn't,' Jo said, matching him for seriousness. 'Those ancestors you're talking about are prehistoric. Haven't you heard of civilization? Mankind has moved on. The great majority of us want a peaceful existence. Yes, there are horrible exceptions, but those who commit them are outcasts and should be treated as such. What do you say, Gem?'

'I say he's winding you up, sweetie.'

'I meant every word,' Rick said. 'Look in any playground and you'll see it in action, the little psychopaths bullying, stealing, lying, fighting. We call it antisocial behaviour as if it doesn't apply to the rest of us, but when he hits me my instinct is to hit him back, not walk away.'

'Rick, you made your point,' Gemma said. 'We're not going to steal your toys, okay? If you and me are going to Portsmouth, isn't it time we thought about leaving?'

* * *

AT HEN'S request, the crime scene investigator who had supervised the search on behalf of Hampshire CID was at Fiona's house. He was in a bandsman's uniform, blue with gold epaulettes and a gold stripe down his trousers. 'I'm a trombonist in the town band and we've got a concert tonight,' he explained.

'Good of you to come. I won't keep you long. I gather this job was dusted and done some days ago?' Hen said after introducing herself.

'The day after the body was found in the Mill Pond.'

'Did anything useful come out of it?'

'Nothing obvious,' he said. 'If there was a struggle it didn't take place in here.'

'What have you taken away for analysis? Plenty of prints, hairs, and fibres?'

'As many as we need. Some of her used clothing. I'll give you the list. We've left enough to keep you interested. The computer, address book, phonepad, camera, handbag.'

'Was she an organised person?'

'She was an accountant, wasn't she? The interior was cleaned regularly. Everything had its place. Even the boy's room is tidy.'

'Did you find out how long she's lived here?'

'Two years, I gather. The place is rented from a firm in Havant. Beautiful location. Probably cost her.'

'Her life,' Hen said.

'Well, yes.'

'Is there any sign she had a visitor before she was murdered? Cups, glasses, tinnies?'

He shook his head.

'No break-in?'

'Only where the plod forced the front door. They left plenty of traces, by the way. No help at all to my team.'

'Not my plod,' she said. 'Emsworth's. I'm from Chichester, where we flit through a scene like butterflies.'

'I'd pay good money to see that.'

In fifteen minutes, she and Gary had the place to themselves. The CSI's zinc dust was everywhere.

'Talk about leaving traces,' she said as they entered the living room. 'Are you any good with computers?'

'Reasonably,' Gary said.

'See what you can bring up. And I don't mean football results. I'll be poking around upstairs.'

The main bedroom said plenty about Fiona. A queen-size divan with pink chiffon draped in an inverted V above the bed head. Lace-edged pillows. Quilt in matching pink, with rosebud motif. Television, phone, radio, bowl of now-wrinkled white grapes. In the bedside drawer, a box of New Berry Fruits, two Danielle Steels, and a Rampant Rabbit vibrator. White laminate kidney-shaped dressing table with triple mirrors on which the SOCOs had excelled themselves. Enough La Prairie products for a month of makeovers, plus some perfumes Hen had never heard of. She was sure of one thing: not-from-your-local-supermarket was written all over them.

The clothes in the wardrobe had been chosen shrewdly for work and play. Several accountant-style suits, formal, sober and expensively lined. A dozen or so dresses that looked frolicsome even on hangers. There wasn't much Hen would have called neutral. The shoes and boots, too, stored in hanging fabric compartments, could be rated as hot and cold, with nothing lukewarm.

She understood what the crime scene chief had meant about tidiness. Everything folded and stacked like a new boutique before the first customers walked in. Easy to use, and easy to examine. Yet Hen had a premonition, soon confirmed, that nothing like a letter or a diary would be tucked under the contents. The knicker drawer was precisely that, twenty or more pairs, sorted by colour. If Fiona had any secrets they wouldn't be here.

She called downstairs to Gary, 'How goes it?'

'It doesn't, guv. You have to know the password to get in. Most people don't bother with one.'

'This lady would,' she said. 'Leave it, then. We'll get a computer geek to do the trick.'

'Want me upstairs?'

She smiled to herself. 'No. I'll be down in a mo.'

Time to take a look at the boy's room. To her credit, Fiona had decorated it with imagination, a ceiling of stars and a wall with spaceships zooming upwards. Another wall had Thomas the Tank Engine wallpaper, and the bed itself was shaped as an engine. There were toys in boxes and some books on a shelf. None of the disorder you expected from a small boy. Hen's guess was that, on the day the child went to stay with his father, Fiona had immediately tidied everything.

Downstairs again, she picked up the large brown leather handbag and emptied the contents onto the kitchen table. 'These look like filing cabinet keys. See if any fit the one in the corner,' she told Gary.

The purse had more than two hundred pounds in notes. She started checking the plastic.

'First one I tried,' Gary announced.

'Good—and are the files nicely labelled, as I would expect?'

'Alphabetical.'

'See what there is under C for car.' Meanwhile Hen was studying the driving licence—a first sight of the dead woman's picture. The red hair looked spectacular even under the laminate. A pale, solemn face, with neat features.

'There's a brochure for a Xsara Picasso,' Gary said.

'A brochure? Nothing else?'

'That's all there is, guv.'

'She had a licence. There must be some documentation. Look under R for registration.'

He wasn't long in announcing, 'Not here.'

At Hen's suggestion he tried C for Citröen, P for Picasso, and X for Xsara, all without success.

'Maybe she keeps all the docs in the car. Did you happen to notice if there was a Picasso in the road outside?' she asked. 'The house doesn't have a garage, so she'd be bound to park it on the street.'

'I didn't see one, guv.'

'Odd. Surely a woman like this would use a car for work. Check the vehicle index on the PNC, would you, Gary?'

Tucked among the credit cards was a photo of a small boy beside a sandcastle. He had red hair and gaps in his teeth. The smile rated high on the aaah-factor.

Gary soon had the information. 'Just as we thought, she owns a Picasso. Silver, two-thousand-six reg.'

'Owned,' Hen said. 'Why don't you take a short walk along the street and see if we missed it somehow?'

While he was outside, she listened to the answerphone. Someone called Gemma from work had called twice asking Fiona to get in touch and enquiring if she was all right. There were various cold calls. Nothing from the ex. Presumably he hadn't needed to call. He would have assumed all was well until he returned the son to the house.

Gary returned, and he had a he-man with him, a middle-aged skinhead with muscles and a confident manner. 'This is Mr Bell, from next door.'

'Francisco,' Mr Bell said with a defiant stare suggesting he wasn't wholly comfortable with the name. 'My old lady is Italian. She always said I could call myself Francis if I didn't like it, but I said that's a girl's name.'

'Frank?' Hen suggested.

'Then the kids at school call you Frankenstein. No thanks. I'll stick with what I was given.'

Gary said, 'I was asking Mr Bell about the victim's car.'

'Nice motor,' Francisco said. 'Two-thousand-six reg. She used to park it out front.'

'It isn't there now,' Hen said. 'We were wondering where it might be.'

'Can't help you.'

'She didn't rent a garage, I suppose?'

'No idea.'

'The keys aren't in the house and neither are the documents.'

'You think someone nicked it? Was that what she was killed for?'

'Too early to say,' Hen said. 'You're from next door, are you, Francisco? Were you here on the day she died?'

'Might have been. If you're asking if I saw anything, I didn't. I work as a security officer in Portsmouth most nights. Catch up on my sleep next day, so I miss a lot of what goes on.'

'You met Fiona, I expect?'

'A few times, yeah.'

'A good neighbour, was she?'

'I s'pose. There wasn't no trouble, if that's what you're asking.'

'Quiet, then?'

'Yeah.'

'Did you notice any visitors?'

'Her ex called once a week with the sprog.'

'Their child, you mean? Did you meet him, the ex-husband?' He shook his head. 'No reason to.'

'What about other callers? Anyone you noticed?'

'What do you think I am, some old git with nothing to do but stare out the window?'

'Perhaps you'd answer my question, Francisco.'

'I didn't see squat, okay?'

'No, it isn't okay,' Hen said. 'I've seen a report stating that you and a work colleague of Fiona's called in to report her missing and you were both outside the house when the patrol car turned up.'

He didn't even blink at that. 'So?'

'So you not only saw one of her callers, but you spoke to the woman and agreed to call nine-nine-nine. Don't tell me you didn't see squat when it's on record that you did.'

He shrugged. 'That babe woke me up, didn't she? I've never seen her, before or since. What's the big deal?'

'Fiona was murdered a few yards from your front door, that's the deal,' Hen said, increasingly impatient with him. His size and looks didn't intimidate her. 'Waste any more of my time and you'll get nicked.'

He held up both hands. 'All right, lady. Stay cool.'

'Do you have a key?'

'Come again.'

'Key—to this house?'

'No. Why should I?'

'Neighbours often do—neighbours who can be trusted.'

'That's below the belt.'

'You say you're a security man. Position of trust. You look like a bouncer to me. Is that what you do?'

'What's wrong with that? Look, I come here voluntary when your boy asked me. I don't have to listen to this.'

'Francisco, it looks as if someone stole Fiona's car. Not only that, but they came inside the house and took the registration certificate and all the documentation relating to the car. They didn't break in. They let themselves in with a key.'

'Got to be the killer, hasn't it?' he said. 'He dumps her in the Mill Pond and grabs her handbag and uses the key to let himself in here. Then he gets into the files, takes the paperwork for the car, and makes his getaway. He can flog the car later.'

'Sounds good,' Hen said, 'but there's a problem with it. If he leaves in her car, what did he do with his own?'

'Didn't have one.'

'How did he get here, then?'

'Dunno. Bus?'

'In all the time I've been investigating crime I've never heard of a killer arriving at the scene by bus.'

'He's local, then.'

'He still drove away in Fiona's Picasso. Where to?'

Francisco scratched his cropped head. 'You've got me there.'

'Not to worry,' Hen said with a smile that took Francisco by surprise. 'Our problem, not yours. That's where a homing device comes in useful.'

'A what?'

'A bug. You'd know all about them, being in security.'

'The car was bugged?'

'Apparently. You can get them on the internet, dinky little things you put out of sight under the dash or in the boot. Fiona must have been proud of that car.'

'How do you know she bugged it?'

'The leaflet is in the files under S for security. The pinpoint tracker. The signals are bounced off a satellite, I gather, and we can access them on her computer. Unfortunately, as Gary will tell you, there's a firewall device on the computer so we have to wait for a whizz-kid to help us.'

'So you don't know where the car is?'

'Tomorrow we will. Maybe later tonight. And of course when we find it we can test for traces of DNA. You can't drive a car without leaving some. Thanks for coming in, Francisco. If we need you again we know where to find you.'

'Right, yes.' He didn't sound enthusiastic. His thoughts were elsewhere.

'Gary will see you out.'

After the door was closed and Gary returned, he said, 'Is that true about the bug?'

'Francisco thinks it is.'

'You made it up?'

She nodded. 'Let's see what he does next.'

twelve

THE CRUSH IN THE Slug and Lettuce was getting too much, so they decided to look for a meal elsewhere. Jo asked Jake if he was vegetarian. He gave his slow smile and said, 'No. Does that surprise you?'

'I was thinking with you being so keen on, em . . . '

'Hugging trees?'

'I wasn't going to say that.'

'I know.'

'What I meant is that you respect living creatures.'

Jake nodded. 'But vegetables have a life, too.'

She wasn't certain if he was serious. The smile had gone.

They went for a Chinese meal in the Hornet and ordered mainly rice and vegetable dishes with some chicken. Using chopsticks, he helped her to some of each, saying this was the custom.

'Have you been to China, then?'

He shook his head. 'I had a Chinese cellmate.'

After some talk about their surroundings, Jo said, 'I'm glad the others didn't want us to spend all evening with them.'

'Me, too.'

'It's not that I dislike them. Just that in company Rick is . . . I don't know what the word is.'

'A gadfly?'

'You've got it. Makes me feel uncomfortable. What was that business about Gemma's boss, when she said he was history now and Rick said he was tomorrow's news, or something like that, and they laughed and went all secretive?'

'Rick went secretive,' Jake said. 'Gemma wanted to let us in on it.'

She recalled the moment now and Jake's memory was spot on. 'Right,' she said. 'Rick closed her down, as if you and I couldn't be trusted. It went from joking to deadly serious. What did he mean by "tomorrow's news"? They know something we don't. I'm sure of that.'

'Sounds as if they expect he'll be found dead.'

'That's what I took it to mean.' She thought about what she was agreeing with and changed it. 'No, it was stronger than that, as if they *know* he's dead.'

'Maybe they do.'

Surprised, she asked, 'How do you mean?'

'The police could have told them to say nothing.'

'Why would they do that?'

'The next of kin are told first.'

'That's what it was about, then.' But in truth she doubted if the police had anything to do with it.

HEN'S CAR was across the street from the Mill Pond, parked in Bridge Road. She and Gary sat waiting in the dark, passing the time listening to a local radio phone-in about policing and how it had changed, mostly for the worse.

Once Hen muttered, 'Give me strength.'

Another time: 'Who *are* these people?'

Finally, after a sharp, impatient breath. 'Any minute now one of them is going to say when he was a boy he was caught nicking apples and the local bobby clipped him round the head and it did him no harm and he's been a model citizen ever since.'

The caller wasn't the next, but the one after. The clip round the head was for letting off a firework in a bus, but the effect was just as long-lasting, about seventy years of blameless living.

Gary stared at Hen wide-eyed, as if she'd picked the Grand National winner. 'How did you know that was coming, guv?'

'It's a gift, Gary.'

'Really?'

'You could pick it up. Listen to enough old coots like that and you'll be as good as I am.' She switched to another station.

Tedious as the wait was, they remained on watch. Their position was ideal. There was only one route away from Fiona's house. Every vehicle had to come towards them and make a turn. They were perfectly placed to follow.

'You tell them good, guv,' Gary said.

'What are you on about now?'

'Porkies. The bug in the car. I believed every word.'

'Good. Let's hope Francisco did.'

'"S for Security" was a brilliant touch.'

'If I'm right,' Hen said, 'he's been into the house and seen inside that filing cabinet. He'll have nicked the registration document from there, so, yes, it ought to worry him.'

'D'you think he killed her, guv?'

'One step at a time, Gary.'

'Step one: he leads us to the car.'

'He could lead us to some nightclub where he's on the door.'

'Christ, I hope not.'

Forty minutes had gone by since they'd driven away from the house and parked here. No way could Francisco have eluded them. Hen thought it possible that up to an hour would pass before he made his move. Even if he was not wholly convinced by her story about the homing device in Fiona's car, it would prey on his mind.

'Do we know what he drives?' Gary asked.

'You saw the cars along there.'

'There were only two anywhere near the house, both of them old heaps really, a yellow 2CV Dolly and a beaten-up green Land Rover.'

'Somehow the Dolly doesn't sound right for a nightclub bouncer.'

A few spots of rain appeared on Hen's windscreen and when she used the wipers the whole thing smeared. She found a cloth and asked Gary to clean up. He was outside and wiping when some headlights approached from the Mill Pond.

'Get back in.'

He wouldn't be recognised in the dark, but they needed to move off sharply if necessary. He was quickly into his seat.

'Can you see what it is?'

'Looks like the Dolly.'

When it turned left they saw the driver. Unless Francisco had disguised himself in false boobs and a blonde wig, he still hadn't made his move.

'If he wanted to be sure of avoiding us,' Gary said twenty minutes later, 'he wouldn't use the car at all. He could walk right round the promenade and come out the other side. He'd reach the High Street that way and we'd never know.'

'And where would he go then?'

'Don't know, and we wouldn't find out.'

'Aren't you a tonic to be with?' She leaned forward. 'We're starting to mist up. Where's that cloth?' She cleaned the inside of the windscreen in time to see another set of headlights approaching. This looked more like the shape of a Land Rover. She started up and watched.

The vehicle waited for a gap in the traffic and swung right, in the Chichester direction. In the short time it was side on, two things became clear. This was a Land Rover and the driver had Francisco's cropped head.

Gary said, 'Go for it!'

Before Hen went for it she had to give way to two others, the second a rented van that blocked any view of the traffic ahead. Hers was a Honda Civic and she was quite attached it. She was also quite attached to her life. She edged to the middle to see if she might overtake. The lights of a steady stream of oncoming traffic showed ahead.

'Don't worry, boss,' Gary said. 'This way, he won't know we're following.'

'All I'm following is this bloody great van.'

'The road opens up later.'

They passed Southbourne and Nutbourne and still there was no break in the traffic. The road was dead straight, allowing no views of the cars ahead, no way of telling if Francisco was similarly hampered or had zoomed a long way ahead.

'I went to a funeral last year and something like this happened,' Gary said. 'The thing was, the service was at the church and after that we were all supposed to follow the hearse to the crematorium. We came to some traffic lights and got left behind and had no idea where to go after that. About thirty of us ended up at some pub. Whoa!'

The van had braked unexpectedly. Hen managed to stop in time, not without leaving some rubber on the road. 'What the hell is this about?'

'You know the Beefeater along here on the left?' Gary said. 'I reckon someone is stopping there.'

'You're wrong,' Hen said. 'Someone is going right and I think it's Francisco. What's down there?'

'Lanes mostly. Chidham, isn't it?'

The van moved off.

'That was a Land Rover for sure,' Hen said. 'I'm following.' She flicked the direction light lever. More cars were approaching. All she could do was wait to make the turn.

'No problem, boss,' Gary said to keep up Hen's spirits. 'We don't want to get too close to him.'

Men and cars, she thought. They get inside one and feel compelled to assert themselves. Even a rookie DC.

When the gap came and they got across, the lane seemed ominously quiet and looked deserted. 'He definitely turned down here,' Hen said. 'Chidham, you said? I don't know it.'

'You wouldn't unless you had a reason,' Gary said. 'We're on a peninsula really, with the sea to right and left. It could be a clever place to keep a stolen car. There's a church somewhere, and a pub called the Old House at Home.'

'No prize for guessing why you came down here.'

'It was lighter than this when I came. Not much to look at, though. A few houses and farm buildings.'

'Like barns, you mean?'

'I know what you're thinking, guv. Not easy finding them in the dark.'

Hen avoided using full beam. Progress had to be cautious and the lanes got more narrow the further south they went. Some sharp bends slowed them even more. At each bend, she half expected to see the Land Rover's tail-lights.

She didn't.

After yet another bend she said, 'I think we're going north again.'

'Probably are.'

They came to a fork. Hen was starting to lose heart. 'Now what?'

'My feeling is left,' Gary said.

More bends, sharp, right-angled. 'I can see lights,' Hen said, her foot on the brake. The road had widened and a car was at the side, on the left.

It was a black Mercedes.

'This is the pub I was telling you about,' Gary said. 'Do you want to check the cars?'

'We'd better.'

They stopped behind the Mercedes and got out. The check didn't take long. Nothing resembling a Land Rover was parked outside. Gary offered to speak to the landlord, but Hen wanted to get back in pursuit.

In a short time they saw the lights of cars crossing the way ahead. They were back to the A259, the main road they'd left.

'Should have taken that right fork,' Hen said. 'Hold on, I'm going to reverse.'

She backed about fifty metres, found a gateway to turn in, and drove back past the parked cars outside the pub. The fork came up and she took the sharp left along a wider, more promising stretch of lane.

'Are you watching both sides?' she asked. 'He could have taken it off the road and switched his lights off.'

'I've only got one pair of eyes, guv.'

She clicked her tongue, but he was right. It was impossible to see everything. She was doing fifty and it felt like eighty. She switched to full beam. 'That any better?'

'A lot.'

'But of course he'll see us coming now.'

They came to a T-junction.

'What now?'

'We're going round in circles,' Gary said. 'If you turn left you'll be heading for the main road again.'

They turned right and recognised the series of bends they'd originally taken.

'We've been right round,' Hen said. 'He's beaten us, the tosser.'

AFTER THE Chinese meal Jake insisted on walking Jo home, the perfect gent. She was sure he didn't expect to be invited in. Their friendship was progressing at an old-fashioned tempo. Wham-bam, thank you, ma'am wasn't this man's style. In a way, Jo approved, yet she was up for a relationship if and when he was.

They waited for a gap in the traffic at St Pancras and when the time came to cross, he took a light grip on her arm and guided her across. The contact encouraged her but he let go when they were on the other side. Fortunately he wasn't sure which way to turn, so she tucked her hand under his arm and said, 'It's up here and to the left.' She held on all the way up Alexandra Road to the house.

At the front gate, he signalled he was about to leave by saying it had been a nice evening.

Jo said, 'You've time for a coffee, haven't you?'

He took a step back and showed her his palms as if she was about to spring at him.

She stepped closer, took his arm again and steered him to the door. 'Live dangerously.'

He gave an uncertain grin.

In the flat she offered wine, but he said black coffee was what he wanted. She said, 'You don't have to worry about missing the last bus. I can easily drive you home when you want to leave.'

He said, 'That might be against my principles.'

'What—leaving a lady at the end of an evening?'

He started to say, 'I meant . . . ' and then stopped, outwitted. Instead of saying his piece about private cars and exhaust fumes he shook his head and laughed.

That was the moment she knew he would spend the night with her.

AT FIRST light, Hen was directing a search of the Chidham peninsula. Every building capable of concealing a car south of the

A259 was assigned to a group of officers. She was convinced Fiona's Picasso was still there somewhere. Last night Francisco had known he was being tailed. He wouldn't have risked moving it. He'd probably searched for the bug and found nothing, but that would only have added to his anxiety. He'd be afraid it was concealed somewhere he hadn't detected.

The task wasn't huge. The whole area amounted to about two square miles, and much of that was open ground. The populated part, containing the roads they'd driven along, was a section in the middle about half a mile across and a mile from north to south. 'He may not have used a building,' Gary pointed out. 'He could have hidden it out of sight down some farm track.'

'Do you think I haven't thought of that?' Hen said. She hadn't fitted in much sleep. 'We'll check the buildings first and then scour the rest of the place.'

Searches are heavy on manpower. Officers have to be diverted from other duties, but a murder enquiry takes priority over most things. Hen had promised everyone it wouldn't take long. In theory she was right, except that the consent of the owners had to be sought at each location, and nothing is quick when members of the public are involved. 'If the ACC should ask what this is about,' she told Stella, who was back at the ranch running things, 'you'd better tell him we're looking for a stolen Picasso. That should silence him.'

THE SAME morning, Jo stirred about six-thirty. In her drowsy state she became aware she wasn't wearing the XXL T-shirt she always slept in. From there her brain reminded her why. He'd been a marvellous lover, discovering what turned her on, treating her gently when she wanted it, and bringing them both to amazing climaxes. She'd felt appreciated, a giver and sharer of passion better than anything she'd ever experienced before.

But had it really happened? She had a worrying suspicion she was alone in the bed and she was scared to turn over and see if he was there. The potential for disappointment was huge. Could she feel the warmth of another body, or was it simply her own? She listened for breathing and couldn't hear any. Then there was a sound from the kitchen, the purring of the kettle. He was out there making coffee.

Modesty took over. She hopped out of bed and snatched some things from the drawer, got under the duvet again and pulled them on just before he entered with two mugs. He was fully dressed.

'I woke you,' he said. 'Sorry.'

'It's all right. I'm not used to getting coffee made for me.'

'You see, I know it's Sunday, but I have to get to work.'

'I'll drive you in.' Oops, she thought. That would be against his principles. 'If I had a bike, you could borrow it, but I don't.'

'I can get the bus.'

'If I drive you, we'll have time for breakfast. And don't you dare say you never eat it.' Oh, hell, she thought, that sounded awfully like nagging.

But cooking for him and driving him to Pagham were important, as if to demonstrate that last night hadn't just been about the sex. If she had remained in bed and let him go out of the door, the whole thing would have seemed like just another one night stand.

In the car he said, 'I'm not used to this.'

'Being driven?' Jo said, knowing he meant something else.

'Sleeping with someone.'

'It didn't show. I mean, it was . . . really special. I'm not promiscuous either, by the way.'

'Nice slogan for a T-shirt.'

'We should get two made. Ah, but imagine what Rick and Gemma would make of it. They'd never let it rest.'

'I expect they spent the night together.'

'I'm not sure. The last time I mentioned it to Gemma she said they hadn't. I think if they had, she'd be only too keen to crow about it.'

'Can't she keep a secret?'

'Gemma?' She laughed at the notion. 'Only when it amuses her to keep people dangling, like they did about her boss and what happened to him.'

'That's just talk,' he said. 'They don't know anything.'

He said this with such certainty that momentarily it crossed

Jo's mind that Jake knew the truth about Mr Cartwright's disappearance. But how could he? She dismissed the idea.

A SILVER Xsara Picasso was found shortly after midday in a field on the west side of the Chidham peninsula. A grey cover was over it. The plates and road fund licence had been removed, but no one had much doubt that it was Fiona's.

'I want this area taped off and nobody else touching the thing until forensics have been by,' Hen said. She'd been confident, but it was still a relief to have found the car.

The searchers who had made the find had folded back the cover from the bonnet to check the make and registration. It's a truism among crime scene investigators that everyone visiting a crime scene brings something to it and takes something away. Fortunately there was a good chance of recovering some DNA from the interior and perhaps from the cover as well.

She called the incident room and asked for Stella. Instead she got Sergeant Murphy. He reminded her that Stella was out at Apuldram searching Cartwright's house.

'Who else is with you?'

'It's Sunday morning, guv. We're down to three.'

She got on to Emsworth and asked for some of that crossborder co-operation. They agreed to send a car to the Millpond to arrest Francisco on suspicion of stealing a vehicle. They would deliver him to Chichester for questioning.

'What's my thinking here?' she asked Gary to see how he was shaping up as a member of CID.

'We let Francisco get the idea it's only the car theft we're interested in and catch him off guard?'

'You can do better than that.'

'We can get a sample of his DNA?'

'We'll do that, yes, but it isn't what I'm driving at.'

He scratched his head. 'I'm not at my sharpest today, guv. I got to bed quite late.'

'Blaming me, are you? Didn't you ever read PACE when you were in uniform? When you arrest someone for a serious offence you can enter and search his house without a warrant.'

'Oh, I knew that.'

'But you didn't say, did you? Get with it, Gary.'

Leaving two uniformed officers to remain with the car until the forensic unit turned up, she drove back to Chichester and had a canteen breakfast.

FRANCISCO WAS already slumped in a chair in Interview Room Two looking as if he needed an Alka Seltzer. Hen and Gary sat opposite. After the preliminaries were spoken, Hen said, 'You know what you're here for?'

'No.' He was trying to stare her out.

'It was explained to you when you were arrested. You're under suspicion of stealing a vehicle. Where did you go last evening?'

'Jongleurs.'

'Come again?'

Gary said, 'It's that nightclub in Portsmouth, guv, Gun Wharf Quay.'

'You're telling us you were in Portsmouth?' she asked Francisco, making clear her disbelief.

'My job, isn't it? Security.'

'We know about that. What hours do you work?'

'Eight till two-thirty.'

'You were never in Portsmouth at eight last night.'

He shrugged. 'I may have gone in later.'

'Cut the crap, Francisco. You were driving round the lanes of Chidham between nine and ten. We were following you.'

Trying to appear cool, he leaned back in the chair with his hands behind his neck. 'What for?'

'Let's spell it out, then. We found Fiona's car in the field at Chidham this morning. You led us there. Forensics are testing for traces of DNA and prints. When we compare them with the samples you've given and checked the tyreprints of your Land Rover, I fully expect to be charging you. I wouldn't try bluffing if I were you. Science has overtaken all that. Follow me now?'

'No.'

'Come on, Francisco. You stole her Xsara Picasso and left it under a cover in a field after removing the plates and licence.

You're her neighbour and she trusted you with a key to her house. You let yourself in and took away the paperwork, all evidence that she ever possessed the car. I'm sure your plan was to wait a few weeks and then get a respray and sell it on.'

'You're talking bollocks.'

She ignored that. 'When the tests results are in, we'll charge you. Then we move to the next stage, proving you murdered her by drowning.'

He sneered. 'Lady, you couldn't be more bloody wrong. Some other person killed her.'

'You had the motive,' Hen said. 'You wanted that car. You live at the scene of the crime, where the body was found. You're a professional, licensed bullyboy. No problem for a man of your strength drowning a woman. You thought it would be taken for an accident, but it wasn't. We found the marks on her neck. You're in deep shit, my friend.'

Francisco altered his posture, sitting forward, elbows on the table. At last he seemed to understand how serious this was. 'Look, I helped you guys. I called the police when that bird came knocking at my door.'

'You reported she was missing, yes, playing the part of the good neighbour. It's amazing how often the person who reports the crime turns out to be the perpetrator.'

He frowned.

'Killer,' Hen said.

'This is so wrong.'

Hen glanced towards Gary as if in two minds. 'Maybe we're getting ahead of ourselves.'

Gary shrugged. 'You said you'd spell it out, ma'am.'

'So I did.'

Gary was making up for earlier failings. He added, 'You believe in telling it like it is.'

'So right, but we'll take it in stages. Step one: We need to prove Francisco nicked the car.'

'Everything follows from that,' Gary said.

'Hang about,' Francisco said. 'Just because I took the car doesn't mean I killed Fiona.'

'You admit to the car theft?' Hen said, saw his reaction and said for the tape, 'The witness nods. We're getting somewhere, then. You took it why?'

'She didn't need it no more.'

'You decided it was up for grabs?'

'Something like that.'

'You thought no one would notice if her car disappeared? That takes some believing.'

He opened his hands as if he didn't care what they believed.

Hen said, 'All right. Let's run with that for a moment, unlikely as it seems. You took the paperwork for the car as well? You had the key and let yourself into the house and raided the filing cabinet?'

He gave an exaggerated yawn.

She spoke to Gary again. 'It does suggest he thought he'd get away with car theft.'

Gary had heard the cautious note and gave only a slight nod.

'On the other hand,' Hen went on, 'he may have wanted to throw suspicion on someone else for the murder of Fiona.'

'How would he do that?' Gary asked as Francisco looked from one to the other.

'Well, his first line of defence was that she drowned accidentally. But just in case that wasn't believed and we discovered she was murdered, he thought if he removed the car from the scene we would mistakenly assume her killer drove off in it, thus deflecting suspicion from himself, the man living next door.'

'Wicked,' Gary said.

'You say I killed her? No way.' Francisco flapped his hand as if swatting a fly.

'Somebody did,' Hen said. 'Did you fancy her, Francisco?'

'Per-lease.'

'You disliked her, then? A bad neighbour? Was she giving you trouble?'

'No.'

'It's easy to see how disputes arise. Loud music late at night getting on your nerves. Well, I guess it couldn't be that because you're used to loud music late at night. It's your job. You're not around most nights. Perhaps it was the reverse. She objected to you coming home in the small hours, banging doors and waking her up. She kept complaining. Drove you round the twist. Is that the truth of it?'

'Are you trying to say I'm mental?'

'Not at all. Angry. Violent. But for a reason.'

'Fuck off, will you?'

'We're about to,' Hen said smoothly. A delay would be useful. This had gone as far as it could for the present. If Francisco was the killer, there would be more to throw at him after his house was searched.

Hen stood. 'I'm keeping you under arrest. When we brought you in for questioning it was in connection with the theft of a vehicle. You're now under suspicion of murder.'

thirteen

'Do you reckon Francisco slept with Fiona?' Hen asked Gary.

Gary weighed the question for a moment before shaking his head.

'Or wanted to?'

He answered with a smile and a shrug that said he wasn't a mind-reader.

'They were on close terms,' Hen pointed out. 'Must have been if she gave him a key.'

'With respect, guv, that doesn't mean a lot these days. They were neighbours,' Gary said, making Hen feel about ninety.

'You see where I'm heading with this?' she said. 'I know he's not Mastermind, but he'd be an idiot to kill her for the bloody car. What other motive is there?'

'Maybe she kept a load of money lying around the house.'

'Maybe she didn't. She was an accountant. They keep it in interest-bearing accounts.'

'She had something on him, then?'

'Blackmail, you mean? I suppose he may have had secrets she got to know about. But he doesn't have a record. We checked.'

'All that means is that he's not been caught.'

'Okay, but I can't see Fiona as a blackmailer.'

'She knew how to get what she wanted.'

'You mean what we heard from the people who worked with her? Cosying up to the boss? Yes, they made her sound like the office whore. But she was up to something smarter, known to us women as maximising your assets.'

'This wasn't the office,' Gary said. 'This was the bloke next door.'

'How did it work, then?'

Gary hesitated. He was new in the job, but he already knew he'd better not look smarter than the boss. 'I'm guessing, but let's say he was into something dodgy.'

'Such as?'

'Nicking cars and doing them up. Fiona watches the comings and goings, follows him one day, finds out, and sees a way of turning a profit.'

'By threatening to tell all? She'd be taking a mega risk demanding money from a hard man like Francisco.'

'She did. We know the result,' he said.

'Not bad, Gary,' Hen said, 'not bad at all. I've only got one problem with it. We're investigating two drownings. If he killed Fiona because she was blackmailing him, how do we explain the killing of Meredith Sentinel?'

Gary actually looked relieved, like a driver who has wound down the window and been told he was speeding and had better improve his driving next time. 'You've got me there, guv.'

Hen said, 'It's back to the sexual motive.'

She'd lost Gary altogether now. He was frowning. 'I didn't think either woman was assaulted.'

'I'm not suggesting they were. It's more about what was going on in Francisco's mind.'

He still looked baffled.

'Picture the scene on the beach,' Hen went on. 'Meredith starts stripping off. They both do, I guess. Suppose Francisco's secret is that he's impotent.'

Gary blinked, disbelieving. 'A muscleman like that?'

'It's not so unusual. Agreed, he pumps iron and shaves his head and wears tattoos to suggest the opposite. He persuades himself that if he finds the right woman he'll turn into a full-blown stud. He's on a quest to find her. And each time it doesn't happen he goes into a red mist and kills them. It's not just that he blames them for his failure, it's that he can't bear them knowing. They have to die.'

'Wow.'

'But now you're going to tell me Fiona—unlike Meredith—

was fully dressed when she was found. Picture the situation. It's late at night outside her house beside the Mill Pond. The two of them have been for a drink, or just a walk. The classic dilemma. Just a goodnight peck or an invitation inside? She's confident with men. She gives him the come-on, kisses, some fumblings. He knows he's going to disappoint and he panics.'

Gary completed it for her. 'Pushes her over the edge and drowns her. Hell, yes.'

He was so impressed that Hen felt compelled to add, 'It's a possibility, no more.'

'How would we find out? He's never going to admit it.'

'We ambush him. But let's not leap ahead. If there's anything in this, he may have killed before. Has Sergeant Murphy finished checking all the drownings I asked him to?'

'He was still working on it this morning.'

'Tell him to snap it up.'

GEMMA PHONED about eleven and said she was going to the Island after lunch on a secret mission and why didn't Jo join her. She made it sound like another adventure for the Famous Five.

'Which island?'

'Which do you think, my innocent? Tasmania? Madagascar? The jolly old Isle of Wight, of course.'

Jo wasn't sure. The trip across the Solent was only ten minutes or so by hovercraft from Southsea, but you didn't take it unless you meant to stay some hours. The last thing she wanted was one of Gemma's interrogations about the night before, especially after what had happened. Even so, she was curious. Against her better judgement she heard herself saying, 'What are you wearing?'

'Smart casual.'

'It's not the beach, then?'

INSIDE THE hovercraft, when Gemma unzipped her white suede jacket it was clear she was dressed for an evening out, all spangle and cleavage.

'What's this, girls' night out?' Jo said, a little peeved. She was in a cashmere top and skinny jeans. 'You could have warned me.'

'You'll be fine.'

'So what's the occasion?'

'Today is my two hundredth birthday.'

'Oh, God, Gem, you're the bloody limit. I haven't got you a present or anything.'

'No probs. Buy me a drink instead.'

'A bottle of fizz?'

'I won't say no to that.'

'Is anyone else coming?' She was already wondering why Rick wasn't in the party.

'Only Brad Pitt and Hugh Grant.'

Be mysterious, then, she thought. 'Which one is mine? Can I put in a request for Liam Neeson?'

Gemma giggled. 'The tall, silent type. Yes, we know about you. How was last night, by the way?'

The question she'd been expecting. 'Okay. And yours?'

'Better than okay.' There was no doubt what Gemma's eyes were saying.

'I knew he wouldn't keep you waiting much longer.' This was going well, the emphasis on what Rick had been like.

'How do you know it wasn't me keeping him waiting?'

'Put it this way,' Jo said. 'You wouldn't look a gift horse in the mouth.'

Gemma gave a hearty laugh. 'A stud, darling, a rampant stud.'

'Attagirl.' The moment to steer the talk away from last night's intimacies. 'You did go to Jongleurs? Who was playing?'

'Some boy band just out of nappies. Very noisy. Rick seemed to think they were hot. His taste isn't the same as mine. I've never thought any band was hot since Duran Duran.'

Jo enjoyed this disclosure. 'You were one of the new romantics?'

'A fully paid up member of the tribe. Batwing jumpers, peroxide fringe. I could do it all again, no probs.'

'I wouldn't advise it.'

'How about you? Did you do the dressing up thing?'

'You bet I did.'

'Stop,' Gemma said. 'Let me guess. You were a goth. Dreadlocks and ripped fishnets.'

'Do you mind?'

'Tell me, then.'

'Studded belt, pixie boots, and lycra leggings.'

'God help us, Jo! Who were you following, dressed like that? '

'Depeche Mode. Still do on the quiet, but I don't wear the gear.'

They were silent for a while, indulging in nostalgia, and only jerked out of it when the hovercraft hit a larger wave.

'The sea's getting up,' Jo said. 'If it gets any worse we could be spending all night on the Island.'

'I know. The forecast isn't great, but sod it, this is my birthday.'

'I still can't believe you kept quiet about that for so long.'

'At my age you do, ducky.'

'Did you get any cards at all—apart from the one from the Queen, of course?'

'Aunt Jessica always sends. She's nearly eighty and lives in Singleton.'

'Where I work.'

'Is that where your garden centre is?' Gemma said. 'I never even knew one was there. Shows how much I care about gardening. My aunt's quite an expert, though. She's got a dinky little cottage garden like the cards she sends, all hollyhocks and roses. Funny old dear. Wears a hideous pink hat, indoors and outdoors.'

Jo smiled. 'I think I might know her, then. Would her name be Miss Peabody?'

'Sweet Jesus! You've met Aunt Jessica.'

'She's the bane of our lives. Comes in every day and points out the plants that are ailing.'

'Brilliant. That's my Aunt Jess. Small world, huh?'

'Don't you have any close family?'

Gemma shook her head. 'My parents died young and so did my kid brother Terry.'

'Sorry.'

'Don't be. I'm well-adjusted. Or, as they say in the office, a hard bitch.'

'No cards from your workmates, then?'

'I wouldn't want one from that bunch of tossers and they

wouldn't bother anyway. I'm too stuck-up for them. They've got their teeth into more meaty stuff, what with Fiona being murdered and the boss going AWOL. We've all been questioned.'

'What's going to happen to the business?'

'Don't know. All I can do is make sure we complete the current orders.'

'You're wishing Mr Cartwright was back?'

'He won't be.' She sounded definite.

'But if you lose your job over it?'

'I'm pinning my hopes on someone taking us over. There are plenty of print firms in the area.'

AT RYDE, they went for a drink in the first pub they reached. Jo asked if she should order the birthday champagne, but Gemma said later would be better. She was still being mysterious about what was to come.

Some men at another table started trying to get attention by spinning beer mats and shouting. They weren't bad-looking and they weren't teenagers either, but Gemma showed no interest. When one of the mats landed on the table she tossed it back without a glance at them, provoking hoots of derision.

'Let's go,' she said to Jo.

'It's a bit of fun, Gem.'

'We've got bigger fish to fry.'

Outside, Jo remembered another saying: Better a small fish than an empty dish. This didn't seem the time to mention it.

They went for a pizza.

'I may as well tell you. We're meeting Rick,' Gemma said.

Great, Jo thought. What am I doing here, playing gooseberry?

'Anyone else?'

'No. You're the two lucky campers I want to be with on my birthday.'

'That'll be nice,' she lied. 'Why didn't Rick come on the hovercraft with us?'

'Sally.'

She had to think. Sally was Rick's Sunday lunch date, that older woman he insisted on seeing. 'He's still at it?'

'Don't know what you mean by "at it,"' Gemma said. 'She cooks for him, that's all.'

If she really believed that, she'd believe anything.

'It's been going on for years. One of those arrangements you can't suddenly end without hurting feelings.'

'Have you met her?'

'Wouldn't want to. A right little Mary Poppins, by the sound of her.'

'So what time are we meeting Rick?'

Gemma looked her watch. 'About an hour. Make your margarita last. We don't want the embarrassment of getting there first.'

A SHORT taxi ride brought them to the secret venue, a spanking new nightclub on the seafront called Cliffs—and nothing to do with Sir Cliff, Gemma confided. Even so, the people who thronged the entrance didn't look right. They weren't straight out of school. They were grown-ups, more like first nighters in the West End than clubbers.

'First we find my prize stallion,' Gemma said, 'and I see him. Over there by the palm tree.'

'Can that be real?'

'The palm or Rick? They both look plastic to me.' Gemma shrieked at her own wit. She meant to enjoy her birthday.

Rick was in a new leather jacket and was carrying a gift bag that was obviously expensive chocs. He knew what the occasion was.

'Before we go in,' Gemma announced after they had all kissed, 'this is my treat, guys. I brought you here and I know what the tab is.'

It was a good thing she warned them, because it cost a ton a head to get in. No wonder the teenagers weren't there in force.

'Who's playing, Madonna?' Rick said to Jo while Gemma was keying in her PIN number. 'Did you see the ticket price?'

'Don't rock the boat,' Jo muttered. 'The birthday girl planned this.'

Inside, the smell of fresh paint competed with the perfumes worn by the clubbers. Complimentary cocktails were being handed out by gorgeous creatures wearing peacock feathers and little else. The heavy beat of retro rock music beckoned from across the carpeted foyer.

Jo noticed some of the new arrivals being taken aside to a sales area where hip clothes and shoes were on offer. It seemed there was a dress code for the men. Suits and chinos were out, designer drainpipes and T-shirts *de rigeur*. The girls were treated more indulgently. Gemma had been right about smart casual. The skinny jeans did nicely, and it was only right that the birthday girl had the party frock.

They collected drinks and moved inside, where a DJ was emoting about the acts in prospect, including a stand-up comic. Basically, the dance area was dark and huge, even the lighting upmarket compared to clubs Jo had seen before. A guitar band started playing and with a whoop of joy Gemma grabbed Rick and Jo and drew them into the fray. The tempo was just right for this early stage of the evening.

After two numbers Jo was ready to sit one out, except that seating was not a feature of Cliffs. Rick and Gemma joined her at the ledge where they had stowed their drinks. Bangers and mash and some kind of risotto were now being handed out by the peacocks, all included in the cover price. Rick took a large plateful, and the girls regretted the pizza they'd had.

'I didn't know this place existed,' Jo said.

'You like it?'

'Love it. For a special night out it's ideal. Wicked. Jongleurs will never seem the same.'

'Slick marketing,' Rick said in his man-about-town voice. 'People of our age are going to go for this, and we have the money to splash out—well, Gemma does. But have you noticed the sprinkling of under-twenties, all bright-eyed and beautiful? I wouldn't mind betting they're on complimentary tickets.'

'To glam up the ambience? You could be right.'

'I bet they're models on ten times our salary,' Gemma said.

'Or city traders earning millions,' Jo said.

'But we're not envious, are we?' Rick said. 'We're achievers, too. It's just that our talents aren't rewarded.'

'What talents are those?' Gemma said.

'Show you later.' He gave a sexy smirk and Jo felt like the hanger-on she'd not wanted to become. She was already thinking about strategies for leaving.

Out of Rick's hearing range, Gemma said, 'Promises, promises.'

Another band was playing. A heavier beat.

'Let's you and me strut our stuff and leave him to finish his nosh,' Gemma said, taking Jo's hand. 'Sally's Sunday lunch couldn't have been much, judging by the amount he's wolfing down.'

'If you two want to be alone I can slip away any time,' Jo offered.

'Don't you dare. We're a threesome. End of story—unless you get lucky with one of these millionaires.'

Jo laughed. 'Better exercise my hips, then.' She appreciated Gemma's friendship, and when the music stopped insisted on ordering the champagne she'd promised, in spite of Gemma warning her it would cost an arm and a leg in this place. She used her credit card and avoided looking at the tab.

They went back to Rick.

'Still struggling with that risotto?' Gemma said.

'Second helping.'

'You won't be fit for anything. Look, Jo's bought some fizz to help it go down. We're on a bender now.'

Jo filled the three glasses and said, 'Here's to the birthday girl. I think we should all make a wish. I'm going to wish Gemma not only keeps her job, but gets promoted to manager.'

Rick said, 'I'll drink to that.'

'No you won't,' Gemma said. 'Not before you've told us your wish.'

'All right.' He squeezed his eyes for inspiration. 'I wish to bring you guys here on my next birthday.'

'When's that?' Jo said.

'August.'

'Nearly a year away.'

'I need time to save up. What's your wish, Gem?'

She giggled a bit and gave Rick a look. 'I wish . . . I wish that we get away with it.'

'With what?' Jo said.

Rick's eyes had narrowed menacingly.

Gemma said to him, 'Are you going to tell her, or shall I?'

He gave an impatient sigh and looked away.

'It *is* my birthday.'

Rick said, 'This is between you and me.'

'How can it be? We all discussed it.' She turned to Jo. 'Rick's too modest. He did the business.'

'I don't know what you're on about,' Jo said.

'He did away with Denis Cartwright. Totalled him.'

'Your boss?' Jo felt the blood draining from her veins.

'But the beauty part is—go on, Rick, tell her what you did.'

He was silent.

'*Tell* her.'

With distinct reluctance, Rick said, 'This mustn't go any further. Cartwright is no more. Literally. After I'd bashed him I took the body to a paper mill in Kent. I know it because I once did a survey there. He went into the pulping mechanism. There's nothing left of him. No clues. Nothing.'

Gemma added, 'Which is why it was so comical in the Slug last night when Rick said he was tomorrow's news. Geddit? Mr Cartwright's in the paper.' She shook with laughter.

Jo didn't laugh. She'd just heard a confession of murder and she was appalled. She couldn't believe Gemma found it funny. A man was dead.

'As a matter of fact, he'd only just told me when you came along. Well, shortly before Jake arrived. He'd been holding out all this time. I wouldn't play poker with him if I were you. Lighten up, darling,' Gemma told her. 'Drink up and have a good laugh.'

'How can you say that?' Jo said. 'You must be out of your mind.'

Rick turned to Gemma and said, 'Didn't I warn you?'

Gemma said, 'Don't make an issue out of this, Jo.'

'Don't make an issue!' Jo hurled the words back as her shock found an outlet in anger. 'Have a good laugh? I don't think so!'

'You knew it was being talked about. You joined in. We're the Headhunters, the three of us and Jake.'

'Don't involve me in this,' Jo said. 'Or Jake. We were joking when we said those things. It was never serious.'

'It was for me, ducky. I had to put up with sodding Cartwright every day. You didn't even meet him, so you don't have to feel sorry for him.'

'Feel sorry! What I feel isn't important. This is cold-blooded murder, Gem. It's a crime, the worst of all crimes, taking some-one's life. I don't care who he was, you can't do that.'

'It's a bit bloody late to be saying so.'

'I'd have said the same thing when we first discussed it if I'd believed you had the slightest intention of carrying it out.'

'I was serious,' Rick said. 'Did anyone see me laughing at the time?'

Gemma took him by the arm and looked admiringly into his face. 'He said he could carry out the perfect murder, and now he's proved it.'

'Just as long as nobody shops us,' Rick said.

Jo was getting the shakes. She put her glass on the ledge. 'I can't stay and listen to you two. I'm leaving.'

'You want to ruin everything?' Gemma said, red-faced.

'It wasn't me who ruined it.'

Rick said, 'Keep this to yourself, Jo.'

She felt like spitting in his murderous face. Without another word she turned and walked off, out of the dance area, across the foyer, and towards the fresh air. She needed some.

Rick shouted after her, 'Remember what I said. Keep your bloody mouth shut.'

SHE RAN to the nearest taxi and got in. At this time of the evening the last hovercraft had left. The only way back to the mainland was by the ferry a couple of miles west of Ryde. That had always been their intended route home. The steamships sailed into the small hours.

Grateful that the driver wasn't the talkative sort, Jo huddled in the back, gripping her arms, and tried to get control of her thoughts. The way Gemma and Rick had spoken about the killing and disposal of Denis Cartwright—as if it was something to be proud of—was chilling. To be strictly truthful, it was Gemma who'd wanted to crow about the murder. She'd had to force the admission from Rick. Yet it was obvious from the way he'd spoken that he, too, thought of it as some sort of achievement, the so-called perfect murder.

They'd been expecting congratulations.

How do you get into a mindset like that? Horrible as it was to contemplate, the killing must have been kindled out of their relationship. Rick had done it to please Gemma. He *must* have. He had nothing personal against Mr Cartwright. Like Jo herself, Rick didn't know the man when they'd all talked in that ludicrous way about methods of disposing of him.

Gemma had said more than once that she hadn't yet slept with Rick. Had she offered sex as the reward for killing her boss? The thought was grotesque, but what else could have motivated Rick? Arrogant as he was, he hadn't stooped to murder just to prove a point.

Gemma was triumphant. That was why she'd found it impossible to keep the knowledge to the two of them. She wanted it known that this guy was so in thrall that he'd killed for her.

They couldn't call it a perfect murder any more.

'We're there, love.'

It was the driver breaking into her thoughts. She paid him and walked over to the ferry and bought her ticket. This would be the last crossing tonight, the man told her. The sea was "churning up a bit" and there was a storm coming in.

Rick and Gemma would be stuck on the Island for the night. Not a problem for those two, Jo thought. They'd share a bed somewhere and wallow in their cleverness.

She was so glad she'd left when she had.

fourteen

SOMETIMES A NIGHT IN custody softens up a suspect.

'Have you thought about what I was asking you last night?' Hen asked Francisco.

'Yes.'

'And?'

'And I'm saying sod all without a lawyer.'

Sometimes not.

The problem, as Hen well knew, was that he would say sod all *with* a lawyer. Trying not to show annoyance, she asked if he had one.

'Come on,' he said. 'I'm a good boy, ain't I? Never needed one till you came along.'

She sent Gary to fetch the list.

THE FALLOUT from Rick's confession of murder had troubled Jo all night long. 'Confession' wasn't the word; there was no contrition in it. He'd explained what he'd done in that spine-chilling matter-of-fact manner that left Jo in no doubt it was true.

What now? Her moral duty was to report him, but this wasn't so simple. Her dealings with the police over the body on Selsey beach had left her feeling more of a hindrance than a help. Without any evidence that Rick had killed Cartwright, it would be her word against Rick's and Gemma's. Those two would deny everything. That Chief Inspector Mallin already thought she was a time-waster.

And she couldn't forget the threat from Rick, shouted at her back when she quit the nightclub. Behind his tough words was a desperate man who regretted speaking out. She was at risk. If he decided she was going to shop him to the police, why shouldn't he kill again?

Bloody Gemma had engineered this. By pressing Rick to tell all, she'd made sure she was no longer the only one in on the secret. If Rick was tempted to silence her he'd need to silence Jo as well. So the threat was shared.

What a thicko I've been, she thought. I went out with Rick a few times, snogged, petted, and came horribly near to full sex with him, and failed to see the danger signals. He's always had an edge, the dark quality that is part of the attraction of the man. But I didn't believe in him as a killer, even after he revealed his interest in murder.

What drove him to do it? Rick had nothing personal against Cartwright. He hadn't met the man when he'd started talking about disposing of him. His motive was to impress Gemma. Had to be. Clearly there was a sexual element. Gem had confided more than once that she hadn't slept with him when they'd started going out. He'd listened to her stupid talk about killing the boss and taken it seriously. He knew the sure way to pull her.

As for Gemma, she gloried so much in the murder that she couldn't keep it to herself. The logic of her behaviour was that she had a share of the guilt. She was—what did they call it?—a conspirator. A latter-day Lady Macbeth. She hadn't struck the fatal blow, but she'd urged him on. She'd made killing Cartwright a test of Rick's passion and rewarded him with sex.

If Gemma's up to her eyes in this, Jo thought, then what about me? I was never serious. I wasn't involved. But I am now. I know about this crime and I'm not telling the police.

Before nine, her phone rang. She checked the number. Gemma. She didn't take the call.

FRANCISCO HAD looked down the list and picked a tricksy old solicitor called Woolf, who asked how long the custody clock had been ticking and said he would need time to get up with the case. Hen told him his new client had already admitted to stealing the dead woman's car. Woolf wasn't fazed. He said in that case he'd need to listen to the tapes of all the interviews so far.

Hen left him to it and said to Stella, 'You know what his game is? He'll keep this going until the twenty-four hours is up.'

'We can ask for an extension.'

'Not with the case we have so far. Nicking the victim's car isn't a serious arrestable offence.'

'And we haven't charged him yet.'

'We're investigating two murders, Stell. I'm not getting side-tracked over the bloody car.'

'You mean there isn't enough to detain him?'

'If we can prove the car theft is linked to the killings we might get somewhere.'

'Like he was disposing of the evidence?'

'That would be terrific, but it doesn't wash. It's not as if he used the car to move the body somewhere. She was drowned a few yards from her front door and his.'

'Suppose he murdered her for the car.'

Hen pulled a face. 'I don't think so. Do you?'

Stella shook her head. 'Not really.'

They returned to the incident room, now dominated by a pin-board featuring photos of the crime scenes.

'A couple of guys from Emsworth CID searched his house,' Hen told Stella. 'There was nothing obvious like a pair of jeans on a clothes rack.'

'I don't follow you.'

'Whoever killed Fiona was in the water with her.'

'But surely he'll have dumped his clothes if he's got half a brain.'

'I'm not sure he has. The longer this goes on, the more it looks to me as if he's nothing else but a failed car thief.'

'He'd have to be an idiot to steal a car belonging to a murder victim.'

'We haven't established when it was taken. It could have been during that time she was away from home and no one suspected she was dead.'

'That makes more sense. Then all hell breaks out because she's murdered and Francisco's got a problem he didn't expect—the victim's motor parked in a field with his fingerprints all over it.'

'He's got no form as a car thief.'

'First offence, maybe. Or he's always got away with it.' Stella looked away, at a pen she was rolling across her desk. 'Mind if I ask something?'

'Fire away.'

'I was told you have an ingenious theory that he's impotent and gets into a murderous rage each time he tries to have sex. Is that right?'

'Are you being sarky?'

'Not at all, boss. It's—well—ingenious. The best we've got.'

'I'll take that. And now you can tell me what's been going on while I've been wasting precious time on bloody Francisco. Did you search the missing manager's house at Apuldram?'

'Yesterday. Quite a nice pad.'

'What did you find there?'

'He's tidy to the point of obsession. No signs of disturbance whatsoever. It was almost eerie. His car's gone. The mail on the mat shows he's been away for over a week.'

'Which we know. Does he have a computer?'

'We took it away. It's being checked. We also picked up the letters and his filing cabinet. There's a photo of him we can use.'

'Neighbours?

'The house is on its own at the end of a lane. The locals don't seem to know him much.'

'You checked the outbuildings, I expect?'

'The patio, the garden shed, the pool. Just about everywhere.'

'Nothing exceptional, then?'

'His collection of bow ties. He has about fifty in his wardrobe, every colour you can think of, and spots, stripes, tartans, florals.'

'We need better than that, Stell.' Hen sighed. 'What would really make my day is a link to Meredith Sentinel.'

'Could be on the computer. If it's there, we'll find it,' Stella said.

'Yes, and find Cartwright himself while you're at it. No clues as to where he might have vanished to? Have we learned any more about the guy, apart from his job and the fact that he's divorced and lives alone?'

'I talked to his staff when the office reopened this morning. It's an open secret that he fancied Fiona. She was doing her best to advance her career.'

'By cosying up to him?'

'Seems so. His PA, Gemma Casey, wasn't thrilled about it. She was left running the business while Cartwright flirted with Fiona.'

'Is he unpopular with all the staff?'

'By no means. "Nice" is the word that keeps coming up. He knows them by name and smiles and opens doors for the ladies.'

'A right old smoothie.'

'I wasn't going to say it, but yes.'

Hen turned towards the visuals on the display board. 'That's two possible suspects, Francisco and Cartwright. I haven't ruled out the others.'

Stella's eyes widened. 'I thought we'd moved on from Dr Sentinel.'

'Well, deputy dear, early in this investigation you suggested he may have hired a hitman. Sounded wild at the time, but I'm not ruling it out.'

'To kill his wife, yes.' Stella was frowning now. 'But there's nothing to link him to Fiona's death, is there?'

'Well . . . ' Hen paused and raised her eyebrows.

'Well, what?'

'What if the hitman happened to be a bouncer called Francisco?'

Stella reddened in surprise. 'How is that possible?'

'Let's say the hitman was hired to kill Meredith Sentinel while her husband was out of the country. He did a fair but not faultless job of faking an accidental drowning. You and I know that Francisco's not the brightest. Maybe he boasts about it, or flashes his blood money around. His neighbour Fiona reads the papers, gets suspicious, and asks a few leading questions. He drowns her, too, and makes her car disappear to give the impression she's gone away.'

'Neat.'

'I wouldn't say so. It's a cock-up.'

'I meant your explanation.'

'Ah.' A quick smile crossed Hen's lips. 'Dr Sentinel returns and plays the distressed husband and is secretly incensed that so much has gone wrong, but he's still not in the frame. We need to know whether Sentinel had any dealings with Francisco.'

'You think Francisco will tell us?'

'If he's allowed to. If not, we may have to get it out of Sentinel himself.'

Stella liked the theory. She was persuaded. 'We've got to pursue this, guv. It explains both killings.'

'And yet,' Hen said, 'I keep coming back to the tree-hugger, Jake Kernow. He's the one with a record of violence. He has local knowledge. He was seen along the beach on the day Meredith was found. He's into fossils and so was she. He drank coffee with her at the museum in London. How much more do we need on this guy?'

'A link to the second drowning.'

'Don't I wish!' She sighed like the young Judy Garland on the road to Oz. 'He's quite a loner. How would he have met Fiona?'

'She visited Pagham Harbour?'

'Did she?' Hen's voice hit a higher register.

'That was a question. A suggestion.'

The disappointment showed.

Stella said, 'I was just thinking it's more likely she would find him than the other way round. She was the go-getter.'

'Agreed. But suppose his line of work gave him some reason to visit the print works.' She snapped her fingers. 'They have posters at nature reserves, don't they? Leaflets, maps, lists of the birds and mammals you're likely to spot. What if he needed some new ones printed?'

'He goes to Kleentext and meets her? It's not impossible, guv.'

'We can check with them. See if they've done any printing of that sort. I'll get Gary onto it. This has been useful, Stell. If only one of these suggestions bears fruit, we'll celebrate in style.'

GETTING THROUGH a day's work at the garden centre had been a minor miracle, Jo thought while driving home. She'd been on autopilot, her mind in ferment. Fortunately, her boss Adrian was like a headless chicken himself because last night's storm had damaged many of the outdoor plants and blown out several panels in the main greenhouse. 'What a wicked night!' he'd said when he first came in, and Jo in her jumpy state had thought he'd somehow got to hear of her trip to the Island.

Still, a low-level task like sweeping up broken glass was a help. She needed to get last night in proportion. Decisions made in anger are usually wrong.

She looked forward to getting home, a simple meal, a quiet hour or two, and an early night. The backlog of missed sleep had caught up with her. Adrian must have seen her yawning because he said she'd been such a help she could leave early.

THE SIGHT of a familiar yellow Smartcar outside the house was not the welcome home she wanted. She said, 'Sod you, Gemma!' and drove straight past. Another face-to-face with that woman would be too much. She drove around the block and drew in between two cars in a neighbouring road, switched off, and banged her head repeatedly against the steering wheel. Ten minutes passed before she told herself she couldn't stay there all night. But what else could she do? She wouldn't go crying on Jake's shoulder. He'd think what a wimp she was. And only an irredeemable wimp would spend the evening sitting in the car, or alone in some pub trying to make a club soda last for hours.

She'd have to tell Gemma to piss off home.

As it worked out, Gemma wasn't waiting on the doorstep when she drove up the second time. The Smartcar had got smart and gone.

Brilliant, she thought. She parked, locked the car, stepped up to the door, and let herself in.

'Here she is,' her neighbour Doreen said. 'I said to your friend you'd be home any minute. You're later than usual.' The old lady was standing in the hallway and Gemma beside her with a sly grin.

What could she do? Give Gemma the bum's rush she would have given her on the other side of the door? Not in front of sweet old Doreen in her frilly apron, smiling as if she'd just baked the perfect Victoria sponge, convinced she'd done the right thing in admitting Gemma.

'I'm not seeing anyone today.'

'Something wrong with the eyesight, then? This can't be put off, Jo dear,' Gemma said in a butter-wouldn't-melt voice meant more for Doreen than her. 'It won't take long and it's very important. I know you weren't expecting me because I've been trying to call you all day. Your mobile must need recharging, or something.'

Switched off to keep you off my back, Jo almost said. What she actually said was, 'I'm too tired.'

'Dear, oh dear,' Doreen said in her most sympathetic tone. 'Can I get you an aspirin, or something?'

'I'll be fine. I just refuse to see a visitor.' She made a move towards the stairs.

'But I don't count as a visitor, do I?' Gemma said. 'I was telling Doreen here, we're the closest of pals. Would you believe, Doreen, she was the only girl at my birthday treat yesterday? Tell you what, Jo, I'll come upstairs and make you a nice cup of tea.'

'No.'

'Don't be so hasty, dear,' Doreen said. 'It's a very kind suggestion. Nothing like a nice cup of tea.'

'Leave me alone,' Jo said to Gemma. 'I've nothing to say to you.'

'But I've something to say to you,' Gemma said, 'and it can't be put off. You really must listen, Jo.'

'You said it all last night. Go away.' She started up the stairs and put her key in the lock.

'We'll leave it like that, then, ' Gemma said, as calm as she'd ever sounded. 'If you don't want to hear it from me, I'll have that nice cup of tea with Doreen and put her in the picture. Then she can tell you later.'

Doreen said at once, 'What a splendid idea. Come in, dear, and I'll get the kettle on.'

Shit and derision. God only knew what Gemma would say to Doreen if she didn't get her way. 'All right,' Jo said, outwitted. 'I'll give you five minutes maximum.'

Gemma beamed at Doreen and followed Jo up the stairs.

'That was underhand,' Jo said as soon as the door was closed, 'taking advantage of an old lady—and of me.'

'Oh, yes?'

'I notice you moved your car to put me off my guard.'

'That isn't fair, Jo. I'm trying to mend fences here. We have to talk. We're friends, for God's sake. Can't leave it as we did last night.'

'So that's why you're here. You're so bloody obvious.'

'I know you wouldn't grass up your friends.'

'Don't count on it.'

But the tone of Jo's voice had given Gemma the reassurance she had come to hear. The relief was written all over her face. 'You obviously got back all right. Was it a rough crossing?'

'I didn't notice.'

'Yes, I could see you were shocked out of your skull, but when a death is involved there's no way of putting it gently. We thought you had a right to know, considering you were in on this from the beginning.'

'Hang about. Don't make me into an accessory,' Jo said. 'Murder was never seriously discussed that night in Chicago Rock, and you know it. What we talked about was just a joke in very bad taste.'

'Too right,' Gemma said. 'Pity Rick didn't cotton on that we were joking.'

'What are you saying now—that you weren't part of it?'

'I bear some responsibility; of course I do. I shouldn't have floated the idea of killing Mr Cartwright, even for a laugh. But we both under-estimated Rick. Jo, he's nuts.'

'You're changing your tune, aren't you?' Jo said. 'Last night you were calling him some sort of genius.'

'That's true. I had to act up. To be honest, he scares me. I don't know what he'd do if I told him I disapproved. Is that weak of me? I suppose it is. I'm worried sick.'

This was a turnaround, and Jo might have been impressed if Gemma had not been so two-faced. 'Report him yourself, then.'

Gemma gaped at the suggestion. 'Turn him in? I daren't. He'd report me. And you, too, I reckon.'

She was hell-bent on spreading the guilt.

'Haven't I made clear that this has nothing to do with me?' Jo said.

'To me, but not to Rick. You and I know we were joking. He doesn't. With his tunnel vision he's convinced he was acting on our suggestions.'

This, at least, had a spark of truth. Rick had never understood the humour in plotting Mr Cartwright's death. He took things literally. All he'd been able to contribute was the grisly story of the woman eaten by pigs. Jo recalled having to shut him up when he'd wanted to repeat it.

'You say he scares you, but you told me last night you'd slept with him.'

'I know.' Gemma shook her head. 'How dumb was that?'

'It's true, then?'

'It was only a shag, Jo.'

'But he'd just told you he was a murderer. How could you do it?'

'You had to be there.'

'No, thanks.'

'Really. I was, like, scared shitless when I realised what he was saying was true, that he'd topped Mr Cartwright. For real. I mean, it was the worst moment of my life. Terrifying. But then he goes, "I took the body to the paper mill and it's gone without trace." I was so relieved that I hugged him. Misery to joy in two seconds flat. Next thing we were ripping each other's clothes off.'

This Jo could believe. The best sex she'd ever had was to make up after a bitter argument. 'So you're hoping no one will ever find out. Haven't you thought that you're an obvious suspect, working for Mr Cartwright, and being treated unfairly?'

'There's no corpse,' Gemma said, folding her arms. 'Nobody can say for sure what happened to him.'

'That's no guarantee. There have been cases of people being convicted without a body turning up.'

A pause. 'You're trying to scare me now.'

'Gemma, I have no interest in scaring you. Why don't you get a grip on reality?'

'What, and run to the police? You haven't, so why should I?'

'That's your decision.'

'I won't shop Rick.'

'You still like him, don't you?'

She plucked at the lobe of her ear. 'He did all this for me, Jo.'

'All this? A cold-blooded killing?'

'He's not cold-blooded with me.'

Amazing, Jo thought, what some women are willing to over-look in men who play around with them. 'You don't know how dangerous this is. I'm telling you now, I don't want to be near him ever again.'

'Your choice.'

'Right—my choice, Gemma. And don't come running to me when your choice gets ugly with you.'

'You just don't get it, do you?' Gemma sighed, shrugged, and turned away as if she was hard done by.

But she'd got what she came for, Jo reckoned: the reassurance that nothing had been said to the police.

The birdbrain left without saying any more. To report to Rick, no doubt.

fifteen

'ARE WE ALL HERE now?' Hen asked. Every space was taken in the incident room for Tuesday's early-morning briefing, but she had a feeling someone was missing.

'Ready to go, guv,' Stella said without quite answering the question. She would always cover up for a colleague.

'Let's crack away, then. Most of you will know that the bouncer has been bounced out of here by his crafty solicitor. Am I bothered? No. We got enough out of Francisco to convince me he was a minor player. We'll do him for car theft later.' She paused, as if to draw a line under Francisco, then spoke in a slow, grave tone she rarely used. 'But the killer remains at liberty and I'm increasingly concerned that someone else is going to die. At our last meeting, somebody—I think it was you, Paddy'—she made brief eye contact with Sergeant Murphy—'suggested we might be dealing with a serial killer and I shot you down in flames because two similar murders doesn't amount to a series.'

Murphy—not normally reticent—had the sense to nod and say nothing. The boss was leading up to something.

Her voice sounded taut. 'Confession time. Paddy's words are starting to haunt me. I can't deny the risk that another drowning may happen, and it's our duty to prevent it. There's an intelligent brain behind these crimes, a cunning, cruel determination to dispose of the victims by a method almost unknown in serial killing. It's cunning because a drowning leaves few traces of the perpetrator. And cruel because it's a slow, agonizing death.' She paused, and there was an extraordinary stillness in the room as each of the team imagined being held under water, fighting for breath, swallowing, struggling, becoming weaker and knowing this was certain death.

'What's so unusual,' Hen continued, 'is that the murderer has to find ingenious ways of getting his victims into water. Meredith Sentinel appears to have gone into the sea by choice, or by invitation. Fiona Halliday was fully dressed, so she must have been forced into the Mill Pond, but the bruising was all related to the drowning.' She paused, then added almost as an afterthought, 'Or maybe he doesn't work like that at all. Pursuing this serial killing idea, the choice of victim may be unimportant. The killer may choose the place of execution and wait, spiderlike, for some hapless woman to come along.'

She took a moment for them to absorb the image. 'I hope and pray it isn't so random, because that will be hell to crack. I'm going to put even more pressure on you all to bring an end to this. I feel in my bones that we're on a countdown and someone else is due to suffer if we can't stop it.' She put her hands to her face and patted her cheeks as if to restore the upbeat persona she usually presented to the world. 'And so, Paddy . . . '

'Ma'am?' DS Murphy had a told-you-so expression.

'I asked you to check all the recent drownings in Sussex and Hampshire. What's the picture?'

His face changed. He hadn't expected to find himself centre stage. He cleared his throat, a sure indicator of loss of nerve. 'I went over five years of records as you asked.'

'And?'

'Thirty-seven drownings, almost all of them accidental and more than half young children.'

'Nothing homicidal?'

'There was that Portsmouth millionaire who drowned his lover in their private pool, but he's doing a life sentence for it. I looked at a couple of cases where open verdicts were returned, but no. In all honesty I couldn't find anything similar to our drownings.'

'A negative report, then?'

'I'm afraid so.'

'After this, how do you feel about your theory?'

Paddy blinked twice. This was like a slapped face after the earlier praise. 'I would have to say it looks less likely.'

'Unless the killer moved here recently.'

'From another county?' The sergeant's features registered relief, but that changed rapidly to panic as he viewed the prospect of checking the figures for the remaining fifty-three counties in England and Wales.

'Or from overseas. If you need civilian help, let me know.' Hen said. 'It's top priority. Meanwhile, we do the business on the suspects we have.' She looked to her left. 'Stella, you were checking the movements of Dr Sentinel—the husband, not the victim—and you got through to someone else at the St Petersburg hotel where he was staying. Update us on that.'

Stella had already told Hen what she'd discovered. This was for the benefit of everyone else. 'Yes, they eventually let me speak to someone from housekeeping, who admitted that after the first night of the conference Sentinel's bed wasn't slept in until the night before he came home.'

'Got him!' someone said from the back of the room.

'Let's not get carried away,' Hen said in a mild, but effective rebuke. 'In theory, he could have got back here and carried out the murder—a scenario we considered before. But Stella also checked every airline passenger list and nobody of his name appears.'

'False passport?' Murphy suggested.

'Possible, but unlikely unless he was into some other racket. Professional criminals know how to acquire false passports. I doubt if an academic wanting to murder his wife would have the contacts.'

'So what was he up to, if he wasn't flying home?' Murphy said.

'Sightseeing,' said Larry Soames, a laid-back DC known for rubbishing everything he deemed farfetched.

'We'll ask him,' Hen said, echoing Larry's throwaway tone. 'He'll be coming to Chichester for the inquest and I've got to be there, too. When's that, Stell?'

'This afternoon.'

'Is it?' Her manner changed. 'God, is it Tuesday already?'

'It's sure to be adjourned.'

'Of course, but it's an opportunity.' She glanced down to see if she was wearing something suitable for the courtroom. Her grey trouser suit would have been better. Maybe she'd slip home at lunchtime. Needing to get her thoughts back on track, she turned towards the display board. 'We have a picture here of the missing man who is also firmly in the frame. Cartwright, the employer of the second victim, Fiona Halliday. He was seen leaving the print works with her on the Friday afternoon and that was the last sighting of either of them alive. Is he another victim, or could he be the killer? Stella, you searched his house in Apuldram.'

'Me, and a CSI team,' Stella said, addressing the team rather than Hen. This process of keeping everyone in the loop was vital. 'It was all in good order. No signs of violence. He's a tidy guy. Even washes up his breakfast things before leaving the house.'

'How do you know it was breakfast?'

'I just assumed he didn't go back to the house after the Friday because of all the mail on the mat.'

'Okay. We're getting nowhere fast. Anything else on Cartwright?'

'They looked especially for traces of Fiona's DNA.'

'Where—in the bed?'

'There, yes, and the sitting room downstairs. The results aren't back yet, of course. For what it's worth, I didn't see anything to suggest he'd had a woman there recently.'

'It's in Apuldram. Do I know the place? I don't think I do.'

'South of Chichester, between the Witterings Road and the harbour. You must have been to the pub at Dell Quay.'

'I have,' Hen said, 'but you don't have to put it as if I'm familiar with every watering hole in the county.'

'Well, Dell Quay is Apuldram,' Stella said.

'Is he a boating type?'

Stella's eyes widened. 'He could be. His bedside reading was some kind of sea story. And some of his clothes are from the chandler's shop at the marina. But they're the kinds of things anyone would wear in cold weather.'

'Better look into it, hadn't we? He could have murdered Fiona and sailed off into the sunset.'

'We didn't find anything really obvious like maritime maps.'

'He'll have taken them with him,' Larry Soames said. He'd never been comfortable serving under this all-woman management, and he saw it as his mission to provide the practicalities only a man would think of.

Hen nodded and glanced Stella's way. 'See if he has a mooring at Apuldram or the marina.'

'Or Emsworth,' Larry Soames chipped in.

'Good thinking, Larry. Your job.'

'Ah.' He'd overdone it this time.

At this point the door handle squeaked. All eyes watched it turn slowly, as if to cause minimal disruption.

'Don't be shy,' Hen called out.

DC Gary Pearce put his youthful face around the door, crimson with embarrassment.

'I had a feeling someone was missing,' Hen said. 'Come in, laddie. What was it—your grandmother's funeral?'

'No, guv. I've been at Fishbourne. You asked me to visit Kleentext, the printers, to ask if they did any work for the nature reserve.'

'So I did. What's the story?'

'I got there too late last night. The office staff had all gone, so I called on my way to work this morning. I thought I'd still make the meeting, but it took longer than I expected. I'm sorry.'

'And did you discover anything to mollify me?'

'To what, guv?'

'To calm the old bat down.'

'Possibly I did. I saw the woman in charge, Miss Gemma Casey. She said all the official Pagham Harbour literature, the maps and guides and things, is done through the County Council and another printer has the contract.'

'Oh, bugger.'

'But she thought Kleentext had done something recently for the nature reserve as a small job, so she printed off a list of clients. I have it here.' Gary was learning quickly how to humour the boss.

'And?'

'Pagham Harbour reserve is on the list. Five hundred Christmas cards.'

'The best news I've had in days. Hand it across.' Hen was given the list and spoke as she was scanning it. 'And did this order involve a visit from one of the wardens?'

'Four altogether.'

'Wardens?'

'No, visits, around the end of August,' Gary said. 'One to make the first enquiry, another to place the order, then returning the proofs and collecting the cards after they were finished.'

'Four visits seems excessive. Things like that are usually put on a van, aren't they?'

'That's what I thought, guv.'

'Did you ask if Fiona dealt with it? I wonder if she was the attraction.'

'I didn't have time. I left with the list and checked it in the car. Then I came straight here for the meeting.'

'So you didn't ask which warden placed the order and kept coming back? No names are listed here.'

'No, guv.'

'I wouldn't mind betting who it was. Nice work, Gary.'

'Have I missed much?'

'Forget it,' Hen said. 'You're my hero. A superstar.' She turned to Stella. 'This gets priority. You and I are shortly off to Kleentext. Meeting over, boys and girls.'

ANOTHER NIGHT without much sleep had left Jo in a frazzled state. She'd already called Adrian at the garden centre to tell him she wasn't coming in. She'd make up time at the weekend. Now that the storm damage was cleared up there wasn't a lot to be done. Sales of horticulture products tail off as winter approaches.

She was still troubled about not reporting Rick to the police. One line of thought argued that he'd committed the worst of all crimes and should be handed over to the law; another, that he was not an obvious danger to the public. If she'd thought other people were at risk she would certainly have done her public duty. But the killing of Mr Cartwright was a one-off crime. She couldn't imagine Rick murdering anyone else. He'd done this to find favour with Gemma—and Gem was too alarmed by it to encourage a repeat.

In an ideal world the police would investigate and solve the crime without any tip-off. Before long Cartwright's disappearance was going to be taken seriously. But in the absence of a body would they ever find out he was murdered?

All of this churned repeatedly in her head. She'd come round to thinking after all she would confide in Jake. He sure wouldn't blurt it about. What was more, he knew the people involved. And he was mentally strong. He'd come through his own hell and was wiser for it. He was the only person she would trust.

And it would be so good to see him.

She got in the car and drove out to the nature reserve. The sharp morning, the clear October sky, and the task of steering the car through the turns of the narrow road gave her a sense that she was doing something positive instead of keeping it all inside. Just being with Jake would lift her.

She hadn't phoned ahead. Far better to turn up and find him. Phoning would call for an explanation and she didn't know how to start telling him all that had happened in the past forty-eight hours.

Pagham Harbour is a southeast facing inlet about a mile across, between Selsey to the south and Bognor to the north. The reserve measures over 1,400 acres, about half of which is water. The shoreline is probably six miles around, with tidal creeks fringed by mudflats and salt marshes, so spotting someone isn't straightforward, even though most of the protected area doesn't extend far beyond the footpath. She thought when she parked by the visitors' centre off the Selsey Road that she should have brought binoculars. She had some at home.

At this time of day no one was around. The centre is staffed only at the weekends. Hers was the only car, not a promising sign. Then she remembered Jake cycled to work from Selsey. But where did he leave the bike? Not here, apparently. She started wavering over her decision not to phone. I didn't even get that right, she thought.

Now that she was here, she had to track him down. Having

circled the buildings and found nothing, she got back in the car, consulted the map, and drove south to approach the reserve by Church Norton, which would be the nearest she'd get by car to the harbour entrance. From there she'd get a view of the shoreline.

She soon located a small car park that also catered to visitors to St Wilfrid's Chapel, a Norman chancel, and a mound where a castle had once stood. You'd think with all those attractions there would be somebody to ask.

Disappointment again. The whole area was deserted. Stepping out along the footpath she passed some pools where wading birds foraged. Plenty of avian life and not a single human being. She could understand why the job appealed to Jake, with his need for open spaces.

The footpath brought her to the start of the bank of shingle that fronted the sea and lifted her spirits. Various plants had managed to flourish here, and she remembered Jake mentioning the shingle plants when he'd come to the garden centre. She wasn't familiar with the names, but the sea-kale, looking like cabbage, was obvious.

Was it too much to hope that he was at work here with the labels he'd bought from her? She couldn't yet see over the ridge. She used the wooden walkway Jake or his employers had provided. It made for easier progress as well as protecting the plants.

Disappointment awaited at the high point. He wasn't anywhere in sight.

She tried to console herself with the broad band of the sea, glittering silver this morning. If nothing else, she was nourishing her mind with some glorious images. The worries of last night were already fading.

Then as she stepped along the shingle spit that was the southern bastion of Pagham Harbour, she turned and saw a movement, distant but unmistakable, a small boat no bigger than a dinghy chugging between the mudflats. She swore at herself for not bringing those binoculars. She could just about make out the single figure steering a course towards the place she'd first called at, where the visitors' centre was. Could this be Jake? He hadn't mentioned using a boat in his work, but then they hadn't talked much about what he did.

Whoever this boatman was, if he came ashore he'd be worth speaking to. He might know where Jake could be found.

She was certain she was visible against the skyline. She waved several times and got no response, so she slid and leapt down the inner bank where the shingle was finer, but just as steep, trying to keep her footing without damaging the plants.

The boat seemed to have turned and was heading in her direction. She could see now that it was an inflatable. And she had a better view of the man.

Her pulse beat faster.

He was wearing a jacket with the hood up.

She completed her dash to the water's edge and waved again with both arms. He put his hand to his eyes and stared back. She felt sure he was Jake. He was big enough.

Wouldn't *anyone* wave back? This man didn't. Her confidence dipped. Was she still visible down here at the water's edge?

She waved again with huge movements as if hailing an aircraft.

Finally he raised a hand in salute like an Indian brave. The hood fell back from his head and she was certain.

'Jake!'

He steered the inflatable in, stopped it in the shallows, turned off the outboard, jumped out, and hugged her. 'Surprise.'

'For me, too,' she said. 'I didn't know you used a boat.'

'We patrol the harbour,' he said. 'There was a grebe that seemed to be in trouble, but it flew off.'

'I thought I wasn't going to find you. I'm supposed to be at work, but I took the day off.'

'Problems?'

'Yes. What's that?' She'd heard voices from somewhere behind. She'd thought the place was deserted. 'Oh, blast. What timing.'

'Visitors, I expect,' he said.

'They may want to ask you things.'

'My job.' He looked in that direction, came to a decision and gripped her arm. 'Okay. In the boat.'

She wasn't dressed for wading through water so she stooped to take off her shoes, but he said, 'Don't bother.' He picked her up easily and carried her. 'Lightweight.'

'You said it. I can't even make decisions.' But her face was close to his and she felt the warmth from him.

He let her down gently on the centre seat, then turned the little craft, stepped in, sat by the outboard, and started the motor. The people still weren't in sight. They'd have to manage without a warden.

Out in the deeper water there was nothing you could call a wave. Only ripples. Well out from the shore he switched off the motor for easier conversation.

'What's up, then?'

She told him everything, reminding him of the ill-fated banter with Gemma and Rick about murdering the boss, and then repeating what those two had admitted in the nightclub, and Gemma's none-too-subtle reining back when she came visiting the next evening.

Jake listened without any change of expression. Finally, when she'd done, he said, 'Obviously you believe him.'

'Believe Rick? Yes, I do, and so does Gemma.'

'Gemma would.'

She heard the remark without fully taking it in. 'Why? What do you mean?'

'She has a stake in this.'

'I don't follow you.'

'She wants the murder to be true. Shows he's nuts about her.'

This was almost telepathic. 'That's the word she used. She said he's nuts.'

'Look at it the other way round,' he said. 'Suppose Rick is lying.'

'She'd go ballistic. He'd have conned her into sleeping with him. She'd hate that.'

'So she believes him because she wants to.'

She understood.

He said, 'You have to make your own judgement. Think about what Rick said, not Gemma.'

'Rick didn't say much at all.'

'But he's the one who knows.'

'You're right. Gemma's only got his words to go on.' She cast her thoughts back. 'Gemma had to drag them from him. He didn't want me to know.'

'And that made it more believable?'

'I'm sure it did. But he was very clear. You couldn't take his words to mean anything else. He said he took the body to a paper mill in Kent and pulped it.'

He nodded. 'Rick's a serious guy. Now see it from his point of view, supposing he made it up about the murder.'

'Just to get her to sleep with him?' She thought about that. Up to now she'd relied heavily on Gemma's account.

'If he felt she was losing interest,' said Jake.

'She *was*,' Jo said, remembering. 'She'd been going on and on to me about Francisco. She even said to me that Rick wouldn't stand a chance if Francisco asked her out.' She thought again. 'But she wouldn't have told Rick.'

'He'd pick it up.'

'You think so?'

'Men do.'

'I suppose he might.' She could see a persuasive cause and effect in what Jake was suggesting with his terse interpretation of the nightmare. 'If he'd made it up about killing Cartwright just to get back in Gem's favour, he wouldn't deny it after she'd slept with him. He'd hope it would be a secret between them.'

'But Gemma can't keep secrets.'

'Right. She insists that Rick confesses to me.'

'So he's forced to repeat the lie.'

Her brain was fizzing with this new possibility, one she wouldn't have considered without Jake's prompting. Like the horrors of childhood, the fear drained away when it was explained.

'I've spent time with men who killed,' he said. 'There's something about them Rick doesn't have.'

'But Mr Cartwright is still missing.'

'He may be dead.' He looked away at a seabird skimming the water. 'Doesn't mean you have to believe Rick. Or Gemma.'

* * *

HEN ALLOWED Gary to drive her to Kleentext, seeing that he was known there. He'd spoken to Gemma Casey, the woman who was running the office while the boss was missing. Hen remembered her as an open talker, freely admitting she'd resented Fiona's too obvious overtures to Cartwright, the manager. Today she was still in her outer office, and looking under strain. No surprise, considering she was just a PA who found herself trying to run a business.

'If you're wondering why we're back so soon,' Hen said, 'you supplied one of my officers with this list of recent clients. I notice you printed some cards for the nature reserve at Pagham.'

'That's right. Geese on the ice. Nice for Christmas.'

'A goose on the plate is better.'

'My thought exactly,' Gemma said, 'but I wouldn't mention it to the client.'

'Who was the client?'

'You said already—the Pagham Harbour people.'

'Yes, but who came here and placed the order?'

'A man called Jake Kernow.'

Hen could gladly have goose-stepped around the room. 'And would he have met Fiona Halliday when he came here?'

Gemma tapped her chin. 'It's possible. I took the order, but Fiona was always hovering around this office.'

'To be noticed by the boss?'

She smiled. 'You have it. She was supposed be in accounts, but she spent more time swanning in and out of here than checking invoices.'

'But you can't say for certain if she and Mr Kernow met on one of his visits?'

'I didn't actually see them together.'

'Was he alone here at any stage?'

'More than once I had to go downstairs and fetch some samples of card or proofs. I made him a coffee and left him for five or ten minutes.'

'In that time he could have met Fiona?'

'I don't see why not.'

'I was told he made four visits here.'

'That's what I recall.'

'Seems a lot.'

Gemma reddened. 'To be perfectly honest, I think he fancied me. Well, I know he did, because we went bowling together.'

'You went out with him?'

'Just the once. I felt sorry for him. He gets a bit tongue-tied, doesn't know what to say to a girl.'

'But he succeeded with you?'

'Depends what you mean by "succeeded," she said with a smile. 'We bowled a few ends. It didn't last. I managed to unload him onto a friend.'

'Not Fiona?'

'Christ, no. I don't like speaking ill of the departed, but she was never a friend. One of my yoga chums.'

'You say you felt sorry for him. It sounds as if he does rather well with girls.'

'Now that you mention it. He's not much of a looker, but he appeals to the caring, maternal thing. Not for long, in my case.'

'Why? Did you have a bad experience with him?'

'Nothing like that. I got bored, that's all.' She held up her forefinger. 'I've just had a thought. When he kept coming back here on any pretext—like insisting on bringing the proof to me in person when he could easily have put it in the post or left it at reception—I took it that he wanted to go out with me. Maybe he was trying to get a date with Fiona.'

'She didn't mention going out with him?'

'She wouldn't. Not to me.'

'Is there anyone else she worked with who might know?'

'Can't think of anybody. She wasn't one to have close friends.'

'But she got on with Mr Cartwright?'

'Huh!' It still rankled evidently. 'She'd be with him behind that door and I'd be told they were not to be interrupted.'

'You think they were having sex?'

She glanced towards Gary. 'Close your ears, Sunny Jim. This is girl talk. I saw the smirk when she came out. She was practically rubbing her hands.'

'You've worked here for how long?' Hen asked.

'Twelve years.'

'And Fiona?'

'Less than two. At first I was sorry for her, a lone parent, young kid to bring up. We got quite friendly. I've had it tough, too, but not in the way she had. She was telling me Mr Cartwright was coming onto her and she didn't know how to give him the old heave-ho. I believed her. Then she started appearing in these ridiculous low-cut dresses and I sussed her out. She'd been trying to pull him from the word go, and wanted to find out if I was a threat.'

'Weren't you?'

She frowned. 'I don't confuse business with pleasure. Besides, he's not my type.'

'So what do you think happened to him?'

'He hasn't absconded with the funds, I'm glad to say. He left here with Fiona looking as if they were off for a quickie, or maybe even the whole weekend. I was really surprised when she was found in the Mill Pond. He's a waste of space and a pain to work for, but in my wildest dreams I've never thought of him as a killer. It says in the papers she was murdered. Are you sure it wasn't some kind of accident?'

'There's no doubt about it,' Hen said. 'She was held down in the water.'

'Horrible.'

'We can agree on that.' She turned to Gary. 'Feel like a trip to the nature reserve?'

JAKE SEEMED in no hurry to return to dry land. He told Jo the harbour had once been so deep that it was navigable by Tudor galleons all the way up to Sidlesham. Centuries of silting had encouraged Victorian landowners to block off the narrow entrance and reclaim hundreds of acres for farming, and they managed it for about forty years, but a great storm in 1910 broke through the defences. 'What the sea wants, it gets,' he said. The nature reserve had been created and now the land grabbers had to look elsewhere.

Here in his own workplace, he had no difficulty stringing

sentences together. He pointed to a formation of birds flying overhead and talked with relish of the latest arrivals, a flock of curlews driven south by the onset of the Arctic winter. 'We see them best at low tide, digging for the lugworm and gilly-crab. Right now the tide's in, so they're resting up. The wildfowl at this time of year are marvellous. Godwits, redshank. We're blessed.'

She knew he was taking her mind off the gruesome stuff she'd grappled with all night, and she was thankful. The panorama from out here in the middle helped get her thoughts in proportion again. He could be right about Rick making it all up to impress Gemma.

A large, dark bird swooped and splashed into the sea close to them. 'What's that one?' she asked.

'Isle of Wight parson.'

'Get away.'

'Cormorant. You have to see him perched on the cliff, like a reverend in his pulpit.' He watched her with such intensity that she became uncomfortable. 'You're very trusting.'

'Why do you say that?'

'Obvious.'

She frowned. 'Not to me.'

'The drownings. I'm the main suspect.'

'That's pants, Jake.'

'The police don't think so.' He gave her another long look with his brown eyes. 'You're taking a risk in a boat with me.'

She tried laughing it off, but he was obviously serious. 'Bit late to warn me, isn't it?'

'Aren't you even slightly worried?'

She dipped her hand in the sea and splashed him. 'Quit teasing me, or I might jump over the side.'

'I meant what I said just now. They're out to get me.'

'Who, the screaming heebie-jeebies?'

'The police.'

She couldn't continue treating it lightly. 'I don't think so, Jake. I understand how you feel after all you've been through, but they'd need proper evidence. They can't charge you just because of something in your past.'

'I met Meredith more than once in London at the museum,' he said, refusing to be persuaded. 'She was a fossil expert. I met the other woman, too. They don't know about that.'

She realised that the roles had switched. He needed reassurance from her. 'That's pure chance, isn't it? Just meeting them is hardly enough to convict you of killing them.'

'I wish . . . ' he began.

'Go on.'

' . . . I hadn't met them.'

'Put it all behind you, Jake. You're a good man. You're innocent.'

He gave a nod. 'Are you getting cold?'

'I'm fine.'

'Want to steer?'

'I'm not much of a sailor.'

'Come and sit beside me.' A sailor's chat-up line. She was amused. He made room and helped her move. He pulled the starter rope and the engine spluttered into life. 'Now try.'

It was easy to steer without getting splashed in this placid sea. She took the inflatable in several directions. 'I'm keeping you from your duties.'

'You're not.'

A faint sound began chiming in with the engine note. Not a natural sound.

'D'you mind?' He switched off the engine. 'My mobile.' He delved into an inner pocket and put the phone to his ear.

Jo didn't say so, but wondered if Jake's boss had spotted him out here in the Conservancy boat with a woman aboard.

His expression wasn't relaxed any more. He went back to monosyllabic mode. 'Yes . . . Ah . . . Right . . . Thanks.' He pocketed the mobile again and there was desperation, if not panic, in his eyes.

'What is it?' Jo asked.

'That was Gemma.'

'Gem? What did she want?'

'She's had the police there, at the printworks. They found out I met Fiona and now they're coming here. They'll arrest me again.'

sixteen

'This time we've got him,' Gary said in the car on the way to Pagham.

Hen gave him a look. 'There's an old saying, Gary. Don't sell the skin till you've caught the bear.'

'New to me.'

'I dare say. But worth remembering.'

'Like don't count your chickens?'

'This one is more bear than chicken.'

She'd visited this part of the coast a few times before without taking in the existence of the nature reserve. All she'd taken in were drunk and disorderlies from the Crab and Lobster at the north end—and that was way back, before it became an upmarket restaurant. Walking and birdwatching were not pursuits of choice for Hen. She studied the map while Gary did the driving. 'Bigger than I thought,' she said after a long silence.

'That bear?'

'The place where he hangs out.'

'His den.' Gary seemed to be enjoying himself.

'The main acreage of the reserve is inland, to the north of us, farmland put to grass by the look of it. Before we look there I want to be certain he isn't on view around the edges of the harbour. The footpath goes right around.'

'Exposed, then?'

'By the looks of it. We'll see if we can spot him from the viewpoint I know. If nothing else, I get to have a smoke,' Hen said.

'In a nature reserve, guv?'

'It's the open air.'

She lit up the moment she stepped out of the car. She'd brought Gary to the rear of the Crab and Lobster at Sidlesham

Quay because she knew they didn't need to walk far to have a panoramic view of the harbour. The pub would also be a good meeting point if reinforcements were needed. Coppers know how to find pubs.

'We're going to need glasses.'

'Plenty in the pub, I reckon,' Gary said.

'Field glasses.'

He opened the boot of his car and handed her a pair of 8x binoculars.

'Good planning. You wouldn't have size five wellies as well? I thought not.' She told him to look through the glasses for a tall, solitary man, possibly hooded. Meanwhile, she found a flat rock and sat inhaling from her cigarillo.

'Any joy?'

'Not yet,' Gary said. 'It's as quiet as the grave this morning. Just a courting couple on the Church Norton side.'

'How do you know they're courting?'

'He's unbuttoning her jacket.'

'They must be good glasses.'

'They're steaming up.'

'Isn't there anyone else in view? Who's that on the other side?'

Gary put the binoculars down to check and then refocused. 'A little bald guy in a shellsuit walking his dog.'

She came to a decision. 'Obviously we can't see all of the harbour from here. We'll have to find another viewpoint.'

'Church Norton?'

'Voyeur.'

'Excuse me?'

'You just want a closer view of that couple.'

'Seriously, guv. Church Norton looks like the best bet. We could follow the footpath.'

'That isn't serious, Gary. It's at least a mile off.'

They returned to the car and used the roads to reach the car park created for birders and visitors to St Wilfrid's Chapel. Theirs was the only vehicle. A short walk in the harbour direction gave them a view right across to Pagham. Nobody of Jake's description was in sight. Even the lovers had disappeared.

Hen lit up again. She was getting anxious. This manhunt wasn't the doddle it had first appeared.

'You know what? This is a job for the Eye in the Sky.'

Gary was wide-eyed. 'The chopper?'

'Think big, lad.'

There was only one helicopter for the whole of Sussex Police, a McDonnell Douglas 902 Explorer, based at Shoreham airfield.

'Get on to the Air Ops Unit and see if it's available. From all I've heard there are four pilots on standby and they spend most of their time playing poker.'

'It costs a bomb to run.'

'Six-fifty an hour. A lot of those hours are spent collecting suicide victims at Beachy Head. This will give the lads a break: a real, live suspect to find. Tell them we'll meet them on the Church Norton shingle spit. Too many trees around this poky little car park. They can put down there, no problem.'

Gary got busy with his personal radio. The chopper would arrive in under twenty minutes, he informed Hen.

'I'm surprised we qualify to use it,' he told her as they stepped out towards the spit, and then added, 'Do we?'

'Leave that for me to sort out,' she said. 'We're dealing with a serious crime here.'

She'd not flown in the helicopter and she was sure Gary hadn't. It was supposed to be used when life was at risk or a serious crime in progress, but she'd once seen a headline in the *Mail on Sunday*: SPY IN THE SKY POLICE AIM TO TRAP SPEEDSTERS. The Sussex chopper was 'bringing more misery to Britain' by reporting speeding motorists, timing them from eight hundred feet between sections of road marked with spots as large as dinner plates. Hen was occasionally tempted to put her foot down. She'd been caught in a speed trap once and only escaped thanks to a good story and a sympathetic traffic officer. If the helicopter crew hadn't got anything better than speeding motorists to occupy them, she reasoned, they could help round up Jake.

The spit was the harbour's bulwark against the sea, an artificial hump of shingle about a hundred metres wide. They reached it with time to spare.

She lit another while they waited. If truth were told, she was a mite uneasy about calling in the helicopter, for all her bravado. The top brass enquired into every mission, and flying over a nature reserve was sure to breach the bylaws. 'Just a thought,' she said to Gary. 'If they ask, he's on the run and dangerous, okay?'

'Okay.'

She undermined this by what she said next. 'Between ourselves, I get the impression Jake is a loner, but I suppose it's possible he has a girlfriend. When you had the glasses on that couple did you look at the guy's face?'

'The lovers? He had his back to me, guv.'

'Could you make a guess at his height?'

'He was horizontal.'

She took a long, thoughtful drag on the cigarillo. Everything seemed so peaceful, too peaceful for an emergency.

'We didn't check inside that pub,' Gary said.

'You're not helping.'

A buzzing from over Bognor heralded H902, the Eye in the Sky. Gary started waving a white handkerchief.

'You don't have to do that,' Hen told him. 'We're pretty damned obvious standing out here.'

The helicopter was yellow and black and noisy. The rotor action lifted some sand off the stones and flattened some of the shingle plants that grew in abundance here. One of the crew beckoned to Hen and Gary to go closer. When the aircraft touched down properly they bowed their heads and got in.

There was seating for eight, but only three crewmen were inside, including the pilot. 'What exactly is the mission?' one of them shouted to Hen.

'A search for a murder suspect. White Caucasian male in his forties, about six foot six, dark, possibly hooded.'

'Has he been sighted?'

'Not yet. He works here. Familiar with the terrain.'

'There's no railway this side of Bognor.'

It *was* hard to hear. 'Never mind.'

'Let's go, then. And chuck the stogie, for Christ's sake.'

She'd forgotten she was still holding the cigar-butt.

The Explorer began a near vertical ascent that left Hen's stomach on the ground.

With the door closed, conversation was possible. She learned that the crew were the pilot, a police observer, and a paramedic.

The pilot reported back to his flight controller in Shoreham and then said, for the benefit of his passengers, 'Let's be methodical. I'll take you to the southern limit of the reserve and back, following the shoreline. Is this guy armed?'

'Could be,' Hen said, giving herself a fright as she realised that a shotgun would be needed by a warden, even in a nature reserve.

An aerial search was ideal for an area as big as this, no question. Happily the visibility was excellent this sharp October morning. They were flying low enough to observe anyone. A birdwatcher had set up his camera above the Severals, one of the shallow pools the waders used, and the sun glinted off the chrome tripod. The entire feathered population of the area took flight, leaving him with nothing to photograph. Hands on hips, he glared upwards. In Park Copse, outside the reserve, a woman was walking a Dalmatian. You could almost have counted the spots.

The pilot about-turned the helicopter and began the systematic tracking of the shoreline. 'Soon as you see anything, scream out,' he said. 'You're the eyes on this job, not me.'

Hen had a seat on the left, looking inland. Gary was watching the shoreline. They passed over a large gabled house. The police observer had a map out and said it was Norton Priory. I wouldn't mind your job, squire, Hen thought. She didn't know such a soft option existed.

Above the car park near the red-roofed chapel they spotted Gary's little Nissan, still the only car in view. A short way on, Hen said, 'Hey ho, cap. There's the couple we saw earlier. Can we get a closer look at the man?' She picked up Gary's binoculars.

The pair had chosen a new spot at the edge of a reed bed.

'Bit early in the day for that, isn't it?' the pilot said.

The couple's movements indicated that they had found a way of lovemaking whilst fully clothed in padded jackets. The presence of a helicopter overhead didn't inhibit the blonde, squatting astride the recumbent man, her long hair dancing with the rhythm.

'The zips would worry me,' the policeman said.

'Just thinking about it makes my eyes water,' Gary said.

'Anyway, he doesn't look as if he's on the run,' the pilot said.

'And he's better-looking than the man we're after,' Hen said. 'Shall we leave them to it?'

They continued in an inland direction along the curve of the shore. It was mostly open land. The Selsey Road, with glittering cars moving in both directions, was ahead.

'There must have been a ferry here one time, where the road crosses the water,' the policeman with the map said. 'That's Ferry Farmhouse coming up.'

'Sidlesham Ferry,' Hen informed them. She knew the main points along the road.

'Visitors' centre on my side,' Gary said. 'Hello, there's something in the car park. Looks like a Panda.'

Nobody said anything about wild animals.

'Probably belonged to that couple,' the pilot said.

'No, they had bikes,' Gary said. 'I saw when we flew over.'

'Does your suspect have a motor?' the pilot asked.

'Not to my knowledge,' Hen said.

They moved on and Sidlesham Quay came up, with the little cluster of cottages around the Crab and Lobster, then a tricky promontory that curled around the inlet where the footpath led along the top of Pagham Wall, one more solid defence against the sea.

The police observer looked up from his map. 'There isn't a lot more after this. A section called Slipe Field and beyond that a holiday village, and then you're getting into the outskirts of Bognor.'

'We'll finish the job,' the pilot said. 'Are you sure your man is down there somewhere?'

'Dead sure,' Hen said. 'He works here.' But behind the confident words, she was beginning to feel this would be viewed as an expensive mistake by the high-ups at headquarters.

The Explorer competed its circuit of the harbour and crossed over Pagham Spit and the narrow channel of water between.

'Want to go round again?' the pilot offered like a fairground attendant.

Hen was about to say it was the only thing to do, but Gary spoke first. 'Can I borrow the glasses, guv? There's an inflatable out in the middle.'

'A boat? I thought the harbour was closed to shipping.'

'It should be—unless it's official. They have to get out and monitor the water levels and stuff like that.'

'Can we get closer?' Hen asked the pilot.

They made a sharp turn and zoomed across the water towards the small craft.

'I think it's him,' Gary said. 'He's wearing the hood.'

Hen sent up a silent prayer that he was right.

The pilot said, 'If I go too close there's a danger of churning up water and sinking him.'

'So?' Hen said. 'He's a big boy. He can swim.'

'We don't work that way.'

They swooped close enough for Hen to see the problem for herself. There was already disturbance on the water below them. 'Is there any way we can round him up?'

'We can try. He's aware of us by now.'

The pilot slowed the helicopter and let it hover to one side of the inflatable, creating a circular pattern of waves but not enough to splash over the sides.

'He's got the idea, I think,' Gary said. 'He's heading for the shore.'

The little boat was chugging towards the Church Norton shoreline.

'Any chance you can put us down?' Hen asked the pilot.

'Do my best.'

From the air it seemed an unequal contest, the helicopter capable of ten times the speed. But they needed a landing area reasonably close to where the inflatable would put ashore. Jake knew the ground better than Hen or Gary, and might easily make a run for it and get away.

She asked Gary if he'd still got his personal radio. He wasn't wearing it on his lapel or anything so obvious.

'Fixed to my belt.'

'Good.' She spoke to the pilot. 'If you track him from the air after you put us down, we can keep in radio contact.'

'Can you run a bit?'

'Gary can.'

'I noticed a car park near the chapel. It's small, and there are trees around, but I think I can put you down there.'

'We know it.'

'Your suspect might have a good start.'

'Gary can do it,' Hen said with confidence.

'Gary and whose army?' Gary said. 'He's six foot six.'

'You've got the law on your side. And I won't be far behind.'

Gary looked at the others in the aircraft for offers of help. The paramedic shook his head. The police observer lifted his trouser-leg a few inches to reveal an artificial limb. 'It's why I was given the job.'

The pilot said, 'The Eye in the Sky will watch over you, son.'

'Thanks a bunch,' Gary said.

Below, the inflatable dinghy continued steadily towards the Church Norton shore. Probably it would take another minute.

'We'll go for it,' the pilot said, veering left, inland, and over the roof of St Wilfrid's Chapel. 'Want me to call up ground rein-forcements?'

'You bet I do,' Hen said. 'You're carrying cuffs, are you, Gary?'

Gary nodded. He was looking pale.

They touched down in the car park and jumped out, Gary first. 'Don't wait for me,' Hen yelled, on her knees. 'Get weaving.'

The helicopter soared again and away over the trees, to keep tabs on Jake.

Hen pulled herself upright and jogged along the footpath some way behind Gary, taking shallow breaths and regretting the years of smoking. Her mouth was dry and her chest hurt, but she made the best speed she could. For all the tough talk she didn't want Gary tackling Jake unaided.

The Eye in the Sky was hovering only about a hundred yards ahead, an encouraging sign. Hen redoubled her efforts, climbed up a small rise and saw that Gary had already reached the inflat-able. But to her amazement, he wasn't struggling with Jake. He hadn't made the arrest or taken out the handcuffs. He was helping to beach the dinghy.

Chest heaving now, she had to walk the last stretch. She could see as she approached that the hooded boatman wasn't tall enough to be Jake. Not a boatman at all, she now discovered, but a boatwoman whose face was familiar.

seventeen

'LADY, YOU'VE GOT SOME explaining to do,' Hen shouted, in competition with the helicopter overhead. She was breathless from running.

This time Jo wasn't going to be unstrung by this assertive little officer. She'd had time to think about what she would say. 'I can't see why. It's not unlawful to be out in a boat.'

'Come on, it's obvious what you were doing. You look ridiculous in the big man's coat. Now where is he?'

'I haven't the foggiest.'

'You don't seem to appreciate how serious this is.' Hen turned and spoke to the young detective beside her. 'Send the chopper on its way, for God's sake, Gary. I'm losing my voice.'

'Don't we need it any more?' he asked.

'Not if the backup are coming. Tell them it's mission accomplished and ta-ra, thanks very much.'

Gary took out his personal radio.

The arrival of the helicopter had alarmed Jo at first and then angered her. She'd couldn't stay floating serenely in the middle of the harbour when the rotor action was churning the water, threatening to sink her. Ideally she would have have sat longer in the boat wearing Jake's hooded jacket. She just hoped she'd bought him enough time. In this vast nature reserve there ought to be hiding places, but she hadn't expected the search from the air and neither had he.

Gary told Hen, 'They've seen she's a woman and they want to stay and find Jake.'

'What else can they do from up there? All right. Ask them to fly over the farmland area and see if he's there. I can't hear myself think.'

Presently the helicopter rose higher, swung about, and crossed the water towards the north. The clatter overhead became less.

'Jake put you up to this, obviously,' Hen said to Jo. 'He's left you deep in shit for helping him to evade arrest. You'd better give straight answers if you don't want to face a serious charge. Where is he?'

'I can't tell you,' Jo said, speaking the truth.

'Do you have any idea what you've got yourself into? I'm investigating two murders and he's the prime suspect.'

'You couldn't be more wrong,' Jo said. 'Jake is a really good guy.'

'How often have I heard that from some crook's besotted woman? Listen. If he was that good he wouldn't need you to cover for him.'

'He had unfair treatment in the past.'

'I know all about his record, dear, and you're coming across as naïve and gullible.'

'He wasn't the man I saw on Selsey beach, and that's the truth.'

Hen's tolerance was under severe strain. 'Interesting, however, that you and he should turn out to be friends. You'll be facing questions about that ID parade he was on. Now tell me precisely what he said when he handed you his coat.'

'He didn't say much at all.'

'His words, Miss Stevens. What were his words?'

'He told me to take care.'

'Was it his bright idea for you to take the boat out?'

Jo shook her head. 'I volunteered.'

'And did he say where he was going next?'

'No.'

'Take off the coat and give it to me. I see you're still wearing your own underneath.'

Jo obeyed. She guessed it would be taken for forensic examination. They really believed Jake was the killer.

From somewhere across the harbour came the two-tone note of a police siren. Then another, chiming in with the first. Hen turned to her assistant. 'Book this woman and stick her in your car, Gary. She's obstructing a murder enquiry.'

HANDCUFFED AND locked in the back seat of the Nissan, Jo watched as two police minibuses drew up and disgorged men and women in uniform. All this activity following the helicopter search showed the high priority being given to Jake's arrest. Yet she refused to believe he had killed anyone. His decency shone through in everything he did. He'd dedicated himself to an ethical life. If she could see that, why couldn't the police? She remembered his words, 'You serve your time, but your record is always there.' How true it was proving.

She hoped he'd found somewhere safe to hide. Those policemen were certain to look in all the obvious places like the bird hides and the chapel and the reed-beds. Thank God he'd said nothing to her about what he planned next. They could question her all day and all night and she'd give nothing away. She doubted if he was right to evade arrest, but she would support him even though she feared he was making things worse for himself. She hadn't experienced the trauma of prison herself, so she had no right to criticise his actions.

She was horrified by what she saw next—the police emerging from the second minibus in black body armour and armed with submachine guns they checked and gripped in a way that left no doubt they meant to use them. Her heart battered her ribcage like a trapped bird. How often she'd heard of innocent men being gunned down in error. Dreadful if Jake fell in a hail of bullets simply because he had a phobia about being arrested.

And while she watched, another police vehicle swung into the car park, a van marked DOGS UNIT. This was massive overkill. Two German shepherds and their handlers joined the searchers. The young plainclothes detective called Gary led the way out of the car park and down the path to where Hen Mallin waited.

Unable to protest, let alone stop the madness, Jo was furious with herself for not doing more. She hadn't played this at all cleverly. The smart move would been to have feigned cooperation and actually sent the search party on some fools' errand miles from where she'd last seen Jake. Instead she was stuck here away from the action with no knowledge of what was happening.

ALMOST AN hour passed before any other vehicle entered the car park, and then it was a mud-spattered old Ford pickup. Two elderly men who were obviously birders got out. They had the woolly hats, anoraks, beards, boots, and binoculars. The humdrum routine of the nature reserve was going on while a manhunt was under way. For some seconds the pair stared in puzzlement at the police vehicles as if they were an unknown species freshly arrived from Siberia. Shaking their heads, they moved off in the direction of the small pool in search of something they would recognise.

Five minutes later, Hen Mallin opened the car door. 'You're steaming up. Step outside and get some air.'

It was good to stretch, even with the cuffs on, but no relief from the mental torment. 'Haven't you found him yet?' Jo said, trying to sound bullish against all the evidence.

'We picked up his bike, which means he can't be far off, unless he got a lift from someone.'

'I wouldn't know about that.'

'And he hasn't borrowed your car, because it's standing by the visitors' centre. We ran a check on your registration.'

'Tax and MOT up to date. You can't do me for that.'

Hen took out a pack of small cigars and lit one. 'Honey, I'll do you for obstructing my murder enquiry.'

'You're so wrong about all this.'

'Run this up your flagpole, Miss Stevens. I could have been fishing your body out of that harbour. We've had two drownings. It won't stop at two. I know the way these psychos act. They seem normal enough, charming at times. But they're extremely cunning because they have no moral sense. And they're brilliant at concealing their true intentions. You've no conception of the risk you took by getting into his boat.'

'I'm still here, aren't I?'

'You're telling me he acted normally?'

'Completely.' She wasn't going to report Jake's heart-to-heart to someone so unsympathetic.

'Right now he's acting the runaway killer. Chew on that. You were definitely in the boat with him?'

There seemed no reason to deny it. Jo gave a nod.

'And then he gave you his coat to wear?'

'Obviously.'

'So he knew we were coming. You told him. Someone tipped you off and you came here to warn him.'

'No,' Jo was able to say truthfully. 'I live twenty minutes away. I would have phoned him, wouldn't I?'

'So how did he find out?'

This was trickier. Jo said nothing.

'And from where? The printer's.'

Hen was answering her own questions and starting to get them right. 'Gemma, the PA. Can't be anyone else. But what's her game, tipping him off? She gave the impression she didn't have much to do with him any more. She went out with him once and passed him on to some other hapless female. You, I presume. So you're a friend of Gemma's.'

Jo took the opportunity to say, 'Like me, she knows he's not a murderer. She's good-hearted. She wouldn't willingly get anyone into trouble.'

'You're a cliquey little lot, by the sound of it. How did you get to know this Gemma?'

'Yoga.'

'On the health kick, are you?'

'We left pretty quickly.'

'We'll walk to the shore and see how the search is going,' Hen said. 'That's if you don't want to meditate in the car.' She set off fast enough to demonstrate that a cigar smoker has functioning lungs, and Jo went with her.

Her sidekick Gary was directing operations using his personal radio. Most of the search team were just in sight, away up the shore.

'What progress, Gary?' Hen asked.

'The tide's on the ebb, which is useful,' he said. 'We found the marks where the dinghy was brought in for him to land, and some of his footsteps. Big feet.'

'Big guy. Where?'

'Just past the point they're searching now. Unfortunately the footprints vanish where the mud ends and the shingle takes over.'

'Are the dogs any use?'

'They sniffed his coat and seemed to get interested in the footprints. We'll see.'

'There's not a lot of cover here. We're bound to find him.' She turned back to Jo. 'What brought you here this morning if it wasn't to tip him off? He's supposed to be at work, not entertaining his new girlfriend. You needed to talk, and urgently, right? What about?'

Hard to resist the temptation to blurt out the whole grisly story she'd got from Rick and Gemma about Cartwright's murder. Whether true or not, it would create a diversion from Jake. But she doubted if anything would shake Hen Mallin's conviction that he was the main man, the psycho who drowned women. Instead she just said, 'I was depressed. I haven't been sleeping well. He's a kind man and a good listener.'

'Are you lovers?'

The question couldn't have been more direct. Jo knew she'd given the answer with her face, whatever words were spoken. 'I don't see what—'

'So you are.' Hen flapped her hand. 'I'm not being nosy for no reason. Need to know who I'm dealing with. Did he also have sex with your friend Gemma?'

'I don't think so.'

'You hope he didn't.'

'She told me they didn't and I believe her.'

Hen shrugged and spoke to Gary as if Jo wasn't there. 'This guy obviously has a way with women, even though he's an ugly brute. I doubt if it's his skill at chatting them up, so what's his secret?'

Gary took this as rhetorical and said nothing.

'Four women,' Hen went on, raising four fingers. 'Our friend here, Gemma, Meredith, and Fiona. He went out with them all.'

'You don't know that,' Jo said, provoked.

'Oh, but I do. You just told me about Gemma and yourself and we already knew about the unfortunate two who were drowned. I'm sorry if I'm trampling on your feelings, Miss Stevens, but you have to face it. He's a ladies' man, and that's the delicate way of putting it.'

'You're making it sound as if they were all his girlfriends, and that just isn't so. He happened to know the woman found at Selsey on a professional level, because of his interest in fossils.'

'He's told you that, has he?' Hen said. 'And did he also explain why Meredith Sentinel came all the way down to Selsey to meet him when her husband was abroad? If that was professional, I'm the tooth fairy.'

Jo tried to stay calm. She knew she was being wound up in the expectation she'd give something away. 'She didn't come to meet him. You're making this up to suit your theories.'

'What, she came for her health, did she? And it was pure coincidence that Jake lives here?'

'I've no idea why she came and neither has he. The first he knew of it was after she was identified, when it came out in the news.'

'Dream on, dear,' Hen said. 'Did he tell you he also knew Fiona, the second victim?'

'We haven't discussed her.'

'Surprise, surprise. How long has he lived in Selsey, by the way?'

'I've never asked.'

'Is he a Sussex man?'

'I believe he's from Cornwall originally.'

Hen snapped her fingers. 'Right on. That's where he kicked the young soldier out of the tree and put him in a wheelchair for the rest of his life. Cornwall it was.' She swung around to Gary. 'Get through to Paddy Murphy now and tell him to pinpoint Cornwall.'

With that sorted, she set off at a sharp pace along the shore towards the searchers. Ignored, Jo thought she had better follow. Making a bid for freedom wasn't a serious option. Besides, she wanted to find out all she could about this misguided police enquiry. Someone had to stand up for Jake's rights, or he'd be crushed.

A cool east breeze had started to disturb the mirror surface of the water, giving the gulls the incentive to swoop and glide. The tide was receding fast. In another hour it would begin reclaiming the foreshore.

The team was spaced at wide intervals across the pebble beach and right up to the scrub above it. The theory was that because Jake had come ashore on the Church Norton side of the harbour he'd holed up there rather than hiking to the opposite side—which, anyway, was more populated. The dog-handlers led, with the main search squad behind and the armed officers bringing up the rear. Progress was brisk. This was a manhunt, not a fingertip search.

Hen caught up with them and spoke to one of the sergeants out of range of Jo's hearing. She seemed to be suggesting a change of method. Some of those closest to the waterline were sent higher up the beach.

'What's going on?' Jo asked Gary, who had caught up.

'They think he could have buried himself under the pebbles, but the boss says there's no point searching so close to the water because it's wet underneath and the stones are too small anyway.'

She hoped against hope that Jake had gone right off the beach and was hiding in the reeds. Yet another part of her knew that the longer he stayed at liberty the more guilty he appeared. That prison experience had left him with a terror of being locked up again. You couldn't argue with someone who has gone through such a trauma.

Her support for him hadn't been shaken by anything Hen Mallin had said.

She crunched through the pebbles, trying to be positive.

Suddenly there was frenzied barking from one of the dogs below a bank of white shingle. The other German shepherd was immediately brought over and joined in the barking. The marksmen ran forward and made a half-circle around the area, crouching with weapons levelled.

From nowhere, it seemed, the helicopter homed in and hovered above.

A knot formed in Jo's stomach.

The dogs were straining at the leash, alternately barking and whimpering, pawing at the stones. Everyone closed in.

Please, God, let it be a dead bird, Jo said to herself.

Hen directed operations, ordering the unarmed searchers to stand back. The weapons team, rigid and ready in their black kevlar body armour, were chilling to behold.

For what seemed minutes, but was probably not more than twenty seconds, nothing happened. The dogs were dragged away by their handlers to give the gunmen a clear line of fire. Trying to be heard above the sound of the rotors, Hen spoke through a loudhailer, apparently to a mound of stones.

'Jake, this is DCI Mallin. It's all over. You're surrounded and we're armed.'

Nothing.

Then one pebble shifted, teetered and toppled from the mound.

'He's in there,' someone yelled.

More pebbles rolled off.

Everyone tensed.

The whole mound moved. A hand emerged from the stones and dragged some of them clear. Jake's pale face appeared, blinking in the light.

'You're nicked,' Hen said through the loudhailer. 'Cuff him.'

Two of the armed squad threw themselves on the mound, totally covering Jake. They scrabbled among the pebbles to get a grip on both arms. They handcuffed him. Then they dragged him from his hiding place. He was in a blue guernsey and jeans.

He must have buried himself more than an hour ago. He'd obviously found this trough in the pebbles and sat in it and heaped more of them over his legs and body like the seaside game played by children. It was not a bad hiding place. If the dogs hadn't been used he might not have been found.

The helicopter performed a kind of victory arc. The pilot waved and showed a thumb up. Gary waved back. Mission completed, the Eye in the Sky swung away towards Bognor.

'Gary, love, the action is down here,' Hen said. 'Give him the caution and let's all get back to somewhere warm.'

But instead of resigning to the inevitable, Jake took a couple of swift steps towards Hen, dragging his captors with him. He was irate and vocal. 'Who brought the fucking helicopter here? Was that you? Do you have the slightest idea of the damage it must have done to the wildlife here? Why do you think this is called a reserve? It's supposed to be a sanctuary for birds and animals and insects. I can't begin to calculate the destruction and panic you've caused to defenceless creatures we spend years trying to protect.'

The words had come freely and with force, he was so incensed. The colour had returned to his face and for a moment his staring eyes shamed Hen and everyone. It was an extraordinary outburst—a revelation of Jake's commitment. Even the gunmen were upstaged.

Hen didn't respond. You can't argue with someone who feels so passionately, and who is right. It had been a destructive act to call in the helicopter, one she would be willing to justify to her superiors, but not present company. He was still the main suspect, a likely murderer, but this had been his moment.

Gary, to his credit, was brave enough to step forward and mouth the words of the official caution. Jake didn't listen, but the formality was observed.

The armed men led Jake away, still muttering and shaking his head. They passed close to where Jo was standing, but he didn't appear to see her. Some tears rolled down her face. With her hands cuffed she couldn't wipe them away.

'Lucky he didn't make a run for it,' Gary said to her.

She couldn't speak.

SHE WASN'T put in a cell at Chichester, as she expected. They sat her on a chair in a side room with filing cabinets where people kept coming in. They removed the handcuffs and gave her coffee. All the interest was concentrated on Jake now, she guessed. She hoped he would hold up.

After about an hour, Gary appeared with a pen and paper. 'The boss wants you to make a statement about this morning and then you're free to go.'

'That's all?'

'She was talking tough on the beach. She's like that.'

'What do I have to do?'

'I'll help you put it down. It's got to be a hundred per cent true because it's evidence. This is the statement form. So we start with your full name.'

*   *   *

HEN WAS at Paddy Murphy's desk in the incident room. 'You got the message about Cornwall? The suspect comes originally from a place called Bugle, north of St Austell.'

'I'm working on it,' he said, pointing at the computer screen. 'I had no idea Cornwall is such a dangerous place. Far more drownings than you find in these parts. So much coast, you see. And rough seas. People get taken by freak waves, strong currents, boating accidents. This can't be done in twenty minutes, guv.'

'I'm not suggesting it can.'

'You're looking over my shoulder.'

'And the reason is that you could nail this guy for me by finding an earlier incident of drowning, one that got past as misadventure. It won't be recent. He left Cornwall after his jail sentence, when he was nineteen, so you're going back twenty years, Okay?'

'That makes it tougher.'

'But you rise to a challenge, don't you?' She raised her voice for everyone in the room. 'Isn't it well known that Paddy rises to a challenge?'

It amused the troops.

Then Paddy said, 'Speaking of challenges, ma'am . . . '

'Yes?'

'What time is that inquest you're attending?'

'Sweet Jesus.'

BACK AT Jo's flat the phone messages had stacked up. The garden centre couldn't trace the paperwork for an order she'd taken last week. Her mother was on the warpath, too, reminding her it was Daddy's birthday and claiming he was practically suicidal because she'd forgotten to call him or even send a card. The least she could do was get onto Interflora and get a bouquet sent round. And Gemma had left a message passing on her bit of news about the police taking an interest in Jake's visits to the print works.

She called her father first and managed to wish him all the best without having to listen to a tirade from his wife which would have gone on for ages. Far from suicidal, the old boy sounded chirpy. She phoned the wine shop next and ordered a case of Beaujolais for him, delivery that afternoon. He'd prefer that to a bunch of chrysanthemums. Then she sorted out the problem at work.

Finally, she thought about the third message. She'd been so angry with Gemma Monday evening when she'd manoeuvred her way into Jo's flat after being told plainly that she wasn't welcome. The business about Mr Cartwright, true or otherwise, had been deeply unsettling. Gemma had come out of it with little credit, looking self-centred and manipulative.

And yet this morning had put all that in a different perspective. Jake—the one reliable friend Jo had—was doubtful if Rick had really killed Cartwright. In his laconic way he'd made the story look paper-thin. It seemed most likely that Rick had been posturing—as usual—and then felt unable to admit the whole thing was invented. Gemma couldn't really be blamed for believing him. She was trusting and he was very plausible.

It was to Gemma's credit that she'd phoned Jake to tell him the police were onto him about Fiona. Over this, she'd behaved as a friend should. There's a responsible side to her, Jo thought, and we've had plenty of laughs together. Maybe we'll get back on speaking terms. Not this morning, though.

Her big concern was Jake. Hiding from the police had been a mistake, however understandable. He'd been incensed by the helicopter and she worried how he would behave under questioning. What's more, he had a fatalistic streak, and he was quite liable to admit to things he hadn't done. When they'd talked that evening in the pub, he seemed to have resigned himself to being fitted up and sent back to prison. 'It's out of our hands,' he'd said. And, 'Crazy things happen to me.' In that frame of mind he wasn't going to fight for his freedom.

Somebody had to.

She was uniquely placed to discover the truth. Events had already brought her closer than she'd liked to one of the murders, and thanks to Gemma's curiosity she'd come pretty close to the other. She knew some of the main suspects. A moment of decision, then.

If no one else was seeking out the killer, she would.

eighteen

HEN'S HECTIC DAY BROUGHT her next to the court building in Chichester. She hadn't had time to change. She hadn't even picked up a sandwich before she appeared at the inquest into Meredith Sentinel's death. So it came as a relief when her favourite coroner rattled through the formalities in under twenty minutes and the inevitable adjournment was declared.

In the corridor outside, she cornered Austen Sentinel before he could slip away and back to London. In court, he'd confirmed in evidence that he'd identified his late wife. Nothing else had been required from him at this stage. In a black pinstripe suit and dark tie, he'd made the right impression, still grieving, yet bearing up bravely. The demeanour became sharply more assertive as soon as he saw who was barring his way. 'I have a train to catch,' he said.

Hen became the party hostess determined to hold on to her guest. 'No panic. Two or three go to London every hour. I'll see that you get home all right.'

'Thanks, but I'm leaving.' He turned towards the main exit.

'Not that way,' she said. 'There's a media scrum outside. I'll show you the back way out.' She was already steering him towards the side door. In the street she asked, 'Have you eaten? The pub across the way does a pie and chips to die for.' Not the best form of words to use to a recently widowed man, but her hunger pangs were extreme.

Even before he turned her down she sensed that he wasn't a pie and chips man. His fine Italian suit wouldn't look right in the Globe. 'Tell you what. The Cloisters Café in the cathedral is five minutes from here. A good class of place. Salads, home-made soups, and local apple juice.'

'I can get myself something on the train.'

'I wouldn't trust the trolley service,' she told him. 'Besides, there are a couple of things I'd like your help on. I'd hate to put you to all the inconvenience of returning tomorrow.'

'I thought we went over it all before,' he said.

They went to the Cloisters. Hen made a phone call along the route and by the time they'd gone through the self-service and arrived with their trays at a table by the window, Gary had nipped round from where he'd been waiting in the Globe and was sitting there.

'You remember DC Pearce from before?' Hen said in a disarming tone to Dr Sentinel.

'What's all this about?'

'Two of us have to be present when a witness is interviewed. It's for your protection really.'

'I didn't agree to an interview.'

'But you aren't refusing? You heard the coroner say it's crucial that everyone cooperates fully with the police investigation.'

'Heaven knows I've done that.'

'It's only clarification at this stage.'

He glared at them both, sat down, and started ripping his croissant to shreds. And he'd looked so amenable when he was giving evidence. 'Go on, then.'

She'd already decided to hit him early with the big one. 'Your St Petersburg trip: Did you attend all the lecture sessions?'

Unprepared, he struggled for the right response. 'One isn't required to.'

'The seminars, the visit to the Hermitage, the formal dinners?'

'I read my paper.'

'What—for two whole weeks? I get through mine in ten minutes over breakfast.'

He looked like a first class passenger forced to use the third-class toilet. 'It's an academic expression. I gave my prepared talk to the conference.'

'I'm glad to hear that. You were sponsored by the British Council, I think you said.'

The blood pressure was rocketing, bringing a patchy orange look to the designer tan. 'Does that have any relevance?'

'Where did you go on all those days off?'

'I fail to see what connection any of this has with my wife's death. This is my professional life you're questioning.'

Hen was unmoved. 'Your hotel room wasn't used most of the time you were booked in.'

That one practically floored him.

Eyes swivelling in panic, he said, 'This is an intrusion on my personal liberty. Have you been checking up on me?'

'On your story,' Hen said as if it was the only reasonable way to go. 'People tell us things and we make sure the information is reliable. You claimed you were in St Petersburg when your wife met her death and now it seems you may not have been. You can clear this up very easily.'

'I gave my paper and did what I was asked.'

'On the first or second day.'

His sigh was more like a rasp. 'I took some time out from the conference to visit a colleague. That isn't a matter for the police, so far as I'm aware.'

'Oh, but it is if you weren't where you said you were. Did you leave St Petersburg?'

A long pause while he seemed to be deciding if he could tell a downright lie and bluff it out. Apparently not. 'Yes.'

'Returning at the end of the three weeks to check out?'

'You're treating me like a schoolboy who played truant.'

'Who was the old colleague, Dr Sentinel?'

'A Finnish geologist. You wouldn't even be able to repeat the name if I gave it to you.'

'Try me.'

'Dr Outi Koskenniemi.'

'You're right.' Hen handed him a pen and one of her personal cards. 'On the back, please.'

Shaking his head at this imposition, Sentinel printed the name.

'Male or female?' Hen asked, looking at the card he'd returned.

He hesitated before saying, 'Female.'

Hen lifted an eyebrow.

His shoulders slumped and all the fight went out of him. 'All right,' he said, 'you've got the picture now. I was playing away, so to speak, and I'm bloody ashamed it should have happened when Merry was being murdered. One can't re-run events, unfortunately.'

'Was this lady at the conference?'

He shook his head. 'She lives in Helsinki.'

'Excuse me. My geography isn't the best.'

'It's a short hop by plane.'

'So you travelled there and stayed with her. You'd better write down the address for me.'

'I don't want Outi involved.'

A fine time for gallantry, Hen thought. 'She's your alibi. You went missing from the conference at a sensitive time.'

Shaking his head, he added the address.

Hen leaned back in her chair. 'You and your friend Outi must have planned this when you got the invitation to St Petersburg. Has it happened before?'

'This was my first visit to Russia.'

'But not to Helsinki?' The answer to that was written all over his face. 'That explains it, then. An affair of the heart. Your marriage to Meredith wasn't roses all the way, in spite of what you told me last time?'

'I was in shock when we spoke.'

'Agreed. And now you can be more frank.'

He felt the knot of his tie as if it was too tight. 'Merry and I stopped sleeping in the same room a long time ago. We continued to live together because neither of us wanted all the hassle and expense of separation.'

'Did she know about your Finnish lady?'

'I expect so. I got to know about some of her male friends. We didn't discuss them, but the signs were there for me to see.'

Hen recalled him accusing her of appalling bad taste for suggesting Meredith might have met someone else. She let it pass, feeling she was on the brink of a breakthrough here. 'Was there a man friend down here in Sussex?'

'Of course.'

'You knew?'

'She didn't come here for the scenery.'

'Who was he?'

'It's obvious.'

'Not to me.' Getting a straight answer was a major challenge. 'I'm asking for his name.'

He shrugged and looked away.

'Don't know?' said Hen, 'Or won't tell?'

He was silent.

'You just said it was obvious who he was.'

'Obvious that some man existed,' he said.

'Isn't there some way of finding out? A name she let slip? Phone calls? Letters?'

If Dr Sentinel was capable of recalling anyone at all, he was in no frame of mind to be helpful. 'I wasn't that inquisitive about her fancy men. "Better not to know," was my philosophy, or you start making comparisons with yourself and losing confidence.'

Hen was so frustrated that she departed from her script. 'You couldn't have missed the man I have in mind. He's six foot six.'

'There you are then,' Sentinel said smoothly. 'I'm five nine. That would be a blow to my self-esteem.'

She wished she'd kept quiet about Jake. A tactical error. 'When we spoke before, you went so far as to suggest that the murderer must be somebody with local knowledge.'

'Obvious, isn't it?' He was recovering some of his poise. And arrogance.

'Yes—and we're working on that assumption.'

'And you have a suspect?'

'More than one,' she said, trying to compensate for the gaffe over Jake.

'Not much of a friend if he murdered her.'

She was trying to keep her cool. 'You'll have read in the papers that we linked this case to another murder by drowning. It's vital that we catch this killer. Any detail about the men she met recently could put us onto him.'

'You're not listening, Chief Inspector. I just told you I didn't wish to know anything about them.'

'Is there a woman friend Meredith might have confided in?'

'I doubt it. Most of her friends were male.'

'Did she keep a diary?'

'Never had the time. Speaking of which . . . ' He looked at his watch. 'I'd like to leave now.'

Hen ignored that. She felt certain there was more to be winkled out from this unpromising source. 'You talked about the time you first visited Selsey, to excavate the mammoth on the beach. Meredith was a Brighton University student who joined the dig, and that's how you met.'

He sighed and shook his head. 'Do we really have to go over this?' He'd taken a near knockout punch, but he was back on his feet and fighting.

'I'd like to know who else was on that dig.'

'Ridiculous,' he said. 'Twenty years ago and you want names?'

She continued to prompt him. Obnoxious as he was, he could provide the crucial link. 'You said the work had to be done fast because of the tides, so you recruited everyone you could get.'

'It was a miracle I found anyone at all. The term hadn't started, so I had to phone around for students I taught and, frankly, any Tom, Dick, or Harry who was up at the university early, as well as locals in Selsey. But if you think I kept a list of their names, you're mistaken.'

'I expect you wrote about the mammoth later for some scientific journal.'

'At some length. It was a major event for this country and I was a young man with a career to pursue. I've lectured on it extensively. Only last June at Brighton in commemoration week I gave the Howard Carter lecture to mark the twentieth year since the dig.'

'As recently as that? Who were the audience?'

'All the VIPs from the vice-chancellor down, plus some experts and enthusiasts. It was a full house, and appreciative, I may add.'

'Good to go back, was it?'

'I'm not sentimental, Chief Inspector.'

'Did you meet any of your original team?'

'There you go again. I've taught hundreds of students since. If

I met them, I wouldn't recall their names.' With his giant ego, he'd wiped them all from his memory.

'With one exception,' Hen said.

'Oh?'

'Your wife.'

'Well, yes,' he conceded without much grace.

'Was she at the lecture?'

'Merry?' he said, as if the idea was preposterous. 'She'd heard it all before. She called it my spiel. No, she was out and about in London being wined and dined by some fossil hunter, no doubt.'

Hen's antennae twitched. 'Fossil hunter? Why do you say that?'

'Because those were the types she was most likely to meet at the museum. In archaeology we often talk of finds. The term had its own special meaning for Merry.'

'No fossil hunter in particular?'

'You'd have to ask her. But of course it's too late now.'

This was like being baited. Each time Hen got close, the lure was jerked out of range. 'Was this lecture of yours illustrated?'

'Certainly.' The words were guaranteed to flow when anything to Sentinel's credit was mentioned. 'I showed a selection of slides and some newsreel footage. The dig was photographed officially and covered by the media as well.'

'You said you wrote about it yourself. With pictures?'

'Some journals like to use illustrations. Some don't.'

'Pictures of the bones, I suppose. Any of the dig in progress?'

'Several.'

'But you wouldn't have captioned them with the names of the diggers?'

He looked pained by this suggestion. 'These are professional journals. The finds are significant, not the finders.'

Hen couldn't resist commenting, 'But I dare say your name appeared.'

'Well, it was my project.'

'You see why I'm so interested?' she said, still trying for cooperation. 'Selsey was where the mammoth was found and where your wife was murdered. We don't know why she came back twenty years later. What time of year was the dig?'

'End of September.'

'Exactly twenty years on.'

'Not significant, in my opinion.'

'I beg to differ,' Hen said. 'A connection is possible, and it's my job to examine it.'

Sentinel was unimpressed. 'Strictly speaking, the anniversary may have been September, but scarcely anybody in a university is up then. The session begins in October, and we're so busy then that a special lecture would be out of the question, I can assure you. And another thing: Merry was only eighteen in nineteen-eighty-seven. I'm damned sure she wasn't having affairs at that age.'

'I'm not suggesting that. But if one of the team from way back resurfaced and got in touch, mightn't Meredith have thought it fun to revisit the place?'

'She had the opportunity in June when I gave the lecture.'

'That was Brighton. Selsey was where it happened.'

'She said nothing to me about going back there.'

'You must have talked about the dig from time to time.'

'It came up sometimes.'

'Are you sure she didn't keep up with any of your team?'

'She kept up with me.' He gave a faint smile. '*Touché.*'

'Nobody else?'

'I wouldn't know unless she told me, and she didn't.'

'Someone must have remembered her. I expect the dig was memorable for the people who took part.'

'Oh, you can be sure of that,' he said with another rush of hubris. 'Not many undergraduates get such an opportunity.'

'You must have been quite young yourself.'

'To be leading such a dig? Twenty-five.'

'Admired by all those little girls in bikinis? I'm sure you were.'

Too obvious. He put up the shutters. 'You're straying into fantasy here, I think.' He drew the chair back from the table. 'I need to go now.'

'When we first discussed this, you said Meredith was one of your team, a fresher. You were very clear about what happened.'

'Nothing happened.'

'Right. You said you noticed her, but that wasn't the start of your romance. That came later. Is that still your position on this?'

'Of course. I'd have been a total idiot to risk my career going to bed with a student. It was a no-no. Didn't I make it clear that we linked up later, after she graduated?'

'I believe you did.' And Hen was forced to admit to herself that his claim rang true. This calculating man was too ambitious to have risked a scandal

In this particular contest, he'd taken some hard knocks and survived them, but Hen, too, had gone through a shaky period. Towards the end, Sentinel had recovered some punching power. Even so, he wasn't behaving with total openness. Hen suspected strongly that he was still holding something back. She'd run out of steam and he was about to escape.

It was infuriating.

'Gary will show you to the station.'

JO NEEDED to prove beyond doubt that somebody other than Jake had carried out the drownings. After a light salad lunch she made herself a strong espresso. Then she planned the rest of her day. First, she faced facts. Jake was the prime suspect for the murder on the beach. The police had got onto him almost from the start, influenced by his previous offence. They'd stacked up plenty of circumstantial evidence against him.

But this wasn't an isolated killing. Fiona had been drowned in a similar way. The police had made it their job to find some link between Jake and Fiona and now they'd got it. He'd almost certainly met her at the print works. But unless they knew something that hadn't yet come out, they were still some way from proving he'd murdered her.

Jo had an alternative theory. If you took the killing of Fiona in isolation there was an obvious suspect in Cartwright, her boss and the man she was last seen with. Fiona had set out to seduce him and succeeded, but only up to a point. Obviously she'd told Cartwright her terms: a top job and maybe even a seat on the board. He'd seen that he'd been set up and must have got angry. She'd died and he'd disappeared. Surely the police must have deduced this much?

The next, more difficult, step was to see if Cartwright could have murdered Meredith as well. Was he one of those unassuming men who live quiet, ordered lives and turn out to be sociopaths? Was the drowning on Selsey beach a trial run for Fiona's murder? Or was there a connection with Meredith that no one had yet discovered?

She needed to know more about Cartwright and it was obvious who to ask.

Time to mend fences.

She called the print works and got through to Gemma. The first contact was terse and untypical, but was bound to be after the hard words they'd exchanged the evening before. 'Thanks for that message you left about Jake. I'm sorry to say he got arrested again.'

'Poor old darling,' Gemma said, trying her best and not quite getting there. 'I saw it coming. We had the plod here on the case at the crack of dawn. They took a copy of the list of clients and it was as certain as death and taxes they'd discover Jake had been here in August and must have met Fiona. Sweetie, you must be gutted.'

'I'm sure he's innocent.'

'Goes without saying,'

'I've got to help him, Gem.'

'I'm with you on that—but what can anyone do if the police have got him?'

'I've got some ideas. Will you help me?'

'How?'

'I'd like to come out and see you?'

'Aren't you at work?'

'I took the day off.'

'Shoot right over, then. You're not interrupting much. I've been doing my toenails.'

THE LAST time she'd come to Kleentext, it was at Gemma's request. This was so different.

They embraced in a token way.

'I was still in shock last night,' Jo said. 'I'm sorry about some of the things I said.'

'And I was out of order, forcing my way in like that,' Gemma told her. 'Pax? Put it there.' She held up her hand for a high five that Jo was pleased to complete. 'So what are we going to do to help Jake?'

'Basically, find out who really did the drownings.'

'Okay.'

'And your boss is the main contender.'

'Wow! Tell me more.' Gemma gestured to Jo to sit down while she perched herself on her desk not a yard away.

After Jo had laid out her theory she added, 'So you see, I've got to find a link to the drowning on the beach. There's no question that this was a double killing. This is where I need your help.'

'And you'll get it if I can think of a damned thing,' Gemma said. 'At this moment I can't. It's not as if the dead woman was one of our clients.'

'It won't be as obvious as that,' Jo said. 'How much do you know about Mr Cartwright's life outside here?'

'Only bits. The divorce happened yonks ago, so I doubt if that has any bearing. He lived at Apuldram and grew roses. Sometimes came in with a rosebud in his buttonhole. He fancied himself as a fashion object, I think, what with the dicky-bows and the brothel creepers. He was way off track.'

'Was he bitter to women?'

'Because of the divorce? I don't think so. Not that you'd notice, anyway. He acted the gent, smiled and put on the charm, like I told you. Mind, when you visit a house you don't ask to see the cesspit.'

'Did he go to university?'

'Never mentioned it.' Gemma raised a finger. 'Ah, you're thinking they could have met as students. Well, I doubt it. I always thought Cartwright left school early to join the printing trade and worked his way up the ladder. Give him his due, he knew every bit of the biz.'

'How about the marriage? Did he talk about that?'

'Not to me, poppet. I'm sorry. I'm not being helpful. How would the marriage make a difference anyway?'

'If his ex was a friend of Meredith.'

'I see.' But there wasn't much enthusiasm in the way Gemma spoke. She hesitated and then said with a tentative smile, 'Jo, are we in danger of clutching at straws?'

Jo nodded. It was fair comment. 'The thing is, I never met the man and you only knew him as your boss. There's a lot more of his life we know nothing about. Did he keep any personal items in the office?'

'Sorry to disappoint. The police took all his stuff away last week. The drawers of his desk, files, a couple of photos, even the calendar off the wall. They had the hard disk out of his computer. Go in and look if you like, but I don't think you'll find anything.'

Jo sighed. This had been the key part of her plan.

'At least it shows they're not ignoring him,' Gemma added.

'Do you think they searched his house as well?'

'It would make sense, wouldn't it?'

'Did they say anything about a search?'

'To me?' Gemma shook her head.

There was a moment of silence while each of them wrestled with her conscience. Then Jo said, 'Are you up for it?'

'If you are.'

APULDRAM WAS an ancient shrunken hamlet a ten-minute drive away, fringing the Fishbourne Channel immediately south of Chichester in an undeveloped area designated as of outstanding scenic interest. The A27 bypass had effectively cut it off from the city. Known for its rose garden and the Crown and Anchor Inn at Dell Quay, it was not a bad place to have a pad, as Gemma remarked.

Jo had always believed in being open with her friends and she wanted to clear the air with Gemma, so as soon as they drove off, she said, 'I'd better tell you, Gem. I've thought about Rick's story and I've got serious doubts.'

Gemma said in a subdued voice, 'Go on.'

'Well, I wonder if he said he'd killed Mr Cartwright just to impress you, almost as an extension of the joking we did about it.

The thing is, Rick is serious-minded and when he says something it doesn't come out as wacky. He doesn't do wacky.'

'That's for sure,' Gemma said.

'So I can't help thinking he got himself into a situation he couldn't find a way out of. He made this claim in such a serious way that you believed him—and so did I when he repeated it to me—and he couldn't go back and say it was all made up.'

'You mean because I had sex with him?'

'Well . . . yes.'

'I told you how it happened, and it was true,' Gemma said. 'It blew my mind when he said he'd murdered Cartwright for real. All the talk about totalling him had been meant in fun, like you're saying. I was really scared, and I felt responsible. He'd never have done it without me opening my big mouth. So when he said the next bit, about doing the perfect murder and making every trace disappear, I can't describe the weight that was lifted from me. Okay, it was still a nightmare, but we'd got away with it. So we shagged like the only two bunnies who made it across the motorway, and that's the truth of it.'

'Do you see where I'm coming from?' Jo said. 'It was your first time with Rick, right? It was a big deal for him.'

'Better be.' Gemma laughed, and it cleared the air a little.

'And then—being Rick—he can't tell you it was all made up.'

'Really?' Gemma scraped her fingers through her hair and pulled some across her mouth.

'In his eyes, he's conned you. He didn't mean to, but that's how it worked out. So he can't bring himself to tell you none of it was true because he's afraid you'll slap his face and tell him to get the hell out of your life.'

'Which I might.'

'The thing is, Cartwright vanished, and as long as he stays vanished, Rick can stick to his story. Mind he's not exactly shouting it from the rooftops. He didn't want me to know until you pushed him to tell me.'

'So I did. . . .' She was shaking her head. 'Poor guy. I never thought. Jo, you're brilliant. A mind-reader. I'm sure you're right. It never happened and I feel so much better.'

Inside herself Jo knew she shouldn't really take the credit. Jake had unravelled Rick's lie, but there were times in life when silence was the right option.

Gemma started singing 'Always Look on the Bright Side of Life,' and Jo joined in until they ran out of lines they remembered.

'There's only one thing,' Gemma said finally.

'What's that?'

'Whatever happened to Mr Cartwright?'

nineteen

'What's your take on Dr Sentinel?' Hen asked Gary when he got back to the police station.

'Shifty as a shithouse rat, guv.'

She smiled. 'You don't have to hold back. Anything in particular?'

'What stood out is the way he talked about his wife. The first time we met him he didn't give a hint she was playing around. I mean, you asked him if the marriage was in difficulty and he practically took a swipe at you.'

'Stay with the facts, Gary. He said my question was in appalling bad taste. We've got it on tape.'

'Yes, and today he says she'd shag anything that moved. Sorry, that's over the top again. I can't stand the guy.'

'That's beginning to come through.'

'He's a bilge-artist, guv. If he was really any use in his job he'd be a professor by now, not a bloody lecturer. On the telly I've seen professors half his age.'

'Concentrate on the case. Did anything in his statements strike a false note?'

'He did his best to cover up the mistress in Helsinki.'

'True.' Hen took the card from her pocket and reminded herself of the name. 'Or was that all a bluff?'

'How do you mean?'

'I wonder if he steered us down that line of questioning.'

Gary frowned. 'Why would he do that?'

'Maybe Outi doesn't exist.'

His eyes gleamed like new coins. 'If she doesn't, he's got about nineteen days to account for.'

'Nineteen days when he could have been back in England

murdering his wife and the other woman. We checked if he flew from St Petersburg to London and drew a blank. We'd better see if he went by way of Helsinki, or any other airport in the region. It's feasible.'

'Mightn't it be quicker to check whether Outi is a real person?'

'The Finn fatale? Yes, you can do that.'

'Do I get a trip to Helsinki?'

'On the budget we're given? You're an optimist. A phonecall, Gary. A phonecall to the Helsinki police. Now I must see how Stella's been getting on with the tree-hugger. First I owe myself a smoke.'

She found Stella at her desk in the incident room and learned that Jake was not co-operating. 'He's still in a strop about the helicopter.'

'At least he's saying something.'

'A silent strop.'

'He's right to be angry,' Hen said in a rare tone of regret. 'I wish I hadn't used the thing. It was the dogs that found him, not the chopper.'

'You weren't to know that, guv.'

'But, Stell, I've got a conscience, too. I care about the world we're destroying and polluting. I hate to think of the rainforest being chainsawed by loggers. I've got my own orangutan I sponsor. And then at the first opportunity of a ride in a bloody helicopter I'm there, causing havoc and destruction in a nature reserve. I should be ashamed and I am.'

'I don't suppose you did too much damage.'

'Where is he now—in the cells?'

'Interview Room Two.'

'Well, I'm choked about what happened, but let's see if I can get one bird to sing again, eh?'

Jake had slumped in the chair and appeared to be asleep when the two detectives went in.

Hen leaned across the table and touched his arm.

His eyes opened, saw her and glowered.

'If you think I'm going to apologise for this morning,' she began, and then paused before adding, 'you're right. I should have thought about the damage a noisy whirlwind of a machine can do to habitats. My decision, my mistake. Without it we'd have taken longer to pull you in, but that's the way I should have gone about it. I was out of order and I'm sorry.'

He remained silent, but the expression in his eyes changed from hostility to suspicion to surprise.

'Like you, I have to work for a living,' Hen carried on, 'and I hope you can respect that, just as I respect you for standing up and telling me what a barbarian I am.' She let that sink in before saying, 'You know why we arrested you. More questions. But this is another chance for you to get a word in. Or two. Or three.'

He didn't appreciate the attempt to humour him. She nodded to Stella to start the tape and speak the official preamble.

When it was done, Hen spread her hands and said, 'We know who you are and by now I reckon you know us, but the stupid tape machine can't remember squat.'

Still no reaction.

She sat back in her chair and studied his face for some time before saying, 'It was plucky of your friend Jo to sit in the inflatable wearing your jacket and hood. Comical, too. I was in the helicopter and she fooled me. I felt sure it was you. At the time I was all for taking the chopper down to about thirty feet, churning up the water and tipping it over. Big guy like you wouldn't be in trouble, I thought. It can't be deep out there. Good thing the pilot didn't approve. We don't know if Jo can swim.'

He still wasn't tempted to comment, so Hen continued, 'Another drowning wouldn't have been good for my reputation. As I was saying, she's a good ally of yours, that young woman. She didn't pick you out in the ID the other day, and even today she insisted you weren't one of the men she saw at Selsey.'

Jake appeared unmoved. Certainly his lips didn't move.

Hen was not discouraged. 'But it turns out that you two are friends, close friends, according to her, and now you have a chance to help her out. We're not going to charge her with wasting police time this morning, but misleading us over the ID parade is a lot more serious. As you know, the parade wasn't controlled by me, or by CID. By law it had to be overseen by a uniform branch inspector. A word from me to him could result in a serious charge for Miss Jo Stevens.'

The bird was persuaded to sing at last. 'She didn't mislead anyone.'

'But she's a friend of yours.'

'She told the truth,' Jake said. 'She didn't see me that morning. I was on the beach, yes, but she didn't see me.'

'What were you doing there?'

'Walking.'

'And did you see Meredith Sentinel, the woman who was drowned?'

'No.'

'You're certain of that?'

'I would have told you.'

If nothing else, the responses were coming now. Hen rested her elbows on the table and supported her chin with her cupped hands. 'I'm going to ask you again, Jake: What were you doing there?'

'Thought I might meet Jo. I didn't.'

'Let me get this right. You knew she was going to be there that morning?'

'She told me she likes to walk there early on a Sunday.'

'What was this—a date?'

He shook his head. 'We weren't dating.'

Hen glanced towards Stella. 'Sounds to me as if the possibility crossed the young lady's mind.'

'We only met the evening before,' Jake said.

'Where?'

'Chichester Gate.'

She was intrigued to know how. She couldn't believe he had a chat-up line. But to ask would have brought the interchange to a juddering halt. 'How did it come about? Were you alone there?'

'With friends.'

'Ah.' This linked up with something she'd learned before. 'Was this the evening you started with Gemma and ended with Jo?'

'Er, yes.' He plucked at an ear lobe. 'Gemma wasn't my girl-friend,' he said, impelled to add something. 'We went bowling, that's all, and met up with the others.'

'Others?'

'Jo and Rick.'

'And who's Rick?'

'A guy playing bowls with Jo.'

'Was anyone else in the party?'

'No.'

'A foursome, then.'

'It didn't start like that.'

'How did it end, Jake? You teamed up with Jo, right? Did Rick and Gemma pair off as well?'

'No. Rick and Jo left in a taxi. He wasn't feeling well, so she made sure he got home.'

'Was he hammered, then?'

A shake of the head. 'There wasn't much drinking done. We saw a film.'

With communication working as well as it was ever likely to, she switched to the matter that interested her most. 'You first met Gemma at her workplace. Kleentext, the printers, am I right?'

He nodded.

'Tell me about it, Jake.'

'Not much to tell. The council said we could get some Christmas cards printed from a photo. I was sent to arrange it.'

'You made a number of visits there. Four, I believe.'

He gave her a dark look. 'All connected with the cards.'

'I'm sure. But it was through this contact that you persuaded Gemma to go bowling with you?'

'You seem to know all about it.'

'I've already spoken to Gemma. Now I'm getting your side of it. Did you also meet Fiona Halliday, the other woman who drowned?'

'Don't know.'

Stella opened the folder in front of her and took out a photo and pushed it across for Jake to inspect.

He took a look. 'She was around, yes.'

'Around? Didn't you speak?'

'Nothing much,' he said.

'But words were spoken? Come on, Jake. You can do better than this.'

'I was in the office one time and she came through. She asked if I was being looked after. I said I was.'

'That was all?'

'Yes.'

'Did you see her on any other occasion?'

'No.'

'At the printers, or anywhere else?'

'No.'

'You understand why I'm asking? You're the only person we know who met both women who were murdered. Can that be coincidence or is there something that hasn't come out yet?'

He moved his shoulders a fraction.

'Are you sure you didn't meet Fiona some other time? A chance encounter when you suddenly remembered she was the young woman who spoke to you at the printer's?'

He shook his head. He was reverting to his silent mode. Some new line of questioning had to be introduced.

'Do you swim, Jake?'

Another suspicious look. 'I can.'

'Where? In the sea?'

'Mostly.'

'This year?'

'A few times.'

'When's the best time? Not when the beach is crowded, I expect.'

'Doesn't matter.'

'Late in the evening? Early morning?'

'Depends.'

'On what, Jake? The tide?'

'How I feel.'

'You're looking at me as if I'm trying to lasso you. It's no big deal, going for a swim in the sea. I reckon at the end of a day's work in the sun in August or September you must welcome a chance to cool off. You live a short walk from the beach, so why not?' She realised as she spoke that this wasn't a productive question, so she followed it with another. 'When did you last have a dip?'

'Two or three weeks ago.'

'You know what I'm going to ask now. Were you alone?'

'Yes.' He put his hand to his mouth and yawned. 'You're wasting your time with me.'

Denis Cartwright's house in Apuldram stood in its own grounds at the end of a lane. Brick built and faced with the local flint and mortar, it was not large, but had a fine position overlooking the inlet known as Fishbourne Channel—a property that spoke of a comfortable income.

Gemma parked on the gravel drive. 'What now?'

Tension was clumping in Jo's ears. 'We look around.'

The front door had been forced and secured again with a padlock. A printed notice from the police stated that anyone with reason to enter should contact them.

'We're a long way behind the fuzz,' Gemma said.

'And we've got to catch up,' Jo said. 'No, I mean overtake.'

Being isolated, the house was easy to walk around without being seen. The paintwork was well cared-for, the climbing rose trimmed, the paths swept. They looked through all the windows they could. The interior looked nicely furnished. At the rear was a rose garden with a patio overlooking a swimming pool already covered for the winter.

'I see there's an alarm system,' Gemma said. 'Do you think it's working?'

'I expect the police disabled it.'

'Do you think they turned it on again?'

'Probably not, going by the way they padlocked the front door,' Jo said, chancing her arm. 'A bit rough and ready, wasn't it?'

Without actually discussing their next move, they looked to see if by chance a window had been left open. But Cartwright was a careful owner.

'Now that the police have been inside and seen what they want, they won't be in a hurry to come back,' Jo said, trying to sound confident. She was supposed to be the leader of this expedition.

'Probably not. What exactly do you expect to find?'

'I don't know exactly. Something they haven't noticed, I suppose.'

'Proving he's the murderer?'

'Well, yes.'

Doubt had crept into Gemma's eyes, but she continued to play along. 'Shall we check the garden shed? That may not be locked.'

'I bet it is, but we can try.' Jo sensed that this was a delaying move from Gemma, dubious about a break-in to the house itself.

The lock on the shed had been forced recently and reattached so loosely that the hasp came away as soon as Jo touched it. The police must have looked inside.

There was a motor mower and some garden tools. Loungers, a sunshade, and some patio furniture.

'What's that hanging on the wall? Looks like a life-jacket,' Gemma said.

'Dusty,' Jo said. 'Hasn't been used for some time.'

'Well, he's not going to offer one to the women he drowns.'

They giggled a bit and it eased the tension.

'Living here so close to the harbour it's quite likely he has a boat,' Jo said. 'You said the other day he could be living on the Costa del Crime, and it's not impossible. Looking around, I get the feeling he's closed the place down and gone.'

'Sailed off into the sunset?'

'Something like that.'

'Smart move.'

'Exactly,' Jo said. 'If I was on the run from the police I'd use a boat if I could. You're more likely to get caught if you go by any other form of transport.'

'Well, have we done the shed?' Gemma asked.

Jo unhooked a wooden mallet from the tools hanging on the wall. 'We're going to need this.'

They closed the door and reattached the lock.

Law-abiding people have to be pushed past endurance to break with a lifetime of conformity. Jo couldn't get out of her mind the sight of Jake being led away in handcuffs to the police cars. She knew he wouldn't be treated fairly with his prison record. He was mentally scarred already. They'd reduce him to despair and he'd be broken, willing to sign anything they put in front of him.

Without another word to Gemma she walked across the patio

to a small leaded window and smashed it. Three blows made a hole big enough for her to reach inside and unfasten the latch.

'Who would've thought it?' Gemma said.

'What?'

'Jo Stevens. Housebreaker.'

'Are you going to help me in?'

They slid a plant tub against the wall and Jo used it to climb up and through the window space. She found herself in a toilet and stepped down by way of the pedestal. She located the living room, unlocked the patio windows, and let Gemma in.

'Hooligan,' Gemma said.

'Accomplice.'

'What happens now?'

'We see what we can find, and preferably something that links him to Meredith Sentinel. Letters, photos, an address book. Anything.'

'Shall I start in here, then?'

'Better,' Jo said. 'I'll do upstairs.'

She felt uneasy walking through someone's home uninvited, but her reason for being there outweighed the reservations. She knew at once that she wouldn't find much in common with Denis Cartwright. The stairs were carpeted in a bright synthetic green only a man would have chosen, and an insensitive man at that.

She found his bedroom. Better start in the most promising place, she decided. The colour scheme here was equally hideous: the walls in khaki with yellow stripes. The bed was king-size, with a brown quilt. A couple of pictures of old sailing ships were on the wall. No personal items on view. Not a single photo. A stack of books by the bed showed he was a reader of C.S.Forester and Patrick O'Brian—more evidence of a maritime interest.

In the wardrobe his bow ties had a drawer all their own. All the clothes were neatly folded and tidily arranged, but gave off a smell that reminded her of charity shops. She opened the bedside cabinet drawer. Cartwright took diazepam and was a chocolate eater. Nothing to suggest he was also a murderer.

The en suite was clean and bare. He'd taken his washing kit with him.

She went to the top of the stairs and leaned over. 'How's it going?'

'Zilch,' Gemma called back. 'I don't think much of his taste in music. It's all brass bands and military stuff.'

'I'll join you shortly.'

She found a small guest bedroom that—at a stretch—might have been meant for a woman to use. The wallpaper was more feminine, sky blue with daisy shapes. A queen-size bed left little space for much else. A white dressing gown made of towelling hung in an otherwise empty built-in wardrobe. The only picture was a cheap print of Dell Quay. Why do people choose to hang pictures in their houses of local scenes they can visit in five minutes? She could find no evidence that any woman had recently used the room. Why would she, if she was the lover? Only, Jo thought, if the lady found his bedroom wallpaper so off-putting that she insisted on doing the business here.

She checked the bathroom and another bedroom converted into a computer room except that the computer had gone. The police must have taken it. There were just some outmoded diskettes, a printer, mouse-mat, mouse, and loose cables.

'The place has been stripped of anything interesting,' she told Gemma downstairs.

'I know. I found a space where a filing cabinet stands. You can see where the sun bleached the wall above it, and there are paper clips on the floor.'

'If he was more untidy I'd hope to find something. Isn't it infuriating?'

'Don't let it get you down,' Gemma said. 'We'll think of another angle. Want a glass of sherry? I found some in a cupboard.'

'I need something for sure.'

Gemma poured amontillado into two glasses. 'We're not too smart, you and me.'

'Why?'

'Leaving our fingerprints everywhere. The break-in wasn't the neatest, either.'

'Is anyone going to care? We haven't nicked anything. I haven't seen anything I'd want to nick.'

'We're drinking his sherry.'

'He owes us,' Jo said, 'for being such a tosser.'

Gemma laughed. 'I'll drink to that.'

The break-in had achieved one good result. The pair were back in harmony again, as united as they'd been when they quit the yoga class together. 'If my parents could see me now,' Jo said, 'they'd die of shame, poor old dears. They're so conventional.'

'Mine are dead,' Gemma said, 'so I can be as shameful as I want and nobody gives a stuff. Actually, I envy you. I'd like to have someone to shock.'

'Rick?'

'He shocks *me*.'

'He's serious, though, and serious people are easy to kid along.'

'Maybe, but they can bite back. I was in a cold sweat when he said he'd killed Denis Cartwright.'

'Me, too,' Jo said.

'I guess you're right about Rick making that up, but this house does have the feel of a place that's lost its owner for good.'

'I know what you mean.'

Somewhere in the far distance a police siren wailed. Gemma looked anxious. Jo shook her head.

'So what's next on the agenda?' Gemma said. 'Any more break-ins planned?'

Another shake of the head from Jo. 'I'm running out of ideas. I'm worried sick about Jake and what's happening to him.'

'I got that message a while ago. You won't be much use to anyone if you get yourself in a state.'

'What would you do, Gem?'

'To help Jake, you mean? I'd chat up some of the guys down at the boat yard, or in the pub at Dell Quay, and see if anyone knows if Cartwright owned a boat and if its still on its mooring. Or gone.'

'Cool. I like it.'

'Shall we go, then?'

They came out through the patio door, which meant leaving it unlocked. Obligations changed after you'd crossed to the criminal side. As Gemma pointed out, if any other housebreakers wanted to go in and leave more fingerprints they were welcome.

The pity of it was that nothing had been achieved except to put them in more trouble. Jo stood on the patio thinking about Cartwright. 'Does he have a car? He must, living out here in the country. Where is it?'

'There's no garage,' Gemma said. 'I reckon he leaves it on the drive.'

'What does he drive?'

'A big old Peugeot Estate. Red.'

'For one guy?'

'He delivers orders. Plenty of room in the back.'

'Is that why you have such a dinky car—so you can't be asked to deliver stuff?'

Gemma smiled.

'If he was sailing off somewhere,' Jo said, 'he may have left his car at the quay.'

'Good thought. Want to look?'

'Before we do,' Jo said, facing the garden, 'there's one other place we ought to check.'

'Where?'

'We haven't seen under the cover.' She went down the steps to the pool, where the sheet of heavy duty blue polypropylene was stretched across the pool and tiled surround and fastened with straps and springs to anchors set in concrete.

'Can we shift it?' Gemma said doubtfully.

Jo walked around the edge and stopped at the far end. 'Some of these springs aren't properly attached. If we can free some more, the whole lot will get loose. There are tools in the shed.' Hang the consequences, she thought. We're here to do a job. She broke in again and chose a metal stake she could use as a crowbar, returned, passed it under one of the six-inch stainless steel springs, and levered it upwards. The looped end slid over the head of the anchor with a twang and the tension eased. She freed two more.

'Keep going,' Gemma said.

'Get another stake from the shed and help me.'

They worked steadily along the pool edges, forcing off the springs.

In a short time the cover began to dip at the centre. The side that had been freed was dragged into the pool and starting to sink.

'This can't be the recommended way,' Gemma said. 'We'll end up with the cover on the bottom.'

'So what?' Jo was too fired up to be concerned. 'Like we said, we're not leaving the place as we found it. Can you free some more on the other side?'

Action of any sort was such a relief.

They progressed along both sides of the pool until the cover was entirely unfastened. It didn't sink.

'There's some air trapped under it,' Gemma said.

Jo wasn't sure. 'Gem, I don't think it is air. Come round this side and help me give it a pull.'

Gemma joined her and they grabbed the edge and hauled, stepping back as far as they could go. The whole thing weighed a lot.

'We're in the flowerbed,' Gemma said.

About a quarter of the cover was out of the water.

'Oh, no!' Jo said. She dropped the cover and ran to the edge of the pool. Every pulse in her body pounded.

The far edge of the cover was undulating in the blue water. A human leg protruded from it.

twenty

JO COULDN'T SPEAK.

Gemma let go of the pool cover and joined her at the water's edge. 'Oh my God, what have we got here?'

Pure panic.

Jo felt as if her throat was gripped by an unseen hand.

'Is it him?' Gemma asked.

Jo found her voice. 'Not unless he paints his toenails.'

A gasp from Gemma. 'Another dead woman?'

'She looks well dead to me.'

'Shall we do a runner?'

'Can't do that again,' Jo said, trying to get a grip. 'The police have got to be told.'

'Who's going to tell them?'

Jo didn't answer. 'I'm not touching her, but I think we should pull the cover off and see who she is.'

'Let's do it then.'

Together they dragged more of the cover back and revealed the gruesome spectacle of a chalk-white female corpse floating face upwards, but mostly submerged, the head low in the water and the abdomen slightly distended and seeming to keep it from sinking. The torso was contained by a pink one-piece swimsuit in nice condition, at odds with the dead flesh.

Gemma said. 'Gross. I feel like covering her up again.'

'That would be difficult.'

There was a shocked silence.

'Well, who is she?' Jo said in an effort to be practical.

'I don't think we're going to find out. Even if we knew her, would we recognise her in this state?'

Jo let out a long, shaky breath.

Neither spoke as each struggled to subdue the nightmare. Finally Gemma spoke again. 'It's your call. What do we do?'

Jo said for the second time, 'Tell the police, of course. If they need proof that Cartwright is a serial killer this is it. Three drownings.'

'They'll get us for the break-in.'

'Bollocks, Gem. This matters more than anything you and I have done. It proves they've got the wrong man. They'll have to let Jake go.'

'What do we say to them?'

'That we did some investigating ourselves because we suspected Cartwright all along.'

'They won't like it.'

'They can lump it.' She took the phone from her pocket. 'Are you with me, or do I do this alone?'

'I'm on the team, kiddo,' Gemma said, 'but I'll vomit if I stay here looking at that.'

'We'll call them from the car.'

THE INCIDENT room was short of senior officers when the call came. Hen and Stella were having another session with Jake in the interview room. Sergeant Murphy, still wrestling with Cornish drowning statistics, found himself dealing with the new emergency. He coped well, got the name of the informant and the Apuldram address, and radioed for a car to speed to the scene. Then he knocked on the door of Interview Room 2.

Hen came out saying this had better be something special.

Paddy Murphy updated her.

Special it was.

She shook her head. 'Another one? I had a gut feeling this might happen. And the body is at Cartwright's place in Apuldram? But we sent a search team there.'

'They didn't look in the pool, apparently. The cover was over it.'

Hen's face turned crimson. 'Morons! That's the first place I would have looked.' She was on the point of demanding names.

Then, appalled, she remembered who she'd put in charge of the search team.

Stella.

Loyal, dependable Stella, who she'd insisted came with her as deputy when she'd transferred to Chichester. How could Stell have missed something as obvious as the pool?

'To be fair, guv,' Murphy was saying, 'the search team were looking for Cartwright, or clues to his whereabouts. He wouldn't have hidden in the pool because he'd never have been able to fit the cover over himself.' He was straining every sinew to cover for Stella. Everyone in the team adored her.

But Murphy's special pleading only forced Hen to counter it more strongly. 'You can't excuse them, Paddy. Someone is going to be hung out to dry for this. Who discovered the body?'

Murphy cleared his throat like a bit-part actor playing to the gallery. 'Two of the women you interviewed: Jo Stevens and Gemma Casey.'

Hen's eyes didn't register much. The long pause was enough to show her reaction. 'This gets worse. Those two?'

'It seems they weren't impressed with our efforts.'

'*They're* not impressed? I'm not impressed.'

'So they did some sleuthing of their own.'

'They had the savvy to search the pool after our team ignored it? Give me strength. Are they still at the scene?'

'I told them to wait. A car will be there by now. I radioed all units as soon as the shout came.'

'I must get out there. Make sure everyone is alerted: crime scene people, pathologist. I'll need anyone from uniform we can raise. Where's Gary?'

'Canteen, I think.'

'Tell him to bring his car to the front, and fast.'

She went back to Stella. The interview was suspended. Jake would remain in custody while the new incident was dealt with. She said nothing to Stella except that a body had been found at Apuldram. The reckoning would have to wait.

She tried to compose herself on the drive. Her anger had to be pushed to the back of her mind while she assessed the new situation. A third body—presumably another homicidal drowning—removed all uncertainty. A serial killer was at large on her patch. She no longer needed to spend time probing motives. Psychopaths killed routinely on the slightest of pretexts. This one was in the habit of drowning women. It could be as simple as that. He'd stake out his locale near water and wait for an opportunity. Or he'd lure the victim to it. They could be charming and persuasive, these nutters.

On the face of it, Cartwright now had centre stage. A body in his pool, his garden, surely clinched it, allowing that he'd gone missing. The manhunt must be stepped up, using Interpol. He'd kill repeatedly until he was caught.

Yet the strange thing was that the search of his house and office hadn't yielded any clue to a fixation with drowning. His hard disk had been picked apart for downloads that would confirm his guilt. He was a sailing enthusiast, admittedly. Looked at the websites, read the books, took the magazines. But floating on water wasn't the same as wanting to be in it with your hands on some poor woman's shoulders, forcing her under for minutes on end until she drowned.

Denis Cartwright appeared to be a loner with no history of mental illness, no previous, whose divorce had left him out of touch with everything except his business, obsessive about tidiness and eccentric in dress (the bow ties), but friendly to his staff, vulnerable to advances from an ambitious young woman like Fiona, yet with no obvious potential for violence. You'd expect to have found something if it existed.

His ex-wife might have given some helpful insights. Unfortunately she'd died of cancer three years after the divorce. There were no children and no close relatives.

Hen felt in her pocket and fingered her pack of cigarillos.

Extra pressure was inevitable now that a third victim had been found. A media frenzy would follow. Just as surely, the high-ups in headquarters would question whether an officer of chief inspector rank was competent to investigate. Trouble was looming about the use of the helicopter this morning. And when they learned that Cartwright's house and garden had been searched previously and the body missed they'd really have something to chew on. She didn't relish the next couple of days.

Sensing, correctly, that this wasn't the right time to comment on victim number three, Gary asked, 'Did you get much out of Jake, guv?'

She stared ahead. Large drops of rain were hitting the windscreen. Typical of the day so far if the crime scene took a drenching that washed away all traces of the killer. 'What did you ask?'

'About Jake.'

The big man still in custody was just one more problem. 'If I tell you he's not saying much, you're going to say, "So what's new?" The latest on Jake is that he's not said anything to incriminate himself. Yet.'

'But he resisted arrest.'

'He's an ex-con. He doesn't expect any favours from us. I don't blame him for that.'

'And what does he say to the fact that he met Fiona as well as the first victim?'

'Nothing sinister in it, according to him. He was at the printer's ordering Christmas cards for the nature reserve. He claims she came by and asked if he was being looked after and he answered yes and those were the only words she ever spoke to him. In fact, he was more interested in Gemma Casey, who we're shortly going to meet again. They went ten-pin bowling together. A cosy little quartet was formed that evening. Jo Stevens was the other woman and she was partnered by a man called Rick, who I haven't met yet. But I'm seeing more than I wish of the two women. They're a pain in the backside.'

'Is Jo the one who acted as a decoy at Pagham this morning?'

'Yes, she's batting for Jake.'

'What does Rick think about that?'

'I just told you I haven't met the guy. I gather he switched to Gemma. And now the same two women turn up in Apuldram sniffing around Cartwright's place and finding the body that my own officers missed. God, I could do with a smoke. Put your foot down, Gary.'

* * *

SHELTERING FROM the downpour under a conifer, she'd got through two of her cigarillos and was lighting a third when the pathologist arrived. The white-clad crime scene officers and uniform PC's had secured the area around the pool with tape and retreated to their transport. Everyone had a valid excuse to stay under cover until the pathologist had done his stuff. Only the dead woman lay exposed to the rain, adrift in the middle of the pool, any parts of the pink costume above the waterline now as saturated and strawberry-coloured as the rest.

Dr Kibblewhite was new to Hen, a tall white-haired man with a stoop and a squeaky voice. He was carrying a huge blue umbrella with the words SAVE TUFTY written on it in white. 'A freebie from a previous case,' he explained to Hen. 'You never know what's coming your way in this job. Tufty was a pedigree bull under threat of slaughter in a bovine TB scare. There was a huge campaign and more tests were ordered and he was saved and it was champagne all round, but one of his supporters was unwise enough to pat him on the head. I did the autopsy. Would you mind holding the brolly over me? Should keep us both dry with any luck.'

They stepped out to the pool's edge and Kibblewhite rubbed some warmth into his surgical gloves and drew them on. 'She's no use to me where she is.'

'That's where she was found,' Hen said.

'If you think I'm going to wade out to see her, you're mistaken,' he said. 'Can someone find a boat hook and pull her to the side?'

A boat hook in a private garden?

Hen called Gary over and explained the problem. He went across to the garden shed and returned with a rake.

'Well done, young man,' Kibblewhite said when the floating corpse had been pulled to the pool edge. 'Now fetch some help and let's see if you can land the beauty.'

Gary shouted for assistance and two uniformed officers came running from under the trees. Ropes were passed under the body and it was hoisted from the pool and gently lowered onto the tiled surround.

With Hen holding the umbrella with one hand and a tissue to her nose with the other, Kibblewhite crouched and began the examination. 'My estimate is that she's been in the water more than two days and less than five,' he said after he'd pulled some hair from the head and examined the wrinkled hands and feet. 'The obvious results of immersion.'

'Drowning?' Hen asked.

'I said immersion. There's a distinction.' Kibblewhite turned to look up at her. 'I can tell you now, Chief Inspector, that you'll hear nothing about drowning from me at this juncture, and you may not hear it at all.'

'And what's the good news?'

'I mean it. After several days have gone by, as they obviously have, it's not easy to form an opinion and I certainly won't give you one at the poolside.' He'd taken a tape recorder from his pocket and started addressing it in a way that brooked no interruption. 'Maceration well under way. Skin tissue deteriorating already.' As if on second thoughts he turned to Hen again. 'Pardon me if that sounded unfriendly. It wasn't meant as such. But don't expect any Quincy–type revelations from me.'

'Did you say Quinsy?'

'Quincy, M.E., as on television. The M.E. standing for medical examiner. You must have seen it. He solves the mystery and outwits the police every time. I first got hooked in the late seventies.'

'Before my time.'

'Isn't it on any more? It was a while ago. I've got the entire series on DVD. The technical stuff is way out of date now, but I enjoy the stories. I expect you watch that CSI thing.'

'Can you say anything that will help us identify her?' Hen asked, not wanting to go any further down the television road.

'Not a lot. The slight distension you see is trapped gas and will have brought the body to the surface. Left any longer the effect will increase markedly. She's small in stature, smaller than you and probably slimmer, if I may be personal. Age fifty, give or take.'

'Give or take how much?'

'Five years. May I continue? Dyed hair and painted nails—which you can see for yourself.'

'Bruising?'

'No chance of finding any. Look at the state of the skin. When I've examined the internal organs I may have more to tell you.' He stood up. 'Where's that young man disappeared to?'

Gary was summoned again.

'Help me turn her over,' Kibblewhite said, producing a second pair of gloves.

Hen said, 'Are you all right with that, Gary?'

'I think so, guv.'

When the manoeuvre was complete, Kibblewhite said, 'No signs of wounding that I can discover. I've done all I can here. I'm going to make a dash for it now. Do me a favour and keep the umbrella over her until they take her away. You can return it to me at the autopsy. '

'When will that be?'

'Tomorrow morning at the mortuary. Be warned. Cases like this take longer than average.'

Hen gave Gary the umbrella to hold. 'You're allowed to take the gloves off now.'

'Will it be for long, guv? I feel such an idiot standing here with everyone watching.'

'Ignore them. You look distinguished, like a butler.'

'A butler?'

'The gloves, Gary. You don't need them. And if I can be personal, do you wear that suit when you're off work?'

'No, guv. T-shirts and jeans mostly. I was told if you want to become a suit, you'd better wear one.'

'It's about ambition, is it? No bad thing. I don't know where you got that advice. It may be true for lawyers and undertakers, but not CID. Our job is about blending in. I won't think any less of you if you come in your jeans tomorrow.'

He looked as if the sun had come out. 'Thanks.'

'Are the two women still out front? I'll speak to them shortly.'

'You first,' Hen said, pointing at Gemma.

'We're in this together,' Jo said.

'Doesn't mean I see you together,' Hen said. 'I want two

witness statements and we'll do it inside, in the dry. I'm going to open the house.'

'It's open already,' Gemma informed her. 'You can get in round the back by the patio doors.' She glanced at Jo. 'We might as well own up, sunshine. They're going to find out sooner or later.'

'You've been inside?' Hen said, resigned to more lawbreaking.

'For a search,' Gemma said.

'Oh, how enterprising.' Hen set off round the house to the rear and saw the smashed window. 'And such subtlety.' She slid the patio door aside. 'Wait here under the canopy, Miss Stevens.'

In the living room she and Gemma sat in armchairs. Gary had finished his stint with the umbrella and joined them.

'What on earth were you doing here?' Hen asked Gemma after going through the preliminaries.

Gemma had wide, persuasive, blue eyes. She tried to make it all sound as sensible as insurance. 'My friend Jo was deeply upset when you arrested Jake yet again. She thinks he's being victimised and she wants to do something to help him.'

'By creating a distraction?'

'Not at all.' Gemma wasn't going to be intimidated. 'This was properly thought through. We talked it over and decided my boss, Mr Cartwright, very likely killed Fiona and maybe the other woman as well, so we came here to look for evidence.'

'You took the law into your own hands and broke in?'

'When the law is heading up a blind alley someone has to point the way,' Gemma said, and folded her arms as if expecting to be challenged.

'Before we go any further,' Hen said, 'I'd like to hear why you in particular suspect Denis Cartwright is capable of murder.'

'We've been over this. I worked with the man. Fiona led him on outrageously and he fell for it.'

'I know all that,' Hen said. 'Didn't you hear my question?'

'He was driven beyond all.'

'So Fiona brought it on herself, did she? The old story.'

'I'm not excusing him,' Gemma said. 'I was putting myself in his shoes. He's a yellow-bellied coward if you really want to know. Anything unpopular with the staff, he asked me to speak to them.

He wanted everyone to think he was mister nice guy. But if he was pushed into a corner I'm sure he'd bite back. That was Fiona's big mistake.'

'She pushed him into a corner?'

'Onto his office floor, to be accurate. And they weren't discussing the petty cash.'

'Are you sure of that?'

'My office is next door. I heard the audio version.'

'Did anyone else know of this?'

'It was all round the office. She wanted a top job and a seat on the board.'

'If this is true, and Cartwright felt pressured, he may have had a motive. But nothing like this happened with the other victims.'

'I can't say, can I? I don't know what went on between them and him.'

'We haven't found any connection. We've searched his house, his computer, his office at work. Nothing. But we're quite sure Fiona's killer also murdered Meredith Sentinel.'

'What about the woman in his pool, then? If that isn't a connection, I don't know what is. That's two out of three.'

Hen didn't challenge the statement. 'When you got here this afternoon, did you break in and search the house first?'

'Yes.'

'Find anything?'

'No.'

'And then you decided to look in the pool. Whose idea was that, yours, or Jo's?'

Gemma frowned. 'I don't think that's important.'

'I'll be the judge,' Hen said.

She shrugged. 'Jo thought of it. Either of us could have done.'

'And was that blue cover in place?'

'Right across the pool, but we managed to shift it. One end wasn't properly attached, and that helped.'

'What do you mean, not properly attached?'

'Some of the springs weren't fixed to the bolt things. That made it easier to get a start.'

'What did you expect to find?'

'We were looking for Mr Cartwright, weren't we? He's the missing person, after all. We didn't know anyone else was missing. Have you found out who she is?'

'Not yet.'

'We did the decent thing reporting it,' Gemma said in a too-obvious attempt to excuse their conduct. 'We shouldn't have broken into the house, but we found the body for you.'

Hen wasn't giving votes of thanks. 'Have you been in trouble before?'

'What—with the police? Certainly not. You can check your records.'

'You're local, are you?'

'I've lived here all my life.'

'Do you have family down here in Sussex, then?'

'Only an old aunt and I don't see much of her. My parents died in a crash when I was nine. And in case you're wondering, I wasn't the maladjusted kid who turned to crime. I was with foster parents until I was seventeen.'

'And then?'

'A flat of my own. I went to Chichester Tech, as it was known then, got myself an Ordinary National Diploma in business studies, and took the job at Fishbourne. If you let me off with a caution I won't trouble you again.'

Right now Hen had more on her mind than Gemma's misdemeanour. 'This man Rick is the fourth member of your little clique.'

'Rick's got nothing to do with this,' she said at once.

'You're in a relationship with him.'

'I wouldn't call it that. He's a friend. We've been out a few times. We don't live together.'

'You four band together and help each other out, is that right?'

'Isn't that what friends do?'

'Provided it's legal. But if you had serious doubts about one of your friends it wouldn't be wise to cover for them. Loyalty is one thing. Conspiracy to cover up a crime is something else. Do you follow me?'

Gemma nodded.

'Gary will help you with your written statement. You'll have to give evidence at the inquest as well. Make sure it's accurate.'

The next one could wait.

Hen went out to check on the search she'd organised of the garden area around the pool. The chance of a smoke was incidental to her supervisory duty.

About twenty unfortunate officers in uniform were moving slowly with heads down across the sodden turf in the unrelenting rain. She found the senior man from the crime scene investigators and asked if there was any chance of recovering DNA from the pool cover.

'You think the killer handled it?' the man said.

'I'm sure of it. The body was hidden underneath and the two women found the cover in place, but one end had a few springs loose. He must have tried to fasten part of it at least to the things that keep it stretched.'

'The anchors.'

'Right. You'll take it to the lab?'

'Of course. But you must allow that the house owner would have handled it on a number of occasions. If we find any trace of his DNA, that doesn't mean he's guilty. And of course the women who found the body will have left some of their skin tissue on the fabric. It's not so simple as it might appear.'

'Nothing ever is.'

She went back to the house and questioned Jo for ten minutes. Little came out of it except the repeated insistence that Jake was innocent and should be released. At such times Hen despaired of her own sex.

Back in the garden she checked with the searchers and shook her head when she saw the result: a few rusty nails and the plastic cap from a tube of sunscreen. She watched the body being stretchered away to the mortuary van. The most pressing need was to identify the victim. But how? The face was too far gone to use in a photo appeal. The woman hadn't been wearing a ring, or jewellery. The pink swimming costume looked like a standard garment unlikely to yield much.

She pondered the possible events leading up to the murder.

The woman was most unlikely to have arrived at the house in a swimming costume. Logic suggested she'd changed out of her day clothes in the house. None had been found, but that was surely because the killer disposed of them, just as he'd disposed of Meredith Sentinel's clothes the night he'd murdered her on Selsey beach. He'd realise they would help with identification.

If the latest victim had been persuaded to change for a swim she must have trusted her killer. You don't get into a private pool with a stranger. She must have known him and come to the house. Who else could her host have been but Denis Cartwright? He'd got into the water with her and drowned her.

No.

Something was wrong here. Cartwright had been missing for almost two weeks. This body had been in the water for a much shorter interval—two to five days, the pathologist had estimated.

Was Cartwright alive, then? Had he returned to the house with this woman, persuaded her to join him for a swim, and drowned her?

Any other scenario was too far fetched. The killer pretends he owns the house and pool and makes elaborate arrangements to fool the woman into visiting? No chance.

Hold on, she thought. I'm assuming too much here. Kibblewhite spoke of immersion, but refused to say the woman had drowned, or anyone had drowned her. Did she die accidentally? A sudden heart attack while in the water?

Were other people present? A swimming party? Drinks, larking about, and she hits her head on the stone surround and nobody notices until it's too late?

Whichever elaborate story you dream up, you're faced with the fact that the woman's death was concealed. Nobody pulls a cover across a small private pool without noticing a body in the water. It was a hidden crime, hidden with the expectation that nothing would be found until next year when the weather was warm enough for swimming.

The bottom line was this: Cartwright's pool, in Cartwright's garden, and Cartwright was missing.

twenty-one

THE MANHUNT WAS STEPPED UP.

Cartwright was no longer just a missing person. The official line, that he was wanted for questioning in connection with the deaths of three women, was sent out with a 'not for publication' note that he was believed to be a psychopath likely to kill again.

Hen's morning started at the mortuary. She'd never been squeamish about attending autopsies. It was the tough-talking men—bless their little cotton socks—who were liable to faint as soon as the pathologist picked up the scalpel. Even so, this one was a severe test, definitely a face mask and tic tac occasion. The well-prepared Dr Kibblewhite had brought two cans of air freshener and they were put to good use from the start.

To put everyone at ease while cutting away the pink swimsuit, he talked with affection about one of Dr Quincy's television episodes. 'You didn't see the dissection. Never did in those days. The only bits of the body you saw were the feet or the face. All very wholesome. So I can't say for certain if Quincy would have destroyed a perfectly good costume as I'm doing here, but, if you think about it, even if I removed it without damage I doubt if anyone would wear it.' He cut off the label and handed it to Hen. Speedo was so common a make that it was almost no help at all.

Photos had to be taken at each stage, prolonging the operation. Kibblewhite stressed that drowning is difficult, if not impossible, to diagnose at post mortem when the body is no longer fresh. No question that water was in the lungs and would be sent for analysis with the other samples, but he doubted if he could state the cause of death even when the results came back. And with the sodden skin deteriorating and no other injuries apparent, he could find no external evidence that the woman's demise had been homicidal.

Neither were there any useful clues to identity. No scars. She was aged about fifty, give or take five years, and she looked after her hair and nails, like a million other women. Two of the fingernails on the right hand were torn, but Kibblewhite said it would not be wise to read too much into that. They may have been damaged when the body was taken from the pool. 'They go soft, you see.'

'My lads lifted her out,' Hen said. 'I was watching them.'

'So was I. It's so easily done.'

'I notice you just tugged out some hair at the roots.'

'Deliberately. Another indication of the amount of time she spent in the water,' Kibblewhite told her. 'The hair loosens.'

'Are you sticking with your estimate of two to five days?'

'I am.'

'You can't be more precise than that?'

'Too many variables.'

'That hair you just removed. If you bag some up for me, I'll ask for an immediate DNA test.'

'You're an optimist.'

'I'm sure Quincy would take the trouble,' she said, unable to resist the dig.

'Quincy didn't know about DNA.' He used tweezers to put some hairs into an evidence bag and handed it to her. 'Don't forget to label it.'

The dissection was more productive, or so Kibblewhite claimed. He went so far as to mention the word 'drowning' as a possibility after finding froth in the main air passages and over-distension of the lungs. Only after he'd seen the results of lab tests would he know if he could say more.

Hen came away thinking she could have been better employed at the nick. Outside, the rain was belting down again. She sprinted through the puddles to her car. When she got there she swore mildly. The SAVE TUFTY umbrella was still on the back seat, neatly furled. She ran all the way back and returned the precious souvenir to its owner as he came out of the door.

'But you're drenched,' Kibblewhite said. 'Why didn't you use it?'

THERE WAS better news when she got back to the incident room. Cartwright's red Peugeot Estate had been found near the boatyard at Dell Quay. The registration had been checked with Swansea and the car transported to Chichester for forensic examination.

'Hey, that's the first good thing I've heard today. There's sure to be evidence inside.'

'Remember who we're dealing with, guv. His middle names are spick and span,' Paddy Murphy told her. 'It's as clean as a Buckingham Palace loo.'

Hen tried to stay upbeat. 'We'll get something back from the Motor Investigation Unit, if it's only grit from his shoes. It's safe to assume, then, that he put to sea.'

'Well, his boat hasn't been found.'

'What sort is it?'

'Quite modest. A twelve-metre yacht called *Nonpareil*.'

'Called what?'

'Did I say it wrong? It's written on the board over there. Gary says it's a printing term, a typeface.'

'I think it also means the best. I wouldn't call that modest.'

'He was proud of the boat when he named her, I expect,' Paddy said. 'She isn't in top nick, according to the locals, but seaworthy enough to cross the channel. A full description went out with the call to Interpol.'

'At twelve metres, it has a sleeping berth, no doubt. He could lay up in some French port for weeks and not be noticed.'

'Not for much longer.'

'Let's hope.' A shadow crossed Hen's face. 'I can see some unfortunate Frenchwoman being invited aboard and becoming victim number four.'

'Sweet Jesus. I hope not.' Paddy passed a hand thoughtfully through his silver hair. 'Most crimes I can understand, even when they're evil. This one is a mystery to me. What's in it for him?'

'Better ask a shrink, Paddy. Pulling them in is my job.'

'Yes, but we need to know the motive.'

'With psychos you can't tell. Some kill out of boredom. That's not a motive. In this case we've got a pattern and we're collecting evidence and we know who we're looking for. Enough to be going on with.'

She walked across to the display board where the name of Cartwright's yacht had been written. It was below his head and shoulders picture—one they'd found in his house and distributed to the press. He looked inoffensive and trying to appear likeable, like some local election candidate, hair parted in an old-fashioned style, eyes wide and hopeful, lips curved in a diffident smile. The check bow tie was the only remarkable feature. Did it reveal humour? Self-regard? Or a nut? Whichever, you would look in vain for signs of violence.

Hen wasn't fooled. She'd seen killers in real life. Maybe one in twenty looked the person you wouldn't share a lift with.

The other two mugshots on display—Dr Sentinel and Jake Kernow—were more believable as murderers, Jake especially. Sentinel's thin lips arched in a cruel way. As for Jake, well, he'd curdle the milk by looking at it.

He was still in custody. She'd have to come to a decision soon.

'Call for you, ma'am,' one of the civilian staff said.

Hope rising, she picked up a phone, and wished she hadn't. Headquarters. The Deputy Chief Constable himself.

She took a deep breath and listened.

'We've been following this enquiry into the drownings. You appear to have someone in the frame now, this print manager.'

'Cartwright.'

'He's being sought in all the French ports as well as our own. Is that correct?' The voice was so courteous, so reasonable.

Ominously so.

'Yes, sir. We found a third body yesterday afternoon, concealed in Cartwright's swimming pool. I'm waiting for confirmation that she was drowned. It raises the stakes. There's no question in my mind that we're pursuing a serial murderer, so I alerted Interpol.'

'No problem with that. But is it a fact that this was the second search of Cartwright's house and garden?'

The knife unsheathed. Stella, you dozy mare, I'm walking the plank for you, she thought. 'That's true. The first search was Sunday morning, after the second victim was found. The last sight of her was leaving the Fishbourne office with Cartwright. Neither of them was seen alive after that, so I obtained a warrant and sent a team to the house.'

'Didn't you take charge yourself?'

'I accept responsibility, but, no. I wasn't there. I was following up another lead.' Francisco. Please don't ask, she thought.

'Did your people take a passing glance at the pool?'

She couldn't bluff her way through this. 'I believe not.'

'Don't you know for certain?'

'I haven't had time to check with the inspector who led the search. I've just come from the post mortem.'

'You're obviously under a lot of pressure.'

Dangerous to concede. 'But on top of the job.'

'I would say it's pretty obvious something was wrong with the search because the body was in that pool for up to five days.'

'Two to five, yes.'

'If the team had done its job, the hunt for Cartwright might be over by now.'

'Conceivably.'

'Somebody goofed, Chief Inspector. I wouldn't go out of my way to cover for them if I were you. Being an effective leader matters more than loyalty to a colleague.'

From deep in her subconscious she dredged up an old saying. 'But if you can't ride two horses at once, you shouldn't be in the circus.'

It stopped him in his tracks.

He took a few seconds to think about it before saying, 'Another thing: you're still holding this man, Kernow. Why?'

'He's been under strong suspicion for some time. He knew the first victim, Meredith Sentinel, and met her in London. And we've established that he visited the print works and spoke to victim number two, Fiona Halliday. What is more, he served two years for GBH.'

'I know all that, but if Cartwright is your man—as everything

seems to suggest—Kernow can reasonably claim wrongful deten-
tion. I'm not his solicitor, but if I were, I know what I'd be doing.'

How could she explain the feeling in her bones that
Cartwright was not the killer, even in the face of all the evidence?

'I'll bear that in mind, sir.'

'This has become a high profile investigation. I can bring in
some big hitters from another division.'

'No thanks.'

'It may be necessary.'

'It isn't, and I don't expect it to become so,' Hen said with all
the authority she could muster.

After cradling the phone she went outside the building. Some
people keep going on caffeine. She knew what her fix was.

By standing with her back in the open doorway she had some
protection from the rain. How the anti-smoking brigade would
view this, she didn't like to think. Some of the fumes would certainly drift over her shoulder into the building, try as she did to
blow them across the car park.

She'd been there about a minute when she was aware of someone standing behind her. She edged to one side and said, 'There's
room.'

They didn't squeeze by, so she turned and saw it was Stella,
looking uncomfortable, as well she might.

'Come to clear the air, have you?' Hen said. 'You'll have a job.'

'They're saying upstairs that you took some flak from headquarters because of me,' Stella said. She continued to stand inside
at a safe distance.

'A little.' Hen was forced to turned her head to exhale.

'I'm sorry.'

'You know what it's about?'

'Paddy phoned me at home last night. I didn't get much sleep.'

'What amazes me, Stell, is that I can generally bank on you to
carry out a search. It was so bloody obvious, that pool with the
ghastly blue cover. I don't know how you missed it.'

'I didn't,' she said.

'Even those two wretched women. . . . What did you just say?'

'I looked in the pool. I had Sergeant Malcolm from uniform

lift the cover at both ends. We didn't take it off completely because I could see it would be a major operation putting it back. Stupid. Everything was so tidy in the house that I got into a mindset of leaving the place as we found it.'

'Go over it again.'

'We switched on the lights and I knelt down and looked under the cover and couldn't see anything. The sergeant did the same. Don't ask me how, but we must have missed the body.'

'You were sure the pool was empty?'

'I really thought so.'

'And you had lights on? Could you see to the other end?'

'I thought so at the time. I'm really sorry.'

'And when it was over, you put it all back in place?'

'Tried to. It's quite technical. Sergeant Malcolm said you need an Allen key to adjust the bolt things that hold the springs in place. We had to leave some of them undone.'

She recalled Gemma Casey saying one end had not been fixed properly. Stella wasn't making this up. 'If the body was lying on the bottom would you have missed it?'

'I can't understand how, with the lights on as well.'

'How deep is it?'

'Not much over two metres. The water was clear.'

'I saw.' Hen puffed on her skinny cigar. 'I thought you must have failed to notice the pool. You failed to notice the body.'

'That's worse,' Stella said.

'I wasn't going to say it, but you're right.'

'Don't know about you,' Gemma said to Jo as they drove away from Apuldram, 'but I don't feel like going back to work after that.'

'Starbucks?'

'Great suggestion.'

'Some people call them pigs,' Jo said.

'The police, you mean?'

'Yes. I've always thought it was unfair. Until today. That's what they are—pigs. They're disgusting. We do the public-spirited thing and report what we found in the pool, proving Cartwright must be the killer and what do we get in return? The third degree. Anyone would think we were murderers.'

'And they're still holding Jake.'

'It breaks me up, Gem. It's sadistic.'

THEY EACH had a black espresso and an almond croissant, to restore the blood sugar, as Gemma put it.

Jo hadn't finished her diatribe against the police. 'It was insulting. The Hen woman was questioning me about my background, how long I've lived here, all kinds of stuff you only ask of criminals.'

'We did break into a house, matey.'

'Not to steal.'

'We were in the wrong, Jo. She gave me a going-over, too. It wasn't about us actually. It was about her annoyance that we discovered something she missed.'

'Do you think so?'

'Good thing she doesn't know the whole truth.'

Jo frowned. 'What's that?'

'Us being the first to find Fiona's body.'

'Christ Almighty, yes. Keep your voice down, Gem.'

'In fact, you found all three bodies.'

Jo blinked and gasped. 'That's true.'

Gemma gave her conspiratorial grin. 'And we associate with a man who confessed to murdering a fourth.'

'Rick.' Jo's throat was dry. 'But we don't believe him, do we?'

'I think we'll find out soon. Mallin knows about him. She calls us a clique and she warned me not to cover up for my friends. I don't think she meant you.'

'She meant Jake.'

'I doubt it. I think she'll soon be knocking on Rick's door.'

'You're making me nervous,' Jo said. 'This was supposed to calm us down. I don't like to think what Rick might say under questioning.'

'He's rock solid. Don't worry.'

twenty-two

HEN DIDN'T BOTHER MUCH with snail mail. Everything that mattered reached her by phone, email, or internal memo. The few letters with her name on them got dropped into a tray on her desk and could stay unopened through the day. Most were junk. A few were from attention-seekers who'd seen her on television or in the press. Rarely anything worth troubling over.

So it wasn't unusual that a typed envelope with a London postmark didn't get opened until mid-afternoon.

It wasn't even a proper letter.

She almost tossed it aside without reading it.

The sender had scribbled a few words on a Post-it attached to a white invitation card. 'Found this among Merry's papers,' was all Austen Sentinel had written before adding his initials.

The wording couldn't have made more impact if it had grabbed Hen by the throat. Embossed lettering on fine, cream-coloured board.

In September, 1987, the skeleton of a mammoth was uncovered on Selsey's East Beach and excavated by a team from Brighton University, assisted by volunteers. To mark the twentieth anniversary of this notable event you are invited to a reunion barbecue on the section of beach where the dig took place.

Saturday 15 September, 8.30 p.m. Free food, drink, and eighties music.

No reply necessary. To have fun with old friends just turn up . . . like the mammoth did.

She now knew why Meredith Sentinel had returned to Selsey for the first time in twenty years.

Heart racing, she snatched up her phone and dialled Sentinel's number. He answered at once.

'Hen Mallin, Chichester CID,' she said. 'Just read your note. Quite a discovery.'

'Yes, it answers one question and begs some others,' he said as if he were talking about an essay topic instead of the invitation that had led to his wife's death. 'I thought you should see it for yourself.'

'You found it among her papers?'

'A few items I'd overlooked when I went through her belongings last week. She sometimes put letters and such things in a glass cabinet where we keep the silverware. It served as her PENDING tray. After she'd dealt with them she threw them out.'

'Was the invitation in an envelope?'

'Not when I found it. She got rid of envelopes.'

'You're certain of that?'

'Didn't I just explain? I don't understand why it matters.'

'Because I need to know who was behind this invitation. It may be crucial to find out. We can get DNA from an envelope. We might get some from the card itself, but the envelope would be better. And the postmark would be useful. There's no return address or name on the card.'

'I noticed that. No RSVP. Unusual.'

'You're telling me there's no chance at all of finding the envelope? Not even with a special search?'

'Sorry to disappoint you. My wife was well organised. She didn't keep wrappers of any kind. And she made a point of using the shredder.' The voice sounded smug, as if he enjoyed frustrating the investigation.

Hen let it pass. There was more to prise out from this obnoxious man. 'How would they have traced her? She'd have been known by her maiden name in 1987.'

'Through the university, I expect. They have an alumni association. Their magazine publishes news of former students and there are always reunions being organised.'

'She was in her first year when it took place, you said?'

'A fresher, yes.'

'How many other people would have received one of these invites?'

'How would I know?'

She felt a surge of fury. 'You were in charge, for God's sake. You'd know how many were involved in the dig.'

'Can't be precise. Anything from twenty to forty.'

'I'm going to need their names and addresses.'

'Don't ask me. I couldn't even begin to remember. I told you before, they were just willing hands as far as I was concerned.' His attitude was breathtaking.

'Where could I find a list?'

'God knows, all these years later. I don't suppose one exists.'

She was trying to suppress her annoyance and not succeeding. 'You told me you published some illustrated articles about the dig. Get them out, please, look at them and see if you recognise anyone in the photos. Where can I get copies for myself?'

'The university library ought to have them.'

'Thanks. You must have had one of these invitations yourself.'

'I don't recall one.'

'Come on, Dr Sentinel. You led the dig. It would have been *Hamlet* without the Prince.'

'Ha. That's a point.' He seemed to enjoy that. 'But the Prince was missing. I don't need to remind you I was in St Petersburg at the time.'

'Or Helsinki.'

'Er, yes.' Not quite so bumptious.

Hen played to his vanity. 'It seems odd for anyone to have organised a reunion without consulting you first about the arrangements.'

'Going by the wording on the invitation, I'm not surprised. It was my dig, my show, but they don't mention me by name. I get the impression this was an undergraduates-only event.'

'They're not undergraduates any more. They'll be forty-year-olds with their own careers.'

'You don't understand, do you? I was in the senior common room in nineteen-eighty-seven.'

Hen couldn't see how that made a blind bit of difference.

'Something else you can do for me immediately after you put down the phone, Dr Sentinel. Look through your own correspondence and see if you can find the invitation to you, preferably still in the envelope. Handle it as little as possible. Get back to me at once and we'll arrange to pick it up.'

Immediately after the call she announced the breakthrough to the team. Spirits had not been high since the blunder over the body in the pool and it was a huge relief to have a new lead. There was spontaneous applause.

'The priority now is to get hold of some more of these invitations,' Hen told them. 'There could be as many as forty in circulation. Some will have been thrown out by now, but some people keep such things as souvenirs. What I'd dearly like to find is one in its original envelope that we can get forensically tested.'

'So we discover who was behind it?' Paddy Murphy said.

'That would be a start.'

Hen explained about the alumni association and said she would speak to them herself. She asked Gary to check with Brighton University library for articles and references to the mammoth excavation. 'Don't get bogged down with the technicalities. It's the people who interest us.'

Stella said, 'If I remember, Dr Sentinel said the dig was before the start of term, so he was recruiting anyone he could get hold of, including locals.'

'Good point. We can go on local radio tonight and ask for help. The listeners are good at responding to that sort of appeal. Would you take care of that?'

'Absolutely.'

Hen knew it would be done well. 'One other thing, Stell. When we were searching the beach at Selsey, do you recall seeing signs of a recent barbecue? Blackened stones, ash, bits of tinfoil lying about?'

'Can't say I do, guv.'

'Must have been another section.' She snapped her fingers. 'They told us where it was. Paddy, find out the exact place where the mammoth was found.'

The alumni association proved to be the ideal means of

contacting ex-students. Once Hen had explained to the secretary who she was and why she needed the information, she was supplied with contact numbers for seventeen archaeologists from the late 1980s.

'Great. We'll have some witnesses soon,' she announced to the team.

In the next hour the incident room resembled a call centre as attempts were made to reach former students. A thumb would be raised in the air each time contact was made.

But the initial response was disappointing. Most remembered the mammoth dig, but hadn't taken part because it was all over before they arrived for the new term. The third woman Hen managed to contact was more helpful. Like the others she'd missed the dig, but she recalled the name of a friend who took part. Although they hadn't seen each other in years, she had a phone number.

Hen raised both thumbs.

The woman was home and confirmed that she'd joined in the dig. Her name was Brenda Sutton and she sounded intelligent and keen to help. 'Yes, I remember the whole thing. It was fascinating. I was so lucky to be part of it because I was reading English, not archaeology. I just happened to be up at the uni early looking for a flat, which—with more good luck—I found on the first day. Dr Sentinel was in the refectory asking for volunteers and I jumped at the chance. There must have been twenty of us being bussed out to Selsey each morning.'

'Do you remember an American fresher called Merry or Meredith?'

'Not by name, but yes, there was an American girl with a marked Southern drawl. I was with a couple of friends and we tended to stay together, so I don't recall the other people's names.'

Even so, this was real progress: someone who had been there in 1987. 'And did you go to the reunion in September?'

'No,' she said, her voice rising in surprise. 'Was there one?'

Hen's hopes plunged again. 'For the twentieth anniversary. A barbecue.'

'I missed that, I'm afraid. Pity.'

'Invitations were sent out.'

'I've moved recently. Perhaps mine got returned to the sender.'

'You spoke of a couple of friends on the dig. Have you kept up with them?'

'Noreen Chick and Peter Schooley. Wait a moment while I get my address book.'

Across the room, Paddy was waving. He'd traced another of the diggers. In the next half hour a list of Dr Sentinel's team began to emerge. Fourteen names were scribbled on the display board, most with phone numbers.

Unfortunately, of the first eight questioned on the phone, not one had come to the barbecue or even received an invitation.

Paddy spoke for everyone when he commented that it was a real downer. They'd contacted twenty per cent of the original group and drawn a blank.

'We keep trying,' Hen said.

She'd had another idea. Jake Kernow was still in a cell downstairs. He'd been questioned in three long sessions about his links to the second victim, Fiona, and little of significance had emerged. The custody clock was ticking. Because murder was a serious arrestable offence he could be held for up to thirty-six hours without charge, but a warrant would be needed after that.

She had him brought to an interview room. Stella was sitting in this time.

'You can do yourself some good now,' Hen said to Jake. 'This isn't connected with what we talked about before. It's about Meredith Sentinel, and you freely admit you met her. In fact you texted us and made a voluntary statement when you heard she was the dead woman on the beach. I appreciated that. This is safe territory, Jake.' To underline the confidence-giving, she was entirely candid with him, telling him all she knew about the barbecue invitation.

He listened in silence as she expected, but there was more than a flicker of interest.

'I'll get to the point,' she said. 'You met Meredith more than once in London, at the Natural History Museum. I asked if she talked about coming to Selsey and you said she didn't. Does that answer still hold?'

He gave his trademark nod.

'You drank coffee together and talked about the rainforests and the ecology, but you must have touched on some personal matters as well. When people meet for the first time they look for things in common. She must have asked where you live, am I right?'

After some hesitation, another nod.

Leading the witness like this would be inadmissible in any court, but what else could you do with such a reticent man? 'And then she would surely have said something like, "I've been to Selsey. I was there for a dig twenty years ago." Is that what she told you, Jake?'

'Yes.'

A small triumph.

'Right. I need your help here. Did she tell you anything else about the dig?'

'It was done in a hurry.'

He'd actually crafted a sentence.

'Because of the tides, yes. Did she mention anyone else who was there?'

'Dr Sentinel.'

'No others? We're trying to trace people. We believe she was murdered at the reunion.'

He leaned forward and his voice was more animated. 'Why?'

'That isn't clear. We may be looking at a motiveless murder. A psychotic killer who takes any opportunity to strike. As you know, a second woman was drowned at Emsworth. And you won't yet have heard that another body was found today in a private swimming pool in Apuldram.'

'A woman?'

'Not yet identified. She was discovered by two of your friends, Jo and Gemma.'

He released a long deep breath that developed into a sigh. He looked personally troubled.

'Do you know anything about this, Jake?' Hen asked.

'No.'

'If you do, and someone else is killed, she could be on your conscience for the rest of your days.'

Silence. He'd retreated into non-communication again.

She exchanged a look with Stella, who rolled her eyes.

'Jake,' Hen said, 'I'm going to release you without charge. I'm sorry all this has been necessary, but you can't deny that you acted suspiciously trying to avoid arrest. You'll be driven back to your home. Get some sleep. If you can think of anything you haven't mentioned, call me.'

He continued to sit there, deep in thought.

Hen was on her feet. 'Come on, fellow, let's get you out of here.'

He looked up, the dark eyes haunted by something unspeakable. 'Have you . . . ' The words faltered.

'Have I what?' she asked.

He got it out. 'Spoken to Rick?'

On Southern Counties Radio the same evening the lines buzzed with Selsey residents who remembered the finding of the mammoth. In the nature of chat shows, the focus of discussion kept changing. Some had watched from the promenade. One caller remembered a photographer falling over in the water. Another spoke about the fisherman who had first noticed the bones and thought he should have been given more credit and this started a spate of comments. Among all these, two of the original volunteers phoned in with their memories. Stella spoke to them later. Neither knew anything about the barbecue.

Hen was alone in the incident room when Stella returned.

'I listened in to most of it. Worth trying.'

'This barbecue is a mystery,' Stella said. 'Did we find out which stretch of the beach they used?'

'The invitation was clear on that: the section where the dig was done. Paddy looked it up. The strange thing is, it was right where the body was found.'

'I don't see what's strange,' Stella said. 'We're assuming she was murdered at the barbecue.'

Patiently, Hen explained her thinking. 'Picture it, Stell. The barbecue going. Music. Beer. Smoke. Some people standing about or sitting on the pebbles talking about what they've done in the past twenty years. The moon is up, and a nearly full moon at that, so they can see what's going on. What do you reckon happens next?'

'Someone suggests a swim?'

'My thought exactly. They don't have costumes, so they skinny-dip, or strip to their undies.'

'All of them?'

'This is the problem. In a party of people you'll get a few bold souls, but not all will want to go in. The others watch. They may even come down to the water's edge and shout encouragement. With all that happening, how does the killer carry out a drowning that can take up to five minutes?'

Stella tilted her head. 'Tell me, then.'

'It can't have happened in the presence of everyone else, can it?'

'Not the way you tell it, boss. I suppose they paired off— Meredith and the killer—and snuck away to another bit of the beach where they could be alone. He suggested a dip and they went in and he attacked her.'

'Reasonable, except for two things. She was found on the exact section of beach where the original dig took place. And there was no evidence of a barbecue there.'

'The tide must have washed over it.'

'These things tend to be held high up the beach where the water rarely reaches.'

'Well, I can't think of anything better.'

'Try this, then,' Hen said. 'What if the barbecue never happened?'

Stella blinked. 'You've lost me now.'

'We've been trying for hours to trace people who were there. Yes, we found about a dozen from the original dig who could have come. Not one of them did. They didn't get invitations. And the reason is that there *was* no barbecue. It was never going to happen.'

Stella thought a moment and frowned. 'Invented by the killer?'

'Exactly. He's devious. There was only ever one invitation and we've seen it. The killer sent it to Meredith as bait, to lure her to Selsey. Handsomely printed, official-looking, friendly. She was tempted. Her husband would be away, enjoying himself in Moscow or wherever. The dig had been a highlight of her student life, and now she makes her living as a fossil expert. Why not join in the fun and meet some friends from way back?'

'It's vile,' Stella said. 'In her shoes, I would have gone.'

'Me, too. What precisely happened in the hours before she was murdered we can only guess. I see her arriving at the beach around eight-thirty and finding nobody. Then he appears and says he, too, received an invitation. Whether he really *was* around in nineteen-eighty-seven is uncertain. Probably not. But he's done his research and he knows she was there. He says the event must have been cancelled and nobody told them. He has wine with him and something to eat. He suggests they sit on the beach and drink the wine. If Austen Sentinel can be believed, Meredith likes men.'

'I think you've sussed it, guv. He suggests a moonlit dip. She's game, but she keeps her pants on, as I would. And he does what he's been planning all along, grabs her in the water and drowns her.'

'And because he's a cold-hearted calculating killer, he gathers up her clothes and bag and removes them from the scene. His hope is that she'll be taken for someone who died at sea and was washed up by the tide.'

'That could easily have happened. The planning that went into this!'

'I know. It makes me wonder if the other killings were equally premeditated.'

'Are you certain Jake isn't the killer? I know he admitted being a friend of Meredith as soon as the news broke, but that could have been a smart move to wrong-foot us.'

'If you're right, I shouldn't have let him go. But I think it suits the real killer to have Jake in the frame. We're dealing with someone of exceptional guile. What you see with Jake is what you get.'

'He was pretty upset at the end of that last interview.'

'You noticed it, too? I think it was when I told him Jo and Gemma found the body at Cartwright's place. There's something he's holding back.'

'About Rick?'

Hen nodded. 'It's high time we spoke to that young man.'

'But we've got nothing on him. He's been in the background all along.'

'Yes, and up to now Jake has taken all the flak. Our first move tomorrow is to see Rick.'

twenty-three

THE RAIN WAS STAMPEDING across the roof when Jo woke from a troubled dream and looked at the clock. Still only 1.15 a.m. She got out, pulled back the curtain, and watched water pouring down the front of the house opposite. The gutters couldn't cope. On TV last night the local weatherman had issued a flood warning. There was a small river north of the city called the Lavant that always dried up in the summer and yet caused huge problems in conditions like this.

Unable to go back to sleep, she put the kettle on for a cup of tea. Always when extreme weather arrived she found herself thinking about global warming and its effects. Drought was not the whole story. Temperate countries could expect more of this monsoon–type weather that they weren't equipped to cope with. Jake would know the science, exactly why it occurred

And so her thoughts returned, as they often did now, to Jake. She assumed he was still in police custody. She'd heard no more from him. How could the police be so short-sighted when it was obvious that Cartwright was the murderer, the body in his own pool sealing his guilt?

The body in the pool proved also that Rick's horrifying claim had been moonshine. Far from being dead and pulped, Cartwright was alive and well and murdering women.

Jake had been right about that. In the morning she would call him and see if the police had come to their senses.

She made the tea and went back to bed.

HEN HAD slept through last night's downpour. She had the ability to shut eyes and shut off, even when dealing with serial murders. Perhaps it was not an ability, just exhaustion. She drove into work without really paying attention to the amount of water lying on the roads. Coming out of Bognor she sprayed a postman and had to get out and apologise. Not the best start to her day. Or his.

Better news greeted her at the nick. Stella was waving a piece of paper from across the incident room. 'Report from the lab, guv. We've got a match for victim number three.'

'You're kidding.'

'Honest. She's local, too. Lives at Bosham, or did. Named Sally Frith.'

'I don't understand. How did her name come up?'

'She's on the DNA register because she was fencing stolen antiques two years ago. Fined five hundred pounds and put on probation as it was a first offence.'

In the CID, good fortune is treated with suspicion. 'What's going on, Stell? Are the fates toying with us, or is this on the level? Is the age right?'

'Fifty-three.'

'I wonder who dealt with it. You and I were still working out of Bognor CID two years back.'

'I'll get the file up.'

'No, I'll check the paperwork You'd better get out to Bosham right away and see what you can find at the house apart from dodgy Chippendale chairs. Take Paddy with you.'

'Paddy?' The silver-haired sergeant was the one fixed point in the incident room.

'He needs to get out more.'

'You don't want to come?'

'I've got other fish to fry.'

'Meaning this guy Rick?'

'Spot on. We've got nothing on him, but he swims into view every once in a while.'

'The one that got away?'

'Or a red herring. I'll let you know.'

Light words, but behind them, serious intent.

First, she accessed Sally Frith's file. The case had been handled by a DI who had since moved on to Brighton CID, and he'd written a useful account of the case. Frith, twice divorced and with a small fortune from the second marriage, seemed to have become a soft touch for a fraudster. She'd met a slippery character called Fu Chin and allowed him to store antique pottery in her large house in Bosham. The items turned out to have been stolen from a museum in Brussels. Fu Chin had spun her some yarn about needing cash for medical treatment for one of his children in Hong Kong and she'd found buyers for five of the pieces and transferred the money to his numbered account. Described by the judge as a foolish and gullible woman, she'd taken the rap. Fu Chin was still at liberty.

Hen recalled the lily-white body floating in the pool. You see dead flesh and know nothing of the personal story behind it. This hapless woman had been conned again, putting on her swimsuit for a dip with a serial killer. How foolish and gullible is that?

More urgently, what did it say about the killer?

He must have persuaded two of his three victims to go into the water. There wasn't any evidence of compulsion about the apparent way Meredith had stripped to her undies and walked into the sea. And Sally Frith must have put on the pink swimsuit before going into the pool. Had they been charmed to their deaths? At a stretch Hen could imagine taking a midnight bathe on a warm September night with Jack Nicholson about the time he made *Easy Rider*, but a dip in an outdoor pool in an English October was something else. Not sexy old Jack nor any man alive could have talked her into getting her kit off in those conditions. She could only suppose the murderer had turned on the heating well in advance.

Such thoughtfulness.

A little shudder ran through her body.

She told Gary to get his coat on. Rick Graham's office was in West Street. 'Normally I'd walk,' she said, 'but look at that sky. It's going to tip down again any minute. Fetch your car. I'll see you out front.'

'What's Rick's connection with the case?' Gary asked when they were in motion, staring through the wipers at the lights of the car ahead.

'Yet to be discovered,' Hen told him. 'He's one of the pain-in-the-bum quartet.'

'Jake, Gemma, Jo, and Rick?'

'Friends, swingers, clubbers. None of them married. Between them Jake, Gemma, and Jo link up in some way with each of the killings. They knew one or more of the victims or they discovered one or more of the bodies. Rick stays in the background but he may have things to tell us.'

Not many cars were parked in West Street so early in the day. Gary steered into a spot right outside the Georgian doorway of the surveyor's. 'Does he know we're coming?'

Hen shook her head. 'Watch how he reacts. You may learn something.'

She flashed the warrant card and instructed the receptionist not to announce them over the intercom. She didn't want Rick leaping out of a top floor window.

His name was on the door at the top of the stairs: Richard O. Graham, member of this and fellow of that, a string of qualifications that didn't include immunity from investigation. Hen turned the handle and they went in.

He was reading the *Daily Mail*. Guiltily, he slammed it into a drawer. His blue eyes blinked nervously. Unruly hair poked up like a tussock of sun-bleached grass. It didn't look right for the grey suit.

Hen gave a kickstart to the interview. 'Were you reading about the body your friends found in the pool? We're CID, by the way. DCI Mallin and DC Pearce.'

'Oh.'

'That was a question.'

'Er, no. I get it for the business pages.'

'Didn't the latest murder make the national press? It will tomorrow. She's a local woman.'

Wanting to get over the shock of their sudden appearance, Rick tried letting them know that they'd invaded his territory. In a prim tone he said, 'I have an appointment shortly.'

'Not until this one is through.'

'What exactly do you want?'

'Information. You're the listening post. Heard it all: dead bodies, an ID parade, a chase, an arrest.'

'If you're talking about Jake, I scarcely know the guy,' he said. 'He's just a hanger-on.'

'Hanging on to Jo as I understand it,' Hen said. 'She was your girlfriend and he took her over.'

'I wouldn't call her a girlfriend. He's welcome to her.'

'How very gracious that sounds. Didn't she give you what you wanted? You swapped her for Gemma, I was told. Tricky when they're close friends, I imagine. Leads to all kinds of comparisons.'

He reddened, either with anger or embarrassment. 'I can't see what relevance this has.'

'All right, Rick, I'll stop being personal. Tell me about your work.'

More signs of panic. He was out on the highwire again, and teetering. 'Like what?'

'Like does it get you out, looking at people's houses?'

'That's part of it.'

'Someone plans to move away, so they ask you to survey the property in line with the new government legislation. You should be telling *me* this. Have you been invited to do a job in Apuldram in the last three weeks? Desirable country house with swimming pool?'

'Certainly not.'

'The owner seems to have gone. I wonder who did the survey. Tell me, Rick, if you were surveying a house and the winter cover was over the swimming pool would you lift the end to inspect underneath?'

He started to bluster. 'I know exactly what you're talking about and why. I've never been to Cartwright's house. I had nothing to do with what happened in Apuldram.'

'Except by association,' Hen said. 'You're sleeping with one of the women who found the body and the other is your ex.'

'You said you'd stop being personal.'

An interruption: Hen's phone gave its call note. 'This had better be earth-shaking,' she said to Gary, looking round for a place with more privacy. She settled for an armchair across the room from Rick's desk.

The caller was Stella. 'Sorry to disturb you, guv, but you ought to know this. We're at Bosham, Sally Frith's house. Huge place with an amazing harbour view. We started in her bedroom and almost the first thing we found beside the bed was this photo of a guy in swimming trunks, and written across it is—wait for it— "All My Love, Rick."'

'Have you got it there now?'

'In my hand.'

'Describe him.'

'Ten years younger than her, I'd say. Blue eyes, hair bleached blond by the look of it and cut in a style of—what shall I say?— more Rod Stewart than David Beckham, if you know what I mean.'

Hen's heart had doubled its rate, but she was keeping her responses bland, trying not to give too much away to Rick. 'Thanks, Stell. You did the right thing calling me.'

'Boss, don't go yet.'

'What?'

'Something else you ought to know. The place has a large indoor swimming pool.'

'Has it?' Keeping a poker face was difficult. 'Worth noting. See you later.' For a moment after switching off, she paused to let her brain catch up with what she'd heard. Deciding to go for broke, she crossed the room and said in a sharp, accusing tone, 'Sally Frith of Bosham. One of your women, right?'

'Huh?' Rick swayed back as if she'd aimed a blow at him.

She spoke the name a second time.

'What's happened?' he said, giving a fair rendering of shock.

'Answer the question, Rick. Is Sally Frith your lover?'

'I see her sometimes, yes. What is it?'

'She was the body found at Apuldram.'

A stunned silence.

Slowly his hand went to his throat and clasped it. 'Sally?' He'd turned ashen. His voice was reduced to a murmur. 'I can't believe this.'

'Can't believe it happened, or can't believe I know about it?'

'Are you certain?'

Hen gave a nod. 'That was my colleague speaking from the house.' She waited briefly, then said, 'You've done the surprised bit now, Rick. You can answer some questions, like how long have you known the lady?'

He shifted in his chair and dragged his fingers across his mouth, surely aware of the trouble he was in. 'I don't know. Eighteen months, maybe. I did some work for her, a survey for some reconstruction at the house. We formed a friendship. This is so hard to believe.'

'She was some years older than you.'

'It didn't matter. We didn't discuss our ages. She was a sweet person.'

'You know she had a criminal record?'

'She told me. She was badly let down.' He took in a sharp breath. 'Do you think he did this—the bastard who got her into all that trouble?'

'The last we heard, he was in Hong Kong. It's unlikely he'd risk setting foot in Britain again.'

'One of his cronies, then?'

'What would be the point? Everything came out at her trial.'

'Was anything stolen from the house?'

'Too early to say. When did you see her last?'

He gave the question some thought. 'About ten days ago. I used to visit her most Sundays.'

'Not for church, I dare say.'

He glared back. 'She cooked us a roast lunch. It was a regular thing. I made no secret of it. Jo knew all about it, and so did Gemma.'

'And we don't need to ask what was for afters. This arrangement lasted eighteen months. You appreciate being mothered, obviously.'

'That's unfair.'

'Ten days ago, you say. Weren't you there on Sunday?'

He hesitated, weighing the options. 'I called at the house, but there was no answer.'

'When was this?'

'Around midday.'

'Had you spoken to her on the phone?'

'No. I just turned up at the usual time. I was surprised and a bit concerned actually. I waited for a while and walked around the outside. It was all locked up.'

'Everything in order?'

'It seemed to be. There was no sign of a break-in. Nobody else was about. The house is detached in its own grounds, so it was no use asking neighbours. I tried phoning her and got no answer. After about forty minutes, I gave up and came away.'

'Pretty pissed off at missing your Sunday treat?'

'A bit, if I'm honest. I tried calling her later. I was thinking she'd gone out for the day and forgotten to tell me.'

'So what did you do for lunch?'

'Sandwich.'

'Where? A local pub?'

'I went home.'

'Pity. If you'd eaten out we might have a till receipt, or even someone who remembers you.'

'I'm telling you the truth. I didn't hang about because I was meeting some friends later. A birthday.'

'And you forgot all about Sally? Where was the party?'

'On the Isle of Wight.'

'Anyone I know?'

'Gemma. It was her birthday. We went to a club. And Jo was there, too.'

'While Sally lay dead in Cartwright's pool.'

He shouted, 'I didn't know that. I've never been near the fucking place.'

Gary pointed a finger and said, 'Cool it.'

'Okay,' Hen said in a calm, measured tone, 'let's explore what happened according to what you've told us. Sally wasn't there when you arrived, and she turns up dead in Cartwright's pool on Tuesday afternoon. The pathologist estimates she'd been dead for two to five days, probably drowned. The day of death was therefore Friday, Saturday, or Sunday. She was in a pink swimsuit. Did you ever swim with her?'

'Never. I don't like swimming.'

'But Sally must have enjoyed it. She had a pool of her own.'

'She told me she swam before breakfast every day. She believed in keeping fit.'

'She'd need to,' Hen said, and added, 'All that cooking. What I can't get my head round is why she'd go to an outdoor pool in October when she was used to swimming indoors and at home. Any suggestions?'

'Cartwright must be alive.'

'Did Sally know Cartwright?'

'I couldn't tell you.'

'She didn't ever mention him?'

'She wouldn't, would she?'

Watching for his reaction, Hen said, 'Are you suggesting she was promiscuous?'

He shifted in his chair. 'I'm not saying anything else without my solicitor being present.'

'Good thinking,' Hen said, untroubled. 'Let's all go back to the nick and do this properly in an interview room.'

AFTER HER disturbed night, Jo woke later than usual. The phone by the bed was going. She snatched it up, hoping to hear Jake.

The voice was male, and for a moment she was fooled into saying, 'Sweet Jesus, I can't tell you how worried I've been about you.'

The caller nervously announced himself as Adrian, her boss. 'Have I woken you up? Sorry. You won't have heard about the flooding. The road is under four feet of water at Singleton. There's no way I can get in to work this morning, so I'm phoning round to see who can make it.'

Adrian lived at Midhurst, north of Singleton. Jo was south of the flooded area, and so was the garden centre. 'I'll try and get in.'

'I'd be so grateful. Karen's going to try as well. I'm not expecting customers in weather like this. My worry is that we may have flood damage ourselves. It could ruin the stock.'

'I'll call you if and when I get there,' she said.

She tried Jake's number next. No answer.

* * *

AT THE police station, Hen left Rick in a side room with his solicitor. The law's delay was one of the few certainties in police work.
She was not downhearted. More needed to be uncovered before she
could make real inroads with this guy. Smart questioning uncovers
the truth, but it has to be rooted in good detective work.

Still on her desk in the interview room in its transparent evidence bag was the invitation card that had lured Meredith
Sentinel to her death. She picked it up and ran her fingertips
across the embossed lettering. An elaborate con. No other cards
had been traced and she was confident of her theory that this one
was unique, an invitation to a non-existent reunion. If she could
prove Rick had sent it, she'd be well armed for the next round.

But he couldn't have sent it to a woman he didn't know.

Was there a connection to Meredith, something yet to be discovered? Either he'd been around in 1987 and met her at the dig
and fantasised about her ever since, or he'd got to know her
more recently. Through his work? He belonged to various professional societies, and they would have meetings in London,
where Meredith lived and worked. A chance encounter? She did
some work for the World Wildlife Fund, her husband had mentioned. Was Rick involved in that in some capacity? He didn't
seem the sort.

She examined the card again. The embossed lettering hadn't
been done on a computer. This was a printer's work.

Kleentext Print Solutions?

She called their number and asked to speak to Gemma Casey.
The receptionist said she'd try. Some of the staff weren't in
because of the flooding.

Fortunately, Gemma answered, and Hen explained about the
card and its importance to the case. 'We think it likely that only
one was printed. It's nicely done on cream-coloured card with
embossed lettering.'

'Swanky. We do that kind of work, mainly as wedding sta-
tionery,' Gemma said, 'but I doubt if this was ours. Only one, you
say? It would be uneconomic.'

'Depends if the client was willing to stump up,' Hen pointed out.

'You're talking fifty pounds minimum for one card.'

'Understood,' Hen said. 'Well, maybe he had about fifty printed and destroyed all but one. They didn't get sent out. I'm sure of that.'

'Anyway, we'd have a record of it,' Gemma said. 'The proof would have come through my office and I can't recall the wording you just read out. If you hang on, I'll check to be certain. We keep a copy of everything.' In under five minutes she was back. 'No, it was definitely done by another printer. We don't usually give out the names of our rivals, but in this case . . . '

Hen noted them. 'And while you're on the line,' she said to Gemma, 'has your friend Rick ever spoken to you about the Selsey mammoth?'

'The what?'

'A mammoth was excavated in 1987.'

'What's it got to do with Rick?'

'I'm wondering if he took part in the dig.'

'All those years ago? I doubt it. I'm sure he would have boasted about it. You know what blokes are like. Jake's the expert on things like that. He's a fossil-hunter.'

'True, but he wasn't on the dig. What about you, Gemma? You were local. Did you volunteer?'

'Me? I was only fifteen in 1987. Simon Le Bon grabbed me more than bones on a beach.'

'Duran Duran? Didn't they cover "Watching the Detectives" ?'

'Hey, you're a new romantic.'

She tried the other local printers. No one remembered taking on the work. The fancy invitation wasn't the clincher it had promised to be. If that bloody man Sentinel had found the envelope it came in, the whole investigation might have been over by now.

THERE WAS real danger of aquaplaning in several places where the road dipped between Mid Lavant and West Dean. Jo slowed and hoped she wouldn't stall. The A286 runs alongside the River Lavant all the way up to Singleton, and there are sections where it can easily burst its banks. Fortunately everyone seemed to be treating the conditions with respect and she covered the six miles to the garden centre without mishap.

Karen from the sales staff was the only one there.

'Any damage?'

'Nothing serious that I've noticed,' Karen said. 'Some leaking from the roof where the glass blew out the other day. We've lost a few winter pansies, and that's about it.'

'Have you called Adrian?'

'Not yet. Should we?'

'He was practically having kittens when he called me an hour ago. I'll give him a call now.'

AT MID-MORNING, Hen called Stella for another progress report on the search at the Bosham house.

'Like I said, we started upstairs. The main bedroom,' Stella told her. After the Apuldram fiasco she was going to miss nothing. 'The quilt was turned back for airing. Some of her clothes on a chair. Nightdress hanging in the bathroom. I get the impression she had a night's sleep and got up and had a shower.'

'Have you checked the pool area?'

'Not properly.'

'Do it next. According to Rick, she was in the habit of taking an early morning swim.'

'Rick. What does he know about it?'

She updated Stella on the Sunday lunch routine.

Stella whistled and said, 'He really had it made. Do you think he killed her?'

'I'm taking this step by step. Have you looked for signs of a recent meal?'

'There's nothing obvious. If he was here, everything is cleared away. It's extremely tidy. We'll start our search of the kitchen shortly.'

'Look in the fridge for the remains of a roast joint. And I expect there's a dishwasher. See if that's loaded. Oh, and be sure to check the rubbish, too.'

Stella wouldn't normally need to be told. She may have felt she was being picked on for the past error. Hen wasn't leaving anything to chance.

There was no complaint from Stella. She promised to call back shortly.

*   *   *

ADRIAN SAID he was 'mightily relieved' to know that the pansies were the only casualties. In his state of euphoria he suggested that Jo close at midday.

She passed on the good news to Karen.

'Great,' Karen said. 'To tell you the truth, I found it quite eerie being alone here before you arrived. It's weird, getting spooked by a garden centre, but I actually came out in goose pimples. I've never been here on my own before today. I was so pleased to hear you drive up.'

'Yes, the place has a different feel to it,' Jo said. 'We haven't even got Miss Peabody stalking us round the aisles.'

'I can do without her,' Karen said, grinning. 'She lives up the road in Singleton, doesn't she? Poor old soul, she's probably under four feet of water.'

Singleton is the downland village where the Lavant first makes itself apparent. This sometime river (so benign in the summer months that it dries to an empty ditch) has its source in nearby East Dean. Serious flood problems affect the village in a specially wet winter because of a spring known as the Fountain, fed by another valley from the north.

Jo's conscience stirred. 'She's my friend's aunt. Maybe I should check and see if she's all right.'

'I expect the emergency people are doing that,' Karen said. 'You might get in their way.'

'I don't know. I think I owe it to Gemma to take a look. I could take the old lady some milk and bread from the Down Tools. They won't be using any today. Luckily I put my wellies in the car in case I got stranded. I think it's the first cottage you come to. We can see it from here.'

'You can also see the flood water,' Karen said. 'Rather you than me.' She laughed. 'If you spot a pink hat floating past, you'd better give up and come back.'

STELLA WAS quick to phone back. 'I checked the kitchen, guv. The dishwasher had been emptied. There is a large joint of beef in the fridge.'

'Hey, that's what I needed to know,' Hen said.

'Uncooked.'

'What?'

'Looking at the sell-by date, it's probably still okay. It doesn't smell off.'

'So she *was* expecting to cook.'

'That's for sure. There are fresh parsnips and carrots, greens, a marrow, and a packet of runner beans.'

'Rick told the truth about that, then. She didn't cook his Sunday lunch. She must have gone before then. She was probably dead.'

'I also looked at the pool area, as you asked, and there's one of those white bathrobes made of towelling.'

'Where?'

'Draped over a lounger, plus a spare towel.'

'Flip-flops?'

'Yes. Beside the lounger.'

Hen's thoughts were in overdrive. 'Stella, listen carefully. Don't touch anything else. I want the pool area taped off as a crime scene. Get the white zipsuits out to the house as soon as possible. I'm almost certain she was drowned in her own pool and moved to Apuldram.'

'The body was moved? Why?'

'Shift the corpse and you shift the suspicion. We assumed the killer was Cartwright. Big mistake.'

twenty-four

RICK'S SOLICITOR HAD DELAYED as long as he reasonably could and now the so-called voluntary statement was under way again.

Hen wasn't wasting words. 'What do you drive?'

Rick said, 'An E Class Mercedes.'

'On the street outside?'

'Yes.'

'The keys, please.'

'Just a moment, officer,' the lawyer said with a smile at Hen's apparent naivety. 'You can't do that. My client is assisting with your enquiries. If you want the power to search his vehicle, you'll have to arrest him.'

'Is that the way you want to play it?'

'Why do you need to search my car?' Rick asked.

'I believe Sally Frith was drowned in her own swimming pool and then transported to Apuldram and put in the pool in Mr Cartwright's garden.'

'And you think I did this?' Some outrage showed in Rick's response. Not enough for Hen's liking.

'If you did, there will be traces in your car. You can prove you didn't by allowing us to make a forensic examination.'

The solicitor put a restraining hand on Rick's arm. 'I don't advise it.'

'I've nothing to hide,' Rick said.

'Let me put it this way,' the solicitor said. 'Impressed as I am with our estimable forensic science service and its painstaking methods, one hears of the occasional mistake being made through no one's fault, of course, and leading to a wrongful conviction.'

'Have it your way,' Hen said without rising to the sarcasm.

'Richard Graham, I am arresting you on suspicion of murder. You do not have to say anything—'

'Hang on,' Rick interrupted, swinging to face his adviser. 'If they do that, they can take my DNA and fingerprints and I'm on their bloody database for the rest of my life.' He pulled the car keys from his pocket and and tossed them across the table to Hen. 'You won't find jack shit. Sally never even had a ride in my car.'

The solicitor said, 'You could regret this.'

'Get lost.'

The man was on his feet at once. 'If that's how you feel, Mr Graham, I'll take you at your word. Find someone else.'

Hen groaned.

Another delay.

THE RAIN had eased, so Jo had put on her Wellington boots and was striding through the puddles. Ahead were a barrier and a sign that the road was closed to traffic. It was no mystery why this valley flooded. To her right rose the great chalk hill called the Trundle, a favourite viewpoint. Left of her, purple-grey, with low cloud obscuring the highest point, a wooded stretch of the South Downs, the most significant upland range in Sussex.

From behind her the tinny notes of Colonel Bogey sounded.

She jerked the backpack from her shoulder and fumbled among cartons of milk and packs of sandwiches, found the phone and put it to her ear.

'Darling, is that you?' It was her mother's all-too-familiar strident voice.

Jo almost slung the thing into the floodwater. 'Hi.'

'You don't sound like your usual self. Are you keeping dry in this dreadful weather?'

'More or less. Can I call you back later?'

'Your father and I have been worried out of our minds about you. What's going on, Jo? Your name's in the paper again.'

'Pure bad luck, Mummy. No need to be alarmed.'

'But this is an appalling case, by the sound of it. All these drowned women, and the man still at liberty. I don't know how it happened, but you seem to be up to your neck in it.'

Not the happiest choice of phrase. She was already up to her shins in it.

'Don't trust anyone,' Mummy ranted on. 'You've got that mobile phone with you? Well, obviously you have.'

'I'll use it if necessary.'

'No, I'm telling you, Jo darling, that these fancy phones are a mixed blessing. You take a call from someone and you have no way of knowing where he is. He could be lying in wait round the next corner and you think he's speaking from miles away.'

'I'll bear it in mind, Mummy. Must go. 'bye.' She switched off.

Immediately, it rang again.

Give it a rest, Mother, she thought. 'Yes?'

'Jo?' This time it really was the voice she hoped to hear.

'Jake, I thought you were someone else. I've been trying to reach you. Did they let you go?'

'For now.'

'Thank God for that.'

'They still don't trust me.'

She sidestepped that. 'When was this? Last night?'

'I didn't call you from home. They can listen in.'

She was about to point out that nothing he could say would incriminate either of them, and then thought better of it. Wouldn't anyone feel paranoid after hours of questioning? 'Are you at home?'

'No, I came to work.'

'What's it like there after the rain?'

'Not very different.'

God, she'd been aching to hear his voice and now they were talking banalities. 'When can I see you, Jake? Tonight?'

A pause. 'I'd like that. I'll come to you.'

'Some of the roads are impassable.'

'Not on a bike. Did you get in to work?'

'Yes, but we just closed the shop. I could do with your dinghy right now. I'm on a mercy mission, walking—well, wading—into Singleton to see if an old lady is all right. She's Gemma's aunt.'

'Be careful.'

'Would you mind calling Gem and telling her I'm checking on Aunt Jessica? Saves her coming out from Fishbourne.'

After the call she was so much happier that she burst into
'*Singin' in the Rain*.'

OUT AT Bosham, a crucial find was made. Leaving nothing to
chance this time, Stella called the incident room while Hen was
arranging for Rick's car to be taken away.

'Boss, the crime scene people are saying there's a strong
chance Sally was attacked here, in the shallow end of the pool.
They picked up quite a clump of hair that was pulled out at the
roots, and I'm certain it matches the colour of hers. There was
also the tip of a broken fingernail.'

'Was there? Two of her nails were damaged for sure. This
could clinch it, Stell. If she was driven to Apuldram, we're going
to find traces in someone's car. You can't move a corpse without
leaving something behind.'

'You can clean up a car.'

'That in itself would be suspicious. Besides, how many of our
suspects have transport? Jake rides a bike. Dr Sentinel uses the
train to get here. Cartwright's car is already impounded.'

'What about Francisco?'

'He's out of the reckoning.'

'That leaves Rick.'

The logistics interested Hen more at this moment. 'I'm thinking about how it was done. Actually, *when* it was done.'

'Is that important?'

'The contents of the fridge—the meat and fresh veg you told
me about—suggest she was killed before she could prepare the
lunch. I think she got out of bed Sunday morning, put on her
swimsuit and bathrobe, and went downstairs to the pool for her
morning swim. The killer was waiting there.'

'Rick. The bastard. I know you don't want to finger anyone at
this point, but who else knew about her daily swim?'

Hen refused to be sidetracked. She was explaining the timing.
'I couldn't understand how you failed to notice the body when
you searched the Apuldram pool on Monday morning.'

'Me neither.'

'I believe the body was moved there *after* you checked the pool.'

'You're saying he left her here overnight and then came back for her?'

'Late Monday.'

The line went silent while Stella took this in. 'That's cool,' she said finally. 'And so cunning. I sound the all clear and he moves in with the corpse. It could have stayed under cover all winter if the two women hadn't come snooping.'

'And it shifted suspicion to Cartwright.'

'This has got to be someone with inside knowledge, guv. Rick must have heard about the search. From his girlfriend Gemma, no doubt.'

At her end of the phone, Hen smiled. Stell had really got it in for Rick. 'What was his motive, then?'

'He'd tired of Sally. He was passionate about Gemma. He wanted to escape from the Sunday lunch routine.'

'I'm not convinced, Stell. He didn't need to kill her. He could have told her it was over and stopped going.'

'Some people do anything to avoid a face-to-face row.'

'Murder?'

'Don't forget there are two other victims. Murder is no big deal when you've done it before. He reckoned he had a foolproof method, drowning them.'

'I'd be more impressed if we could link Rick to the other murders. I don't know what connection he had to Meredith or Fiona.'

Stella continued to stoke the flames of her suspicion. 'He's been around from the beginning. Jo found Meredith's body and who was it who happened to be dating Jo at the time? Rick. Then he started dating Gemma, who worked with Fiona. There is a link, you see.'

'We can say much the same for Jake.'

'Guv, Jake had nothing to do with Sally. She was Rick's woman.'

Hen saw sense in that. 'I'll have another try with him.'

JO HAD reached a point in the mercy mission where she felt rather foolish. If she went any further, the water would come over the tops of her wellies, so she was forced to take them off and carry them, wading barefoot with her skirt pulled up to her thighs. Even so, her mood was buoyant. She'd see Jake tonight and have a good laugh about this.

Not far ahead was the timber-framed flint cottage she knew to be Miss Peabody's, and it was on higher ground than she remembered. Some water might have penetrated to the ground floor, but this wasn't the emergency she'd pictured. She waded through the remaining surface water and up a definite incline to the front door. A sandbag was across it.

RICK HAD decided he didn't need a solicitor. 'When you find the inside of my car is clean, you'll have to let me walk.' he told Hen.

'I'll be frank with you,' she told him. 'I'm interested in other deaths as well as Sally's.'

Alarm briefly visited Rick's eyes. He passed both hands over his bleached hair, smoothing it. 'Oh that,' he said with a too-obvious effort to sound unflustered. 'You've been talking to Jo and Gemma. I made that up, about killing Cartwright. It was a running joke that got out of hand when Jo took it seriously. No sense of humour, that woman.'

Killing Cartwright? This was a whole new angle on the case.

Up to now, Hen hadn't got Rick down as a humorist. He appeared to want to talk, so she and Gary listened.

'The beginning of it was that Gem couldn't stand her boss, so we all got to thinking up weird ways of getting rid of him. Fun ways. I don't think Jake joined in, but he's got as much fun in him as a bowl of cold porridge. He was listening, though.' Rick's eyes widened as a thought struck him. 'Was it bloody Jake who put you on to me? He'd take anything as gospel, that guy. Anyway, I made up this story about bashing Cartwright's head in and disposing of the body at a papermill, turning it into pulp, so he'd be in the news. In the news. Joke, right?'

Hen had failed to smile, but she gave a nod.

'It was a touch too realistic for Jo and freaked her out. Gemma believed me too, but she didn't take it the same way. I think she really did want to see the back of Cartwright. But for Christ's sake, it was a joke.'

Hen turned to Gary. 'It must be the way he tells 'em.'

'Only a bloody joke,' Rick insisted.

'A poor taste joke.'

'This all started with the girls,' he said in his defence. 'They were having a laugh about it before any of the bodies were found. I joined in, like you do, to keep the conversation going. I suppose it got out of hand later, but don't believe a word of it. Nothing happened, right?'

'Have you finished?' Hen enquired.

'Er, I suppose so.'

'Now let's talk about Meredith Sentinel.'

He blinked, as if the switch to another victim had derailed him. 'Can't help you. Didn't meet the woman, don't know anything about her.'

'I'll fill you in, then,' Hen said. 'She came to Selsey expecting to attend a beach barbecue, a reunion of the mammoth excavation twenty years ago. A proper invitation was sent to her.' She took the bagged card from her desk drawer and held it for Rick to see.

He gave it a glance. 'Nothing to do with me.'

'Twenty years ago, Meredith was a new student at Brighton. She was part of the dig. A great experience for her. A good memory. She expected to meet old friends when she returned here in September. Instead, all she met was her murderer. The grand reunion was a hoax. I notice you have an impressive string of letters after your name. Where did you do your studies, Rick?'

He took a deep breath, kept her waiting and finally gave a broad grin. 'Edinburgh.' Who said he didn't have a sense of humour?

'All of them?'

'That's where I was living until nineteen-ninety-two.'

It wasn't the triumph Rick expected. Mentally, Hen excluded him. Suddenly she'd cut off. She still had the invitation in her hand and she stared at it as if she hadn't seen it before. An entirely new line of thought had popped into her brain. She was tempted to end the interview there. But there was a chink of light ahead, and she decided to go for it. She restored her full attention to Rick.

'You and Gemma are pretty close? An item, as they say?'

'Good friends.'

'Very good friends, according to her. She's a local lass. She tells me she was only fifteen in the year the mammoth was dug up. It must have made an impression, though. It was a big deal in Selsey at the time. Some of the local kids joined in. The weather was really good by all accounts. A chance to show off their bikinis and meet some students. Has she told you about it?'

This was invention on Hen's part. Nothing about the stronger attraction of Duran Duran. She had some expectation that he would answer yes.

He didn't. Instead he said, 'She told me once that she had more hands-on experience of fossils than Jake would ever have. I thought it was a joke. You don't find out with Gem. I guess she could have meant the mammoth dig.'

THERE WAS no answer to Jo's persistent knocking. Worrying. She put her wellies beside the sandbag and tried the doorknob. It turned and she was able to step inside. The mat was damp to the touch of her bare feet. Some flood water, at least, had seeped into the cottage.

The interior was dark and smelt musty. But as her eyes adjusted she could see that it had been kept tidy. There was no hallway. You stepped straight into the living room. She could make out the traditional stone fireplace and stove, which was both cooker and water heater. Glass-fronted cupboards were stacked with china. The little kitchen was across the room to one side of the hearth. She felt the squelch of the carpet as she moved over it.

A small fridge was in the kitchen. The electrics didn't seem to be working and she wasn't going to risk trying them. She took off her backpack and put the milk and sandwiches into the fridge. To her right was a door that might have led somewhere, but on opening it she saw only steps almost entirely immersed in black water. A cellar, she supposed. This place would take months to dry out.

She stepped back, felt her heel touch something soft, and almost lost balance. She'd trodden on a dishcloth. In reaching out for support, she knocked a plate off the draining board into the sink.

A voice said, 'Is someone there?'

She wasn't sure where it came from, but she called out, 'Miss Peabody, are you all right?'

'I'm upstairs.'

Through the living room on the opposite side she found the staircase. 'It's all right,' she called, to set the old lady's mind at rest. 'It's only Jo from the garden centre, come to see if you need any help.'

She mounted the stairs.

'THIS CAME to me when we were interviewing Rick,' Hen told Gary. She was pink-faced with excitement. 'It turns the whole case on its head. Everything has a different interpretation. This.' She brandished the invitation card. 'This was never intended to bring Meredith to Selsey and lure her to her death. I made a false assumption. The envelope was addressed to Dr Sentinel and intended for him. He led the dig. He should have been the guest of honour at the reunion. But of course Meredith was a D.Sc as well. She was Dr Sentinel, too, a brilliant student who got a first and went on to take her doctorate at University College. She thought the envelope was addressed to her. Her husband was away in St Petersburg and couldn't possibly attend. The way it was worded would have appealed to anyone. Listen to this: "Free food, drink and eighties music. No reply necessary. To have fun with old friends just turn up . . . like the mammoth did." Imagine Meredith reading that at a time when old sobersides was out of the country. A chance of a night out. She was up for anything. She got on a train and came down here.'

'Why was she murdered?'

'Question of the day, Gary. Get me Sentinel's number.'

MISS PEABODY was wearing her pink hat. A hat in your own home? Odd, certainly, but just because she was eccentric didn't mean the poor old duck should be left to fend for herself. The blue twinset didn't go too well with the hat. The tweed skirt? Well, it had seen better days.

'The door was open,' Jo explained.

'I left it open deliberately, in case someone came,' the old lady said. 'When the water started to come in downstairs I collected any precious things I had and brought them up here.'

They were in her bedroom and the narrow single bed was heaped with letters, newspapers, books, and a few dry groceries.

'Sensible,' Jo said.

'It's not the first time. I've had three major floods in my lifetime, so I know what to do. It's the clearing up that I hate. It takes months to dry out, even with help from the council.'

'It's deep in that cellar below the kitchen.'

'That always floods first. It was used as an ice-store once, but I've got no use for it except to grow mushrooms. The walls leak. That's the trouble.'

'I heard the forecast on the car radio. I don't think it will get much worse, if that's any consolation.'

She stared at Jo's feet. 'Don't you wear shoes?'

'Wellies.' Jo smiled. 'Left them on the step. Can I make you some coffee while I'm here? I tucked a few things in the fridge.'

'Tea would be nice. Milk and no sugar. The kettle is on the stove, so it should be hot. Have we met before?'

'The garden centre.'

'Oh, yes.' She was a little forgetful.

When Jo returned with the tea on a tray, she said, 'I have a friend called Gemma and you're her Aunt Jessica.'

'You know Gemma?'

'We've done quite a lot together.' And how! 'I expect she would have come to make sure you're all right, but I'm just up the road so I offered to look in.'

'I don't see a lot of Gemma these days.'

The very thing Mummy would say, given the opportunity. The older generation like to portray themselves as neglected. 'She's been really busy at work, having to take over from the manager.'

'I'm her only living relative.'

Cue the plaintive violin music. 'She told me.'

'Her parents died when she was quite a small girl, you know. Killed in a car crash. Dreadful. Her mother was my sister, Angela. A lovely young woman. I've got a picture of her somewhere. It's among the things I carried upstairs for safety. My photo album was the first thing I made sure was safe. You can't replace such a thing and it holds so many memories.' She spilt some of her tea turning to look over the old-fashioned eiderdown. 'There it is. The big red book. Could you hand it to me carefully so that nothing falls out?'

Old people and old photos. Jo could see this taking longer than she'd expected. She didn't really want to be looking at ancient snaps for the next hour.

'I haven't stuck them all in,' Miss Peabody said, seating herself on the bed and opening the album on her lap. She'd drunk the tea hot and placed the empty cup back on the tray. 'I've been promising myself for years that I'd do it. Well, that's a bit of luck.' She'd picked up a small snap in colours so faded that they were almost monochrome. 'Here they are on their wedding day. They were married in that tiny little church at Upwaltham. A lovely setting for a wedding.'

Jo gave it a polite glance. 'She was a beautiful bride.'

'I was the maid of honour. I didn't want to be called the bridesmaid. They're usually much younger than I was. I had a pink headdress and a matching pink bouquet.'

That figures, Jo thought, wondering if the pink hat went back to those days. She handed back the photo and glanced at her watch. She'd been in the cottage twenty minutes already.

'Carnations mainly.' Miss Peabody was still on about the bouquet. 'A hardy plant, the carnation. It can survive mild frost conditions and under glass it will flower all the year round.' She started sorting through a mass of pictures. 'Here's one that will amuse you. Gemma at five years old with Terry. Look at her expression, as if she really could be doing something better than being made to pose for a picture with her little brother. Isn't it a scream?'

Jo tried to show some enthusiasm. The small girl with chubby arms folded did have a pout, as if she would rather have been elsewhere. The curly-headed boy had managed a cute smile for the camera. 'Very amusing.'

'She was rather put out when Terry came along. It can be difficult for the older child.'

Fifteen minutes more passed and they'd only started on the photo collection. Jo was trying to think of ways of bringing this to an end without being hurtful. Outside she heard a vehicle stopping somewhere near. With any luck it would be the fire service or the police and they would take over.

No one knocked.

'Oh, dear. Here's the *Chichester Observer* report of the accident,' Miss Peabody said, handing across a yellow press clipping. 'It's family history, so I kept it, but I didn't know it was among the photos.'

Jo scanned it rapidly and then read it a second time:

TWO DIE IN SOUTH MUNDHAM CAR CRASH

A fatal car crash in South Mundham on Tuesday evening has shocked the village. The victims were named as Patrick and Angela Casey, both aged 27. Their overturned Ford Cortina was found by office cleaner David Allday close to Limekiln Barn in Runcton Lane. He was returning from his late shift at 1.45 a.m. The couple appeared to have died instantly, a police spokesman said. 'No other vehicle seems to have been involved. There was ice on the road and they may have taken a turn too fast.'

The Caseys are survived by one daughter, Gemma, aged 8. Their son Terry died in another tragic incident in 1978, when he drowned in their garden pond at the age of 3.

'So sad, isn't it?' Miss Peabody said. 'Gemma had to be fostered. My health wasn't good, or I would have taken her on. Between you and me, she was quite a handful. Very wilful. Still is, from what I see of her.'

'And the little brother drowned?'

'Yes, that was awful. One August afternoon the children were playing in the garden. I think Angela was watching television. Gemma came in and said Terry was lying in the pond and wasn't moving. She'd tried to lift him, poor mite. Her little dress was soaking. When Angela got out there it was too late.'

twenty-five

Austen Sentinel was his usual unfriendly self. 'Some other time. I'm interviewing students,' he told Hen on the phone.

'Fine,' she said, prepared for this. 'Finish your interview. We'll have a car pick you up in twenty minutes.'

With an impatient sigh, he said, 'What is it?'

'Cast your mind back to nineteen-eighty-seven. The dig at Selsey. You told me you were only twenty-five at the time.'

'That's correct.'

'Young, energetic, and with leadership qualities.'

'I don't remember claiming all that.'

'In short, attractive.'

'That was for others to judge.'

'You mentioned all those young girls in bikinis.'

'Ha.' From the satisfied sound, he might have been a chess player whose opponent has at last revealed her strategy. 'You won't get me on that. I behaved myself.'

'I believe you. You told me after the inquest—I'm quoting you now—you would have been a total idiot to risk your career by going to bed with a student.'

'And I stand by that.'

'You also said that the ratio of women to men at the university meant you were the proverbial kid in the teashop.'

'There's no contradiction there. One can look at the sweets without sampling them.'

'But what about the sweetshop across the street?'

'I don't follow you.'

'You said you recruited local people for the dig as well as students. It wouldn't have broken university rules to chat up some of the local totty.'

'So why are you raising it?'

'Because one of the Selsey lasses apparently took a shine to you. And I dare say you encouraged her.'

'If I did, the memory has faded.'

'Hers didn't fade. She carried a torch for you for twenty years.'

'Oh, what nonsense.'

'It wasn't nonsense to her. She formed a plan. She'd have a reunion with you, a private one. Just the two of you, at Selsey, letting you believe it was a beach barbecue for everyone who took part. She went to all the trouble of getting an invitation printed— just for you—and sent it.'

'You're mistaken. That invite wasn't meant for me.'

'It was.'

'My wife opened it. I told you.'

'Because it was addressed to Dr Sentinel. You both had doctorates.'

Some seconds of silence followed.

Hen resumed, 'Unluckily for the sender, you were booked for St Petersburg, and Helsinki. If you saw the invitation, you chucked it aside.'

'So what are you accusing me of?'

'Nothing. I'm telling you why your wife was murdered. She found the invitation. She may have been the one who opened it. If so, I'm sure she found it tempting.'

'Oh, she would, knowing Merry.'

'She decided to go.'

'We know that.'

'Right. But this is the crux. When Merry got there it was a tremendous shock for your old flame, expecting you to turn up. And when Merry said who she was—your wife—the shock must have been seismic. I doubt if the wretched woman knew you were married. People who harbour fantasies for many years don't move on mentally. She pictured you as you were in nineteen-eighty-seven, young, amorous, and hers alone. The existence of a wife would have been unthinkable.'

'This deluded creature murdered Merry? Is that what you're saying?'

'The two women meet for a non-existent barbecue. They wait on the beach for others, who, of course, don't turn up. They drink some wine—she's sure to have brought some to make the evening a success, and Merry may have brought some, too—and it all appears friendly, swapping their memories of nineteen-eighty-seven. Finally, Merry is invited for a moonlit swim.'

'And she was attacked in the water and drowned?'

'She made two fatal mistakes. The first was going there at all.'

'And the second?'

'Admitting she was your wife.'

He took a sharp breath. 'What kind of lunatic was behind this?'

'An attractive young woman you loved and left who developed an obsession about you.'

'Grotesque.'

From all she had seen of Austen Sentinel, Hen was inclined to agree. Actually, the man sounded as close to genuine regret as he was ever likely to get.

The right moment for Hen to take it a stage further. 'Think back and tell me if there was anyone who might match up.'

'God, what an impossible question! In those days I was sleeping with hundreds of women.'

Talk about delusions, Hen thought.

He was wrestling with the impossible. 'Someone from the dig? All I can recall at the moment are summer nights after the tide was in and we'd salvaged and stored our finds. We used to adjourn to a pub close to the beach near the lifeboat station.'

'It's called the Lifeboat Inn.'

'We'd drink the evening away. We were young people, warmed by the sun, pleased with a good day's work. I have a faint recollection of slipping away from the crowd with a local girl and indulging in a few kisses on the beach.'

'Only kisses?'

'It may have led to something more intimate.'

'"May have"? Who are you kidding?'

She'd massaged his ego. 'Two or three times. Once in the back of the van, I think, because doing it on pebbles is not ideal. But if you're asking me to remember the girl's name, I'm stumped. Certainly I wouldn't have expected her to fantasise about me later.'

'She would have been young, younger than your students.'

'You obviously have someone in mind.'

'I do. And so do you, Dr Sentinel. Tell me some more about her.'

It seemed for a moment as if he would try and hold out, but then he clicked his tongue and said, 'Not her name. That's gone. Yes, there was a local girl, young and not too experienced.'

'A virgin?'

'Well . . . yes.'

Jo WAS looking for an excuse to escape from Miss Peabody and her photo collection. She'd been in the cottage longer than she intended. Nearly an hour, now. She'd looked at shots of Gemma and her family till she felt ready to climb the walls.

'You could sort these out and put them in some kind of order,' she said, preparing to move. 'If you're stuck at home for a few days it may be a good time to do it.'

'How sensible. I've been meaning to make the effort. The oldest ones at the beginning, and so on. It's a pity I don't have any of Gemma as an older child.'

'Didn't the foster parents take any?'

'Oh, they were devoted to her, always taking photos. They were lovely people. So caring. They took her everywhere, along with the other children. I had pictures of her at Disneyland and in Paris. But after she was fostered again, when she was twelve, she came to see me and went through the album and removed every single one I had of her with that family. I didn't make a fuss; I expect she wanted to start her own collection.'

'Why was she refostered if it was working so well?'

Miss Peabody shook her head. 'It was awfully sad for the parents. They took on a new child, a little girl of about eight called Janice. Gemma's first foster sister. She had four brothers, but they wanted another girl in the family. Within weeks the parents took the children on holiday in Portugal. They went to some kind of amusement park and the boys went on that up and down thing.'

'The rollercoaster?'

'Yes, Gemma would have loved to go on that. She's always been adventurous. But her new foster sister was nervous, so the girls were given a ride on some kind of boat thing, a two-seater shaped like a swan.'

'A pedalo?'

'No it wasn't that. It was driven by something under the water so that it went in a circuit, and there was a stretch where it was enclosed. Really I think the ride was meant for young couples, a chance for a cuddle without people watching.'

'The tunnel of love.'

'That sounds like it. The two girls had a boat to themselves. Sadly, the young one, Janice, fell out while it was going through the tunnel. It seemed she had a fear of the dark. She must have stood up, I suppose. She was caught under the machinery and drowned. Well, the poor foster parents were held to be negligent and all the children were taken away from them.'

Two deaths by drowning: a brother and a foster sister. A pulse had started hammering in Jo's head. 'I've got to leave, I'm afraid. I'm getting a headache.'

'What a shame. Do you want something for it?'

'No. I'll be all right.'

She crossed to the stairs, went down, remembered her backpack and went to collect it. A shock awaited.

Somebody was in the kitchen.

Gemma.

With a meat mallet raised.

A different Gemma to the person she knew, a wild-eyed, angry Gemma, practically spitting her words. 'Stupid interfering bitch. My so-called friend, spying on me, squeezing every sodding detail from the old crone.' She stepped closer, bracing herself to wield the mallet. It was a heavy wooden thing with sharp ridges to break the meat fibres.

Jo stepped back, horrified.

Gemma made a sideways move across the doorway, blocking the exit. 'Get back, shithead.'

'Gem, what are you doing? I came to help your aunt. I *am* your friend.'

'Some friend!' She lunged forward. She meant to use the mallet.

Jo backed off again. As she did so, her foot dipped into a cavity and she felt her balance go. She'd taken a step down into the flooded cellar. Her foot was in water to above the ankle.

Gemma swung the mallet.

Jo raised her arm, swayed, ducked the blow, lost balance entirely and fell backwards, splashing into filthy water so deep that her head went under. She came up for air and felt a huge restraint on her shoulder.

Gemma was forcing her down with her foot.

She couldn't withstand the weight. She felt herself go right under again. Air was escaping from her mouth, bubbling upwards.

This was the pattern of the killings, pressing the victim under until her lungs filled and she drowned.

Her limbs were leaden. Her eyes bulged. She was trying to resist and the strength wasn't there. Drowning, she knew, places a massive strain on the heart. The shock can be instantaneous. The inrush of cold water to the mouth and nasal passages can cause cardiac arrest. If you survive that, the drowning takes minutes rather than seconds. The struggle to survive is instinctive, but in a small space you can't battle with someone who has a foot on your shoulder.

She had never known pain like this. Her eardrums felt ready to explode. She tried to hold her breath but the water surged through her nostrils, causing her to gulp more of the foul liquid.

All the time, Gemma's foot bore down. The bundle of nerves giving so much pain in Jo's shoulder stiffened. All sensation was going. Every cell in her body screamed for oxygen.

twenty-six

SUSSEX AND HAMPSHIRE POLICE forces combined in the hunt for Gemma Casey. An all units call was broadcast after it was reported that she'd driven away from the Kleentext print works in the unmarked silver Mercedes van owned by the company. Hillie, the sharp-eyed receptionist there, had seen her go. Her yellow Smartcar was still in front of the building.

The shout came at 11.50 a.m. A sighting on the A286 near West Dean. The van was heading north towards Midhurst.

'She won't get past Singleton without oars or wings,' Hen said to Gary. 'The road's impassable.'

'You know what's up there, don't you?' Gary said. 'She'll be holed up in the garden centre where her friend Jo works.'

'You think so?'

'I reckon she knows we're closing in.'

'Leave the reckoning to me and put your foot down. We're not keeping up.' They'd left Chichester with two police cars that were powering ahead using their 'twos and blues.' One was an armed response vehicle.

'I can't get close, guv. They're kicking up too much spray.'

'Overtake. They're only Fords. You've got the speed, haven't you?'

'Not that much.'

'Joke, Gary.'

'Ah.' He forced himself to smile.

'Try not to lose them altogether. Why didn't I think of the delivery van? Sometimes you miss the obvious things. One of the reasons it's taken me this long to suspect Gemma is the little yellow car she drives. I couldn't see how she could transport Sally's body from Bosham to Apuldram in that sawn-off two-seater.'

'If it were down to me, we'd still be after Jake,' Gary said. 'I assumed it was a man all along.'

'A woman is well capable of holding another woman under water.'

'Maybe, but she came back and lugged her out and moved her. She had to be strong.'

'In the first place, Sally was a lightweight, really petite. Then I talked to Stella about the layout at Bosham. The pool is an extension to the house with its own external door, which wasn't kept locked. Gemma would have backed the van up to it. She seems to have improvised by using the lounger as a trolley. It was on wheels, you see.'

'Cool.'

'She is. And I expect the van is equipped with a hand trolley that she put to use at Apuldram.'

'What put you onto her?'

'Keep your eyes on the road. It twists a bit up ahead. The breakthrough for me was realising who that invitation was meant for.'

'Not Meredith Sentinel, but her husband?'

'Which made it likely a woman had sent it. Imagine the shock it must have been for Gemma when Meredith showed up for the so-called reunion. Instead of her first love, the glamorous young man who initiated her into sex and who she'd dreamed about for years, a woman appears and announces she's his *wife*.'

'So the motive was jealousy?'

'Raw, green-eyed jealousy. Here was a beautiful, accomplished woman who'd been another member of the dig all those years ago and who'd managed to grab the star prize and marry him.'

'Not much of a prize, as it turned out,' Gary said.

'Gemma didn't know that. To her, he was still the gorgeous young lecturer of twenty years back, and hers by right. Could you put the wipers on fast speed? I'm losing sight of the others.'

Gary obliged. 'But why did she drown Fiona? That was a big risk, surely.'

'To be honest, I don't know yet. My best guess is that Fiona caught her out. The woman was an obvious enemy, in and out of the office, pushing her aside and cosying up to the boss.'

'Jealousy again?'

'Probably not. I think it had to do with the special invitation Gemma had printed.'

'That was printed at Kleentext?'

'I'm certain it was. Gemma denied it when we asked, but she would, wouldn't she? The job was embossed work. It couldn't have been done on a home computer. A good accountant knows what's going on in a business, officially and unofficially. Fiona found a proof copy, or the plate it was made from. By questioning Gemma about it, she sealed her fate.'

'Gemma thought Fiona would blow the whistle on her?'

'And she would have done, given the chance. Gemma went to Emsworth and waited outside Fiona's house. The location couldn't have been better situated for her. The Mill Pond was ideal for another drowning.'

They were touching ninety in the straight stretch leading up to West Dean. The trees close to the road made it seem faster.

'So it wasn't serial killing in the usual sense?' Gary said.

Hen was starting to wish he'd give all his attention to the driving. 'What do you mean?'

'Different motives.'

'Right. The motivation wasn't the same in Fiona's case. But the method—the drowning—suggests a serial mentality.'

'Why did she kill Sally, then? Jealousy again?'

'Basically. Even she realised that Sentinel was unattainable now. If she pursued him after murdering his wife, her motive would be laid bare and she'd be the obvious suspect, so all that pent-up obsession had to be transferred elsewhere, and Rick was the recipient—to Sally's cost. Gemma wasn't willing to share him with another woman. And after killing Sally, she had the neat idea of transporting the body to Apuldram and so bringing Cartwright under more suspicion.'

'Victim number three.'

'Or four, or five. Whenever anyone caused Gemma a serious problem she drowned them. Same pattern. She may well have killed others. I know the searches didn't turn up any, but drowning is a brute to detect. Previous murders could have been dismissed as accidents.'

Hen's personal radio buzzed. The first response car was in touch. 'Oscar Six to Bravo One. We're coming to the garden centre, ma'am, but I don't see the van outside. Do you want us to make a search? Over.'

'I'd rather push on.'

'There isn't much road left before Singleton.'

'Where's the van disappeared to, then? We'll go right up to where the flood is. She could have stopped there and made a run for it.'

'Hang on, ma'am. Something is coming towards us.'

'Stop it, then.'

In the next second she saw headlights and a vast slipstream of spray. She could barely make out the outline, but it was being driven at speed, whatever it was. 'Block the road,' she yelled into the radio.

There wasn't time. The Mercedes van emerged from the spray, snaked past the flashing beacons of the police cars, and headed towards Gary's small Nissan. Bravely or recklessly he braked, put the car into a skid and turned crosswise to block as much of the road as possible.

Yards away from crashing into them, the van rocked erratically and skidded. Sparks flew from under it. One of the marksmen had got a shot into a tyre. The brakes screamed as the stricken vehicle slid off the road and came to a jolting halt in a ditch not twenty yards from Gary's car.

'Leave this to us, ma'am,' a voice said over the radio.

'You bet I will,' Hen said.

'Go, go, go!'

Three officers armed with sniper rifles sprinted to positions either side of the van and flung themselves on the ground. One had a loudhailer. 'Armed police. Armed police. You're surrounded. Turn off the engine, throw out the key, step outside and lie face down on the ground.'

There was some hesitation.

'I don't want any more shooting,' Hen radioed in the hope that she'd be heard. 'She won't be armed.'

'She's turned off the engine,' Gary said.

The van door opened. The keys were thrown out. The door opened fully, but no one got out.

Inside, behind the steering wheel, was an old woman in a pink hat.

AFTER MISS Peabody had been helped out of the van, she said, 'If you think I'm going to lie on the ground you're mistaken.'

Hen had run forward and gestured to everyone to hold their fire. 'No need, madam.'

'I'm very shaken up. Something must be wrong with the steering. I know that was the first driving I've done in over thirty years, but I still have a licence.'

'Where's the woman who drove the van up here?' Hen asked.

'My niece Gemma? In my cottage being stupid. That's why I came looking for help. She's going to kill the nice woman who came to help me out—if she hasn't done so already.'

'Call an ambulance,' Hen said to the nearest policeman.

They got in the cars and burned rubber for the extra three hundred yards or so, some way past the barrier, when they were forced to get out and wade through water.

GEMMA FACED them defiantly from the cottage doorway with arms folded. 'Here come the plod, too late, as usual.'

Hen shoved her towards an officer who had the cuffs out and ready.

In the poorly lit interior Hen looked about her and saw nothing. She dashed through to the kitchen and discovered the body half submerged in black water. With Gary's help she lifted it from the hole.

'It's Jo.'

She tilted the head back and cleared the airways as well as she could.

'Feel for a pulse.'

Gary tried. 'I don't think there is one.'

Hen pinched the nose shut and gave two slow breaths into the mouth. Jo's chest gently inflated.

'Check again.'

Gary shook his head.

Hen started chest compressions, the lifesaving method now preferred to the kiss of life.

After half a minute Gary said, 'There's a faint pulse, guv.'

Hen continued. There was a rattle from Jo's chest. They turned her on her side and she debouched some water.

'She's breathing now.'

When the paramedics arrived they said Hen's action had saved Jo's life. It remained to be seen if the drowning had caused permanent brain damage.

JO'S FIRST visitor in hospital was Jake. Totally out of character, he was saying more than she was, trying to explain what he'd heard from the police. She had little memory of the attack, and his version was second-hand, but by degrees it became clear that she was thinking straight. She gripped his hand and didn't let go even when her second visitor entered the ward: her mother, with Daddy in tow.

Up to now Jo had dreaded the day when Jake met her parents, but it didn't seem to matter any more. All went miraculously well, and Mummy approved. 'What I like most about the young man is that he's a good listener, like your father.'

Daddy just winked.

IN VIEW of Jo's amnesia, Miss Peabody's recollection of the attack in the cottage was vital. The old lady made a long and lucid statement not only about the day's events, but about Gemma's childhood. She mentioned what was known about the drownings of the small brother Terry and the foster sister Janice. But she was scrupulous in declining to draw conclusions.

For Hen, it was confirmation of the suspicion she already held, but no less disturbing. Cases of killing by children are not unknown. Fortunately, they are rare.

* * *

GEMMA, WHEN questioned about the murders, was unrepentant, even eager to be heard. To her unbalanced way of thinking, the grievances were still open sores. Meredith, she said, must have been fated to come to Selsey. This harpy had turned up instead of the lovely man who should have come. She'd brazenly admitted who she was and it became clear that she'd trapped Austen Sentinel into a disastrous marriage. That evening on Selsey beach the two women had shared a bottle of wine and Merry had admitted to serial adultery. She'd mocked Austen's failings as lover and careerist, and admitted no fault in herself. She'd destroyed two people's happiness, and didn't see it. Half drunk and laughing, she'd walked hand-in-hand into the sea with Gemma and justice had been done.

Fiona's demise had been a consequence of her unstoppable desire to undermine Gemma. She'd discovered that one of the printing staff had put aside some top quality cream-coloured card at Gemma's request. It swiftly became Fiona's chief mission to find out what was going on. She'd picked her moment to sit at Gemma's desk and search her computer files. In the recycle bin she'd found an early draft of the invitation Gemma had thought she'd fully deleted. Triumphantly she'd accused Gemma of doing private work in office time. This interfering bitch couldn't be allowed to live. It was fortunate that she had a week off work coming up, because Gemma was responsible for the staff vacation roster. No one else except the boss knew that Fiona had time off. Gemma picked her evening to drive to Bosham and waited. Late in the evening, madam stepped out of her car and was helped into the Mill Pond and held down and ceased to be a nuisance.

As for Sally, she was a rich older woman keeping up with a toyboy who happened to be Gemma's consolation after the shocks of the past few weeks. Being a gentleman, Rick couldn't bring himself to ditch the old crone, though it was obvious he was weary of her. Gemma wasn't of a mind to be just another member of a harem. She needed sole possession. The problem had to be removed. It was just a matter of visiting the pool at the time of the daily swim. Sally had fought quite well for a lightweight. The idea of moving her to Cartwright's house was an afterthought. At the time it had seemed rather smart.

'All this is on record now,' Hen said. 'Are you aiming to plead guilty at the trial?'

'Why not?' Gemma said. 'I don't want anyone to think I'm sane. I can't wait to be deconstructed by some fascinating shrink.'

HEN CALLED a meeting of her team and thanked them. She said Gemma's full history could not have been discovered from the records they'd searched. Nobody had suspected until now that she'd drowned her own brother and her foster sister. Both events had been regarded as accidents, and her link to them had not been reported at the time. With hindsight it was clear that jealousy had been the main factor in each. After getting away with those juvenile crimes, she was always liable to repeat them if the motivation and opportunity arose. She was a well-concealed murderess, articulate, witty, and good at her job, but with a potential to take life whenever she was thwarted.

THE TEAM celebrated the same evening at the Crown and Anchor at Dell Quay. Unnoticed by them—a mere stone's throw away—a small yacht called the *Nonpareil* glided serenely back to its mooring. It had also been missed by Interpol, the coastguard, and the harbour police. Denis Cartwright looked fit and tanned after two weeks in the south of France. He knew nothing of what had been going on. By his own decision he'd been out of contact, the only way he was guaranteed a chance to relax. When interviewed later wearing one of his trademark bow ties, he was surprised by all the fuss over his so-called disappearance. 'I told my personal assistant I was off sailing for a couple of weeks. I can't understand why she didn't let everyone know. She's usually so reliable.'

Tailpiece for the Mammoth

THE NOVEL YOU HAVE just read is a work of fiction. No mammoth was discovered at Selsey in 1987. But a real find of much earlier provided the idea. The distinguished local historian, Edward Heron-Allen, recalled the event:

In March, 1909, a heavy easterly gale of some days duration stripped the shingle from the steep East shore of Selsey Bill and brought to light a mass of Mammoth bones. Unfortunately, the entire population of Selsey fell upon them like one man and a boy (in the hope of gain), and the greater part of the skeleton, which was only get-at-able at extreme low tide for about three days, was wrenched out of the clays in a thousand fragments. Prof. Gregory, Dr. A. Smith Woodward, and myself were present at this barbarous demolition, but I was fortunately able to secure afterwards (for gain) the major portion of the recovered bones, which are now in the Natural History Museum at South Kensington. The measurements of the kneecaps, a toe bone, and four teeth, which were all perfect, enable us to say that this was a young Mammoth standing about nine feet high.

Nature and History at Selsey Bill: a Lecture delivered in London on the 17th of January, 1911, and in Chichester on the 4th of February, 1911. Edward Heron-Allen (Selsey: Elizabeth Gardner, 1911)